Penguin Books
An End to Running

Lynne Reid Banks, who is the daughter of a Scots doctor and an Irish actress, was born in London and was evacuated to the Canadian prairies during the war. On her return to England she studied for the stage at R.A.D.A. and then had several years' experience with repertory companies all over the country. The first play she wrote was produced by a number of rep companies and later performed on B.B.C. television. She wrote and had published many other plays, one having been put on in a London 'little theatre' and several others performed on radio and television. She was one of the first women reporters on British television. She worked for I.T.N. for seven years – from its inception until 1962 – initially as a reporter and later as a scriptwriter.

Her first novel, *The L-Shaped Room*, appeared in 1960 and was made into a successful film. She published *An End to Running* in 1962, *Children at the Gate* in 1968, her fourth novel *The Backward Shadow* (a sequel to *The L-Shaped Room*) in 1970 and *Two is Lonely* (the concluding book of the trilogy of *The L-Shaped Room*) in 1974. She has also written *The Farthest-Away Mountain*, a children's book, *One More River*, *Sarah and After* and *My Darling Villain*, all for young adults, *The Adventures of King Midas* (1976), *Dark Quartet: The Story of the Brontës* (1976) and a sequel *Path to the Silent Country: Charlotte Brontë's Years of Fame* (1977). *Dark Quartet* won a Yorkshire Arts Association award in 1977 for an outstanding book connected with a Yorkshire writer. After leaving I.T.N. she went to live in Israel (the scene of several of her novels) where she married a sculptor. She and her husband lived on a kibbutz in Galilee for eight and a half years. They have three sons, and now live in London.

Lynne Reid Banks

An End to Running

Penguin Books
in association with Chatto & Windus

Penguin Books Ltd, Harmondsworth, Middlesex, England
Viking Penguin Inc., 40 West 23rd Street, New York, New York 10010, U.S.A.
Penguin Books Australia Ltd, Ringwood, Victoria, Australia
Penguin Books Canada Ltd, 2801 John Street, Markham, Ontario, Canada L3R 1B4
Penguin Books (N.Z.) Ltd, 182–190 Wairau Road, Auckland 10, New Zealand

First published by Chatto & Windus 1962
Published in Penguin Books 1966
Reprinted 1966, 1975, 1976, 1977, 1978, 1980, 1982, 1984

Set, printed and bound in Great Britain by
Cox & Wyman Ltd, Reading
Set in Monotype Times

Author's Note

While I would like to thank my friends on
several Kibbutzin for helping me with the
background for Part Two of this novel, I want to
stress that Kibbutz Beit Hashoresh is entirely
fictitious and is not based on any existing
one, nor are any of the characters in the book
based on real people.

Part One: Martha

For Pat

Chapter One

It was a good shop. Even without looking in the windows, one could tell by the door. It was all glass with a copper handle shaped like a boomerang, and as I pushed it open it made a very polite squeak, like a fat rich woman being pinched and liking it. It was the kind of squeak made by the kind of door which will only be allowed to squeak once.

Sure enough, as I put my foot on the carpet, thick and springy as a golf-green, a woman's voice said peremptorily, 'Dan, the hinge!' Then she came briskly out of a little cubicle. She was a thin woman, whippy as a willow twig, wearing bishop sleeves to hide her knobbly elbows. Her hair was cut like a man's, only with a heavy, rigid kiss-curl on her bony forehead. She wore tinted glasses with an Oriental cast and big pearl earrings which made her ears seem to be sprouting button-mushrooms. She had the hooked nose and bright beady eyes of a parrot.

She looked me up and down almost imperceptibly, and saw at once that I didn't match the shop. 'Can I help you, madam?' she asked notwithstanding.

'I've come to see Aaron Franks.'

She swayed like a poplar, her long thin feet in low heels planted firmly in the green carpet. 'Have you an appointment?'

'Yes,' I said. I disliked her instantly. It wasn't a thing which often happened to me.

'Your name?'

'Martha Fletcher.'

Her brow cleared, and I realized she had read the letter I had sent in answer to the advertisement. Now she had placed me, and she almost smiled, but in a patronizing way as if I should have sought out the tradesman's entrance. 'Wait here a moment,' she said, and went back into the cubicle.

A well-fleshed young man with smooth, inflated features had tiptoed round behind me and was oiling the hinge on the glass

9

door. Every tight circle of his clothing – collar, cuffs, belt – was a bottleneck to the flesh it enclosed. I felt the oilcan was unnecessary – a squeeze of his fat fist over the offending hinge would have done. But when he smiled at me I felt ashamed of this unkind thought. His smile had all the warmth his colleague's lacked.

I could hear her talking on the internal telephone, in a crisp, dictatorial voice. I looked round the shop. It was difficult to know what was for sale, as everything was new and splendid and there were no price tags. You were expected just to select things without needing to know the price; that was the sort of place it was. Among other things there was a cone-shaped chair of lime-green velvet with a purple cushion in it; beside it grew a sort of tree-stump of white metal hoops, between which little shelves were wedged at irregular distances, like fungus-growths; on the shelves were many strange and useless, but often quite beautiful, objects in glass and jade and enamel. There was a mock fireplace, or rather a grimace-shaped hole in the wall in which glowing bars stretched, like red-hot teeth braces, and above it was a narrow ledge of curved glass on which an arrangement of plates stood uncomfortably on edge. Above that, and slightly to one side, was a painting in a triangular frame. It was a pattern in three shades of a grey with a small red thing in one corner which looked more like a snail than anything else, or perhaps it was one of those 'Sold' stickers they put on pictures in art galleries. The whiter-than-daylight neon glinted silkily off the glazed surfaces, making me feel dowdy and hatless.

'My brother will see you now.' The parrot had stolen soundlessly up on me. 'This way.'

She showed me a narrow flight of stairs leading into the basement. 'Mind your head,' she said grudgingly.

Downstairs, the aspect changed immediately. To begin with, there was no heating down here; the floors were stone, and there was a dry chill in the air. It was also badly lit, and I nearly stumbled over a tea-chest at the foot of the stairs. There were boxes and crates littered everywhere, and each wall was made up of cubby-holes in which I caught glimpses of precious things packed in straw.

A man's voice, curt, and chill as the stony air, guided me

through the maze. 'I'm here.' I squeezed through a narrow space between two packing-cases and saw Aaron Franks for the first time.

He was sitting over a table facing away from me. I could see only a narrow back in buff suède, white shirtsleeves, the top of a black head, and ears, rather pointed, and flaming red as if with anger. He was typing, urgently, concentratedly, with two fingers. As I entered the area – it wasn't a room, just part of the cellar demarcated by shelves and crates – he struck two keys at once, and thus the first word he spoke in my presence was the only one left that no one will print.

The next were: 'Sit here.'

I came round to the front of the table and sat where he indicated, in an upright chair that bounced a little as it took my weight. I shivered – partly from the tube metal striking its iciness through my thin blouse and partly from an indefinable uneasiness which the front of Aaron Franks gave me.

He went on typing for a minute longer and then tore the page out of the machine and pushed it towards me.

The lower half of it was covered with words. I had trouble reading them, partly because they were mostly mis-spelled and full of overtypes, but chiefly due to their having little or no relation to each other. The writing was a mixture of disjointed phrases, onomatopoeic successions of letters, and odd words, rather like *Finnegans Wake* only not so intelligible.

'I'll give you five minutes,' said Aaron Franks, 'to read the half-page you cannot see.'

I clutched the sheet of paper, peering at its blank top half desperately, almost as if I hoped that concentration would fill it with words which I could understand and make some sensible comment on. The unmarked whiteness glared back at me derisively. I could feel sweat begin to prickle my palms.

'Now read the visible section.'

With a silly sense of relief I looked again at the typing. But in the interim it had lost what little significance it had had for me when I first glanced at it. It was now a tangle of black squiggles. I inanely let my eyes follow each line, back and forth, to the bottom. It was entirely possible that this was some esoteric joke, and that if I looked up I should find him laughing

11

at me. This would be quite in keeping with the rest of my life; people constantly regarded me as a source of amusement. Sometimes I could join in their merriment; sometimes not. Often not. It's an odd feeling to live one's life behind a face which makes other people laugh. It started early. 'Funny-face . . .' Even my parents never called me Martha. It doesn't suit me. It sounds dark and sober with downward lines. All my lines are asymmetrical, wayward – comic.

'Well?'

I forced my eyes up beyond the top of the page. My throat felt tight and painful. The eyes that met mine were sleepy; only a portion of the strange, pale irises was visible. They were set on either side of a strong, beaky nose under sharply winged eyebrows. His face was both bony and sensual; his mouth, semitically full and yet somehow austere, was closed in a firm, almost cruel curve. His hair was black, silky, brushed forward from the crown, cut to lie flat on his head like a little boy in the streets of Paris. His hands lay on the table on either side of the typewriter, palms pressed flat, but relaxed. He wore a blank, waiting expression; not one that might turn into laughter.

'Well?' he said again, expectantly.

'Well what?' I asked, feeling the stirrings of anger.

'Have you nothing to say about my work?'

'You can't type.'

The curve of the mouth turned up faintly at one side.

'That's what you'd be for. Anything else?'

'What sort of comment do you want from me?'

'I want you to criticize my work. It's the last time I shall allow it, if you do come to work for me, so make the most of your opportunity.'

I felt the anger grow like indigestion in my stomach. It threw up a sour taste into my mouth. I was twenty-five; no one had the right any longer to make me feel so impotent, so ineffectual. I needed the job; there wouldn't be another at this price – but no price paid for this sick, cold feeling of being out of my depth. It was too familiar, too recently grown out of. I stared back into those light, narrow, non-committal eyes with cold dislike.

'I think it's a lot of meaningless rubbish,' I said deliberately.

I expected something violent to happen to the blurry wedge in front of me, but it hardly stirred. One thin hand moved and picked up another piece of paper.

'And this?'

My hand shook as I took the paper.

> A song of special moment to my fame
> is the beleaguered swinings of a hound
> all torn upon his latest carrion.
> My heart should be as lusty as this lord
> over the foal and ferret in my pound.
> Instead it is a broken, brainless thing,
> unused to slaughter as a peony;
> pinioned beneath a whirring wheel of doves
> unstinting and soft-breasted as the air;
> fit for the rusty howlings of this world
> as are the catches on the milky breath
> of an unlicensed child.

When I'd finished this, my heart had stopped beating in high reproach against my rashness in saying 'meaningless rubbish', and I was ready to say it again. But this time I was less angry and less sure.

'Well?'

'I don't understand this either. It has no sense, but it does have rhythm. It feels as if it ought to mean something, but as far as I'm concerned it just doesn't.'

The opaque eyes stared at me for a moment longer, then he seemed to relax. He leaned back and lit a cigarette without offering one to me.

'Do you know what my sister thinks of the first thing I showed you?'

'No.'

He inhaled deeply and looked at me again. Now an expression of laughter had come into his face, but it was not directed against me. 'She thinks it's a work of pure genius.'

I wanted a cigarette. I said nothing.

'That's why she's willing to engage a secretary for me. Oh, you didn't imagine I'd be engaging you? I don't engage anybody, or decide anything. That's no part of my job, I'm told. Do you like her?' he shot at me suddenly. I was taken aback and couldn't think of a polite answer, but he didn't wait long for one. 'Well, you'd better. She's the boss.'

He sat smoking silently for a while. The cold of the place was eating through my flesh and I shivered. His eyes flicked over me.

'You wouldn't have to work down here for long. This is just temporary. There's going to be a flat above the shop which will be – metaphorically of course – a fountain-head; from it will flow the prose and poetry my sister is convinced will gladden the souls of a more percipient posterity. She has a theory, you see, that I'm ahead of my time. She has another theory to the effect that radioactive fall-out is not going to increase the incidence of idiocy, but stimulate the brains of the unborn to superhuman proportions – to the point, in fact, where they'll be almost equal to mine.'

He leaned forward across the desk and pressed the tips of his fingers together. He let his eyelids droop and his lips caved in as if he had no teeth.

'Well now, my dear,' he said in the slow, lecherous voice of a rather dirty old man, 'and how would a pretty girl like you like to work for a superman? Eh?'

'Do *you* think you're a genius?' I asked him.

He was still leaning across the desk, but now the old-man look disappeared and he was staring into my face with cold, hard eyes. A little left-over smoke trickled out of his nostrils. He said very quietly, 'I'm nothing.'

He suddenly flopped back in his chair, throwing one arm carelessly over the back of it and letting his cigarette dangle from his lips. He looked like a different person– the tension of cynicism was gone, and he just looked limp, crafty and rather stupid, like a teddy-boy.

'Personally, I couldn't care less whether you come or don't. It doesn't matter a good god-damn to me one way or the other. I'll be landed with somebody, whether I like it or not; whether it's you or someone else makes not a blind bit of difference.'

'I really don't think I want to work for you, or your sister,' I said, struck anew with dislike, of a different sort this time. Every facet of this strange young man seemed more repellent than the last – but there was something fascinating about him

14

which made me suspect that every attitude was somehow a distortion of whatever he really was.

He shrugged, and that odd mouth of his curled disdainfully. 'Good for you. Never work for Jews. They'll always do you dirt eventually.'

I was shocked. He looked at my face, and said, deliberately misunderstanding the cause of my dismay, 'Oh! Didn't you know we were Jews?'

'With a name like yours I could hardly have thought you were anything else.'

'True.' His eyes kept me pinioned. 'So what are you looking like that for? Don't you like to hear anti-Semitism expressed so freely?'

'Not by a Semite.'

'Who better qualified?'

The sour taste was back. I swallowed it and stood up. He followed me with mocking eyes. 'Don't think much of me, do you?'

'Not much.'

'It seems a pity you've decided to go, when we have so many opinions in common."

I stopped. 'What do you mean?'

He shrugged again. 'You don't like my sister. I loathe the bitch. You think my work stinks. I know it does. You don't like me. How right you are!' He grinned. 'Stick around, why don't you? We'll get on well together.'

I was once told as a child that you could tell a good man from a bad one because when a good man smiles it improves his face, whereas a smile merely lights up the evil in the face of a bad man. I used this criterion, more or less unconsciously, for years, and it still gave me a shock to see that Aaron Franks's smile gave him a look of contempt, violence and despair, like the grimace of a soul in hell.

Chapter Two

Going back to my flat on a bus after this interview, I was dazed and bewildered at having agreed to work for this unlikely and unlikeable employer. I tried to find a reason for it. There was, of course, the matter of money. But it couldn't have been altogether that, because although I was alone in the world and quite dependent on myself since my father died, I lived within my means and had money saved for between-job periods. Tempting as Miss Franks's offer was, it wasn't enough to be miserable for. I had a rooted distaste for accepting money, even for services rendered, from someone I disliked; and I did dislike her. After I'd changed my mind, her brother had called her downstairs and announced that he wanted me – as a spoilt child might point out, with arrogant hauteur, the toy it's chosen; and I watched with a shiver of new dismay how those parrot-eyes half hooded themselves and the mouth, a thin parody of his, tightened and turned downwards in a look of disapproval, of cold authority that brooked, in advance, no challenge. Really, it was a look of warning, and I wished now that I had heeded it and fled.

Why hadn't I? There was something palpably un-normal and disquieting about the relationship between brother and sister, and although it half-frightened me, I was intrigued. The whole atmosphere of the shop was electric with dis-ease and animosity, with the clashing of personalities. There's no hate like the hate between close blood relations, and when it exists it's surely something for outsiders to keep well clear of. But there had been something in that smile – that tortured smile – that was as tangible an appeal as if he'd seized my arm to prevent me from leaving.

I was still shivering from the cold of the cellar, though it was high summer. The flat was stifling, but I put a cardigan on as soon as I got in. I switched the radio on at once, too, as I always did. Both the girls I shared with were out at work, and I set about getting a meal ready for them, still rehashing in my mind the incredible details of the interview. Whenever I came to the bit where he had said, 'Never work for Jews. They'll always do you dirt eventually,' my face slid automatically into a grimace of disgust and I found it that much more difficult to explain to myself why I'd agreed to go back tomorrow, and presumably for many days after that, to submit myself to that arrogant woman and that self-hating, unattractive young man, who embodied, by turns, just about every personal quality I loathed.

When the food was in the oven, the table laid and my window-box watered, I was left with nothing to do. This was nemesis to me; my recurrent and insoluble problem. I stood at the window looking out over the roofs of West Kensington to the hump of Earl's Court Exhibition; my mind was almost a total blank, except for the thin prickle of disquiet that was always there when nothing else was. *Don't just stand there. Do something. Learn something. Think something.* But as always my mind hung stalely; my body stood, numb with inertia, waiting for some order, receiving none because there was no routine, prescribed chore to give it.

After some time I realized the evening paper would have come. With an ashamed lift of the heart I hurried to get it, spurred by a false sense of purpose. Out of duty I chased my eyes swiftly over the headlines before turning to the crossword. I usually did two crosswords a day – the *Telegraph* and the *Standard*. It took me a fortnight of doing the *Telegraph* one every day to get sufficiently into the compiler's mind to finish it; but the victory when at last I did so was very hollow. It was a token of wasted hours. Disgusted with myself, I would resolve never to do it again; but I would go back to it like a drug, the next time my mind fell into that vacant staleness of boredom.

I settled down, scanning the *Standard*'s clues with an addict's eagerness, and for a few minutes I was occupied and at peace. But it was soon done; I'd been doing them regularly for weeks. *Of all the futile, fruitless wastes of time!* I thought as I threw it aside. This inner rage was part of the pattern. *What's the matter with me? Why can't I bear to be alone?* I moved about restlessly,

17

looking at my watch. Half an hour at least before I could expect the girls. It stretched ahead like the time before a child's party.

Read, I thought grimly. That's what other people do when they're at a loose end. But my resolution had flagged before I even reached the bookcase. The challenges it presented were either too big (*Dr Zhivago*, bought in a high-minded moment and never read by any of us) or too small (endless paperback Nigel Balchins and Monica Dickenses and Nancy Mitfords, read and re-read until just to open them brought home to me the self-indulgent squirrel-wheel which was my mental exercise).

Determinedly I took down a book of plays which someone had given to one of the girls. But it had a flavour of homework; I couldn't concentrate on it. I lay back and thought with a sort of dull desperation, *Perhaps this new job will fill my mind and my time with something solid, something worth while. I should be able to do it for myself, but I can't. I never could. I'm not a rebel without a cause. I'm not even a rebel. I'm just a lump that has to be fed all the time with work and artificial distractions. I have no real education, which is a pity: I've got no talent, which is worse. But the real trouble is the saddest lack of all – I've got no enthusiasms.* That wasn't quite true. I was enthusiastic about growing things. But what use was that, when I had no outlet for it except a single window-box?

The girls returned at last, tired and querulous from the day's work. One of them, Gwen, was a secretary working for a television news company; the other, Jill, worked in the Times Bookshop. Both were frustrated actresses and hated their jobs, but apart from that they were very easy to get on with and we lived together in as much harmony as is possible for three unmarried women under one rather small and shabby roof.

'Did you get it?' they asked one after the other as they came in.

I told them I'd got it, and then they wanted to Know All, which in the normal course of events I would have enjoyed relating. We were very good audiences for each other's stories, whether they concerned love, work, families, or, in Jill's case, even dreams, with which she regaled us each morning while we drank our coffee in half-asleep patient silence. But as I couldn't

18

explain it to myself, I certainly couldn't undertake to explain it to them. It would sound most odd if I said, 'The woman who's paying me is bitchy-looking and hated me on sight, and the man I'm working for is a sneery little savage one minute and an affected show-off the next: he hates his race, his sister, and himself, his work's no good and he knows it – and I start tomorrow.' So instead I said, with restraint, that it seemed like an interesting set-up and that my boss, so far as I could gather, belonged to the *avant-garde* school of writers. Then they told me about the trials of their respective days, and that took up most of the evening.

At nine o'clock or thereabouts my solitary current admirer phoned. His name was Jim Maxwell. I'd met him in the most conventional way, at a party, about three months before, and he had been courting me sedately ever since. He was 32 and a shipbroker (I still wasn't very clear what that was) and I liked him, but sometimes I grew impatient with him and was unkind, which was upsetting to us both. I never wanted to hurt him and was always painfully sorry afterwards, but that didn't stop me at the time. This evening was one of the times.

We chatted desultorily for a while; my mind was still very much occupied by the encounters of the afternoon. I told Jim something about my new job. I usually told Jim about things, chiefly because I was trying very hard to fall in love with him and it seemed important that I should be able to confide in him; but I was for ever aware of something lacking. He listened obligingly and made encouraging noises, but he never laughed at the funny bits or gave useful advice or seemed to enter into the thing as I would have liked. It's fair to say I was hard put to it to laugh at his City jokes or to understand the finer points of his stories about shares and things. The reason I wanted to fall in love with him (which may seem obscure at this point) was because he was so very *nice*, and it was rare for a nice man to be seriously interested in me. Usually men treated me like a cross between a puppy and a small sister, and the only men who had got 'serious' about me so far had been – not to put too fine a point on it – bastards. Jim was not a bastard and he did take me seriously, and that, as I mentioned, was a very rare and important factor.

I told him more about the job than I had told the girls, and his reaction was exactly what I should have expected.

'It sounds impossible,' he said. 'How can you work well if you don't believe in what you're doing? Chap sounds a queer sort of fish – can't bear these arty types. What did you say he was called?'

I told him again.

'Jew-boy, eh? Well, there you are.' I felt the cold hand of my personal demon stealing over my vitals. 'Why can't you find some normal, sensible, English chap to work for? In some civilized business house? They're crying out for good secretaries. Matter of fact, Blaistow needs a new girl – his leaves next week. Why don't I put in a word for you, and you ring this pansy writer chappie up and –'

'It's fixed now,' I said, trying to stifle my unreasonable annoyance. After all, as Gwen had pointed out after the last flare-up, 'You'd be jolly miz if you had no one who cared enough to make helpful suggestions – even if they *are* n.b.g.'

'You can unfix it,' he said with one of his sudden outbreaks of manly firmness. 'I'll talk to old Blaistow tomorrow. He's quite an elderly chap, probably mumbles a bit dictating and so on, but you could soon get used to that. Very decent old boy; anyway, I'll be there to keep an eye on you . . .'

'But, Jim, I don't want to work in the City. It's miles to go, and anyway, what do I know about shipbroking?'

'Quite a lot, I should hope, after three months of me. You'll get fascinated by it after a few weeks of learning the ropes. You only have to pick up a few technical terms, anyway, and I'll soon teach you those . . .'

I had a trapped feeling. 'Jim, don't go so fast. I've told you, I've agreed to do this other –'

'But you can get out of it,' he persisted reasonably. 'You can't *want* to work for a character like that?'

'Well I'd rather work for an artist, however weird, than some bumbling, dreary old –' I caught myself short, but it was too late. There was a long, hurt silence from the other end. This was a constantly recurring point of conflict between us. Briefly, Jim worked on the basis that all artists, in whatever field, were pansies and parasites. He couldn't pass in the street a man whose hair needed cutting or who was a bit unconventionally

20

dressed without remarking that what he needed was six months in the Brigade of Guards. I used to try and divert his attention if I saw one coming, because his reaction invariably made me furious. My demon already had me hard in his clutches, but I managed to say, 'I'm sorry, Jim, I didn't mean to be rude.'

'Blaistow's the salt of the earth.'

My demon let out a shriek of gleeful anguish and dug his claws into me.

'Have you ever tried to work for a lump of salt?'

'Now, don't be so silly, Martha. You know what a bee you've got in your bonnet about this artist thing.'

That was another item on the debit side of Jim – clichés. At moments like this it was hard to remember how long was the list on the credit side, or indeed to bring to mind a solitary point in his favour.

'I haven't got a *bee* in my *bonnet*,' I retorted loudly, laying heavy and cruel emphasis on the hackneyed words.

'Don't get ratty, dear,' he said, with maddening mildness. 'I'm only trying to help.'

This was unspeakably true. It always was. I had a stone-cold-sober moment when I saw the futility of Jim and me struggling to bridge a gap as wide as the Arctic Ocean and just as cheerless. I knew I ought to hang on to this knowledge and give the whole thing up – give us both a chance to find other people. But the gaps between my people are always so long and miserable. I put the moment of clarity away from me.

'I'm sorry, Jim,' I said contritely. 'I tell you what, let me have a go, and then if it's too frightful after a week or so, we'll talk about Mr Blaistow again.'

He was completely mollified and cheered up at once. 'Good. What about a flick tomorrow? This new "Carry On" thing sounds pretty tolerable.'

'Oh, Jim – not a "Carry On" thing.'

'Don't you like them? I think they're damn funny.'

'Yes, only . . . let's go to a theatre instead.'

'Oh . . . right-o. A nice light comedy, eh? I'll get my girl to book seats in the morning.'

I sighed. I was pretty sure we'd wind up at the Palladium.

• • • • •

I lay awake much of the night in an agony of trepidation. My imaginings were concerned much more with the sister than the brother. After jerking my way through several aggressive duologues with her in my thoughts, I realized to my alarm that I was actually afraid of her. It was an instinct, and no amount of reasoning would reassure me that she was not lethal.

However, she greeted me on my arrival without visibly baring her teeth; though she did give her watch a pointed glance. I was exactly on time, but from the way her eyebrows flickered I realized that five minutes' margin would have been wise.

I caught the eye of Dan, Dan, the oil-can man, and was mildly encouraged by his fat, happy smile. That, I thought, was the way to be – placid, fat and nerveless. I hurried downstairs.

Aaron Franks was waiting for me.

'You're late,' he shot at me instantly.

'One minute.'

'Lateness, like chastity, isn't a matter of degree. Either one is or one isn't.'

'Aren't you ever?'

He looked at me coldly. 'I doubt if I would be, the first day at a new job,' he said. He waited for me to answer back, and when I didn't he seemed disappointed. 'All right, sit down and let's get cracking,' he said tersely, dropping into a chair.

The work we did the first morning was something I hadn't bargained for. It was boring. Or at least, it would have been if my boss hadn't kept me lively by alternating between a dictation speed of 250 words a minute and a slow-witted mumble which Mr Blaistow could hardly have equalled from the brink of the grave. The actual material was not *avant-garde* – or *derrière-garde* – or anything very much. It was just a dreary monologue apparently spoken by some beatnik in a coffee-bar and was full of 'mans' and 'cools' and 'daddys' which went on and on and on. Sometimes he would put on an appropriate American accent; other times, he would go very county-English or occasionally break into Mittel-European, slipping in a few incongruous 'alreadys' or 'yets' accompanied by 'oy-voy's' and Yiddish gestures. I think I was meant to laugh, but it was just too unfunny and pointless.

Dictation went on for three hours almost solid, broken only

once when he looked at his watch at about noon and said, 'I want to phone my bit of crumpet. Go up to the shop and make sure she doesn't listen in on the extension.'

'How do you suggest I stop her?'

'That's your problem.'

I located the extension at the top of the stairs, in Parrot-face's cubby-hole office. She wasn't on it; she was serving a customer. I stood about awkwardly until I heard the ping of the phone being hung up; at the same moment the customer left and Parrot-face turned to me.

'You want me?' she said, hooding her eyes.

'No. Mr Franks was making a phone-call.' She glanced at the extension and her fingers twitched. It gave me quite a small pleasure to be able to add, 'I think he's finished now.'

I went back downstairs, leaving her with frustration clear on her face. My shortly-to-be-ex-boss was lighting a cigarette.

'Any trouble?'

'No.'

'Good girl. That'll be one of your regular duties from now on . . . seeing to it that I get a bit of privacy in which to phone my floosies.'

'It won't be one of my regular duties after the end of the week.'

'Quitting already?'

'Yes.'

He leaned forward to look at some notes he'd made. 'Do you think there are maybe too many "alreadys" in that last part?' he asked suddenly.

'I really wouldn't know. I lost the message about an hour ago.'

'You've got it all down, though?'

'Oh yes.'

'Can you read it back?'

I quailed at the thought of the hours and hours this would take. 'I imagine so.'

'Good. Come on then, let's get the rest of it down before lunch.'

He dictated more of the same until one o'clock, by which time I'd filled about half my notebook with the drivel and got

23

beyond caring. At long last it stopped. Aaron Franks stubbed out his fifteenth cigarette into the exquisite overflowing ashtray and stood up.

He slipped into a beautifully tailored suède jacket. 'I am now going,' he said, 'to baste the kid in the milk of its mother. I think today . . . shrimp cocktail – roast pork – and a glass of milk. That's about as proscribed a combination as even the most prurient rabbi could imagine. I trust you've brought a packet of sandwiches, nice Christian ones?'

'I'm going out for lunch.'

'You'll find everything round here pretty pricey.' He disappeared round an elevation of packing-cases and then put his head back into sight. 'Are you sure you can read all that back?'

'Yes.'

'What a clever little secretary!'

I sat, limp with tiredness, and fought back irritation. My fingers were cramped and had deep red grooves in them where the pencil had pressed. I looked through the thick wodge of pages, covered with squiggles, and thought suddenly, *To hell with the end of the week. I'm off now.*

I threw the notebook down and almost ran up the wooden stairs. Parrot-face was waiting for me at the top.

'Could you spare a moment?' she asked with a courtesy I entirely mistrusted.

She led me into her cubby-hole and closed the glass door. There was barely room for the two of us in there. She sat and I stood facing her, our knees almost touching. I could smell her scent, which was not quite strong enough.

'I wanted to have a little private word,' she began cosily, and for a moment I feared she would add 'woman to woman'. But she left that implied. 'Perhaps with an intelligent girl like you, it's unnecessary; but I feel it's only fair . . . in case anything my brother says or does should . . . I do believe so strongly in the Doctrine of Importance, don't you?'

This *non-sequitur* took me aback. The horrifying thing was, I did believe in *a* Doctrine of Importance; I just had to hope hers was something quite different. There's nothing worse than hearing your own opinions emerging from somebody you can't bear. I didn't answer; just waited for her to go on.

'. . . Of Important People, I mean. Now, my brother is – as I'm sure you've noticed – a very gifted, I might say phenomenally gifted writer.' I blew a mental raspberry, but my face betrayed nothing. 'Such a gift is rare, it's precious, and it must be nurtured and – and fostered. Taken care of,' she added kindly, as if I might not know what 'nurtured' and 'fostered' meant. 'Important People are not like the rest of us. It's such nonsense to talk about people being created equal. If that were true, there'd be nobody like my brother – or Einstein – or Myra Hess – or – er – Karl Marx.' I was bewildered by this curious combination of talent, until I realized something interesting – they were all Jews. I was giving her my full attention now. It was fascinating and horrible to hear these words, these theories, from her. They were like my own, and yet somehow not. My trouble was that I couldn't quite see the difference yet – except that I certainly wouldn't have included Aaron Franks in my list of Important People.

'Of course you've read *The Insanity of Genius*?' I shook my head. '*Not?* Oh, but you *must*! It would help you so much when you come into contact with exceptional people like my brother. Of course, it simply confirms what I've always said – brilliant people aren't normal. Well, of course, that's obvious, isn't it? But I mean, they're not just abnormal mentally, that would be absurd – like a normal-sized person with just one enormous feature. Big people are big in all sorts of ways – extreme in lots of directions. It would be unreasonable to expect a great talent to develop in a person who was otherwise just like anybody else. What I'm saying,' she continued, smiling at me winningly, 'is simply this. My brother is – well, I won't say a genius; not yet. But he is brilliant – quite brilliant. So that means he's a man from whom it would not be fair to expect perfectly ordinary, everyday behaviour. I've known him since he was born, I've always known there was something special about him, and I've made allowances. Our father did the same. He realized Aaron couldn't be treated just like a normal child, so he – and I – protected him, shielded him from mundane things like – well, money matters, or emotional entanglements which might – distract him or interfere with his ability to concentrate on his writing. Would you like a cigarette?'

I took one gratefully. A puff each, and the little glassed-in room was as solid as an aquarium filled with milk.

'As a result,' she went on, leaning her head back to reveal a very unattractive, turkey-like throat, 'he's still a child in some ways. Someone less perceptive than you might say he was spoilt. Personally I don't think conventional manners and that sort of thing matter particularly compared with a talent which will carry a name into the future.' She looked at me, her bright bird's-eyes piercing the smoke-screen between us.

'I see what you mean,' I said, which was true. The name that was carried into the future, *if* it was, would also be hers.

'I knew you would. In any case, it's just a question of getting used to his ways. The first few weeks will be the hardest,' she said with a thin smile, 'after that, you'll begin to take a pride in working for him. Not quite like the pride I feel – being part of his family – but a satisfaction just the same. Well worth it,' she concluded inexplicitly. She coughed and flapped her hand. 'Dear oh dear, it's getting thick in here! Open the door, would you, Miss Er –'

I thought I was dismissed, and backed out with great willingness. But she apparently had a second thought, and beckoned me back.

'If my brother *should* do anything which distresses you – for instance, if you should hear him talking on the telephone in a way which – or if any of his letters strike you as – perhaps you'll tell me.' She saw the expression which sprang to my face in spite of myself, and continued hastily, 'Don't imagine I'm spying on him or anything like it. It's simply for his own protection. I'm sure I can count on you.'

I found a sort of superior workmen's café in a side-street not far away. Or at least, that's what it looked like. I ordered the cheapest meal I could think of – a plain omelette, some french bread and butter, and an orange – and it was extremely good, as it damn well ought to have been for 9s. 6d. I decided to bring sandwiches in future. The petty irritation with my employer for having been right about eating-places dominated, temporarily, the other annoyances he'd given rise to. I think this was due to my being filled with loathing for his sister, who, by her hateful attempt to recruit me, had unwittingly enlisted me in the one-man ranks of the opposing force.

In my enthusiasm for the fight, I'd forgotten the fatigues. The sight of my drivel-stuffed notebook lying awry where I'd tossed it, never expecting to be faced with it again, made me groan aloud. However, having once joined up, it's no use wincing at the 'bull', so I picked it up, put some paper in the typewriter, and got to work.

The Onlie Begetter arrived back half an hour later. I stopped typing, the better to listen to an argument that was going on at the top of the stairs. It seemed to be about some party she wanted him to go to. Her voice became shrill.

'You must leave these decisions to me,' she said. 'Madeleine Craven's going, and she could be very helpful if she takes to you.'

'Why the hell should she?'

'You can be charming enough when you like.'

'I don't like – not where that fat bitch is concerned. Or her greaseball of a husband.' He was keeping his voice down; I had to creep round a non-acoustical packing-case to hear.

'What nonsense you talk, Aaron! Theo Craven's one of the most witty, delightful –'

'– Crafty, dishonourable, sharp-dealing smarmy bastards in the business.'

'Ah, but it's a business you're very interested in.'

'You mean, you are.'

'Don't you want to get your play on?'

'What play?'

Her voice suddenly dropped and changed. It became overtly menacing. 'The play you're going to write, starting this afternoon – starting now.' I felt a cold shiver pass down my spine. There was no wheedling, no humouring left in that voice. It was stripped of everything except steely command. 'I haven't let you engage that girl to give you an available bottom to pinch,' she went on. 'You're going to get to work, and I'm going to see to it that you work hard. If not . . .'

I was tense in every muscle. Now for it. Now I'd find out what held him, a mass of defiant wriggles, firmly under her bony thumb. But, to my disappointment, the conversation was over, and I was hard put to it to make the guilty dash back to the desk in time to avoid being caught by my boss as he came softly down the stairs in his crêpe-soled shoes.

I sat virtuously puzzling over a difficult outline as he came into sight, and barely glanced up; but that glance shocked me. His face was livid and there were dark pulled-in shadows under his high cheek-bones. His mouth was ugly and taut, and his thin hands, fumbling for cigarettes and lighter, were shaking noticeably. He caught my eyes before I could look away.

'Did you hear any of that?'

Too taken aback to lie, I nodded.

'Always listen when you can. It'll save me having to repeat things.' He made a small stifled motion of his head as if checking the urge to glance over his shoulder; I'd noticed him doing that before, without understanding what it meant. Now I realized that he was perpetually controlling the desire to make sure she was not behind him.

'What's that you're doing?'

'Transcribing what you gave me this morning.'

'Scrub it. I was only killing time. You don't think there's anything worth salvaging out of that lot, do you?'

'I thought you weren't going to ask my opinion about your work.'

'That isn't work, it's crap.'

'Was what you showed me yesterday, work?'

'No. Well . . . perhaps the poem, a little. It had something – nothing intelligible, but something from somewhere other than the top of my head. *She* didn't care for it. Said it was brilliant, but too sentimental. She can always detect a trace of quality, however overlaid, and demolish it with her disapproval . . .'

'But doesn't she want you to be good?' I ventured.

'*Her* way. And she knows nothing. She only knows what she thinks will make me famous, talked-about.'

'Then I'd have thought she'd want you to write with absolute clarity so that everyone could understand.'

'Clarity isn't what makes you talked-about these days. I'm unique – I'll create my own following – my esoteric style will soon be the fashion – etcetera. Etcetera.' A tiny sound – probably a mouse among the straw – made him start, and turn his

28

head so sharply he ricked his neck. 'Christ, I'll be glad when I have a door I can lock! If only one could instal sound-proofing without anyone knowing about it. Just spread it on like paint. What an invention that would be! If I could figure out a way to do that, my name would really deserve to go down in history. Franks's Privacy Emulsion. Specially effective in close-knit Jewish matriarchies.' He put both his feet, neat and small in suède shoes, up on the desk and leaned back in his chair, closing his eyes. His face – on which I'd already seen a dozen personalities – now wore a negative look of peace. Turned up towards the cold strip-lighting, the lines and shadows vanished, and it looked like the face of a child. Or a corpse. It was quite innocent of any viciousness or unhappiness or hatred.

He roused himself, lit another cigarette, and sat silently for a while. I waited, patient and intrigued. Finally he said, 'Let's see if I can dictate for you to take straight down on to the machine. It'll save time.'

I put some papers and carbons into the typewriter and sat waiting. He got up and started to move about. There was a nervous urgency about him now; the languorous insolence was quite gone. He was prowling and struggling. He stopped moving and opened his mouth as if to speak, his eyes narrowed against the smoke. Then his cheek muscles twitched impatiently and he started pacing again.

'Listen,' he said suddenly. 'Don't take it down, just listen. There's a Jew, an English-born, English-bred, English-thinking Jew. He's never been persecuted; nobody's ever called him "dirty Jew"; his parents were rich, he went to a good school, everyone treated him on his merits, which were average. He doesn't specially think of himself as a Jew – right? He's English. Been in the war and so on. But said all the old prayers, if I forget thee, oh Jerusalem and all that, family liberal but devout . . .' He stared at the ceiling, thinking, his breath coming short. 'When he was a kid he put pennies in the blue box, thirteen trees planted in Palestine at his Bar Mitzvah . . . you don't know anything about that; anyway, it's just background. Actually Zionism doesn't mean a row of beans to him. He's English, like a Canadian is a Canadian even if he does still talk about some other place as the Old Country. Are you with me?'

'Yes?'

'So he settles down, gets married, buys a house, inherits the business ... roots, roots, roots, deep in English soil. So he *thinks*. And he goes on giving money to the National Fund, he supports Israeli charities, and so on; wife goes to Zionist meetings, listens to lectures, comes back all hipped up – we ought to make a trip – just for a year – do our bit. But by now the State's been going for years. Pioneering's finished; no fighting, no glamour. Besides, it's hot there; besides, the kids are settled at school; besides ... Anyway, they don't go. But all the time, as he gets older, something's nagging at him, something's not right. He's missing something somehow. He's not sure what it is, won't let himself be sure; dimly he feels it's too late. He doesn't even talk about it. And then his son says he wants to marry a non-Jewish girl. He catches his daughter trying to pass herself off as a Gentile. He's not very strict, but he doesn't like that. He begins to feel his Jewishness again, as he hasn't since the massacres during the war. The swastika-daubing crops up around the same time. Eichmann's caught. Other things happen ... I haven't worked out what yet; maybe he tries to be a Free-mason and doesn't find it all that easy to get in. Anyway ... he suddenly knows what he wants. He wants to go home.'

He spun round to look at me. His eyes were on fire.

'Go on,' I said. 'Is this the play?'

'Of course not,' he said, and now it was clear he was getting more and more excited. 'That's what happens before the play starts. Well – no, perhaps that's the first act – the son and daughter, the pressures that make him suddenly realize, suddenly wake up to it. It happened to my father. Not all of it, but the final realization, when he was quite old, that he wanted to go to Israel – to "go back", he said, although he'd never been. He wanted it as he'd never wanted anything in his life – he told me so. But he didn't go. Things stopped him. That's my play – the things that stopped him; the claims of his business, his wife, his kids, his *roots*. He gets more and more desperate, he fights harder and harder, against – not so much solid opposition, as a frustrating soggy non-cooperation, a reflection of his own pro-crastinating semi-indifference over the years. Everyone smiles tolerantly, saying "You can't be serious! At your age? You'd never adjust yourself!" His kids aren't interested; his wife can't face it. Even the immigration authorities aren't keen. They discourage him gently – they want young men. And he's got his own inertia to contend with. In the end he realizes he can't make it. It *is* too late for him, just as it was for my father. He should have gone years and years before. When he was my age.'

He stood immobile, the tension of his idea working in him like a powerful yeast. Suddenly it exploded; he jumped into the air with a whoop, and landed on his feet on the desk, scattering papers and kicking his portable typewriter a skidding blow; I just saved it from falling. I stared up at him; his slim legs were planted apart; quivering from head to foot, he towered high above my head. I had a moment's awe; I had caught the thrill of creation from him. It shook in my throat; I wanted to echo his exultant shout.

He crouched swiftly and took my hands.

'Say it's good,' he commanded.

'It's good. Only –'

'Only *what*?'

'Only it sounds more like a novel.'

He tossed this aside. 'It has to be a play, that's my brief,' he said.

He stared first into one of my eyes, then into the other, searchingly. 'You're not sure yet,' he said, 'but you will be. You're not Jewish, but I'll make you feel it, just as if you were. I'll make them all feel it. Just the way my father did me.' He let me go and sat cross-legged on the desk where the typewriter, which I was still nursing, had been. He was trembling with excitement all over, like a dog. 'I've had this idea at the back of my mind for three years,' he said. 'Since my father died. He died a very rich, very successful, very popular and very unhappy man. He'd achieved everything he set out to do; he was loved; he had nothing to be ashamed of – but none of it rated, in the end. He died disappointed.'

He withdrew from me without moving. His eyes narrowed; his limbs seemed to gather themselves closer to his body; his head sank between his shoulders. Only his hand, groping blindly and ineffectively for a cigarette, seemed to be part of the here and now. I lit a cigarette and put it between his lips. We sat silent for a long time.

At last his eyes came back from long distances and focused on me.

'At least you can sit still,' he said, and smiled. The smile no longer made him ugly. 'And now,' he added, getting stiffly off the desk, 'we'll begin.'

Chapter Three

Jim picked me up sharp at 7, which was when he had said he would. This promptness was one of the reassuring things about him; it bespoke a well-ordered mind, something I notably lacked.

'What are we seeing?' I asked, hiding misgivings.

He looked smug. 'The one at the Royal Court.'

'A straight play?' I asked with some incredulity.

'No good?'

'On the contrary, very good. Thank you. But won't you be bored?'

A little hurt, he said, 'Of course not. I'm not an all-comedy man.'

We had a very quick dinner first, where we always did. The steaks there are good and I didn't have to worry about the size of the bill (Jim cared rather a lot about money) but I hated those little tables where you never quite know where to put your roll or your bowl of salad – or your elbows, for that matter. They serve carafe wine with a great deal of fuss and expect you to taste and savour it as if it were some rare vintage. Still, Jim liked it.

'Well! How did you get on today?'

One second's reflection told me this was not a moment to confide in Jim. I would only get more of Mr Blaistow's saltiness rubbed in my wounds. So I just said, 'Oh, all right. He's started to write a play.'

Jim sniffed, but it could have been due to a slight cold. 'What's it about?'

This was difficult to answer in a word. 'He's only done the first scene.'

'Well what happens in that?'

I cut off a piece of steak, keeping my elbows well in to my sides, and hoped the subject would change, but it didn't. 'Must be about *something*.'

'So far, not very much.'

'What's the setting?' Jim asked knowledgeably.

'A living-room in Wimbledon.'

'Sounds a mite conventional. The piece we're seeing tonight is something quite out of the common.' He had evidently gone the whole hog.

It was called *The World at My Window*, and was a very long play translated from the Flemish about a red-haired prostitute in the slums of Brussels. She sat in the window of a dingy place called Café des Sports and watched the passing parade for three acts without moving. She talked a lot, though I personally couldn't follow much of the conversation, which suggested that the author had torn the pages of his script down the middle and reshuffled them. Characters wandered in, exchanged their involved philosophies with each other and the prostitute, and wandered off, never to be seen again. The first two acts ended just in time to prevent the audience watching the girl actually engaged in her profession. At the end one learned she was paralysed from the waist down.

'Charming,' said Jim, thin-lipped.

I searched for something to say which would encourage him to try another straight play some time in the distant future.

'It was interesting in a way . . .'

'It was bloody meaningless from start to finish. *And* obscene.'

'Well . . .'

We walked out of the theatre. All round us, fellow members of the audience were talking animatedly.

'. . . *did* enjoy it. Critics were right for once. "The author's put his fingers on the pulse of society . . ." Which of them said that?'

'. . . Freudian overtones . . . the paralysis was symbolic, of course. Untouched by her own degradation . . .'

'. . . Only wish they'd played it in the original. One's bound to lose a lot of the poetry even in the best translation . . .'

'Of course, as Maurice said, she was a latter-day Maya – all things to all men.'

'No, nonsense. Alistair was right. She's an extension of Blanche du Bois. Mankind's whipping-girl and sin-eater –'

34

'That's right, because remember how the banker *and* the navvy both used the same phrase about feeling "cleansed and fresh from the womb" after they'd practised their pet perversions on her?'

'Bosh, the girl wasn't passive, that was the whole point. Although she couldn't feel anything sexual, I mean *because* she couldn't she was able to exploit a sort of *spiritual* lust in herself. To degrade men far more than if she'd merely . . .'

Jim was listening with a puzzled frown. He turned to me when we reached the street.

'Did *you* get any of that?'

'No.'

'Did you get anything out of it at all?'

'I thought the girl was very good – within the limits of the play.'

'That was the whole trouble. It hadn't any limits. It was just a – an amorphous stream of words. Pretentious bloody drivel.'

'It's making a packet of money for someone.'

'Because people are snobs. It's the current thing to see. If you haven't seen it, you're out of the conversation.' Secretly I agreed with him, but I hadn't enough faith in my own judgement to commit myself. I'd hated *Ulysses* too – what I'd managed to read of it – *and* Belá Bartok. And most of Picasso, come to that. But obviously one couldn't say so, when so many people would take it as an earmark of the very suburbanism one was trying to get away from. Well, no; I had to be honest. I wasn't trying to get away from it; I was just trying to hide it.

'I only hope,' Jim was saying, 'that your Yiddish boss isn't one of these new wave wallas.'

I said nothing, feeling miserable. At least Jim had the courage to say what he thought, to be what he was. I wondered why admiration didn't flow out of this knowledge. Admiration, like love, didn't seem to have much to do with facts or deserving. It was just there, or it wasn't.

Next morning, Aaron Franks didn't appear.

I sat for half an hour doing nothing. Then I wandered about and looked into the packing-cases, drawing aside the shavings gingerly for fear of giving Parrot-face the least excuse to complain, and admired the wonders of art and craft that lay there, trembling in their expensive beauty like new laid Fabergé eggs. When I'd looked at everything that was open to inspection, I was cold from the chill of the cellar away from the small heated cubby-hole area where the desk was, and wanted coffee; and like a fat genie Dan appeared, waddling carefully down the narrow stairs, balancing an exquisite cup on an exquisite saucer and preceded by an exquisite aroma.

'Is that, I hope, for me?' I asked.

'I thought you'd like a cup,' he said diffidently, smiling his friendly, happy smile as he gave it to me. Like most fat men he had a child-like face, innocent and bland and rosy. 'I didn't know about sugar, so I put some in the saucer.'

'Thanks, I don't. I'm so grateful for this,' I drank some and felt its comforting warmth permeate my nervous, chilly system.

'Aaron not here yet?'

'No . . . where do you suppose he is?'

'Sleeping, I should think, lucky little perisher.' He watched me, grinning at my obvious pleasure in the coffee. 'By the way, how did you get out last night? Polly came down to look for you and was quite annoyed she'd missed you.'

'She can't possibly be called Polly.'

'Why not?'

I didn't know him well enough to say 'Because she looks exactly like a parrot,' so I just mumbled something about its not suiting her – an inversion of the truth.

'Her real name's Paula, but Aaron's always called her Polly. She hates it, but it sticks.'

'What do you mean, she was annoyed?'

'What? Oh, last night . . . Yes, she was a bit tetchy. Nothing serious.'

'Did she want to see me about something?'

'I shouldn't think so. She just likes to keep tabs.'

'I let myself out through the back door.'

'So she guessed. I expect you'll find that line of retreat cut off from now on.'

'Oh?'

'She got me here early this morning, fixing a bolt to the outside.' He saw my expression and grimaced sympathetically. 'Sorry.'

I began to suspect I had a covert ally in Dan.

'How long have you been here?' I asked.

'Oh, years. As long as the shop, almost. I came straight from Oxford ... Aaron and I were mates there, hard as that seems now to credit.'

It did indeed. 'I should have thought you were older.'

'So I am, but only three years. I wasn't stupid, he was bright – one of the youngest they'd ever had up there. He was all right, in those days, Aaron was. Really a good bloke – I mean *really*. He was like something let out of a cage – went bull-headed at everything, books, sport, tutorials, parties, talk, girls, the lot. He positively revelled. Of course, lots of people enjoy themselves at university, but Aaron set a new high for sheer *joie de vivre*. Have you ever watched a puppy sink his teeth into a woolly toy and go *gr-rr-rr-rr*?' He shook his head violently from side to side and did, in fact, look very much like a bulldog puppy shaking a toy rat. 'Well, that was Aaron and Oxford.'

'Funny. He doesn't seem to enjoy life much now.'

'No, well ... he's back in the cage again.'

Parrot-face's parrot voice shrilled from upstairs. 'Dan! Come *along*, dear, what are you doing?' Dan rose guiltily.

'I must run.'

'Thanks for the coffee.'

'See you.'

He hurried away, and I sat and thought about a younger Aaron Franks, not a mass of conflicting inconsistencies and poses, but a whole personality. I knew I had seen a bit of it the day before, when the poseur had vanished for four straight hours and he had worked with a demonic intensity which was the exact antithesis of his previous languid, smutty-sneery demeanour. For those hours I had forgotten myself and the world, in the all-absorbing frenzy of keeping pace with the quickest, most dynamic brain I had ever met.

I was surprised and disappointed that he was not as eager to get on this morning as he had been reluctant to stop last night. He had had to go to dinner with his sister, but his last words to me had been 'Don't be late tomorrow.' And now he was late – an hour and a half late. I took out the key he had given me and unlocked the drawer where he'd told me to leave the many pages representing yesterday's output. 'Be sure it's locked,' he'd said. I re-read what we'd done. It still seemed exciting and good; but I felt the pressure of what the dialogue hadn't been able to incorporate – the thoughts and memories of these characters which Aaron had not the skill, or a play the depth to explore.

It ought to be a novel, I thought again. And remembered his answer: 'A play's my brief.' His brief! Who was she to give him orders? I felt the bewilderment fermenting in my head, slow bubbles of protest and anger rising to the surface. But I reminded myself it was none of my business.

I put the pages back. They shared the drawer with a great many other bits of paper, many crumpled or folded from having had other things stuffed in on top of them. I began to neaten them – sorting them was out of the question; they seemed to bear no relation to each other. Some were scribbled poems; others were the beginnings of short stories that never got beyond the first few paragraphs. This seemed an ill-omen. Perhaps he lacked staying-power for everything.

After a while I heard heels clacking down the steps and Parrot-face poked her head round the packing-case boundary. Instinctively I thrust the new play into the back of the drawer.

'On a warm day like this!' were her first words, as she bent to deprive me of my electric fire.

'It's not warm down here,' I said.

'You'll put yourself to sleep," she said. 'What are you up to?'

Silly to resent a phrase which from anyone else would have seemed a harmless idiom. 'I'm tidying these drawers,' I said.

'Oh yes, my brother's wildly untidy. Don't throw anything away, will you? You never know when even a snatch of something may develop – or even have an intrinsic value. Why do you smile?'

'No reason. I'm not throwing anything away.'

'My brother just telephoned – I said I'd give you a message. He's in bed today. Nothing serious – a little biliousness. He wants you to bring the typewriter and what you were working on yesterday, and go to our house. I'll give you the address.'

'Right.' I stood up and began to cover the machine. She watched me until I took out the previous day's pages.

'Is that the beginning of the play?' she asked, drawing nearer like a vulture waiting for a death.

'Yes,' I said shortly, and slipped them into a manuscript envelope.

'You go and call a taxi,' she suggested. 'I'll get Dan to bring the things up. That machine's too heavy for you.'

'Thank you.' I put the envelope down in order to get into my coat and pick up my bag. When I turned back, it was in her hand.

It wasn't easy to decide, in a flash, what to do. She was smiling at me quite peaceably, as if enmity between us were unthought of. So sure of herself and her position was she that she actually opened the envelope and drew out the papers without even waiting for me to go upstairs.

When I conceive an instinctive dislike for someone I am always in a state of suppressed – what? Hate, anger, fear? – in their presence, and this disarms me. I knew with complete certainty that the last thing Aaron wanted was for his sister to see the play in its raw, barely-begun state. But I lacked the courage to take it from her hands.

Raging at my own ineffectiveness, I blundered upstairs. Dan was dusting china.

'Dan,' I said, 'I've got to go over to the Franks's house. Will you bring the typewriter and that big envelope up here for me?' And I added in a low voice, 'Now. And get the envelope away from her.'

He looked startled, but didn't argue. I went out into the strong sunlight of Regent Street; the brilliance was startling to my eyes, as if I'd emerged, like a fakir, from thirty years in a tomb. The sun caught the glossy corners of the taxi I hailed, and flashed hearteningly.

'Just a moment,' I said, and went back into the shop.

Dan came up the stairs with the heavy machine under one massive arm.

'Where's the envelope?' I asked sharply.

He shrugged and pointed downward with his thumb. I felt suddenly able to go down and take it away from her. It was the effect of the sun on the taxi, plus a sudden anger, stronger than nervousness.

She was deep in it, her back to me as I came round the packing-case. I didn't bother with excuse-me's or preambles.

'I'll have that now, if I may.'

She swung round, one eyebrow disappearing under the kiss-curl. I wondered fleetingly if anyone had ever kissed her. I thought not. Her face seemed to have hardened a few degrees even in the last five minutes.

'Pardon?' she said coldly.

'I must be going, and I need what you're reading.'

'There's no hurry,' she said after a moment, and went calmly back to the typed pages in her hand.

It was war. Of course I'd known it from the start. This just happened to be the first will-to-will battle, and she held all the weapons. The most powerful was my knowledge that, in the last analysis, Aaron couldn't stand up to her if she decided I ought to be sacked.

As I stood frustrated and helpless, the phone rang. Automatically I reached for it.

'Mr Franks, please,' said a shrill little female voice.

'He's not here today,' I said. That was as far as I got. Parrot-face almost snatched the receiver from my hand.

'This is Miss Franks, who is that? Who? But I must have your name if I'm to tell my brother ... Well, he'll certainly want to know who – No, I'm sorry, you can't have his home number. Of course, if I knew your name ... Oh, very well!' She slammed down the receiver angrily. 'Common slut,' she muttered furiously. Then she remembered me. But by that time I had the manuscript in my hand; she'd been foolish enough to put it on the desk for a moment.

'Good morning,' I said politely, and made my exit.

The Franks *mènage à deux* was a large and beautiful house – almost a mansion – on Hampstead Hill. It was all but invisible among its guardian trees until one circled a central island of chestnuts in the key-shaped drive. A breathtaking display of wistaria and roses, intertwined on a whitewashed wall, surrounded a Regency front door with an elaborate fanlight. There were many and varied windows, through which I caught glimpses of elegance – the gleam of silver, reflected in wide light mirrors; patches of sunlight subtly embossing a yellow carpet, and many flowers. Jewels of light glowed deep in heavy glass bowls.

I rang the bell, and a woman came to the door. She was short and ugly with tiny, needle-sharp eyes almost lost in powdery folds of skin. I told her who I was, and she peered up at me. The little eyes were piggy, disconcerting. They focused on something beyond me.

'Better pay that thieving taxi,' she said in an almost stage-Yiddish accent. 'All robbers, what you want with a taxi, young thing like you?'

'I had a heavy typewriter to bring.'

'Then go get it out and pay him,' she ordered. 'Letting it mount up! If you was paying it would be a different story.'

Somehow there was no offence about her, though. I did what she told me and came staggering up the steps with the typewriter.

'Young devil, making you bring that great thing,' she scolded. 'Here, I help you up the stairs with it.'

'I can manage –'

'No – you want to ruin yourself? So don't be silly. For me the damage is done years ago.' She grabbed one end of the typewriter and between us, with much more difficulty than if I'd carried it alone, we tugged and lugged it up the wide shallow stairs, with her grumbling all the way.

'Great heavy monster – what you want with such a thing? His handwriting is beautiful, if he should be bothered with it, but no. Lazy young pig, you should pardon the expression, I don't know why I wasted my time to teach him to write when he was only three years old –' She stopped half-way up to get her breath. 'Three years old he was only! Writing already like an angel – his name, my name – oy, such writing, perfect, like a child of ten! And not content for long with names. Stories, poems, everything. Bella, he would say to me, I read to you. So darling, I say, read to me, read. No matter what I'm doing, always I stop and listen.' She stood for a moment longer, her little hand, like a powdered claw, pressed to her side. I took as

41

much of the weight of the typewriter as she would let me and we edged on upward like crabs.

At the top was a spectacular landing, close-carpeted in almond green, with gleaming white doors leading off it; above hung a chandelier, and above that was a glass dome through which sunlight streamed. Some of the glass was deep blue, and the winking coruscations from the chandelier were bi-coloured, splashing the white walls magically.

'He's in here, the lazy boychik – sick, he says! Sick from drinking too much . . .'

She entered without knocking. It was a large, pleasant room, but too feminine to suit Aaron, who lay in bed under the wide windows with a pad on his knee, scribbling. He looked up, and his dark, wedge-shaped face lit up.

'At long bloody last!'

'Don't you swear, you wicked boy, you want I should beat you?' said Bella threateningly.

'Go on, you terrifying old crone, I dare you!'

She let go of the typewriter and crossed the room with surprising agility, in quick hopping motions, like a nimble old flea. She boxed him around the ears until he caught hold of her two stick-wrists in one hand and pulled her down till she was sitting, helpless, on the edge of the bed.

'You should be ashamed, to bully a poor old woman!'

'I should be ashamed! What about you? Don't you know I'm practically dying?'

'Dying – such nonsense! You're too idle to get up, that's all, you make this poor girl to come all this way with that great monster –'

'Put it on the table, Martha –'

'And anyway, to talk about dying is foolish. Bad luck, it's asking for trouble.'

Aaron let her go and sank wanly back on the pillows.

'I am dying, Egypt!' he croaked.

'You are not dying. And who?'

'Egypt, you ignorant old woman.'

'Is that nice?' she said, and then appealed to me. 'Is that nice, calling me names? What shall I do to him?'

'I tell you what you can do, if you're determined to be

obliging,' said Aaron, sitting up again. 'You can go down and get Martha and me some lunch. A good, rich, exciting, Polish meal. Not Kosher.'

'So when did I ever cook not Kosher, you blasphemer? What you eat when you are outside I don't want to know about, but when you eat in your own house, you eat Kosher. Finish.'

She got up, with a tight-lipped look of being deeply offended. He grabbed her hand.

'Angry?'

'Angry? To be told, not Kosher? What you think I should be?'

'Angry.'

'Well I am not.' She clasped his face in both hands and kissed him with a great mwoomphing sound. 'But only because I am so good-natured, and a foolish old fool. I go cook. And no carryings-on while my back is turned!'

'Carryings-on, indeed! I'm far too weak, and Martha's far too virtuous.'

'Good, good, but the first I don't believe.' She looked at me appraisingly, as if trying to decide if she believed the second. Her needle-eyes bored into my past. 'Hmph, I go cook,' she said, and went, abruptly.

'So did you bring it?' Aaron demanded at once, eagerly.

I gave it to him, but guiltily, knowing what his question would be and ashamed that I couldn't give the right answer.

'She didn't see it, did she?'

'I'm afraid so.' His face darkened, 'I couldn't stop her,' I added miserably.

'Well you should have damn well stopped her! Why didn't you?' His eyes were cold and furious.

'Why do *you* let her –'

'That's enough.'

'All right, then, don't bark at me. At least I stopped her getting too far with it. Please don't forget, she pays me.'

He muttered something and stared at the envelope, his long hands touching it protectively. He seemed to have lapsed back into his lethargy, from which he was trying to rouse himself. 'So have you re-read it? How does it seem this morning?'

'Good.'

'There's a "but" in your voice.'

'Only the "but" that it's in the wrong form.'

'Still harping on your novel idea? I wrote a novel at Oxford,' he said suddenly. 'I found it the other day. Not bad. Of course I'd nothing very much to say in those days – still. It had something. Excitement and vigour. It kept going, even through the trivialities that seem important at 18. It was *haya*.'

'What's that?'

'Alive.' He sat in a silence that seemed despairing. 'You don't think I'm dying, do you?' he said shockingly.

'Good Lord! What do you mean?'

'I don't mean physically.'

I went and sat on the edge of the bed. He looked at me. He was not joking or posing. His eyes were darkened by some deep disquiet.

'Why do you think you might be?'

'I don't know,' he said listlessly. 'Various indications. Rereading that novel I wrote, and feeling as if it were written by somebody else – not able to recapture the – the joy of living I felt then. But remembering it, the way you remember the dead, with pangs.' He drew the pages slowly from the envelope and sat staring at them blindly. I marvelled at the quick changes in him. He had seemed so vital while Bella was in the room. It was the knowledge that his sister had read some of the manuscript that had deadened everything for him.

'Talk to me,' I said impulsively.

He looked up in surprise, and his eyes narrowed with the old measuring distrustful look. 'What about?'

'Her.'

'There's nothing to say.'

'There *must* be.'

'You mean, why I stay, why I let her scare the pants off me? Yes, I'm sure you must find it very extraordinary. You're probably imagining all sorts of turgid dramas – a wicked past she holds over me, some hypnotic influence. Eh? It's nothing of the sort. If it were, I'd probably jump at the chance of unburdening myself. Something really dramatic – something shocking, terrible – if it only were!' He leaned back against the pillows, the long wedge of a face turned away from me. 'You know what I told you about my father?' he said. 'Why he didn't go to Israel? Didn't all those nebulous reasons strike you as insufficient?'

'No . . . it's the little barriers that are sometimes the hardest to get over.'

His head snapped round. 'You understand that!'

'Of course.'

He stared at me for a moment, and then thrust his arm at me. 'Feel that sleeve,' he ordered. I felt it. 'The finest silk. Nothing else ever touches my skin, which is consequently very sensitive. You may have noticed my clothes – suède jackets, Jaques Fath ties, Italian shoes – the best, nothing but the best, ever. Even my underpants are the spit of the world's most blue-blooded silk-worms. There's never less than a couple of hundred pounds on my back when I step out of this house. But when I want the price of a bottle of scotch, I have to go to her on my bended bespoke-tailored knees, and then she doesn't give it to me.'

'You mean, she has the money.'

'Father left it all to her, every penny. She talked him into it. It's in trust for me, until I'm 30 – that's another six years. That's because when I was at Oxford I went a bit wild and "proved" I couldn't handle the stuff. And she managed to persuade him that if I had a lump of it to fling around, I'd fling it, and get no work done – not her sort of work.'

'Was it his sort, too?'

'Poppa didn't know a book from a back axle. His bent lay in quite another direction. Perhaps that was why he was so impressed by my sister's assertions that he'd spawned a literary genius . . . and by her claim that she alone understood the best way to handle me. Of course I didn't find out about this private arrangement between them until after he'd died.'

'But I still don't understand. So, she's got the money. It's not the only money in the world. Why can't you get out and earn some of your own? You're not a cripple.'

'Have you ever lived like this?'

'Like what?'

'Like this.' He indicated the room, the house, the grounds, the silk pyjamas, in one comprehensive gesture.

'Do you mean, in luxury? – No.'

'It does things to you.'

'Saps your courage, softens your backbone?' I couldn't keep the edge of mockery out of my voice.

'You don't think so?'

'I don't know – it might. But if you *know* that's what's the matter with you, you ought to do something about it before it –' I stopped jarringly.

'Before it kills me. Quite.'

We sat in silence. He'd withdrawn from me, and I felt ashamed. Nothing that had happened in the short time we'd known each other gave me the right to speak to him like a friend. Or so I was admonishing myself, until he said distantly, 'You might as well go home. I don't feel like doing any work.' Whereupon I promptly threw my new-born deference aside and renewed the attack.

'And I don't feel like going home,' I said crisply. 'Come on, let's get on with it.'

'Who do you think you are?' he asked angrily.

'Your secretary – in name only, it would seem.'

His mouth twitched. 'You've got your nerve. I've got a good mind to fire you.'

'Okay, but hurry up before I get too interested in the play to want to leave.'

The tension relaxed suddenly.

'Do you *really* think it could be good?'

'Yes, for heaven's sake, *yes*! How many more times do you need to hear me say it? Only so far it's in its infancy. Come on.'

I settled myself in front of the typewriter, inserted paper, and sat erect, looking at him with nannyish expectancy. A grin irresistibly demolished his authority.

'All right, you win. But don't get above yourself.'

We worked till lunch, and through lunch, and most of the afternoon. The pile of pages grew, and with them Aaron's concentration and suppressed excitement. When a phone call came for him at about 4 o'clock, he told Bella to say he was out. We finished the draft of Act I.

At six o'clock we were taking a breather when the door opened and Parrot-face walked in.

'Still here?' were her first words.

'Martha's staying for dinner.'

'Oh? Oh, but I'm afraid she can't. Rafe and Miriam are coming.'

'So what? She'll eat up here with me.'

She looked at me. I quailed inwardly.

'I don't think I'd better,' I said cravenly to Aaron, and was rewarded —or rather, blighted – by a thin-lipped smile from my hostess.

'But I want you to,' Aaron said.

'Miss Fletcher knows her own business best,' said Parrot-face with finality. 'Now tell me how you've been getting on. You should have got a great deal done,' she said, looking pointedly at the time.

'We have.'

'May I see it?'

'It's not ready to be seen yet. It's only a rough draft.'

'Never mind, I can use my imagination.'

The pages were face down on the table beside the typewriter. I instinctively put my hand on them, pressing hard. This time I would be all right – this time I had Aaron to back me up, I needn't give them to her. But I heard Aaron say fumblingly 'All right then, but it's not very good,' and I felt a surge of fury against the brother so strong it drowned my dislike for the sister.

After reading a page or two she sat down in my chair, heavily, and said 'Cigarette, Aaron'. He clambered out of bed to give her one, trying to catch my eye as he did so, but my nostrils felt waxy and I refused to exchange looks with him. He leaned against the foot of the bed, looking very tall and rangy in the monogrammed silk pyjamas; his ankles were crossed and he smoked with an air of negligence, but he was watching her face like a sparrow-hawk and his thin fingers bit deep shadowy dents into the white counterpane.

She read all the pages we had done, slowly and carefully, and then laid them face down on the bed. She stubbed out her cigarette without looking up, and then she did look up – straight into his face, and her eyes were remorselessly cold.

'It won't do,' she said.

He stiffened and straightened up slowly. His face was white. 'What's wrong with it?'

She glanced at me. 'Put your dressing-gown on, Aaron,' she said sharply.

He didn't move. 'What's wrong with it?'

'A great deal. It's slow-moving – actionless, really. It's too conventional in form – not at all what I expect from you; it lacks your originality, your flare for the unusual, your –'

'My talent for meaningless bilge.'

'Miss Fletcher, I think we can say good night to you.'

'Don't go, Martha. What else is wrong with it?'

She gave me a harsh, dismissive glance, and seeing that it had no effect, she sighed deeply. 'Why on earth are you writing about a Jew?'

'Now you've surprised me. I thought whatever else you criticized, you'd be pleased about that aspect.'

'Why should I be? Miss Fletcher, will you please go?'

'I think I'd better, Aaron.'

'I'd rather you called my brother Mr Franks.' Her voice was a pistol-shot.

'I'd rather you minded your own bloody business!' he shot back. My spirits lifted. 'Martha, I want you to hear this, if you can stand the strain of a few more minutes of this charming family scene.' His face was all bumpy white muscles and drawn sinews of rage, and his ears were scarlet. 'Go on, Poll. Why not Jews? I want to understand this.'

'Primarily because we want the play to be a success.'

'Why should Jewish characters hinder that?'

'Because it's esoteric. It's all right to put shaggy old East End pawnbrokers or sharp-nosed shysters or hand-spreading fat crooks into a play for laughs or a gentle tear or two. But you can't write a serious play exploring Jewish feelings and expect anybody but Jews to understand it.'

'Mankowitz has done all right – and Wesker –'

'Mankowitz's Jews are all caricatures; he's clever enough to know what the public will stomach. As for Wesker, his Jews aren't Jews, particularly; they're just people; their problems are universal. You're trying to write about a specifically Jewish problem, regarded in a Jewish way, which couldn't happen to anyone but a Jew. And anyway, why expose a thing like this? It's – it's indecent. It's an intrusion on privacy. Altogether apart from being outrageously disloyal.'

'Disloyal?'

'Do you think I'm so stupid I can't see where you got it all from? Have you no respect for your father's memory, that you can expose his pathetic feelings in a play?'

'I don't see anything pathetic about them.'

'I say that because I don't choose to call them wicked.' Aaron's eyes narrowed, but she went on: 'You know what Mother felt about Father wanting to go to Palestine –'

'Israel.'

'Palestine. You know what I felt, even as a child, and what I feel now. It was – well, it was his weakness; every man has one, and that was his. It only came when he was old and getting feeble –'

'Are you suggesting Father's Zionism was some sort of senile aberration?'

'You twist my words.'

'That is what you think, though, isn't it?'

'I hate the whole business, it's unlawful and abominable, and if you went to *schule* a bit more often you'd feel the same!'

'I wouldn't give the time of day to any crack-brained rabbi who preached that Israel shouldn't have been founded in the absence of the bloody Messiah! You know, you really should have let Father go. You should have gone with him, and settled down in Mea Shearim. That's your spiritual home, after all. Perhaps instead of that incongruous kiss-curl you could have had a shaven pate, like the other female fanatics . . .'

'*Aaron!*'

'Why not? At this very moment you could have been throwing stones at some Shabbos-breaker, or spitting in the face of some girl with bare legs . . .'

I'd completely lost the sense of the conversation, and I wanted to understand it, because it was important. He was standing up to her, fighting back, abusing her, and although he

49

wasn't fighting for the play directly, I felt it was all bound up together.

She was trembling as she sat in the chair, her bony, masculine hands pressed down on the arms in an effort to control herself. 'It's no use discussing that,' she said coldly. 'I've long ago given up trying to make a good Jew out of you. But your writing is something different. I will not have you using your talent to turn your father into a laughing-stock. If you go on with this play, and if by any chance it were accepted, everyone we know would recognize him.'

'Does that matter?'

She looked at him as if he were growing horns. 'Of course it *matters*,' she said, as if the words burned her. 'He was your father.'

'And I loved him very much, and I understood him, and admired him. And now I want to write about him. Do you honestly think he'd mind?'

She stood up, as tall as he, her wiry body quivering.

'*I* mind,' she said harshly.

They stared across the narrow space between them into each other's eyes. His dropped first, and with them my hopes. I turned away; I couldn't watch.

'This isn't what I want from you, Aaron; it's a waste of your time and your great talent. You are not to write as other people write. You are to develop something new, something entirely your own.'

'This is my own,' he said, but it was a defeated mutter.

'No, it's not. In any case Theo wouldn't look at it. Madeleine told you last night what he's after – something different –'

'Something so intellectually obscure he can't understand it.'

'Understanding it isn't important. What matters is that people should talk about it. Who really understood *Waiting for Godot*? Who understood *The Caretaker*? *The World at My Window*? That ludicrous dustbin thing? Nobody. Probably not even their authors. They were controversial. People felt they had to see them, or be out of the swim. That's what gets people into the theatre these days. That, or trash. And I won't allow you to write trash.'

There was a long silence. I stared out of the wide windows

50

across a vista of smooth lawns and painting-book trees. Birds were singing their evening song. Hampstead Heath looked acid-yellow in the evening sun.

'So what do you want me to do?'

'Scrap all this nonsense and start again.'

My teeth made an ugly squeaking noise as I clenched them violently. *Don't. Don't let her. Don't.*

'All right then. If you really think –'

I turned round. She had won. She was all smiling affability.

'Do stay if you'd like to, Miss Fletcher. I could ask Bella to bring you something on a tray.'

She walked out of the silence and closed the door. The silence went on and on. He came over to the window and stood beside me, looking out into the tranquil evening.

'Say it,' he said at last.

I turned to him and caught my breath sharply to call him a bloody coward. But when I looked at him there was no question of saying it. He'd said it to himself already.

'What now?' I asked instead.

He shrugged and leaned on the window-sill. After a long time he said, 'I'm going to give her what she wants.'

'A nonsense-play.'

'Why not? It'll be quite a satisfying gesture, in a way. An insult to her, and to Theo Craven, if he's fool enough to be taken in by it, and anyone else who thinks it means something. But most of all, to her. It's what she deserves, it's what they all deserve, miserable pretentious sods who think nothing can be good or important if they can understand it. They despise themselves so much in their secret souls, they only dare admire what's beyond them. Right, I'll give them something that's beyond them, and they can stuff it down their throats or up their noses or into whatever bodily aperture seems best suited to it. It won't be meant for their brains because they haven't any.' He spoke with a deadly cold contempt, and only a very slight tremor in the silk covering his arm showed me that most of it was for himself.

Chapter Four

'Has he made a pass at you yet?'

Jill's well-projected voice rang from the kitchenette. Jim, sitting at table with Gwen and myself waiting for the next course, grew sharp-eyed. This was an out-of-the-blue Jillism which could have referred to anything and anyone, and neither Gwen nor I was willing to commit ourselves until Jill made herself clear.

She emerged, carrying a tray of her dainty desserts which were always more for show than for blow.

'Well?'

'Has who made a pass at who yet?' Jim asked jovially.

Jill looked, as always, surprised that we hadn't been following the silent workings of her mind. 'Aaron Franks, of course.'

Jim looked at me, and for some reason, certainly not guilt, I blushed. 'Don't be absurd,' I said.

'If it's so absurd, why are you embarrassed?'

'I'm not.'

'You are.'

Jill really could be infuriating sometimes.

'All right, have it your own way. I am. Now let's eat, or we'll miss the play.' The girls had just browbeaten me into paying for a third of a television set, and we were still at the stage of first-month-total-immersion.

Jim, however, had had a set of his own for some time, and quite rightly despised our indiscriminate goggle-eyed absorption.

'Oh Lord, we're not going to sit gawping at the Idiot's Lantern all the evening, are we?' he groaned. 'That's not what I came over for.'

'You can have what you came over for after Gwen and I retire,' said Jill sweetly. Normally this sort of remark would only have made me laugh; Jill and Gwen knew perfectly well that Jim and I behaved with unremitting propriety when we

52

were alone. But my nerves were ragged, and so I snapped back, 'Do you have to make that sort of smutty remark?' and she looked hurt and astonished and said 'Oh don't be a twerp, I didn't mean anything,' which resulted in an awkward silence. Gwen broke it by saying 'We'd better give the set time to warm up,' and before long we were crouched in a semi-circle with our sweets on our knees, staring at the lighted square like beings in a trance.

During the first commercial, Jim went out of the room and I said to Jill, 'What on earth made you suddenly ask that about Aaron?'

'What? – Oh, that. I'd been thinking about it during dinner. It seemed a natural question. After all, you've been with him for four weeks now, and you never seem to stop talking about him . . .'

'What absolute bloody nonsense, I scarcely ever mention him!'

'You *are* in a narky mood tonight!'

'You have narky moods yourself sometimes.'

'Never without a good reason.'

'Well, I have a good reason. I've been working damned hard.'

'Damned late, anyway. This is the first evening you've been home before nine for weeks, and this is Sunday. I should think poor old Jimbo's getting pretty cheesed off about it.'

'So, did you have to ask your personal question in front of him and make things worse?'

Typically, Jill immediately went into reverse and nearly turned herself inside out apologizing. 'Honey, what a fool I am! What a total creep. Gosh, I'm sorry. You know what I am, I just don't stop to *think*. I haven't really made things worse, have I? Do say you forgive me! – Oh look, here's the Esso Blue man, I'm mad about him; turn the sound up, Gwen!'

After the last programme, and not a moment before, the two girls went off to bed, leaving Jim and me to do the dishes. I couldn't really blame him for being a bit surly.

'Couldn't we leave them for once?'

'House-rule. Whoever doesn't cook, washes up.'

'But I want to talk.'

'So, talk.'

'What's all this "so" stuff?'

'So stuff? What are you talking about?'

'You start all your sentences with "so",' he complained.

'Rubbish.'

'It's not rubbish.'

'Stop arguing already and dry the dishes.'

'And that's another thing!'

'What is?' (knowing very well and cursing myself).

'"Already".'

'It's just a way of talking,' I said, washing each item with meticulous care. Why was I being deliberately slow? Surely not to postpone the time when I would have to sit with Jim on the sofa?

'A Yiddish way of talking,' he corrected.

'So? I mean, what if it is?'

'You're picking it up from Franks.'

'Well, why not? It's natural enough. We're together all day.'

'And most of the night, it seems.'

'Oh, Jim!'

'Well, it's true, isn't it? I never heard of any secretary being worked such long hours. He doesn't own all your time, does he?'

'I don't *have* to work late.'

'Then why do you?'

'I enjoy it. I'm interested in what he's doing.'

'What *is* he doing, anyway, that takes until ten o'clock at night?'

'Writing.'

'Bilge.'

'What do you mean by that?' I asked coldly.

'Nobody writes for nine hours a day.'

'We take breaks.'

'I'll bet you do!' he said sarcastically. 'Clean breaks?'

'Jim, you're beginning to annoy me.'

'All right, I'm sorry. But you must admit it sounds extraordinary. At that rate his play'd have been finished in a few days.'

'It is nearly finished.'

'I hope it's bloody well brilliant.'

54

I said nothing.

'Well – is it?'

'I don't know,' I said shortly.

He pounced. 'You don't know if it's good or not, and yet you're prepared to give nine hours a day to working on it! Pretty odd.'

'Can't we shut up about it? You often work late.'

'Yes, because I'm *really* keen on my job.'

'So am I!'

'Or your boss?'

'Oh God!' I was beginning to feel exhausted. 'It's what he's *doing* that fascinates me. I've told you.'

'Yes, and in the next breath you told me you don't even know whether the play's any good.'

'It's not the play I'm interested in.'

Blast him. He'd made me say it.

'Oh! So there's something besides the play!'

'What does it matter, Jim? Why can't you leave it alone?'

'Because I never see you and I want to know why. What else is he working on besides the play?'

'Why should it help to know that – A novel. Now are you satisfied?'

'What, you mean he works on the novel in the evenings?'

'*Yes*,' I said wearily. 'He works on the novel in the evenings.'

'Like a hobby.'

I turned on him. '*Not* like a hobby. The novel's his real work. Now I'm going to stop discussing it. Talk about something else or go home.'

We washed and dried in unfriendly silence for a few minutes and then he said 'Has he?'

'What?'

'What Jill asked during dinner.'

I couldn't help admiring, in an infuriated way, the sheer British bulldog tenacity of him. 'He's got plenty of girl-friends to make passes at, far more cooperative than me.'

'How does he know how cooperative you are till he tries? Besides, that type can't bear to see a decent girl within range without having a go.'

I said nothing. My face burned.

'What are you blushing for? You blushed at dinner. He *has* made a pass at you, hasn't he? The bloody cheek of him –'

I could feel myself shaking with irritation as I turned to him. 'Jim, will you stop it? I'm his secretary, that's how he thinks of me and how he treats me. And what do you mean "that type"? You've never set eyes on him!'

'Yes I have, I saw him when I came to pick you up at the shop the other night. I know the type, all right. Bloody over-sexed little sheeny!'

I felt rage explode in my face like a jug of ice-water hitting me. 'He's taller than you are!' I shouted idiotically. 'And don't use that word, if you don't want me to start calling you a bloody under-sexed little Anglo-Saxon!'

He stared at me for a moment and then said indistinctly 'I can't stand this', and made a groping movement to put his arms round me. One of his hands still clutched the limp dish-towel, and it should have been funny and touching, but my mouth was full of anger and my throat hurt with a sudden genuine hatred for him. I pushed past him into the hall and grabbed his coat and hat. As he came to the door of the kitchen I shoved them into his arms. He started to say something, his face blurred with bewilderment and the beginnings of apology, but I went straight into the living-room and slammed the door like a child. I flung myself into a chair and clung to its arms until, what seemed like an age later, I heard the front door of the flat close. Then the hard pain in my throat dissolved into tears. But they didn't heal my anger, though I cried for a long time.

When I went into the shop the next day, Dan met me. 'The new office, you'll be glad to hear, is now ready. Up, not down, them stairs today.'

From his uninhibited good cheer, I knew at once that Miss Franks wasn't anywhere about.

'Where's the boss-lady today?'

'In bed ill.'

'Nothing trivial, I hope?'

Dan looked shocked. 'Only a sty,' he said, with a chilliness that shamed me.

Aaron was waiting for me. He didn't have his usual morning aura of grim rebellion. He grabbed my hand as I came through the door at the top of the spiral staircase and exclaimed, 'Look, isn't it gorgeous? Oh God, what a room to work in! And did you notice, the stairs creak? I've tested them all sorts of ways; no one can avoid making a bit of noise coming up. She can't bloody well creep up on us here, unless she rigs up a pulley and gets Dan to fly her like Peter Pan!'

The room was indeed very pleasant and conducive. The walls and ceiling were pale grey; the carpet slightly darker. The long window looked over Regent Street; the sun streamed in, lending a fine fresh warmth to the room, a marvellous contrast to the artificial white light and dank chill of the cellar. There was an austerity about the furnishings which evidently pleased Aaron as much as the sunlight and air pleased me.

'Look!' He led me to a tall grey filing cabinet and stroked it as if it had been a priceless antique. 'It has a double lock,' he said tenderly, 'on every drawer.'

'Maybe she's kept duplicate keys.'

He grinned and shook his head. 'I bought this myself. Only two keys in the world. One I've got here.' He jangled his key-ring in front of me. 'The other –' He produced it out of his pocket and closed my hand over it. 'With your life,' he said, not wholly facetiously.

He held my hand between both his for a moment and looked down into my eyes. He was happy, I could tell. After a month I was beginning to know with reasonable certainty when he was acting, which was still frequently, but I could also tell quite often what was the antithesis of the act, what genuine mood lay beneath the façade at any given time. Now there was no act. He was quite simply happy, like a boy with a new hide-out. I'd noticed that when he was not acting, he was often more like a child in some ways than an adult.

'She's away today,' he said conspiratorially. 'We can do the real one all day.'

'Good.' I withdrew my hand and sat down at the desk. I unlocked his brief-case, which was lying by the typewriter. He brought 'the real one' to the shop in the locked brief-case every day because he was never parted from it; but we seldom got a chance to work on it except at night, after the shop had shut and Parrot-face had gone home. She thought we were staying on to work on the play.

A thought struck me as I was sorting last Friday's output. 'When you go home tonight, won't she want to see what we're supposed to have been doing all day?'

'Don't spoil today with your damned feminine practicality,' he said. 'I'll figure out some lie when the time comes. Today's mine. We're going to baptize this room with real work, whatever has to be done in it later. Okay?'

'Okay by me.'

Three hours later he straightened his tired back and I did the same, making dead, curled-legged spiders out of my cramped hands and laughing.

'Let's go and have lunch somewhere splendid,' he said.

'What, together?'

'Please – if you'd like it.'

'I would.' But then I remembered to look at his diary. 'Oh – you've got a date.'

'I have? Who the hell with?'

'Someone called Anne-Marie Bjoegenson. You told me to arrange it that day she kept ringing and you weren't in the mood for her.'

'Oh Jesus, yes. Oh, hell's *bloody* bells. I know what – I'll put her off.'

'You can't do that. It's nearly one now. She'll have left.'

'Where am I meant to be meeting her?'

'The Coq au Vin.'

'Right. Come on.'

'What do you mean? I'm not coming!'

'Yes you are. It's time you learned the facts of my life.'

I went on protesting, but he wouldn't listen. I found myself in a taxi seeping through thick traffic towards Jermyn Street.

'What on earth is Miss Bejugglehorn or whatever her name is going to think?'

'Should be funny to see. Don't worry, she isn't important.'

'Then why do you waste your time?'

He shrugged and looked out into the lunch-hour-crowded

streets. People were sitting round the steps of Eros on single sheets of newspaper. As usual the fountain seemed to have leaked, and long broad streams of water streaked the plinth and made the paper cushions soggy.

'I wonder why people sit there? It's not really a meeting-place; they just squat like flies among all the dirt and damp and litter and exhaust fumes, and stare at the wheels of cars going past . . .'

'Why do you waste your time, if she's not important?' I persisted.

'I like her to sleep with,' he said matter-of-factly, but without turning his head.

'Sleep with? Doesn't your sister want to know where you've been if you're away all night?'

'Bloody silly euphemism, isn't it? I meant, lie with. That's what they say in Hebrew, did you know that? Modern Hebrew, I mean. Just the same as in the Bible. If you want to say a girl is promiscuous, like Anne-Marie for instance, you don't say she "sleeps around", you say she "lies down". Much more precise, I think.'

'Do you know Hebrew?' I asked, to cover my embarrassment.

'Bits and pieces. Father tried to teach himself when he thought he might be going to Israel.'

'He seems to have taught himself some rather singular expressions,' I couldn't help remarking.

Aaron laughed. '*I* taught him that one. Picked it up from a kibbutznik at Oxford.'

'What's a kibbutznik?'

'Someone from a kibbutz, of course.' Kibbutzes, I remembered from somewhere, were some kind of communistic settlements in Israel, where children were raised away from their parents and nobody owned anything. 'I'll be interested to hear what you think of Anne-Marie.'

'I can tell you now what I think of her,' I retorted.

'What, prejudging the girl just because she "lies down"?' He was looking at me, quizzically and coldly.

'You've hardly gone out of your way to make her sound admirable.' Then I remembered that phone-call I had heard him take, the first day, and asked, 'Is she your bit of crumpet?'

'She's *a* bit of crumpet, certainly,' he replied promptly. 'Try and judge her in the light of your own natural crumpetishness, repressed though it doubtless is. Although I said she was un-important, that doesn't mean she isn't nice. Ah, here we are.'

I climbed out of the taxi on shaking legs, and stood staring aloofly down Jermyn Street while Aaron paid the taxi. I felt jolted and as upset as if he'd just seen me in my bath. Yet it was such a petty thing that I was angry with myself for minding. Certainly I mustn't let him see that he had got under my skin. I made excuses for myself by thinking my skin was probably thinner than usual today because of my row with Jim, and subsequent all-but-sleepless night, the night before. All the same I would have given a great deal to be able to run away and not have to meet this nice, unimportant, unrepressed bit of crumpet who was waiting for us. I pictured her as the sort of girl you find at the Lyceum at lunch-time hops – white-faced, dead-lipped, blacked-out-eyed and winkle-picker-shod, with a balloon skirt swinging like a church-bell from well-oiled hips. I pictured all Aaron's girls in this way. It didn't occur to me until we walked into the Coq au Vin and I saw Anne-Marie sitting waiting that, however contemptuously he might talk about his 'floosies', it would have been quite incongruous if they had really been witless and vulgar.

She rose, smiling at him, and put out her left hand palm down for him to hold. She was an Ingmar Bergman blonde; her silvery hair fell straight to her shoulders on either side of a face like a white cherry – creamy where it wasn't stained with too much rouge and lipstick, but undeniably luscious-looking and pretty with very blue eyes and straight, pale brows which she had left alone. She wore a simple blue dress, close-fitting over a full bosom and hips, with an artificial rose under her chin, demure between white lapels.

My heart gave a painful jolt as he bent to kiss her cheek, and another when she turned his head with her free hand and planted her full mouth on his deliberately. The ordinariness of her plump little face was hidden from me by the back of his head; that miraculous hair shimmering against the blue dress was all I could see.

Then he drew back, and, still holding her hand, said, 'Oh Anne-Marie, this is Martha. She's my amanuensis, and she's going to have lunch with us. Martha, Anne-Marie.'

The hand she gave me was cold and limp, and her eyes were as bright and dead as blue Day-glo.

'How do you do,' I said.

'Hello,' she said distantly, and turned immediately back to Aaron. I saw her show her teeth at him furiously. I walked to the counter to leave my coat, and heard her whisper, 'But I wanted to talk with you! How could you bring her, you *peeg*?' to which Aaron replied in his normal voice, 'Nothing in the world to stop you talking. Martha's discretion itself – aren't you, Martha? Come along, ladies, I'm famished.'

I shared her anger. He was thoroughly enjoying her frustration and my embarrassment. On impulse I drew my coat back over the counter just as the man was pinning a ticket to it.

'I wish the cloakroom,' said Anne-Marie suddenly. 'I will meet you at the table.' I caught a glimpse of blurring eyes and a pink-tipped nose as she swung away from him and walked quickly past me.

Aaron stood grinning with his hands in his pockets. 'See what I mean? Unimportant, but nice.'

'Which is more than anyone could say of you.'

He regarded me blandly. 'I think I'm very nice.'

'Well I don't.' I was putting my coat on again.

'Don't you approve of my taste?'

'I've nothing to say about your taste, it's your manners I object to.'

'Sorry, nanny, don't scold me.'

I went close to him and said in a very quiet voice, 'If she's good enough for you to go to bed with – sorry, lie down with – she's good enough to talk to over lunch. Personally I'd rather lunch by myself than stay here and annoy her.'

If I'd hoped for a more or less violent reaction, I was disappointed. He smiled amiably and said, 'Oh, okay. See you later, then,' and turned away with a casual wave of his hand, leaving me standing alone.

I wandered helplessly about the streets for a while, stifling tears and wondering if I'd gone raving mad, or what, to make such a fool of myself over nothing at all. What on earth was the matter with me? First Jim last night, and now this. I couldn't make sense of my own behaviour, and felt as if I were vulnerable to every small eddy of my own subconscious emotions. The frightening thing was that if Anne-Marie had turned out to be the sort of dim-witted little trollop I'd expected, I'd have sat through lunch feeling superior and not turning a hair at the thought of Aaron making love to her. Because she didn't look either dim-witted or specially trollopy, I'd had this violent reaction. Every time I thought of his thin hands caressing that beautiful hair I felt sick.

I caught sight of myself in an angled plate-glass window. My own hair, common-brown and short and up-curling, had blown, as was its wont, into two points above my head; I looked like a large horned owl. Those huge eyes that I'd always thought were my only claim to beauty now looked like a panda's eye-patches in my white face. My figure was positively undeveloped by comparison with Anne-Marie's.

Shut up, shut up, what does it matter? I mentally kicked myself. I walked back to the shop, dreading the afternoon, dreading the new insight into me that my ludicrous outburst would have given him, arming him with weapons of scorn and sarcasm. No doubt his fabulous conceit would lead him to imagine I was madly in love with him. The poor, mousy, repressed little secretary ... what fun he would have, patronizing me. And now he probably *would* make a languid attempt to seduce me, just for the hell of it, just to do me a favour ... I couldn't face it. Raging inwardly, I got on a bus and went home.

I had hardly closed the door of the flat behind me when the phone started ringing. It was Aaron, of course.

'Where are you?' he asked, sounding more curious than angry.

'At the Tower of London, feeding the ravens.'

'Don't be silly, I mean what are you up to? I've been waiting half an hour for you. I want to get on.'

'I didn't feel like working this afternoon, so I came home.'

There was a silence, and then he said 'Aren't you well?' There was something very like concern in his voice. There was nothing for me to do but lie.

'No, not very,' I said, muffled by a sense of cheating and absconding.

'You poor little thing, why didn't you say something? Is there anyone there to look after you?'

Sarcastic beast, as if he gives a damn! I thought angrily. 'I'm quite all right,' I said stiffly. 'I'm going to bed.'

'I'm coming over,' he said. Before I could react to what sounded like a smutty riposte, he added 'I can't work without you anyway. I'll sit and hold your hand and keep your morale up, like you did mine that time I was laid up.'

He hung up before I could protest, and I was left standing, the receiver in my hand, trapped by my own stupidity, my own ludicrous over-sensitivity. The row in the Coq au Vin obviously had not registered with him at all! And now I was left in the silly position of having to get undressed, get into bed, and play sick to bolster up the results of my folly.

I nearly ran away again, but the thing was becoming farcical. Feeling a complete idiot I got into the decentest nightgown I could find and propped myself up in bed with a lot of pillows. I had never felt less ill in my life. I was furiously angry with myself, but at the same time, as I sat there practising looking pale, it began to seem rather funny, somehow. When he arrived and I let him in and saw the look of comic solicitude on his face, I could hardly help bursting into guilty laughter.

'What are you grinning at? You're supposed to be ill.'

'I don't know – it all seems a bit silly.'

He stopped dead in the act of taking off his jacket and peered hard at me. 'Wait a minute,' he said slowly. 'Did you run out on me because you were sulking?'

'No of course not!' I protested, but without conviction.

'Were you really upset with me at the Coq? I thought you were joking.'

I felt panicky. The situation would soon be what I had imagined it was before. 'Look, I'm ill, I tell you!' I said with deadly sincerity.

He took hold of my shoulders and pushed me over to the bedroom window. 'Hm,' he commented dubiously, examining my face. 'You look suspiciously healthy to me.'

'You looked pretty healthy the day you were supposed to be ill,' I countered.

'Touché,' he said, letting me go.

'May I get into bed now, please?'

'Show me where the kitchen is first, and I'll make some tea.'

'Do you know how?'

'You sarcastic wretch, I'm not that spoiled! Bella taught me how to cook like a little Kosher angel.'

I got into bed and he shouted from the kitchen, 'What did you think of Anne-Marie?'

'She's very pretty,' I shouted back.

'She loathed you.'

'Even after I left? I think that's a bit ungrateful.'

'She thinks I'm having a "beeg theeng" with you.'

'I hope you disabused her of that idea.'

'On the contrary, I assured her you were the beegest theeng in my life to date. That's why I was back at the office so quickly. The lunch didn't get beyond the potted-shrimp stage.'

He came into the bedroom with a tea-tray, looking smug, sat down on the bed and clasped my hand to his heart. 'Let us have a beeg theeng and make an honest man of me,' he said with heavy Italian passion.

'What a little swine you are,' I said sharply, snatching my hand away. He looked surprised. 'Now what have I done?'

'That poor girl. You make love to her as long as it suits you and then tell her outright lies to get rid of her.'

'Well it wasn't more than a token lie. I mean, I am having "theengs" with other girls besides her; just not with you, and not anything "beeg", that's all.'

I looked at him curiously. He had a rather satyrish face, at that. 'Don't you ever get into trouble?'

'No, and neither do they. I see to that.'

'I meant emotional trouble.'

'No, because I'm very careful to pick girls like Anne-Marie who – well, who lie down. The way men do, I mean – for fun, for their health, out of *joie d'esprit* or *de corps* or whatever.'

'Do such girls exist in large numbers?'

'I find they do. Sufficient numbers so that one never has to trespass on to dangerous ground, anyway.'

'Dangerous ground?'

'The sort of ground pain grows in.'

He looked at me for a moment and then went to pour the tea. 'Pity I didn't bring the stuff over,' he said after a short silence. 'You're obviously quite well enough to work.'

'Where did you leave it?'

'Up there. Oh, not to worry, she won't be in today, she's got her conjunctivitis; that's always good for two days' freedom at least.'

'Has she really not got a clue that you're doing something besides the play?'-

'Not a clue. I'm sure of it. She hasn't been so pleased with me in years. Can't you tell the difference yourself? All those becks and smiles and wanton wiles . . . she's been quite human.'

'And so have you,' I said without thinking. I was feeling very much at ease with him.

He was quite still for a moment, and then turned slowly to face me. 'Meaning?'

'I don't know –'

'Yes you do. Say it.'

'You're happier. I think that's what I meant. You don't do your acts all the time any more.'

'My – *acts*?'

He looked suddenly different, and dangerous. I found myself stammering. 'You know what I mean.'

'I'll be f——ed if I do.'

We stared at each other through air dancing with his antagonism. I felt as if I'd been walking through a peaceful meadow and suddenly discovered it was a minefield.

'I want to know what you meant,' he said.

'You're so unpredictable! I abuse your manners, call you names, take all sorts of liberties, and your reaction is nil. Suddenly you're looking as if you'd like to kill me.'

'I would like to kill you, you offensive bitch! Who do you think you are? Just because I've taken you into my confidence, just because I let you talk me into trying to write a bloody novel, doesn't mean you can pry and comment and behave like my bloody psychoanalyst, for Christ's sake!'

I sat numbly. He stood in the middle of the room, holding his cup of tea. The cup began to rattle in the saucer and with a sudden, infantile gesture he flung it at the wall. We stared at the running stain, trickling down towards the broken pieces of china by the skirting boards, as if at the evidence of some disaster which had attacked us both from outside. He looked down at the hand which had thrown the cup and then at me with a dazed expression.

'It's all right, Aaron.'

I started to get out of bed and go towards him. But with a sudden trapped gesture he shook his head violently and, doubling up, rushed past me and into the hall. It had a number of doors leading off it and I watched helplessly as he blundered about, trying to find the right one to get him out of his trap. *He's crazy*, I thought suddenly. *He even moves like a lunatic.* I wanted to close my door against him, to leave him alone as one would leave some dangerous wild creature to batter itself into exhaustion and passivity; I really was afraid of him. But suddenly he found the right door and flung it open and I had a great sense of personal relief as I thought, *Thank God, he's found the way out; now what happens to him is not my business.* Only he didn't go out. He stopped in the doorway, his thin shoulders heaving, his head hanging forward, both hands clutching the door-frame and his legs quivering. I thought, *If I call him now, anything might happen, he might turn round and come at me. I don't even know him any more.* But without willing it I found myself walking to him, I found myself touching his back; and as he turned round, I saw that his face was his own face again, only quite helpless, and with tears on it. I stood in front of him and said quietly, 'It's all right. It was my fault.' His arms came up slowly and he put them round me and held me with my face against his shirt. I could feel him trembling violently, but his voice above my head was almost steady as he said, 'No, it was mine. Only I couldn't help it. Can it be one's own fault when one can't help it?'

He held me quite still in his arms for a long moment, and I held him. He didn't say anything else and gradually the trembling stopped, and his arms relaxed, and I moved out of them. I didn't look at him because I knew he hadn't had a chance to deal with his tears. Instead I went into my bedroom and got his jacket and brought it out to him. By that time he was looking almost all right again.

He turned round and I helped him put the jacket on. He moved stiffly and slowly, like an old man. He seemed to be gathering himself together for a great effort as he turned round again.

'Is there anything I can say that will make you forget it?' he asked.

'I'll try,' I said helplessly.

'Did I frighten you?'

'A little.'

'I'm sorry. How inadequate! Please don't worry. It doesn't often happen now.'

'But what – what was it?'

He looked at the floor. 'In a child, you'd call it nothing more solemn-sounding than a tantrum. I don't know what you'd call it in a grown-up.' He made a sound like a laugh. 'Not an act, anyway, of that I do assure you.' He looked up quickly, caught my anxious look fixed on his face, and turned away. 'I must be off. Do you think you'll be well enough to come to work to-morrow?'

'Yes.'

'Perhaps you'd rather not come again, after this.'

'Of course I don't feel that.'

'Good.' He kicked at the door-jamb for a moment and then said, 'What about the mess?'

'The what? Oh, that. Don't worry, I'll do it.'

He didn't argue. 'Well . . .' He started to go without looking at me again.

'Where are you going now?'

Standing out in the hall, he rubbed his hand over his cropped hair, forward from the crown and down over his face. 'I'm going to see Anne-Marie,' he said. 'Do you mind?'

My bewilderment was completed by the way he asked this. There was nothing sarcastic in it. It was as if he were genuinely asking my permission.

'No,' I said. 'I don't mind.'

. . . . .

After he'd gone I got a damp cloth and a dustpan and brush and knelt in my bedroom facing the wall. I rubbed the cloth over the wallpaper and some of the tea came off, but not all. I could see it was going to leave a mark, which would defeat me in my promised efforts to forget what had caused it. I picked up the bits of broken china. My hands were shaking. There's something very sad about anything broken. Usually I get rid of the pieces quickly without thinking about it, but now it was like a little death. I'd been very fond of that particular cup, but that wasn't the worst of it. I kept seeing the abrupt switch into violence, the wild ungoverned gestures, the thin angry fingers letting the inoffensive cup lash the wall and go down in pieces. *Like a child*, I kept thinking. *Just like a spoilt child*. I tried to feel tolerant and quietly understanding about it, but I could only think about him holding Anne-Marie in his arms. I felt a raging sorrow that made me lean against the tea-stained wall and weep.

Chapter Five

'*Man, beseechingly:* "But don't you see, Alf? Oh, why can't anyone understand? I can't participate, I can't submerge, I can't be committed! And why? – because I can't lay my hands on the particles of my individuality and reassemble them into a recognizable entity. How can you commit what is nothing but confusion? My identity is intangible, spread through the world like dust-motes. There is nothing unique about me except universality. The only part of me that's real is the part which gravity ties to the earth, eternally. How can one fight when the very laws of nature disseminate and diffuse one's inner syndrome until it becomes mere atoms spread through the human equation?"

'*Alf, dousing his chips in vinegar:* "Quit your bloody whining. You're alive, ain't you? You can breathe, eat, drink, screw? So what's your problem?"

'*Man, lying down sobbing on floor between tables:* "I want my mother! I want my mother!"

'*Alf finishes his chips, crumples newspaper into a ball and tosses it down beside Man. Teddy-boy, jeering:* "'Ere, litter-lout! Pick up yer rubbish or the Beak'll fine you ten quid!" *Alf, as he leaves:* "Go and stuff yourself."

'*Curtain.*'

Aaron was laughing so hard by the time he finished dictating that he could barely choke out the final words. He put his head down on the window-sill and groaned with the pain of laughing. At last he stood up, wiping his eyes, and tottered over to where I was typing 'Curtain' at the bottom of the page. As soon as it was done, he dragged me from my chair, and went into a short routine he had taught me.

'Jack the Ripper was Poet Laureate to Catharine of Russia. True or false?'

'False!'

'Valse! Valse? I'd love to!'

'Da – da – de-dum ... Da – da – de-dum ...' We whirled briefly round the room to the strains of the Blue Danube, then he stopped suddenly, nearly pitching me on my face, and said sternly, 'Of course Jack the Ripper wasn't Poet Laureate to Catharine of Russia. Jack the Ripper *was* Catharine of Russia. How could you be so dense?'

'Dence? Dence? I'd love to!'

'Da – da – de-dum ... Daaaa – da – de-dum ...'

We drew up at last, hot and panting with laughter. He sagged at the knees; I caught him under the arms and tried to hold him up, but he was a dead weight and slid like a corpse to the floor, dragging me with him. We lay in a hysterical heap.

'Finished – finished – finished! My master-work is born! My travail is done! Oh, you lucky people!'

'Let me up, will you, you dim-wit, you're ruining my dress!'

'Ah, now me vile passions are aroused! Did you think I would let you go, Maria, knowing the fearful truth? Knowing that I am Tod Slaughter giving the worst performance of my life? Never! One last kiss, then into a home-made grave ...'

'Would it be any harm to ask what is going on up here?'

A silence fell that was grave-like indeed. Aaron rolled away and we both lay there, propped on our elbows, looking aghast at Parrot-face standing like Nemesis in the doorway with a face like the kiss of death.

Aaron recovered first, and scrambled to his feet. I felt too weak to move. The situation was so awful and ludicrous that more laughter was gathering irresistibly in my throat when she said frigidly, 'Either get up, Miss Fletcher, or pull your skirt down. My brother may find your suspenders an attractive sight, but personally I find them rather revolting.'

Anger and outrage winded me. I lay there, gaping at her. 'Poll, for God's sake! Don't make a fool of yourself.'

'*You* say that to *me*?' she asked with acid dignity.

'Of course! You can't seriously imagine –'

'No imagination is necessary.'

Aaron tried to laugh, but it died in his throat. He turned abruptly and helped me to my feet. His face was drawn. 'We were only fooling about,' he muttered angrily.

'Rather noisily. There are customers in the shop who must be wondering whether I run a brothel. I sometimes wonder myself.'

She turned and walked out. The fun and the excitement lay around us, killed stone dead.

Aaron suddenly struck the desk with his fist, with all his strength. 'I'll kill that bitch one day,' he said between clenched teeth.

My own outrage died when I realized the futility of his. 'Look Aaron, she hates me. I knew it from the first moment she saw me. It's something deep-seated and feminine and there's nothing one can do about it.'

'Deep-seated and feminine my arse. It's just a pure, un-varnished, prejudiced horror of the thought of me having any-thing to do with a *shiksa*. It's what your family might feel if they thought you were making love to some handsome black buck from the Congo jungle. That, and the fact that she is just a bitch. A would-be matriarch who'll always be frustrated be-cause she can't let a man touch her. Oh Christ,' he said with sudden weariness. 'I suppose I should feel sorry for her. I should make allowances. Write her off as a howling neurotic and stop caring . . .'

'Sounds good in theory. What's stopping you?'

'Fear, I suppose. Something very primitive that I can't do anything about. I was wetting my pants because of her when I was three years old and she was thirteen and undertook to be "a little mother" to me.'

'What about your real mother?'

'Having *me* did for her, poor old love. She was nearly fifty when I cropped up.' He sat staring glumly at the floor. 'One day I'll get away,' he said, but without conviction. 'I'll just say to hell with her, to hell with the money and the house and every-thing else – I'll just shog off.' He looked up at me sharply. 'I know what you think – you think I should have done it years ago. Listen, it's not just the luxury, believe me, it's not just that. It's – it's everything. That house. What did you think of it?'

'It's beautiful.'

'She's got taste. I'll give her that. Not about art, but about décor. Mother had it, and she's got it. It's all cold, since Father died, cold but perfect. But I like the perfection and Bella warms it into a home for me. I love that house – you know? My roots are there. I know every bit of it, every bush in the garden, they're all worked into me like my bones. Father bought it for Mother before Poll was born. They married very late in life and I've heard they were just like young lovers; some of their friends say they used to get a bit embarrassed, watching them holding hands and having private jokes and kissing when they thought no one was noticing. They only had about twelve years together, but by God, I'd rather have twelve years of –'

He broke off as if he'd startled himself, and quickly lit a cigarette. He offered one to me, nervously, as if I'd become dangerous through having learned too much. 'Anyway,' he went on at last, 'I couldn't bear to lose my chance of getting the house. And I could. She could will it away – it's hers – if I didn't toe the line . . .'

'You'll have to toe it for a long time at that rate.'

'Well, you never know. Perhaps . . . I always think, perhaps if I do everything her way until I get my money, if I've achieved whatever it is she wants me to achieve, then she'll let me go my own way after that . . .'

'She can't very well stop you. She couldn't stop you now.'

'I know . . . it's just that, somehow, your life gets a stranglehold and you can't make that wrenching effort to escape . . . Specially when you don't even know what sort of person you want to be . . .'

'Better the devil you know . . .'

'That's it.'

'And what's "the devil you don't"?'

'Myself. Without the trappings.'

We sat and smoked our cigarettes to the end, and both reached at the same moment to stub them out in the crowded ashtray. He took hold of my hand and said more gaily, 'Well, never mind. We've finished the Horror, anyway. She'll be pleased about that.'

'What tyranny *is* this? She'll be pleased!'

'Things are better when she's pleased. You don't know. You don't have to live with her.'

I bit back the retort obvious, and said instead: 'Do you honestly think you're going to get away with it, Aaron?'

He stood up and stretched. 'I wouldn't be surprised. They're all just daft enough to swallow it. Did I tell you friend Theo's just taken a lease on some old theatre in the suburbs which has a glorious past and is now a hatching-house for TV commercials and is proposing to resuscitate it? Going to make a latter-day Royal Court out of it, get the intelligentsia streaming across the river to worship at a new shrine. He's got the workmen in now, tearing out all the expensive sound-proofing and putting back the stage that the TV boys tore out five years ago. And he's looking for a wildly new, madly *avant-garde*, insanely angry and young and dirty-minded playwright to launch the venture with a suitable bang. At the moment he's toying with a play which was written in Mohawk by a Caughrawaga Indian, in between slapping red-hot rivets into the top of a skyscraper in Chicago. It's all about life on a reservation – sort of a modern Western. But I don't think Poll will stand for that. She's so impressed by our Acts 1 and 2 that she's already nudging Mad Craven's elbow at the bridge-table and dropping great sledge-hammer hints . . .' He chuckled. 'What a howl if he took it! What a bloody joke. God, I'd sit in the stalls on opening-night and look at their stupid faces, and at all those bogus Method boys on the stage knocking their witless guts out pretending they were getting the message, and I'd laugh myself unconscious.'

'Would you?'

'Why not? – But they probably won't take it. I'm probably underestimating them. Even that fat phoney Theo must occasionally spot when he's having his leg pulled. Still, it won't hurt to try.' He was looking at me idly, but suddenly he frowned. 'You look worn out,' he said.

'Rubbish.'

'I work you like a bloody slave, I know that perfectly well. But I couldn't do any of it without you . . .'

'Thanks,' I said – dryly, to hide a sudden elation.

'I must be wrecking your private life.'

'You probably would if I had one, but I haven't.'

'Why, what happened to that bloke who used to pick you up here? The sandy one with duck's disease?'

'Ducks can fly, and he flew.'

'Did you mind?'

How to answer this truthfully? On second thoughts, why answer it truthfully, or at all? I shrugged and changed the subject.

'When are you going to show it to her – Act 3?'

'Tonight, if she's receptive. She's throwing a big party on Thursday night – big in importance, anyway. The Cravens are bidden; whether they'll come of course depends on whether they've got anything better to do. If Polly likes it, she might thrust it into his hot little hands right then and there.'

'I'd better start fair-typing it first thing tomorrow.'

'No, listen, Martha, don't come in tomorrow. You really deserve a rest; I feel suddenly guilty about you. Take a couple of days off.'

'I wouldn't know what to do with them.'

'Rest or go to a movie or something.'

'And what about the evening work?'

'I'll get on with it long-hand; you can catch me up later.' His voice instinctively dropped, although we were touching so obliquely on the subject.

'I thought you said you couldn't do anything without me?'

'Well, that's what's worrying me. I'm getting too dependent on having someone to dictate to and discuss things with. Surely real creative work should be done entirely alone?'

'Are you saying the book so far isn't real creative work?'

'Is it?'

There it was again, the insatiable hunger for praise and reassurance. He's worse than a woman in love, I thought. 'Don't you know if it's good?' I asked, detachedly.

'I feel it is, but – I don't know . . .'

'Well, don't sink into a gloom,' I said briskly after a pause. 'If you really won't need me, I can't pretend there aren't plenty of things I'd like to do at home. Let me know when you're ready for me.'

Three days and nights of attenuated boredom and useless loneliness passed. I spent the days meandering about the flat, tending my window-box, reading desultorily or cooking meals for the girls and myself. I started doing crosswords again. I hated this return to stagnation, but I couldn't help it. In the evenings I crouched, glassy-eyed and slack-jawed, in front of the goggle-box. I was aware of a sour feeling of self-disgust during all the most absorbing pieces of entertainment. But it was the self-disgust felt by drinkers and dope-takers for a habit that helps them bear life. The self-disgust is part of the price of numbness.

'Oh, for heaven's sake, why don't you phone him?' asked Jill at dinner on the third evening, flinging down her knife and fork into the middle of what I realized had been a long introverted silence.

'He said he'd phone me when he wanted me back,' I said.

'Well, of all the nerve! Just like that! So you sit around being miz until he decides he's forgiven you.'

I realized jarringly that she meant Jim. 'I thought you were talking about Aaron,' I said before I could stop myself.

Jill and Gwen exchanged glances. 'Don't you even miss old Jim?' asked Gwen curiously.

'Sometimes.'

'But not enough to make you try and patch things up.'

'The same goes for him, apparently.' In the last few days I had had time to brood on this and to suffer the pangs of hurt pride about it for the first time.

'Seems a bit rash to let such a solid citizen get away without at least an effort ...' Gwen's taste in men ran to penniless artists, but, wistfully, she was the first to appreciate the merits of grey flannel suits and regular incomes.

'It really wouldn't have done. We didn't match.'

'Still ...'

Still – better than nothing. But that, I felt, was a pretty unattractive, not to say defeatist, attitude. And I didn't *really* miss him. Only at times like this. As we drew our chairs round the set, I suffered a sinking feeling as if there were a vacuum inside me. How appalling to be so empty of private resources! I was utterly dependent on other people for an escape from loneliness. *I live in the second and third persons*, I thought. *I'm not a three-dimensional individual, I'm a mirror.* I pushed this disquieting knowledge of myself away and concentrated on the tasteless antics of some dim *farceur*.

But later came an orchestral programme, and during it I went off into a reverie about Aaron's play. When he had first started it, before I'd persuaded him to syphon off his aggressiveness into the secret evening project, he had been so bitterly resentful that the results had reminded me of that 'picture' of Picasso's, through which rusty nails are driven, points out, to tear the hands of anyone who tries to touch it. He spat out words so full of scorn and fury that it hurt me to read them back to him; it was like beating him with his own whips. After a few days of this, with us both growing more and more depressed and exhausted, he buried his face in his hands one afternoon and said, 'It's no good, is it? I mean, it's not even good *bad*.' When I had no answer, he took a deep breath and said, quite calmly, 'If I'm going to make a rude gesture, it might as well be an effective one. Even Theo wouldn't fall for this crap. So, tear it up, and let's start again.'

After that it was very different. The nonsense began to have a diabolical thread of reason running through it. It was called *Man in a Hole*. On one level it was just what he'd intended it to be – a subtle take-off of all the new-wave playwrights he despised for writing as if half-baked ideas and demotic rhetoric counted more than craftsmanship and having something important to say. But on another level, it was something more. It abounded in hints of hidden meanings. It was full of fascinating off-beat characters and sparkling snatches of dialogue – but they were all disconnected from the plot, if you could call it a plot. Following the progress of this was fascinating and infuriating – like watching an energetic retriever with a flea; he'd chase along madly, nose to the scent, with a great air of being confident there was something up ahead – and then suddenly leap round to bite at his own rump before starting forward again in a totally different direction.

One day when this happened I uttered a wail of frustration and flung my pencil across the room.

'What's eating you?'

'You're driving me crazy! It was just starting to add up.'

'I know. I realized it just in time. Nearly scared the wits out of me.'

'But it could be something good – something *real*!'

'You show dangerous symptoms of forgetting the object of the exercise.'

But after we started to work on the novel in the evenings, the days' irritations ceased to count. They were just something to be got through before we could bring the pile of pages out of the locked brief-case and get down to what really mattered. At first Aaron had doubted his ability to do two things concurrently, but the scheme worked well. The play gave him a rest from the novel, which he came to all the more freshly and enthusiastically after a day of wrestling with the mental gymnastics of *Man in a Hole*.

For me, it was like working with two different men – during the day a verbal gymnast, and in the evening a creative and serious writer. All the other confusing aspects of his personality took sides with one or the other of his writing selves. The rebellion, the smuttiness, the sneering, the languid self-disgust all amalgamated into the smoothly contemptuous daytime self; the seriousness, the humour, the vitality and the eager creative absorption welded together into the evening whole. I wondered from time to time what would happen to the evil daytime genius when the play was finished.

And now it *was* finished. Tonight was Thursday, the night of the party. Tonight it might be shown to Theo Craven. I felt a shiver go through me at the thought of a stranger reading it. It was as if I were thinking about Aaron, defenceless and stripped, delivered over to judgement, with a condemning revelation of immaturity or malice hung round his neck.

The phone rang. Without taking her eyes from the screen, Jill reached across and picked it up. 'For you,' she said, passing the receiver blindly in my general direction.

'Oh *don't* take it in here!' Gwen implored, hitching her chair forward until she was nestling almost to the bosom of the set.

But I was too lazy to move. 'Hallo?' I whispered.

'Hullo yourself,' Aaron whispered back. 'Are there microphones hidden in your Marie Laurencin, or what?'

I hadn't realized till this moment that I had thought my job with him had somehow come to an end and that I would never see him again.

'The telly's watching us,' I hissed.

'So, how are you?'

'Bored. How are you?'

'Not bored. Listen, what are you doing?'

'Right now? Watching the –'

'Have you just washed your hair or anything?'

'No?'

'Good. Well, get into something stunning and come over.'

'But – but it's the party,' I stammered.

'Exactly. You're invited.' He sounded blithe.

'Who by?'

'Me.'

'I couldn't. She'd strike me down with poisoned basilisks.'

'Then sharpen up a few barbed glances of your own. Get dressed, I'll be over in twenty minutes to fetch you.'

I heard the click as he hung up, and sat numbly, staring at the screen, my mind darting about inside my ill-equipped wardrobe like a trapped rat. My only decent after-six dress had a wine-stain on it dating back to Jim. I clutched Jill's arm and said, 'Can I borrow your new pyramid-line?'

'Have a heart, I haven't worn it myself yet,' she said without moving a muscle.

'Gwen, your lime-green—?'

'Cleaners,' came the tranced reply.

'Oh, oh God! One of you, please help me!'

Jill shook her head as if a fly were buzzing in her ear, Gwen said in a far-away voice, 'My black lace, and if you get one tear in it I'll do you.'

The next few minutes were chaotic. I rushed in and out like a lunatic, skidding and cursing; the girls sat on, impervious. But they came to life when the doorbell rang.

'Who's that?'

'Aaron.'

'*What!*' They both shot to their feet, the set forgotten, and began making lightning adjustments to the room and themselves. 'Why on earth didn't you tell us your exotic boss was coming?'

'Would you have heard? He won't be coming in anyway.'

'You *dare* to not show him to us!'

I had never seen him in a dinner-jacket before. It was a very beautiful one, with touches of discreet eccentricity in the cut; it gave his lean body an air of effortless, almost decadent elegance. We stood staring at each other in the bad light of the tiny hall.

'You look quite lovely,' he said gravely, to which I replied unthinkingly 'So do you.'

His laugh was forced; I saw his eyes flicker uncomfortably round the hall and, unpleasantly, I remembered the last time we had stood in this doorway.

'Come in for a minute,' I said quickly.

'And lay the ghost? All right.' I hadn't thought for a moment that he would speak of it.

We went into the living-room, where I had to suppress a shriek of laughter at the sight of Jill and Gwen, who had been leaping about like dervishes a minute before, now relaxing in graceful attitudes of negligence with books in their hands.

Introductions were solemnly performed and a sherry poured from our joint stock. I had not been embarrassed by the flat when Aaron had been in it before. Now, perhaps because of his elegance, I became aware of its shabbiness and unfightable feminine disorder; of the meagre hospitality exposed by the solitary decanter and half-bottle of Gordon's gin; of the hideous cretonne cover Jill had relentlessly made, and ineptly fitted, on to the aged settee; of the dearth of books or other intellectual equipment; of the absence of any object of real worth, beauty or even intrinsic interest in the whole room. What a limited life we let ourselves lead, I thought despairingly. Not even a decent reproduction, not a souvenir of anywhere more enterprising than Edinburgh! What a horribly commonplace, *bourgeois*, uncreative, uncommitted, unintellectual, dreary little trio we are. I wondered why I'd never noticed it before, never before compared this flat, what it lacked and what it exposed of our limitations, to the homes of more exciting people. Because I didn't know any, presumably. I shrank inwardly from the prospect of tonight, of meeting successful people in the mass for the first time, in surroundings calculated to make me feel like a Poppit necklace in the window of Asprey's.

I excused myself and fled to my room to examine myself again in the mirror. The black lace was probably the safest choice I could have made, even if I'd had a choice. It slimmed my hips and made the most of my shoulders and neck; also it lent an entirely spurious illusion of sophistication. But how badly it needed jewellery! I tried a rather expensive piece of costume junk against the shoulder. Normally I would have thought it pretty. Tonight it looked awful – as anything that wasn't real would have done. I tried my pearls, which were sort of real, but they had a striving, pathetic air ('The only thing she's *got*, poor lamb, that's *quite* obvious') so I discarded them too. No suburban pretensions. The best or nothing. I gave my hair a final brush, and put some perfume on – Gwen's, so I should be able to smell it myself and get a morale boost.

'Put some behind your knees!' hissed Gwen. who had crept in. 'And in your elbows – and there – yes, there, and drops round the hem of your slip.' She knelt at my feet and began to work round me like a dressmaker.

'I'll stink to high heaven!'

'You won't, you'll move in a blissful aura ... of *my* perfume!' she discovered too late. 'Oh well, it's worth it. *Isn't he gorgeous?*'

'What?' I asked, startled.

'A creature from another planet! Those beautiful little hips! That fascinating bony face! Oh, if only one *did* something – painted or wrote – he'd simply be one's inspiration! There.' She stood up and ruefully held her depleted flask to the light. 'He'll be intoxicated by you.'

'Asphyxiated, more probably. But thanks.'

We went back into the other room, where Jill was rather stiltedly holding the fort. Aaron stretched languidly along the settee, smoking through a long cigarette holder and looking dangerous and out of place, like a black mamba lying across the flowered cretonne. He gave me his suave, George-Sanders look and rose slowly and smoothly to his feet. He put out his hand and, when I put my own into it rather bewilderedly, brushed mine with a worldly kiss. I heard Jill give a little gasp of appreciation. Then Aaron straightened up and said, 'Cor, you don't 'alf ponk. Where'd you fink you're goin' then, the Pally? Come on, don't muck about.'

'I could kill you,' I said succinctly when we were luxuriously ensconced in the back of the hired car. 'You ruined the whole effect.'

'My favourite thing,' he replied cheerfully. 'They were looking at me like something from outer space; I couldn't resist.' He was holding my hand lightly on his knee. He often touched me casually, squeezing my hand or hugging me in a moment of exuberance; till now this unself-conscious sensuality and warmth had seemed merely a pleasant contrast to the average Englishman who never indulges in casual gestures of affection for fear of compromising himself. But even a man one knows very well can seem like a mysterious stranger in the uniform of evening dress. I was suddenly very conscious of Aaron's hand round mine; the touch of his fingers was light, warm and dry; he moved his thumb absently back and forth across my wrist until every nerve in my body seemed to be concentrated there.

I drew my hand away, covering the movement with speech.

'You might tell me a bit about tonight,' I said. 'I'm sure I shouldn't be going. She does expect me, I suppose?'

'Oh yes, she expects you.'

'But why? Why did you invite me?'

He didn't answer for a moment, but sat back, the passing lights making patterns across his face. His eyes were very bright.

'Things have been happening while you've been loafing at home,' he said. 'Much faster than I'd expected. No flies on old Polly.'

'Why, what's happened?'

'You'll see.'

'Oh, tell!'

'Patience.'

What could have happened in three short days? 'She liked the finished article, presumably?' I ventured, fishing for further clues.

His full mouth was pulled tight to his teeth in his effort to keep back laughter. 'You could put it like that,' was all he would say.

The big white house was wide awake; light streamed from every window, striping the drive and the island of chestnuts. There were half a dozen cars drawn up, and as we walked up the steps I could see the party going on in one of the big rooms in the front.

Bella met us in the hall. Her little round face was more powdery than ever, and her unpainted mouth was a straight, harried line. She gave a grunt when I greeted her, and stumped angrily away with my coat.

'Poor Bella. She loathes parties.' Aaron stood before a vast mirror set in the wall and adjusted his tie. I couldn't stop looking at him. He caught my eye in the mirror and grinned.

'Looking forward to it?'

'No. I'm scared.'

He turned round and stared at me. 'Scared? Of *them*? That lot?'

'And her.'

'Oh, well . . .' He shrugged. 'She's in her how-nice-it-is-that-I'm-always-right mood. She's smiling and benevolent as a well-fed anaconda.'

And that bulge in her guts is you, I thought, dropping my eyes so that he shouldn't read my mind. He had a way of doing that which was disconcerting.

He put his hands on my shoulders and said gently, 'Come along, my little pretty.' And he kissed the top of my head and led me into the big, bright room.

The general effect was dazzlingly impressive, the way the shop had been when I first walked into it. It was contemporary in the Design-Centre-then-on-to-Heals sense, which managed not to be incongruous in that Regency room. Everything was light and bright and costly-looking, except the people, who were mostly *heavy* and bright and costly-looking. There were about a dozen of them, including, to my great surprise, Dan. I don't know why I should have been surprised, really; except that she always treated him as an office boy. Somehow despite what he'd told me about having been a friend of Aaron's at Oxford, I hadn't imagined he would be at all involved in the Franks's rather posh social life.

The men stood up as I came in, and Polly's parrot face bent into a horny smile.

'Ah, here's Aaron with his little secretary,' she said with what might have passed for cosiness unless one happened to know better.

I was taken the rounds. Theo Craven was large and florid with bloodshot eyes exactly matching his Bacchanalian lips. His hair was crisply grey and his nails buffed to glossy almonds; a wave of some expensive spicy smell emanated from him with such power that it quite obliterated Gwen's gentle fragrance. His wife Madeleine was small and fat and agonizingly corseted. Her naturally scanty hair had been tortured into a stiff balloon; her general outline suggested a cottage loaf on top of which a third blob of dough has been stuck. She looked me curiously up and down when shaking hands, as if pricing my clothes.

Another couple were the Davidsons. The husband Bill was one of those smooth, well-fed men who could be anything from thirty to fifty. He had a boyish tuft of brown hair that spouted like a recalcitrant weed from the crown of his head, and an unruly lock that need not have flopped engagingly into his eye, necessitating a recurrent toss and upward tilt of his chin, unless he had wanted it to. The chin, untilted, sank insignificantly into a pad of soft flesh. Tilted, it became part of a youthful look-to-the-future mien which reminded me of an advertisement for National Savings.

His wife was vaguely familiar. 'Of course you know Mrs Davidson – Joanne Dickson the actress?' Polly said commandingly, and my heart went out to the young woman when she said warmly, 'Of course she doesn't, why should she? – Hallo.' We shook hands, and she grinned at me. She was tall and slender and beautiful, like a fawn, with a clear-cut wild look. How right I had been not to wear fake jewellery! This girl's starkly simple brown dress was set off by two solid chunks of gold in her ears, and another on her finger. They looked like nuggets, and were so flagrantly big that they could only be real. Mrs Craven and Polly both wore diamonds, Polly discreetly, Mrs Craven not.

Dan brought round drinks. The conversation didn't tax me, in fact it didn't include me at all. I was able to stand apart from the others and get the feel of them. They just made rather commonplace small-talk and gossiped about people

I'd never heard of; but perhaps the brilliance would come later.

Bella stuck her head in like a cranky tortoise and said, 'Dinner's on.'

I drifted in with Dan. He looked compressed and uncomfortable in his dinner-jacket, which appeared to have shrunk. I had a different feeling about him here; he no longer seemed like an ally. I was dying to ask him if he came here often or only in the butling season, but there was a rigidity and formality about him that inhibited me.

'What does Mr Davidson do?' I felt safe in asking.

'Don't you know? He's a producer. Quite famous. Remember, he did *The World at My Window* at Coventry and it came in to town and ran for ages?'

It clicked, then; that was where I'd seen his wife before.

'Miss Dickson played the prostitute.'

'That's right. First big break and all that theatrical clap trap.'

As we entered the dining-room my eye was caught by an extraordinary picture over the fireplace. I call it a picture; actually it was a framed square of canvas which had been slashed diagonally once. The edges of the slash had been drawn inwards and the cut backed with a piece of black material. That was all; that was the picture. Dan saw me staring at it and said diffidently, 'Martha's very taken with your Broggotti, Paula.'

The company turned and stared with me at the meaningless monstrosity.

'Magnificent, isn't it?' Theo Craven said reverently, 'So stark – so elemental. It says it all, in one swift, clean, perfect gesture.'

'And yet if it had been any different –' said someone else, '– an inch to the right, a fraction more perpendicular . . . the clarity would have been blurred.'

'It makes other paintings seem so *fussy*,' said Mrs Craven.

'Other *paintings*?' Joanne Dickson pushed back her short red hair and stood with her ringed hand buried in it, her other hand on her hip, staring upward with a puzzled expression. 'Pardon my naïveté, but where does the paint come in?'

Her husband laughed indulgently. 'Darling, darling, that *literal* mind!'

84

'I meant other works of *art*,' explained Mrs Craven, glancing at her husband for support, and being rewarded by a benign beam.

'Okay then, where does the art come in?'

'You don't care for it?' Polly sounded, very politely, as if Joanne's answer would fix her for all time in her deserved intellectual bracket.

'No, frankly, I think it's a bloody insult to a decent bit of canvas.' She sounded, not rude, just cheerful and confident. I began to like her very much.

'It's not even decorative.'

There was a shocked silence and everyone turned to look at me. None of them was more surprised than myself that I'd spoken.

'What, another little neo-classicist in our midst?' drawled Davidson, thrusting a mocking chin at me.

Polly smiled. I saw what Aaron meant about her how-nice-to-be-always-right mood. 'Not at all,' she purred. 'She's just someone who doesn't know anything about art, but knows what she likes.'

This raised a laugh at my expense and during it I looked at Aaron. He had his hands in his pockets and was staring unhappily at the floor. I had a feeling of desolation. He was almost ghostly in his un-solidity when Polly was anywhere about.

She had taken care to place him as far away from me as possible at table. I sat between Davidson and Dan, and Aaron sat on his sister's right, with Theo Craven on her left. The dinner was full of odd, sour flavours and the pervading dryness which comes of no butter with the bread or on the vegetables. I had to drink rather a lot, both to wash it down, and to keep my end of the conversation anywhere near up. I found Dan abstracted and taciturn; he concentrated mainly on eating, but while chewing each mouthful would stare fixedly down the table at Polly. He had a gentle, cow-like quality about him which the slow glassy-eyed chewing emphasized. Davidson, on the other hand, liked to talk while he ate, principally theatre, about which I knew very little. I was grateful to have learned about *The World at My Window* in time to use it as a gambit.

'What are you working on at the moment?' I asked, when the details of that production were exhausted.

He poked his chin archly in the direction of the Swedish glass candelabra. 'Ah,' he said. 'What indeed!'

'Is it a secret?'

'Not for long. Hey, but on second thoughts – it shouldn't be a secret from you. I understood Aaron to say it was partly your baby.'

Something inside me jumped. I turned to stare at him, a forkful of cold chicken half-way to my mouth.

'You don't mean –'

'Sh! Pa's urn motte,' he said in what I realized after some thought was comedy French.

I could hardly eat the rest of the meal, let alone keep up a merry flow of prattle. Several times I tried to catch Aaron's eye, but what use would it have been? We were acres of polished teak away from each other. The only eye I could catch was Joanne Dickson's. She put some food into her mouth and made a slight grimace at me.

'Look at my wife – she loathes this Kosher muck,' Davidson chortled. 'Even though she's Jewish herself. Paula's is about the only house where one still has to put up with it. Bet you there's not one person here who's tasted Kosher cooking since the last time Paula invited 'em.'

'But –'

Davidson laughed. 'If you can find anyone here except our hostess who's never had bacon for breakfast I'll monjay my shappo.'

'*Please* tell me about the play.'

'The what? – Oh, no mustn't. Can't spoil old Poll's surprise. It'll be announced with the brandy, I expect.'

He was right. As soon as Bella had brought in the coffee, I saw Polly give Aaron a nod. He went to the sideboard and brought out a dusty bottle.

'Damn me – Napoleonic, no less!' whispered my neighbour. 'She *is* going it! Still, I suppose it is a bit of an occasion.'

'Let Dan do it, Aaron,' Polly called in ringing tones. Dan dabbed his lips and rose quickly to his feet. Before long huge bubble-glasses licked with brandy had been set before every guest, and Polly stood up.

She really wasn't a bad-looking woman. Like nearly everyone else she wore black, but expensive black, cut to make the most of her angular body and to soften and conceal the knobs and hollows. The hair was as uncompromisingly severe as ever; even the kiss-curl looked about as feminine as the cow-lick on a Gay Nineties barber. But tonight the diamonds on her hands drew attention to the fact that they were slender and moved with a cool preciseness which was almost graceful; and her face, more carefully made up than usual, had a glow of elation which could easily pass for warmth and even softness. When she looked at Aaron, sitting beside her, the parrot look disappeared; one noticed a full, almost sensual mouth and an air of covert tenderness.

She looked round the table until there was absolute quiet and then said, 'This was going to be just an ordinary party. But yesterday something happened that was not at all ordinary.' She paused and put a ringed hand on to Aaron's shoulder. He sat under it like a statue, staring at his glass. She went on: 'This is a very important moment in my life, a moment I've worked for and looked forward to, and prayed for, though I never doubted it would come.' Bill Davidson made the sort of embarrassed derisive little noise under his breath that non-religious people make when prayer is mentioned. Polly drew a deep breath and picked up her glass with her left hand. 'Within a week of its being completed, Aaron's first play has been chosen by Theo to open his new theatrical venture.' An obliging gasp and a spatter of applause greeted this announcement. 'Bill is to produce it, and Joanne will play the leading woman's part. I'd like you to raise your glasses and drink to its success.'

Everyone stood up and drank, then began chattering like starlings. The brandy fumes hit me in the eyes and made them water. Through a mist of tears I looked down the table and saw Aaron's gaze fixed on me. People were clustering round to shake his hand, laughing admiringly and congratulating him, and Polly's possessive hand still lay on his shoulder as a glittering accolade; but he looked straight at me. And winked.

Chapter Six

I'd always heard that things move with unbelievable slowness in the theatre. You wrote a play; that took months. Then you submitted it to managements and agents; that took more months while the scripts collected dust on some shelf, and then usually you received them back with curt notes. Eventually, perhaps, your play was accepted, but then more months passed while it was cast, a tour arranged, a theatre found. That, at least, was the version drummed into me by Jill and Gwen. But this arrangement, I was able to tell them, was either outdated or completely legendary.

Aaron wrote his nonsense-play (I told myself I must stop thinking of it as that, or the description might slip out by accident) in a little under six weeks, including the angry time which was wasted. It was accepted within two days, and a fortnight later it was in production. Just like that. Of course, it was possible that things might be different for playwrights without direct access to Theo Craven.

Bill Davidson was no hack producer to throw a play together just anyhow. He was a disciple of some mythical Russian, which meant, among other things, seven weeks' rehearsals. He had some trouble convincing Theo Craven that this was not mere wilful eccentricity.

'After all, sweet boy,' said Theo when he, Aaron, Polly, Bill and myself were crowding the little upstairs office at the shop, drinking gin (not me, of course) and discussing the financial side of things, 'the days when you could pay actors three-ten a week for rehearsals are over, more's the pity. And this play – brilliant, Aaron, nothing against it, I'm enchanted with it, but it happens to have a very large cast. Eighteen artists. Of which only twelve or maybe even ten are in the Equity-minimum category. But for the others – your beautiful wife, for instance, Bill – could we in all seriousness offer Joanne a paltry Equity minimum? Even for outer London? £9 rehearsal money at least. And the same for the other leading artists. For seven *weeks*, William. Darling boy, I shall be bankrupt before we begin.'

'In Russia they rehearse for two *years*.'

'Why should I care what those mad Bolshies do? Why should they care either, when the State is paying?'

Polly chipped in. 'In any case, Theo, the theatre won't be ready in under eight weeks, will it?'

'Do we *have* to fill in the whole time till then adding to my bills? I tell you, the *bricks and mortar* of that place are costing a fortune. If they'd turned the *Coliseum* into a television studio, it couldn't cost more to reconvert. For a theatre the size of my bathroom!' He ran his hand over his curly grey hair, seeming to get consolation from the feeling of its crisp abundance. 'Ah well. After being such a fool as to go into this business in the first place, I must expect to be bled white, I suppose. So find your artists, William; start the rehearsals. Hold them in the Savoy Grill with snacks laid on. Pay them a hundred a week, what does it matter? It only means I go broke a few months sooner, that's all.' With a martyred air he drained his gin glass and reached for his pearl-grey homburg. 'Paula, darling, I'm off now to make some money to pay for bringing your brother's baby into the world. He is its father; he conceived it. But I – I am its mother. I bring it forth. For me, the true labour pains. But do I complain? Don't answer, yes I do.'

'And they say *Jews* are stingy,' said Aaron, when he'd gone.

'Dear old Theo, he'll be all right,' said Bill.

'Of course he will,' said Polly. 'Let's all have another drink.' Her whole manner had altered since the play had been finished and accepted. She no longer paid any attention to me at all; I might have been invisible. As for Aaron, now that he had produced the thing she wanted of him, she treated him with the affectionate indulgence of a mother for a clever and obedient child, and let him please himself. Her whole attention was focused on the details of the play and its production.

Aaron, on the other hand, was completely detached from *Man in a Hole* and everything to do with it. He sat in on these early conferences because they were held in his office, but entirely passively. He never contributed anything. When

89

Bill appealed to him for his views on casting or any other point, he would focus his eyes with some difficulty and say vaguely, 'My part of the business is finished. It's in your hands now.'

When Bill had gone off to interview some actors' agents, Polly took Aaron to task, but not sharply or hectoringly as of old. 'It's not natural to take so little interest in the production, Aaron,' she protested quite mildly. 'Don't you care who brings your characters to life?'

'I don't know one actor from another.'

'That just isn't true. I've heard you argue their respective merits for hours on end.'

'It's Bill's business. Far be it from me to interfere. Let them all get on with it, and the best of British luck to them.'

'You're a strange boy,' she said tolerantly. 'You don't seem to realize just what an exceptional thing you've achieved.'

As soon as she was out of earshot, Aaron blew a raspberry.

'What a change is here, my countrymen!' I remarked.

'It won't last,' Aaron said. 'I'm in favour at present because I've produced the son and heir as ordered. If it dies, or when it's forgotten, I'll be *persona non grata* again until I cough up another one. Don't forget, I'm the passport to the Franks family's immortality.' He did a back-bending stretch, his long body seeming to double its length and his chair tilting dangerously. He was as limber and relaxed as a cat since the night of the party. 'Now,' he said, 'I've got work for you.' He got up and opened one of the double-locked filing-cabinet, bringing out a red notebook. 'Enough loafing about, my girl,' he said, throwing it down in front of me. 'Get on with it.'

The book was filled with his childlike, almost illiterate-looking scrawl. 'Can you make it out?' he asked, bending over my shoulder.

'You've done all this in the last week?' I could scarcely believe it. 'There must be eight thousand words here – when have you found the time – and the privacy?'

He chortled gleefully. 'She's been in no mood to notice me scribbling away. I've had hours to myself. It's good, too, Martha – I *know* it's good. And now that other bugger's out of the way, we can work on this all day. She won't bother us. She's got her eyes focused in quite another direction.' Without warning he suddenly added, 'What nice little ears you've got!'

'Oh? Thank you,' I answered, after a moment.

He touched one. 'They haven't got proper lobes. Doesn't it hurt to wear earrings?'

'Yes, sometimes.'

'Then you shouldn't. They're so pretty bare.'

This – I was sure – perfectly casual remark had the most alarming effect on me. He might have been talking about some intimate part of my body. I bent low over the book, pretending to be making sure I could read the writing. I could feel his breath on my ear and I was rigid with the instinctive certainty that he would kiss it. Wanting it or not wanting it formed no part of my confused thoughts; I only knew I couldn't sit quietly and receive it as casually as it was given.

I stood up abruptly, my hands clenched on the book to hide their sudden trembling. 'I'll get on with it right away,' I said in an unfamiliar high voice. My chair swayed and crashed on its back. The noise made me jump like a shot horse.

'No need to break up the happy home,' said Aaron plaintively.

By the time rehearsals started, Aaron was so deeply entrenched in the novel that he scarcely listened when Bill rang him up to give him the details.

'I'm not one of these autocrats who bar the doors to keep the authors out,' I could hear Bill's strident voice declaiming over the phone. 'Voos et ever so bienvenu, any time you like. In fact, we'd be glad to see you, especially at first . . . some of the actors in the small parts are of necessity a bit cretinous, and I've had one or two – er – queries about the script from a couple of them. Nothing I can't sort out during the preliminary read-throughs, but still, I'd be grateful if you'd pop along – full and free discussions about the hidden depths, the lines between the lines, character backgrounds, and so forth . . . I always have about a week of soul-searching before we even start plotting the moves.'

Aaron had the phone propped between chin and shoulder,

and was correcting some pages I'd just typed. I could see he was paying less attention than I was.

'Uh-huh, well, I'll drop by if I can. Don't count on it though.'

He hung up absently, cutting Bill's next speech in half.

'You didn't ask him where the rehearsals are being held,' I mentioned.

'What? – Good God, you don't imagine I'm actually *going*, do you? "Irremediable"? Did I say Irremediable? I meant "Unreversible".'

'It's such an ugly word.'

He looked up. 'Did you change it?' The angry glint could come back in a second any time he was challenged. In between times it was impossible to remember I had ever been afraid of him; at times like this, it was incredible that I could have forgotten.

'I'm sorry.'

'Don't *ever* change what I write. If there's any revision to be done, I'll do it.'

'I said I'm sorry.'

He gave me a cold glance and went back to his work. The silence was like that of an Arctic night. After a few minutes he put the pages down and said 'Cigarette?'

I took one in silence. I always felt rotten while those moods lasted – ill, almost.

'You see the thing is –' he began, then stopped. 'The thing is, it's got to be *mine*. All mine. "Irremediable's" better. I realize that. I might have thought of it myself, if you'd left it alone. Now I'll have to leave it as it was.' We smoked in silence. He was frowning. 'I can't take help from anybody on this, not that kind of help. I – I can't bear the thought that somebody might be able to do even a small bit of it better than me.'

'But that's foolish.'

'Perhaps. It's got to be mine, though. That's all I know. Don't mind me when I go off like that. Come on, what chapter are we up to?'

A week later, Bill rang again. His voice was now not so much strident as shrill.

'I say, mon old cher, when are you going to make your

promised visit? We're all getting a bit bogged down in your symbolism.'

'In my what?'

'Your symbolism,' said Bill, a little less positively. 'I mean, all those men and holes and things.' He laughed uneasily. He waited for Aaron to say something enlightening, but Aaron was lighting a cigarette. After a moment his voice went on, 'Of course it's all perfectly clear to *me*. My view is that there's no such thing as obscurantism; the individual must interpret according to his own needs; one brings one*self* to these things. But when a *collection* of minds is being applied, and a coherent *whole* is aimed at, well of course one must achieve some sort of mass comprehension – an interpretive common denominator, as it were.' He cleared his throat noisily. Aaron held out the phone to me and covered his mouth with his hand; his face was scarlet with suppressed laughter. Bill went gamely on.

'What I'm getting at is, old boy, that it's no good me explaining *my* interpretation, which I'm objective enough to realize may only be right *for me*. A *blanket* coverage is what's required, and that's something that can only properly come from you. After all, only you know what you were really getting at,' he finished, now so rattled he almost gave himself away.

With a titanic effort, Aaron controlled himself long enough to say, in a cold, rather pained voice, 'I'm afraid I simply don't know what you're talking about. The whole thing's as clear as crystal. If it isn't, then either you're all being peculiarly stupid, or I've failed.' He managed it very well, although his voice began to wobble a bit towards the end and he had to cover the mouthpiece immediately.

From the other end came a disconcerted silence. Bill knew he had lost considerable face, and was hard put to it to extricate himself. He decided to bluff it out.

'Well of course, as I say, we're all absolutely clear about our *own* interpretations. It's just that they all seem to be a little different.'

'How can they be different? You might just as well talk about having different interpretations of Mary Had a Little Lamb.'

'Come, come, old boy, it's not that simple!'

'Of course it is. In any case, I've nothing more to add to

what's in the play. If you can't get them all to see it your way, you'd better sack them. Or, better still, let them all do it according to their own ideas. It should be totally chaotic, and increase greatly its chances of success.'

'Er – yes, of course.' Bill laughed nervously, obviously completely at sea. 'Well, er – when can we expect you, then?'

'Oh, I wouldn't. I really don't fancy seeing the thing in any sort of raw state. I'm looking forward to seeing the dress rehearsal.'

Near-panic now sent Bill's voice rocketing up into the soprano register. 'What! But Aaron, you can't do that! I mean, look here, chum, I must speak to you like a – a dutch uncle. I mean, you're brilliant and nobody denies that, but you're pretty new to this business, and you've got to learn to accept advice from people who know the ropes.'

'I thought it was you who wanted my advice.'

Bill spluttered. 'I'm telling you, not many authors have the chance you're getting. Most producers won't let 'em past the door. They beg and plead, but they don't get *in*. They just have to accept what the cast and producer come up with, whether it's what they had in mind or not. Now, when you're lucky enough to strike a cooperative producer, someone like me who appreciates an author's point of view and is willing to listen to it, take my advice, boy. Take advantage of it. Don't miss this chance to watch your play in production! Think what you can learn from it – it's a deeply important part of your career. You don't think *I'm* going to benefit from your coming, do you? This is entirely for *your* sake! Now be a sensible chap and spend as much time with us as you can.'

'Thanks heaps, nunkie,' said Aaron in an Oxford drawl. 'It's jolly D of you to put yourself out like this. But you needn't bother, really, because actually, as a matter of fact, don't y'know, I'm not sodding well coming.'

The spiral stairs creaked before the phone was properly back on the hook. Aaron's face turned from red to white and he darted me a look of wide-eyed sudden terror, like a schoolboy about to be caught in some horrible indecency.

She walked in, as she always did, without knocking. Her face, in the glimpse I got of it as she swooped past me, was not like a

94

parrot's; it had taken on the sharp untamed menace of a hawk. She walked straight up to Aaron and slapped his face as he sat there.

I found myself on my feet before he was. He rose more slowly, rubbing his cheek and staring at her with frozen outrage.

'You impertinent, spoilt, conceited little moron!' she spat at him. 'What a fool I've been not to see this coming! Of course, it's all been too easy for you. You couldn't take your first bit of success like an adult, could you? Oh no, you have to behave like the callow little undergraduate you are! How dare you! You don't deserve Bill's kindness, Theo's generosity, or your father's hard-earned money. You don't deserve the talent that's been given to you!'

She turned away, her shoulders wrenching in spasms, her knuckles white at her sides. Aaron's face turned after her numbly, his eyes glassy. After a moment she pulled herself together a little, and turned back to him, speaking more calmly.

'Listen carefully. You're going to that rehearsal room. You'll apologize to Bill, and you'll put yourself completely at his disposal. I don't pretend to understand how you can do anything but fall on your knees with gratitude for this opportunity, but it really doesn't matter. What matters is that you make the most of it whether you want to or not.'

She turned to the door, and seemed to realize for the first time that I was in the room. She stopped short, and gave me a look of such unconcealed dislike that I felt myself wither. Then she walked out without another glance at either of us.

We sat as far apart as possible in opposite corners of the taxi. My one quick look at his humiliated shoulders had sent such a current of pity through me that I dared not look at him again for fear I would take him in my arms. Or hit him myself. I hate having to pity people, more particularly when I long to admire them.

Where are you? I raged silently. *Where are you, the real, solid, ungetattable person?* The core, the indestructible I, seemed to be missing – in him, as in me. He's a lizard, I thought. He lies in the sun, looking lithe and impervious, snapping up flies like Bill, but let his bloody sister sneak up behind him and pick him up by the tail and suddenly there's only half of him left.

The rehearsal room was off Russell Square. We got stiffly out of the taxi at opposite sides, and Aaron paid it, and then we just stood there silently, several feet apart on the pavement. Behind us, the traffic roared past, as if to cut off retreat. In front stood a dingy brick church hall; its worn signboard carried long-unremarked notices hanging in rain-curled tubes from single nails.

Aaron took a step towards the door and then suddenly turned.

'I'm not going in.'

I breathed deeply and looked away.

'I suppose you think I'm afraid to.'

'Whatever I say will sound wrong.'

He stood for a long moment, looking down the street, his weight on one foot, his arms limp at his sides. The sun was on him; his black hair shone and his finely-boned face was lit as if by a portrait photographer, to the best advantage. His clothes hung so well on him, so casually and well; he always wore his clothes as if he were naked and alone. Again I had to fill my lungs. It hurt to breathe deeply, but I was hollow and empty with some undefined apprehension.

'It's a kind of insanity,' he said at last, as if to himself. 'When I'm away from her I can't make it make sense. And yet when she's there – it's inevitable.'

'It's not insanity, it's fear.'

'But why am I afraid of her? Why?'

'Because you've always been afraid of her.'

Suddenly, without any warning, I burst into tears. He stared at me in amazement as I stood there with ugly violent sobs shaking me.

'What's the matter?'

'How dared she hit you! I hate the wicked bitch, *I hate her*!' I shouted. Hysteria was new to me. It tasted white in my mouth and my stomach was thick with it; it was flung up uncontrollably choking and blinding me. I felt his hands, hard and commanding on my shoulders. I threw myself against him, expecting in some despairing recess of my mind that he would snap and fall

96

backwards like a twig; but he was as solid as a tree. He held my face against his chest; I could feel his hard male strength challenging me back into self-control.

'I'm sorry –' I gasped, coming back to awareness with cold shivers of shame. 'Everyone's staring –'

'So? Come on, let's walk.'

We walked. He had his arm round me and I leaned against his shoulder. Every now and then he tightened his grip. He kept his head bent towards me. He didn't speak and neither did I; we just walked silently, heads together. After going round the square once, I put my arm round his waist, and at the same moment he turned so that we faced each other, and then we kissed. It was extraordinarily simple and mutual, as if our bodies were governed by the same mind. Completely unexpected, it was at the same time an overwhelming relief; a hunger I hadn't even been aware of had been marvellously satisfied, an unrecognized tension released in a flow of warmth that covered me like a wave.

He kissed me twice and then let me go and we walked on side by side, not touching any more, watching the paving-stones slide backwards under our feet. I had no thoughts, only the warm wave receding and leaving me with a clean sense of peace.

After a while we found ourselves outside the church hall again and automatically stopped walking. Aaron said 'When I'm not with her, it seems like a nightmare – you know, the sort where, for no reason at all, all your muscles seem to dissolve. I've got to find the strength to resist her, otherwise eventually she'll destroy me altogether. Martha?'

It was a plea for confirmation. I answered 'Yes, you have.'

'I can't do it except by being by myself, by doing my own sort of writing without fear of her walking in, finding it, reading it. If she did, I couldn't go on with it. It would all be spoilt if she read one single word.'

'What are you going to do?'

'Go away.'

'And when you come back?'

'Perhaps I'll be a person in my own right. Then she can't touch me.'

After a long moment I said 'Where?'

'I don't know yet.' He took hold of my little finger and swung my hand absently, staring at the double-doors behind which the rehearsal of his play was going on. 'Have you any money?' he asked suddenly.

'I have some in the bank.'

'Will you lend it to me?'

'Yes, how much do you want?'

'How much can you spare?'

'I'll write you a cheque.'

I wrote it, using my thigh as a desk. The words flowed steadily from the pen he had lent me. 'Aaron Franks, Fifty Pounds Only.' It was all I had. I had bought a very expensive dress after the party, in case there should ever be another. Now I felt a dull disappointment that I could not add the cost of this futile extravagance to the sum on the cheque. Fifty pounds seemed like nothing.

I handed it to him and he put it in his breast-pocket without looking at the amount and kissed my hand. It was as if he thanked it for its part in this odd little ceremony. 'Don't go back to the shop. Go home. I'll be in touch with you.'

And he turned and walked away, leaving me with his diminishing image in the commonplace sunlight.

Chapter Seven

I was not to go back to the shop. But what was I to do, then? Go home, as he had told me? My impulse was to obey him, but even as I started to walk slowly towards a bus-stop my mind went ahead of me to the shabby, empty flat, so devoid of any means of distraction or comfort for the ill-ease that sickened me. Nor was it the place where I could properly think about that moment, touched with magic, when we had turned to each other, the moment that had been so badly needed and so healing but which had passed and might never be repeated, or even mentioned between us again.

The idleness, the crossword-puzzle staleness, began to shadow me. I dared not go home. I had come away from that limbo, at least a little way; when I was with Aaron I no longer needed cheap superficial distractions, imitation causes: he was my cause. But he'd gone, and I didn't know when I would see him again.

Adrift and suddenly frightened, I turned and hurried back to the last place of anchor – the place where we had last stood together, outside the church hall. The door was open now, and I could hear the sound of voices. Without stopping to think, I went in.

There was a stage, or rather a platform, but they weren't on it. They were standing about in the auditorium part, in groups, chatting. In their hands were thick red manuscripts. The dusty floorboards were marked out with chalk; round the walls were dozens of hard folding chairs, and on one of these at the far side sat Bill, with Joanne beside him. The sun streamed through the dirty curtainless windows and lit up her red hair like a fiery halo. They were having what looked like an argument, and as I walked uncertainly towards them I could hear Bill saying:

'My dearest Jo, it's as clear as crystal; a child could understand it. You might just as well talk about the hidden meanings in Mary Had A Little Lamb.'

99

Joanne saw me before she could reply, and stood up.

'Well, thank God, here comes Martha, anyway. Let's hope she can throw a little light on the subject.'

Bill turned, and waved to me without rising. 'Come to announce the imminence of the young genius?' he asked with forced good humour.

'No, I'm afraid not,' I said.

The other members of the cast, seeing a new-comer, came strolling over, and soon they stood around us in a loose semi-circle. They were all sorts, sizes and ages; I looked round at them, trying to place them in the play. Yes, there was the jeering teddy-boy from the café scene, and there, unmistakably, was the decayed old Countess-turned-café-proprietress, who took dope and had visions of Atlantis. Next to her was the Lolita-figure who turned out to be a middle-aged dwarf in the second act. Bill had plumped for a dwarf who could be made to look younger, rather than a young girl who could look like a dwarf. He would. There were several others I recognized, and a whole lot more who could have been just people called in off the street, except that there was something not quite ordinary about every one of them. I had never seen actors close-to and off-stage before.

Bill was introducing me. 'The author's helpmeet,' he said grandly, and I saw several of them exchange glances. 'You say he *isn't* coming, after all?' he added to me with false joviality.

'No, well, not today, anyway,' I mumbled, feeling inadequate in the face of all these eager, clear-cut, expectant people. 'I – I just thought I'd come along and tell you that he's – he's gone away for a few days.'

'A few *days* – you're sure it's only days?'

'Well –'

'Because we're into the third week of rehearsals, you know. Characterizations are still fluid, but they're bound to harden off pretty soon. If he *wants* to have his say, he'll have to hurry.'

'I don't really think –' I began nervously. Bill turned sharply. 'I mean, I think he wants to leave it to you.'

'Yes, so I gathered.' His boyish face had some ageingly grim lines on it, and he kept flattening the tuft of hair with his hand. He seemed at a loss, and shot a helpless look at his wife, who was standing, her long legs in tight trousers planted apart, her hands on her narrow hips, looking at me measuringly.

'Look, Martha,' she said abruptly. 'You were in at the birth, so to speak. What about it if *you* come to rehearsals, since Aaron won't? If he's out of town, you're free . . . and we'd be damn' grateful, I mean if it's not the hell of an imposition –'

'But what can *I* do?' I asked, panicky but flattered by being told I was in a position to earn the gratitude of this glamorous creature.

'The thing is,' said the 'Countess', 'we're all agreed it's full of marvellous parts, but – well bluntly, we're not awfully clear about what it all *means*. If you could just sort of put us on the right track —'

'We're all going our own sweet ways at the moment, actually,' interjected the teddy-boy in what Gwen would have called a RADA voice.

'But I don't – I mean, I just took it down and typed it.'

'He must have talked to you about it, ducky,' said the female dwarf.

'It's *his* intention we want to be true to,' put in Bill sententiously.

'If only we knew what his intention was.'

I was surrounded by them now; their eyes, their minds were all fixed on me. I had never been the focal-point of interest to so many people before. I knew I should refuse – it was ridiculous; what help could I possibly be, knowing only too well what Aaron's intention had actually been? But the lure of the lime-light, and respectful attention, and even power, was irresistible.

'Well, I'll do my best, only –'

'Attagirl,' said a tall rather raddled actor whose haggard, handsome face I recognized from television. The circle of tension seemed to break up like an ice-floe, and melt into little floating, laughing groups.

Bill immediately took up the reins again. 'Come on, people!' he said, clapping his hands like a kindergarten teacher. 'Allez on! Let's go back to the beginning. Just walk it with your books. Opening-scene – Miggie, where are you, enfant? – Oh there. Set for the café, dear.'

A fat girl of about 16, incredibly shabbily dressed, shuffled through a pile of papers in her hands and then began whisking about the chalk-marked area, moving the hard chairs like gigantic chess men. Bill motioned me to sit beside him at the side. Most of the cast melted away into the shadows near the platform, or came and sat in front with us; but three or four took up their positions around the stage-area. I saw that the haggard actor was to play the Man of the title. There was the teddy-boy, there his girl-friend, there the tramp, sitting in a corner, miming a cup of tea absently with one hand while holding his clumsy script in the other. My eyes automatically sought the Countess, who was soon to enter with the urn of fresh tea; and there she was, standing at one side, waiting to enter when she heard the tramp say the words 'The world's my oyster, and I'm allergic to them.'

Suddenly a shiver of excitement went over me. But this was wonderful! It was thrilling beyond words! There they all were, three-dimensional people, about to bring the paper words to life, bringing their own minds and bodies to bear on the flatness of what had been merely written down. Oh, where was Aaron? He shouldn't miss this, this moment trembling with the magic of birth, the true alchemy of transformation. I gripped my hands together to hide the bursting excitement that was making it hard for me not to leap up and shout the way some people do at football matches.

Then Bill said casually, 'Okay, people, off you go.' And it started.

Almost at once, everything changed. My excitement faded, and was replaced by a species of horror as I watched the actors making those motiveless moves and heard them speaking those maddening, half-meaningful lines. They moved and spoke with a kind of imitation confidence, each afraid to admit his bewilderment, each determined to counterfeit sense and purpose. That was their job, I saw for the first time – to complete, to add the third dimension. But Aaron's play didn't give them a solid, two-dimensional surface to build on. I remembered learning at school that nothing was one-dimensional; even a pencilled dot has breadth. But here, bafflingly, unforgivably, was the geometric impossibility – the shapeless, weightless intangible, having no formula, no continuity; providing no basis for building, not

102

even a foundation of thought. It consisted of a solitary, non-solid dimension – words.

They went through the motions and none of them argued. Occasionally, after some particularly outrageous *non-sequitur*, there would be a small, empty silence, as if the props with which they were struggling to shore up the uncohesive mass had suddenly snapped, and the silence was filled with a feeling of crumbling. It was like shoring up icing sugar or face powder. There was nothing to support, nothing to uphold, nothing to get a grip on.

After a while I could bear it no longer.

Joanne stopped in the middle of a speech as she saw me creeping out.

'Hey, Martha, don't go! We're going to have a session in a minute.'

'I must. There's nothing I can tell you.' An angry sort of loyalty to Aaron confused me. 'It's – it's all there – I mean, there's no use talking about it.'

'How does it look to you? Are we getting it across?'

I looked helplessly at Bill. 'Good God, this is the first time we've done the *moves*!' he exclaimed. 'Getting it across! Give us time, for Christ's sake!' He looked as if he blamed me.

Jo ran after me and caught me up in the dim institutional passage. 'Don't mind my old man,' she said, rubbing her hands up and down against her thighs in a brisk, embarrassed way. 'He's a good old slob really, he just can't admit there's anything he can't grasp first go. Myself, the first words I learned were "I don't know", and I've been using them ever since, at regular five-minute intervals. I don't know what Aaron was getting at, and I don't believe Bill does either, and furthermore I don't think any of the rest of them do, though they'd die before admitting it. Listen, you will come back again tomorrow, won't you? – because you sitting there gave me a kind of quasi-confidence, a tenuous link with the creator, so to speak.'

'But there's nothing I can do,' I said again, desperately.

She stared at me, out of clear wide-apart eyes. 'But it must *have* a meaning,' she said slowly. 'Aaron's a bit of a weirdie – couldn't help being, with the ogress for a sister – but he's too much of a good egg to do a nonsense on us.'

I opened my mouth, looking from one of those square green

eyes to the other. They were like a child's in a way, full of trust and candour.

'Of course it has meaning,' I heard myself say loudly. 'It's just that I can't think how to explain it. Listen –' (How like me to pick up a speech mannerism! The mirror, the tape-recorder, the reflecting nonentity . . . what can I do, what can I say?)

After what seemed like an endless pause, I said 'Listen, I'll read through my notes tonight, the ones I made while he was writing it, and see if I can't come up with something . . .'

The wide bright mouth spread into a curly, jester's smile. 'And then you'll come back tomorrow and tell us?'

'Well – but won't Bill – I mean your husband – won't he –'

'Resent it? Might. Listen, we'll have lunch together, and you can tell *me*. I can pass it on tactfully. Okay? – Only I simply *can't* work on a part I don't understand. Hideously "Method" of me, I know, but there it is.'

'Did you understand *The World at My Window*?' I asked suddenly.

'No,' she said. 'That's how I know I can't do it.'

'I thought you were very good in that,' I mentioned timidly.

She gazed at me with blank astonishment. 'You must be mad,' she said. 'I was bloody lousy.'

It wasn't until I was half-way home on the bus that I remembered the manuscript of the novel.

Aaron had left it on the desk. I was certain of it. Polly had startled him into leaving for the rehearsal immediately after her outburst; there'd been neither time nor thought for putting the novel back in the double-locking filing cabinet. Would she have read it by now? My whole body chilled at the likelihood of her having had a good poke round the moment we had gone.

I jumped off the bus at the next lights, ran across the road and caught another one back the way I'd come. I didn't give myself time to think. If I had, I might have hesitated, quailing at the remembrance of that look of pure hate she had given me as she walked out of the room.

Huddled in the bus, shivering with dread, I tried to tell myself that this was utter nonsense. Who was she, after all? Just a woman, a domineering bitch of a woman. She was not Satan incarnate, nor did she hold the power of life or death over me. What was the worst she could do, the very worst? But there was no reassuring answer. The worst was what she did every day, by brushing the cold, evil tentacles of her life against mine.

I walked through from Piccadilly into Regent Street, lingering to stare blindly and procrastinatingly at some antique silver in one window, a dead lobster in another, the turbaned figure outside Veraswami's . . . my mouth was dry. I felt a moment's fury against Aaron. How could he let me in for this? Easy for him to say 'I'm going', to take my cheque and run away, leaving me to deal with all that he'd left behind. Why should I do it? I asked myself angrily. But there was no reassuring answer to that one either. Only an answer that I turned my head away from, twisting my neck with a jerk as if the words were written in the air in front of me.

The door opened silently; the squeak had been nipped in the bud and had never dared recur. Somewhere, of course, a refined little buzzer buzzed, because immediately Dan appeared, the fat genie.

'Oh, it's you! No sale.' He grinned. I felt relief pour over me like a warm showerbath. I knew at once he had the place to himself.

'She's gone?'

'Left right after you did.' Instinctively he lowered his voice. 'What happened up aloft? She was in a hell of a state, poor love.'

The 'poor love' took me considerably aback, but I didn't have time to register it. The novel was in the forefront of my mind. 'Did she go back upstairs before she went?'

'No, I don't think so – no, I'm sure not.'

I took the spiral stairs two at a time – no mean feat. The pile of typewritten pages lay as we had abandoned it. I found myself hugging it hard, making great creases in the back page, as I carried it downstairs.

Dan was laying dust-sheets over the metal-hoop 'tree' and its fungus shelves. As I was making for the outer door, he unexpectedly called me over.

'What do you honestly think about that painting?'

The grey-tone oil with the red splotch had not yet been sold.

I looked at it unseeingly. 'I don't know,' I said indifferently, supposing he would think me a fool and not giving any special damn.

'I don't either,' he said worriedly. We stood looking up at it for a while, and then he said 'What does that make us, do you suppose?'

'Honest,' I replied.

He turned to me. 'But Paula likes it,' he said. 'She really does.'

'Does she?'

'She *really* does,' he repeated earnestly. 'She has things like it in her own home. Oh, but you saw one – her Broggotti. D'you know what she gave for that?'

'No.'

'Five hundred guineas.'

I reacted despite myself. 'Five –'

'Hundred guineas,' he said solemnly. 'Well, I mean, you don't shell out that kind of lolly for something you don't genuinely like – do you?'

'But it was just a slit in a bit of canvas!'

'She likes it,' he repeated doggedly.

'Then she's even madder than I thought,' I said flatly.

'You – you don't like her, do you?'

There was a hesitancy in his voice, as if he was afraid of my answer. I felt suddenly brave, standing in her territory, left undefended, surrounded by the pretentious objects symbolizing her taste, and with the manuscript safely in my hands. 'I loathe her,' I said distinctly.

He drooped; his cherubic face sagged into half-comic pouches of rue. 'I knew you did. She doesn't like you, either. It's sad, because you know she's really a splendid person in many ways.'

I blew a derisive raspberry. He looked faintly shocked by my vulgarity, and said defensively, 'Oh well, if that's how you feel –'

'I rather thought it was how you felt, too.'

'What gave you that idea?'

'You gave me the impression you were in on the anti-Polly conspiracy.' That wasn't exactly how I'd meant to put it. It

106

sounded sly and unpleasant, even to me, and I saw Dan with-draw.

'I know she's rather difficult at times,' he said stiffly, 'liking to keep tabs on people, and so on, and I know it can't be much fun working for someone who dislikes you, so I thought I'd try to be friendly. But if I ever said anything that . . . I mean, it must have been a joke. I – I admire her tremendously,' he went on, now beginning to stammer and blush like a school-boy, but pushing on determinedly. 'Perhaps you don't realize that she started this place from nothing, and made it into a by-word. She –'

I don't know what made me argue with him. I felt sorry for him actually; his loyalty to her was rather touching, in an abstract way, and his embarrassment was painful to watch. But I couldn't prevent myself. 'Oh come,' I said sarcastically. 'Hardly from *nothing*. Her father left her pretty comfortable, that's quite obvious.'

His round face was a hot red mask, beginning to gleam. 'In T-t-trust,' he stammered. 'Nearly all in Trust. He only left her a thousand pounds of her own, and l-l-look what she's done with it.' He made a jerky gesture, like a nervous amateur actor. 'She knows her business, and she's shrewd, and on top of that, she's artistic. You don't think I'm *proud* of not understanding modern art, do you? It's something lacking in me. And in you, too,' he added fiercely. He was really upset, I could see. His outburst over, he took out a handkerchief and shakily wiped his brow, turning away from me, his fat body swaying a little unsteadily on his stumpy legs.

I was quite unprepared for dealing with this extraordinary attack, from someone I'd though of as an ally. I felt stunned and abashed. 'Dan, I'm sorry,' I mumbled.

After a moment he said, 'S'okay.' Then he turned and walked quickly away down the basement stairs.

I didn't spend the evening worrying about Aaron's where-abouts, or (though it was tempting) re-living the moment in the square. I had a feeling of certainty that he hadn't meant any-thing by it. It was an island in an almost impersonal sea. All I was, all he wanted me to be, was his secretary; and if I was more

107

than a normal secretary to him, it was because he needed something extra, being an extraordinary man. I stored the drop of sweetness in the back of my mind. It was perfect and unrepeatable, I thought, the right thing at the right moment; leave it at that and don't nag at it to be something more.

I had the flat to myself, and I was glad, for once. I turned the radio on automatically, but the nasal ululating of some dimwit grated on me and I turned it off without foraging for another station. The quiet was pleasant, soothing. I made a light meal, and while I ate it on my knee I read through the manuscript I had 'rescued'. It was good enough to re-establish contact with Aaron's decision that nothing mattered except to finish it successfully. Then I put my empty plate aside and went to my bedroom. In the chest-of-drawers, I had a stolen copy of *Man in a Hole*. I had filched it when the copies, neatly bound in red, came back from the duplicators. Aaron, noticing, had laughed.

'Punch a couple of holes and run string through them, and it's all ready to hang in the bog.'

Now I sat on my bed with an eiderdown over me, and a pad and pencil beside me, and read it carefully through. I put aside as much as possible the thought of how it had been written, and why. I thought, if I were Jo, or any of them . . . if my job, or my self-respect, depended on finding some sense in it . . . I remembered something Polly had once said about *Waiting for Godot:* 'As many interpretations as there were members of the audience.' I had read somewhere that Samuel Beckett couldn't, or wouldn't, explain what he had meant by it. Perhaps there was a meaning to anything, if one was prepared to bring enough of oneself to fill in the gaps left by the author's intention. Anyway, that was the slim hope I was working on.

Jo turned up at the snack-bar where we'd arranged to meet, looking like a beautiful spy in an enormous high-collared coat, a Garbo hat and dark glasses.

'Why the disguise?' I felt friendly enough with her to ask.

'I feel furtive and conspiratorial about meeting you,' she explained. 'Bill'd be livid. We had a hell of a morning, just working on the first scene. Poor old Sandra – the Countess – she doesn't know her arse from her elbow about this play. I hope you've come up with something illuminating.'

108

We carried trays of coffee and cheesecake to a corner table. Jo settled down and to my alarm got a notebook and pencil out of her bag with a business-like air. 'Now then, let's have it,' she said briskly.

My nerve failed me. I had a drowning sensation – being out of my depth, with my foot barely touching one shifting, unreliable bit of support which I had dreamed up late last night and which might or might not make sense when I tried to turn it into words.

'Well,' I began uncertainly.

'Is it clear to you? What he was getting at?' she asked eagerly.

Her voice and personality were so incisive, so confident. Yet she was dependent on me in some incredible way. *He's too good an egg to do a nonsense on us* . . . There was no way out. I had to try.

I fixed my eyes on hers and said in the firmest tone I could muster, 'To start with the title.'

'For God's sake let's. What on earth does it mean – except what it sounds like?'

'You see, Aaron sees people as being completely isolated. It's as if everyone on earth had dug himself into an individual fox-hole on a battlefield – or maybe was born in it. There are bullets whistling overhead the whole time; by bullets I mean the hurts other people dish out as soon as you give them half a chance. If you stick your head out of your hole, someone's sure to take a shot at it, just on principle.'

'Too damn true. Go on.'

'Aaron thinks we're all motivated by two opposite instincts which are for ever pulling us apart. One is to save ourselves from pain; the other is to – well, to communicate, to love, if you like. The premise of the play is that you can't obey both instincts, and yet you can't escape from them either.'

The puzzled frown began to smoothe off her face. 'In other words, if you try to come out of your nice safe hole to share yourself with the bod in the hole next door, you're likely to get a bullet in the backside.'

'Exactly.'

She scribbled furiously. 'Yes, okay, I've got that much. So that's what the Man in the play is doing – struggling to decide between not being hurt and not being loved . . .' I felt a sort of quiver of excitement. It began to make sense, even to me. 'So now, tell about the different characters. The Countess, the female dwarf and the rest. And me, please. That's the most important thing.'

I took a sip of coffee and breathed in deeply. From here on, it would have to come right off the top of my head. But it was extraordinary. I opened my mouth and sense of a sort came out.

'He keeps trying different people,' I explained, 'always for a negative reason – that he thinks they may be able to resist hurting him. But Aaron thinks we're all bound to hurt each other – we can't help it; we have to pass on the hurt we've received.'

'Like fagging in school,' said Jo unexpectedly.

'Well . . . anyway. He attaches himself to the Countess because she's kind and motherly. But when he realizes she's equally kind to everyone, he feels offended because he's not special to her. He tries the little girl because he thinks she's too innocent and unworldly to hurt him; but she turns out to be a vicious freak. Then he latches on to the teddy-boy because he thinks he'll be too stupid to be malicious; but the teddy-boy, being stupid, revenges himself on the Man for what his father did to him. The tramp's indifferent, and the Man sees a sort of safety in that; but he finds that's just unsatisfying because he can't make the tramp react to him. Then he finds you, and you're all the things he's always wanted, but by this time he's accumulated so much pain that he has to give some of it back to the world, so he ruins something that could have been marvellous – he starts the hurt-cycle going again by destroying you.'

I stopped. Jo took the dark glasses off and was staring at me with wondering admiration.

'But of course,' she said simply.

Chapter Eight

Polly came round to my flat that night. She didn't phone first; she came in person. I suppose she hoped to take me by surprise, but in fact of course I was half expecting her.

One look at her face told me that she was both very angry and very anxious. I could almost have felt sorry for her, until she showed her teeth at me in one of her curt, half-snarling questions.

'Well. Where is he?'

'I don't know,' I said.

'You must know. Someone must know.' The fury and worry twisted her face two ways at once; her expression was half-way between a sob and a snarl, and rather frightening. Her eyes were wild in her thin, hard face.

'Do you want to come in?'

'No I don't want to come in!' she said loudly. She was staring at me as if trying to read Aaron's whereabouts in my face. 'You wouldn't tell me anyway, would you?' she said suddenly. 'I could have saved myself the trouble of coming.'

She turned to go, but I stopped her. She seemed so distraught.

'There's nothing to worry about,' I said.

She whirled on me; her forehead seemed to bulge more than ever, white and hard through the tight skin. 'Then you *do* know –'

'No, I don't. But I know he's not dead or anything.' I drew a deep breath; her presence always made me feel a little air-starved. 'He's gone away to be by himself.'

She stared at me again, and now I could almost read her thoughts. *He told you, and not me. It's me he wants to get away from and he's let you know it.* Her eyes closed suddenly, the way one snaps down a blind when a prying face appears outside the window. She stood for a moment, perfectly still in the corridor outside my flat, her narrow feet and sharp ankles rigid; then she turned abruptly and walked away on stiff legs. She staggered once, half-way to the stairs, as if she were drunk.

Jo had asked me to keep coming to rehearsals. The 'explanations' I had invented had been rapturously received, apparently; even Bill had been impressed. There was quite a different atmosphere in the dusty church hall; an atmosphere of excitement, of confidence. I was welcomed warmly. It felt so odd; I knew I had earned their respect in a way, but it was all based on lies and phoneyness, so I couldn't completely enjoy it. At the same time, it stimulated me, in the false way drink can. It was exciting without really meaning anything.

Polly sat alone in a corner, chain smoking. She couldn't even bring herself to look at me. Her fingers, khaki-stained, lit one cigarette after another and then let them burn down, forgotten, the smoke streeling up between the flat unpainted nails.

The rehearsals depressed me horribly. I could see how they were putting my 'interpretation' into effect, but it was like watching someone painting a skilful mural on a wall of rice-paper, with you alone knowing it wouldn't outlast the first puff of wind. I felt a sort of sick anger against Aaron, but it wasn't like the anger you usually feel for other people; it was more like guilt, as if I had done the ugly thing myself.

The rehearsals used my days up; I hated them, but I couldn't not go. It was a sort of compulsive masochism. I watched, fascinated, as the bogus skeleton was coated with the flesh of the actors' skill. When they asked me to explain this or that, I opened my mouth and words came out. Quite clever-sounding words. I listened to myself in amazement. Where did it all come from? Some untapped well of perverse logicality which I'd never suspected was in me spouted forth spurious camouflage for the play's lack of solid foundation. They treated me with the deference due to an oracle. Occasionally the horror would leave me and a bubble of hysterical laughter would burst in my throat. But actors are used to reasonless laughter, and nobody thought me odd.

* * * * *

Money started to be a problem by the end of the week. My salary came from Polly, and Polly had of course stopped paying it. I had had about four pounds left in the bank after Aaron cashed my cheque (I wondered where and under what circumstances). The four pounds went on rent and my share of the kitty for the week's expenses at the flat. I was completely broke by Saturday.

I hated to borrow from Jill or Gwen; they lived more or less from hand to mouth, and were both saving for holidays. Besides, they didn't know what had happened. But there just wasn't anybody else I really knew well enough. I sat at rehearsal thinking how I would approach Gwen – somehow I felt it would be easier to ask her than Jill. I hadn't had a proper lunch for three days. Next week I would have to get a temporary job; but that meant missing the last week of rehearsals. This, in prospect, was both a relief and an agony.

Jo came and lay on her back on the chair beside me, her long trousered legs widely extended like a forked branch. 'Any word from the Creator?' she asked.

I shook my head. She glanced at me; her slanting look was oddly perspicacious. 'You're looking a mite deathlike,' she remarked. 'Is this enterprise keeping you awake at nights, too?' Without waiting for a reply, she went on 'If you've nothing better to do this evening, come and have a nibble at our place. Bill's got to see a man about a set.'

I was grateful. The evenings since Aaron left had been hard; I couldn't make use any longer of my old time-killers – even the television seemed part of my old half-life, to which I looked back as a cured drug-addict must upon the time of his addiction, with wariness and disgust. For the most part I'd been sitting alone in my own room, reading books from the library. Recently I'd discovered a whole section on Israel, up in the non-fiction department which I'd never been to before. The dry, scholarly accounts were a kind of link with a bit of Aaron's life. I waded, with fierce determination, through pages dotted with alien, half-comprehended words like Histadrut, Knesset, Palmach, *yishuv*. I read at random. Historical order meant nothing to me. I hardly know whether the Ottoman Rule came before or after the British Mandate, whether Allenby conquered Jerusalem in the first or second war, or whether the first *aliyah* came after the Balfour Declaration or before. Such facts went out of my mind as soon as I'd read them. But the story parts, the early pioneers, the illegal immigrants, the Siege of Jerusalem, these gripped my imagination and involved me so that for hours I could forget everything except what I was reading. I began to be interested in the place for its own sake, not just for the sake of feeling closer to Aaron.

But I was glad of a chance to go out. The Davidsons lived in a big studio flat in Chelsea, full of strange and fascinating objects picked up by Jo from markets and antique shops at home and abroad. I wandered round admiring the attractively blended conglomeration while Jo, in a butcher's apron, cooked spaghetti. We ate companionably beside the open fire. She chatted unceasingly of this and that, in a warm, gossipy way that was as relaxing as a hot bath. I didn't even have to pay attention except on the surface; most of the people she talked about were scarcely even names to me.

But suddenly she began to discuss Polly and Aaron.

'How long have you known them?' I asked.

'Oh, aeons. Aaron was the first little boy I discovered *was* a little boy, if you know what I mean. We used to play together in that blissful garden, until one day when we were about six, Bitch-face discovered us staring interestedly at each other's nudity.

'Oh, it was okay for me, except that she was fiendishly icy and frightening even then; I still remember that sensation of withering on my stalk when she banished me and called me a dirty-minded little guttersnipe.' She gave a hard little chuckle. 'But poor old Aaron really copped it.'

'How do you mean?'

'We heard about it – I think Bella told my mother. The things a sixteen-year-old matriarch can think up! You'd think their father would have had something to say about it, but he was a bit unimaginative and taken up with business. He left Aaron more or less in Polly's charge.'

'But what did she do to him?'

'She left him severely alone for a week – wouldn't speak to

114

him, wouldn't look at him. As if he were beneath disgust. Then, when he was thoroughly upset and demoralized, because of course he worshipped her then, like a mother, she woke him up one night and told him all about sex. Only instead of just telling him, she showed him pictures. God knows where she got them – real Port Said stuff. Told him *that* was what sex was – filth and beastliness. Said she could never feel the same love for him since his "dirtyness" with me in the garden. For ages afterwards, he thought there was something wrong with him, that he was naturally wicked. Think of it! A child of six! One day when he was out with Bella, he met me and my mother. I waved to him and he turned and ran away. He shouted back that he hated me. Bella found him sobbing his soul out, and got the truth out of him. She was horrified, of course. She did what she could to put things straight for him, but she was too embarrassed to say much. She beat the hell out of Polly, though. And that took courage. Polly never forgave her. Not to this day. And afterwards she made Aaron suffer in a hundred little subtle ways for telling on her.'

I sat motionless for a long time, locked into my imagination with the mental pictures and my loathing.

At last I said 'It's a wonder he's not completely unbalanced about sex, after that.'

'Well, he doesn't exactly eschew it, but I can tell you he never makes love to anyone he respects. Always with promiscuous little girls who'll go with almost anybody.' She smoked in silence for a moment, and then said, 'I had a go at him myself, once, years ago. Sort of Tea and Sympathy stuff – thought I'd break the pattern, because I knew he really liked me, and I attract him too, or used to. But he wouldn't. He just laughed and said it would be incestuous. But I knew that was just an excuse. It seems he *can't* make love to anyone who he feels he'd be – I think defiling is the only word.'

I had liked her right from the start, but this confession somehow demolished the last of the barrier of awe. Over coffee I found myself asking her to lend me some money, and without the slightest hesitation she wrote me a large cheque. She didn't even ask me why I needed it.

    •   •   •   •   •

Aaron's telegram was waiting for me on the hall table.

'Meet you Charing Kent Station ten a.m. Sunday bring novel. Aaron.'

I lay awake for three hours, watching the car lights fanning over the ceiling. My feelings were confused and stifling; they seemed to stop me breathing properly. I had intended to tell him what I felt about the play and what he'd done, and I tried to memorize sentences in advance, but when I imagined seeing him again, I could plan no further. That seemed to be an end in itself.

When at last I slept, I dreamed of Aaron; an intimate disturbing dream which generated a physical feeling I had never had in real life, a feeling so strong it woke me in time for the slow, exquisite decrescendo. I lay for a few minutes, distressed in my mind, but with my body languid and at peace. Then I dropped into a deep, tranquil sleep.

My train to Charing was on time; it drew into the little country station with an excess of hissing, and a few doors clapped open and shut. I got out, clasping the manuscript tightly under one arm. It was raining, the soft, misty rain of early autumn; looking through the window on the way I had seen the leaves turning. The country air smelled sweet and good. I had forgotten how dirty London air is till I tasted something fresh in my mouth and lungs.

Aaron was waiting at the ticket barrier. He wore an old khaki sweater and corduroys, and the beginnings of a beard. His beard grew oddly, underneath his jaw, leaving most of his face bare. He had no mackintosh on and the pearly raindrops dampened the frizz of the sweater.

The first thing he did was to take the manuscript from me, as if relieving me of a heavy suitcase. Then he led me by the wrist to a bench under the overhang of the station roof. He took the script out of its envelope and riffled through it quickly, making sure it was all there.

'I had a moment's blind panic when I remembered where I'd left it,' he said. 'But then I realized you'd take care of it.' He hardly looked at me, and he didn't look up, either, when he asked in a rushed, muffled voice, 'She didn't see it, did she? – If she did, for Christ's sake don't tell me.'

116

I was free to laugh. 'Now you won't believe me when I say no!'

'But it is no? Truly?'

'Yes, truly.'

He took my wrist again, and after a moment he stood up. 'Your train back doesn't leave for an hour,' he said. 'You'd better come and have a hot coffee or something.'

I followed him out of the station yard, numb with disappointment. He had only wanted his manuscript! He held it now, carelessly dangling from one corner, as if, having recovered it, it was of no more importance to him. I thought how he had kissed me, and afterwards swung my little finger absently, his mind elsewhere.

We went into a café and sat in the window. The sun came out and sparkled through the fine pattern of raindrops and flowered curtains. Aaron slung the big envelope on the vacant chair beside him and ordered two coffees without consulting me. He seemed preoccupied, but he kept putting his hand over to touch mine as it lay on the oilcloth tabletop, in a nervous unconscious gesture. He didn't seem to want to talk, but there was so much I needed to know.

Timidly I asked where he was living.

'Oh, a room over a pub; I'd show you, only it's a bus-ride away.'

'How did you find it?'

'Chance. Got on a train, got off when I felt I was far enough out, got on a bus . . . it was all quite random and unplanned. It's okay, though. A bit damp and the food's horrible, but it's quiet and the cider's marvellous.'

'Have you been working?'

He answered without looking at me. 'Of course. What do you think I came for?' But I felt he was lying.

'You said –' I stumbled. 'You said you came to find yourself.' The words sounded sententious. I looked fixedly at the plastic salt-cellar. He didn't answer, so to break the silence I said nervously, 'I've been going to rehearsals.'

'You've been *what*?' There was derisive unbelief in his voice.

I looked up at him. He was very handsome, almost beautiful.

117

The sunlight patterned his face, surrounded by the soft, virile black hair. His eyes were hard and enigmatic. The bulky, ugly sweater emphasized the thin elegance of his hands, the youthful tender column of his neck. He was laughing incredulously; his teeth were strong and perfect; I wanted to put my fingers between his warm lips and touch them.

'Aaron, what you've done is horrible.'

His laugh died abruptly, but the shape of it left the beautiful teeth still exposed. I managed to go on. I had to, now.

'Those people who are trying to act it. They're artists. They're doing their job, it's important to them, and what you've done is – is like sending somebody out in a car with no brakes. No, it's more like building a rotten bridge and then letting people walk over it. Besides . . .'

I made myself look into his eyes to see how he was taking it. I feared his sudden rages almost more than I feared Polly's. Hers terrified me, but his hurt me more deeply. But he was not angry yet, only astonished.

I suddenly took hold of his hand, which had just drawn away from mine. 'Aaron, do you understand that that monstrosity you've written is *going to be put on*? That people are going to see it, and judge it, and judge *you*? Haven't you any self-respect?'

He took his hand out of mine. His face had gone quite white and expressionless, like the face of a corpse. I felt it would be cold to touch. He stood up and put his hands slowly into his pockets. He stared out of the window and said distantly 'I'm not interested in that piece of work, any more than I'm interested in my latest fart. She asked for it, and she got it. My only hope is that it chokes her. As for the actors, they're getting paid, which is all that concerns any actors I've ever met. If you're worrying about my reputation, don't. It doesn't exist, so there's nothing to lose.'

'But don't you see, you'll *have* a reputation after this – a bad one!'

'With whom?'

'The public – the critics –'

His mouth turned up at one side and his shoulders gave a short, sneering lift. 'Am I supposed to care?'

'Yes, *yes*!'

He said a short, ugly word and sat down again. The coffee

came. He looked down while he stirred his – his hair had grown, and hung in shining black strands over his forehead. When he looked up he was smiling. Somehow his smile maddened me. There was something so unreachable about it.

'Don't grin like that!' I said sharply.

He reached for my hand, but I snatched it away. 'Look,' he said reasonably. 'Can't I convince you that it just doesn't matter? That I don't give a damn what they say? It can't hurt me, either way. As a matter of fact, it won't be a flop. It's meaningless, yes; but it's well written or Theo wouldn't have bought it and Bill, soft-headed pretentious idiot though he may be, wouldn't have undertaken to direct it. It's got vitality and social comment and symbolism and all that jazz the critics are always raving about. The fact that none of it adds up will make it more intriguing, not less.'

I felt myself beginning to cry. He didn't understand. I was helpless to breach that wall of unimaginative indifference and conceit.

'Don't you see,' I said weakly, putting my hand over my eyes, 'It's *because* it's well-written that what you've done is so wrong. Aren't there enough people who *can't* create anything whole and good, without you deliberately botching something that could have been wonderful?' I was crying now. I couldn't help it. I was so angry and ashamed of him.

He didn't try to comfort me. He just waited until I stopped and then said, 'I suppose we'd better be getting back to the station if you're going to catch that train.'

A blind, reasonless rage possessed me. I would have liked to attack him, with my hands, with my finger-nails. I wanted to hurt him physically, to tear down that imperviousness with pain.

'I could kill you,' I said shakily. 'You stupid, arrogant, patronizing lout!'

He looked at me calmly. 'I'll walk you to the station.'

I stood up, anger weakening my legs to the point where I had to lean on the table. 'No,' I said. 'I don't want you.'

I stumbled out into the sparkling sunlight, my mind blank. It wasn't till I was safely in the train that I realized what I'd said. Perhaps he hadn't noticed.

. . . . .

The district the theatre was in was strange to me. Funny how one comes across bits of London one's never seen, each with its own character, as different from the rest as if it were in another city altogether. It seemed such a long journey on Tube and bus that I thought Theo Craven must have lost his touch. How did he expect people to come all that tiresome way, when most of them wouldn't make the effort to go to a theatre in the West End?

But when I got there, I was astonished by how attractive it was. After all the grimy garishness of the inner suburbs, this district, south of the river, was almost a village. There were some beautiful old houses, and pubs like country inns, and even a pond with swans on it. Near by was the theatre. It still had workmen's ladders leaning against it, and the new paint gleamed. I caught my breath as I saw the title going up on the tiny marquee in black bold letters. There was a big poster, too; Aaron's name jumped off it and stopped me in my tracks. I stood staring at it, feeling the reality, the imminence of it for the first time. A white tide of nervous anxiety passed over me, leaving a dredged emptiness in its wake.

Tomorrow was the opening. It had come upon the theatre before it was completely ready; only the dress rehearsal could be held there. It was this that I had come to see. I was not coming to the first night, I had decided. I couldn't bear it. Besides, Polly would be there.

The cast was already in the building, filling the back part of it with life and tension. I found my way to Jo's dressing-room, which she shared with three of the other actresses. It was appallingly cramped; each woman barely had room for her own sticks of grease-paint on her portion of the dressing-table, and the hanging space for clothes was quite inadequate for more than one. But everything was bright and freshly-painted, and nobody seemed to mind the limitations. They were all joking and laughing and pushing past each other with exaggerated rudeness, putting on accents – 'D'you mind gettin' your great bottom off my appurtenances?' – 'Only a nasty shameless piece like you would admit to ownin' any.'

They seemed pleased to see me. I was almost part of the company now. They made room for me to sit down and let me watch them putting on their make-up. I sat quietly, listening to their shrill, nervous chatter and watching their four varied backs, bare in their slips or caped in towels; their hands, seemingly with a life of their own, went about their intricate business with automatic efficiency while their owners twisted and fidgeted like restless children. Miraculously, the reflected faces altered under the ministrations of those quick fingers. They started as glazed blanks, featureless as currant buns, hair submerged under colourless swathes of chiffon, mouths lipless, eyes lashless; and slowly emerged – evolved into startling poster-size human beings, characteristics emphasized with vivid blacks, reds, greens; lines, shadows, highlights were superimposed; the chiffon came off, the hair beneath was consigned to unfamiliar shapes, framing the strange new faces. It was like watching God at work on the raw material of humanity on a day when he was tired of the commonplace and had decided to be more than usually emphatic.

It was as exciting as a circus, and, to me, just as unreal. *Like children dressing up*, I thought, puzzled, in a faintly contemptuous way, by its importance to them. Yet at the same time, I could feel the vicarious thrill of it fluttering through my own veins . . . the work-force that drives artists and which makes their lives so much more intense and meaningful than most other people's. I knew I wouldn't have been able to understand even enough of it to envy them, if I had not experienced it second-hand through working with Aaron.

I pushed away the gratitude. It threatened to undermine the contempt and anger with which, for the last week, I had been fighting my hunger for him. This, today, coming to the theatre at last, was my first weakness since I had seen him at Charing. I hadn't even been near the dusty church hall, and when Jill had well-meaningly tried to show me the advance publicity in the papers I had been so abrupt that even she, usually not very sensitive, had been tactful and sympathetic.

An unrecognizable Jo finally turned towards me. 'There,' she said, drawing her hands once more down the flattened planes of her hair, its curly flames doused with water and oil. 'How do you like me?' Her beauty was dulled to drabness, her lips thinned, her great square green eyes seemed lustreless in their bed of applied shadows. Even her hands, usually the acme of capable vitality, looked pallid and defeated.

'How can you do that to yourself?' was all I could say, torn between admiration and dismay.

'Do what?'

'Make yourself so – awful.'

She looked at me blankly. 'But it's the girl in the *play*,' she explained patiently, as if to a child.

The shabby little stage manager tramped down the stone corridor and knocked on the door, calling out, 'Beginners, please.' Jo suddenly clutched my hand convulsively. 'Hear that?' she said. 'It's the first time for *years* this little place has heard those words . . .'

'Television commercials, indeed!' said the Countess (who was really the Countess now, complete with curlers). She spoke with a well-bred sniff of disdain, and added in the same tone, 'How utterly buggerish advertising people are! A perfect little gem of a theatre like this!'

Jo said to me, 'I can feel it, coming alive again all round us. It doesn't smell right yet, but it will soon. Oh, I *do* love Theo for buying it – saving it from its hideous commercial fate, cleaning it up and giving it back its self-respect!' She was not being affected, I could see; she was simply hugging herself with pleasure. 'And I love Aaron, too,' she added unexpectedly.

'Why?' I was startled into asking.

'For writing a play that's witty and alive and interesting enough to set people thinking – and talking, and asking questions, and telling their friends, and writing pieces in the papers, and making other people come. Oh darlings, it doesn't *matter* if nobody understands a single word, so long as it *attracts* them.'

'By that reckoning, you might just as well put on "Nudes Not Prudes",' objected one of the others. 'That'd fill the place.'

But Jo was in no mood to be taken literally. 'Good idea!' she exclaimed. 'If "Man in a Hole" as written doesn't fetch 'em, we'll bloody well take all our clothes off and put on an exhibition!'

'We wouldn't even have to change the title,' said the Countess dryly.

Six hours late I crawled home, feeling stunned. The making-up process I had watched had been only a foretaste of what was to come later. The whole production was transformed, lifted into another stratum, by the addition of costumes and sets, the juxtaposition of darkness and bright lights, and by the intervention of the proscenium arch and the tiny, empty orchestra pit. My faculties of criticism were bemused; I could no longer tell with any certainty whether it was nonsense or brilliance. During the infuriating delays and interruptions, like hiccups in the flow of action and speech, I had tried to pull myself together, to shed the illusion, and imagine how an audience would react to a first showing, knowing nothing of its conception or birth-pangs, but seeing it as if it had never been anything but a whole. But as soon as the lights were adjusted or the sticking door fixed, as soon as Bill leapt off the stage and said 'Carry on, chaps!' the magic would seize me again and wonder at the sheer excitement of it would paralyse my judgement.

Polly sat at the very back of the stalls; she was so still throughout the whole long afternoon and evening that one could almost forget she was there, except when a glance over one's shoulder would pick out the dim, expressionless moon of her face through thin horizontal clouds of cigarette smoke.

At one point during a long break for lighting I crept out for plates full of sandwiches and a huge jug of coffee, which the cast accepted abstractedly and bolted like starving foxes. I steeled myself and took some down to Polly. For what seemed like several minutes she ignored me as I stood beside her in the aisle. It was like standing in a cold draft. At last she looked round and our eyes met through the smoke and darkness.

'Coffee, Miss Franks?' I asked formally.

She continued to look at me for a moment, and then said curiously, 'What are you doing here?' – as if she'd only just registered my presence at the rehearsal. I didn't answer. She said, 'Take those things and go away' – but as I turned to go, she added behind my back in a low, almost sensuous voice, 'You won't be here tomorrow evening. I don't want to see you in this theatre tomorrow evening.' The repetition had something hypnotic about it. Thinking over it at home, cuddling a badly-needed cup of hot chocolate and trying to thaw out my cold ankles by the fire, I was surprised that I had gone meekly away without a word, still carrying the food I had foolishly taken her. I was more surprised still that now, away from her, I did not feel any rebellious 'I damn-well-*will*-go-just-for-that' reaction. I knew I wanted desperately to go, but that I would not, and that my fear of Polly was only a small part of the reason.

Chapter Nine

I feared the long hours of the next day, and so made them longer by lying awake most of the night, dreading them. I woke sharply from a shallow sleep, with a painful empty feeling that hot coffee didn't fill.

Stupidly, I had made no plans for occupying the sterile time until the day and the evening should, for better or worse, be over. When Gwen and Jill had left for work, I wandered through the quiet flat idly, irritably, temptation chewing at me with an almost audible sound like a mouse in a wainscot. I desultorily washed up the breakfast things, read the paper, made my bed, tidied up. Then, looking at the time and finding it was only ten o'clock, a sort of rage shook me. How was I expected to bear it, when the time passed with such deliberate slowness? They would just be arriving at the theatre now for the final run-through. There seemed nowhere else in the world where I could be comfortable, except there. It was like an itch one has been ordered not to scratch. But after all, I argued with myself, why not? Why not go? I wasn't that afraid of Polly, surely? No. The reason was that if I went during the day, I would never be able to tear myself away tonight. The hypnotic excitement would get hold of me, and I would just remain. And I didn't want to see other people seeing it; I shrank from the thought of that, as if from a peculiarly cruel retribution for some wrong-doing.

Nevertheless, the magnetic pull towards South London was so strong that I dared not let myself leave the flat. I knew in which direction I would involuntarily turn, as soon as the barrier of the front door closed behind me. I found myself picking up Gwen's *Telegraph*, and my hand fumbled round for a pencil without my order. I flung both aside with a sense of shock. *Not that dead thing again!* I thought fiercely. I tried to read my latest book on Israel, but the words slid past my eyes as meaninglessly as the cracks between paving-stones.

I leaned my head back against the chair and stared at the ceiling. Was I some kind of masochist? Was that why I wanted to go so terribly? I couldn't put it down to Aaron any more, because since my trip to Charing I had stopped caring about Aaron, or so I told myself. No, it was the play itself. It had become a separate entity, with a life and needs of its own. And it needed me. But that was ludicrous. Needed me for what? What new conceit was this? But on this very thought, Jo phoned.

'What's up? Why aren't you here?'

'Why should I be?' I asked with an attempt at casualness.

'We're having a last run-through and everything's to hell. We need our good-luck piece.'

'Oh, rubbish!'

'It's not rubbish,' she insisted with complete seriousness. 'You don't understand. Everything in the theatre's a matter of luck. We have to be superstitious because nothing that happens is under our control.' She waited for a moment, and then said 'Of course you're coming tonight?'

'No, I wasn't planning to . . .'

'But you *must*!' she shouted suddenly, nearly deafening me. She sounded really angry. 'You *must* come! How could you *not*? Please don't upset me like that. I'm not going to mention this to the others. You've got to come, they're expecting you. Everything'll go wrong if you aren't here.' She put down the receiver before I could speak.

I paced the flat, literally wringing my hands. Why had she had to phone and talk in that absurd way? Why did she put everything on to me, suggesting it would be my fault if the play went badly? Right from the beginning she'd turned to me like some kind of talisman. How ridiculous and emotional theatre people were! As if I could affect things – who knew nothing about plays really, who was plain and commonplace and who had never been looked at with admiration in my life. *Before*, amended some inner honesty. That brought me up cold and sharp. So it was just self-importance, was it? The thrill of my first taste of power, going to my head and there having to rationalize itself into a feeling of responsibility? I felt disgusted and ashamed. I would not go – now there would be no temptation to go, since I had uncovered the ugly, selfish reason for wanting to. I became suddenly brisk and controlled. I left the flat and did the shopping, giving my orders with crisp confidence. Know thyself, that was the true and effective answer to everything. I didn't even want to go now. In the afternoon I went out again, this time to the cinema. It was a very good film and while watching it I forgot everything else. By the time I came out, it was seven forty-five. The curtain had been up for fifteen minutes.

I had a bath and went to bed early. The girls had both gone to a late party. The quiet of the flat didn't seem disturbing now; I had defeated my devil, and bed felt good, warm and rewarding like a mother's hug. I built up a backrest with cushions from the living-room, and snuggled up, my feet on a bottle, with a hot drink and supper on a tray and my cigarettes beside me. I gave the theatre and the play a swift, glancing thought. It seemed remote, like the memory of a man you've fallen out of love with . . . *What was all that about?* I asked myself tolerantly. It would be interesting to read the notices in the morning though . . . I started to read my book. The words came into my head perfectly now. It was all about the early pioneers, really fascinating.

When the bell rang, I was annoyed. Who on earth could it be, at this hour? Then I realized it wasn't awfully late, only about a quarter to ten. Probably some friend of Jill's, they were always popping round uninvited . . . I was putting on my dressing-gown when the noisy thing pealed again 'Shut up, can't you?' I said to it irritably. But it went on ringing with a mindless, monotonous sound, like the thin toneless scream of a lunatic. I felt a shiver of anger and unease, and actually shouted 'Shut up!' again as I ran into the hall, quite loudly enough for whoever was outside to hear.

It was Aaron.

He looked so ill and unnatural that for a second I didn't recognize him. Even after I opened the door he still stood there, his finger on the bell with his full weight behind it; he seemed to be concentrating all his strength and attention on it, as if keeping the sound going was the only thing that would save his reason. His whole arm shook with the effort and his teeth, clenched and bared in a grimace showing some tremendous inner struggle, made him look almost as terrifying as if he really were a madman.

I instinctively dragged at his arm to stop the incessant, hideous ringing, and that seemed to break whatever spell held him. He went limp, and looked at me, as if bewildered to find me there. He was panting. Suddenly he flung himself forward, forcing me backwards, and dragged the door to behind him with one arm as if using me as a shield. I remembered in my dazed numbness how this had happened before; only then, the worst had been over when he put his arms round me. Now I had a sense of terror, of some great weight about to fall on me, and we trembled against each other for a long terrifying moment.

Then he released me, and took my wrist tightly in his hand, holding it with all his strength, and said faintly: 'I've got to tell you. Please let me.' I knew something appalling had happened to him, something he couldn't bear alone, and even through my fear I felt a piercing lightness of heart that he had come to me and to no one else. 'Come in here,' I said, and led him like a blind man through into my bedroom.

He sat down on the bed and began to shiver uncontrollably; I wrapped my eiderdown round him and he looked rakish and absurd, but somehow all the more touching and alarming because of it. He didn't look at me, but stared at his hands, from one to the other, as they lay palms-up on his knees.

'Would you like anything?' I asked. 'A drink?'

He didn't answer. Slowly his breathing became quieter and suddenly he began to talk.

'I went to see it,' he said. 'It was because of what you said. At the time it didn't mean anything, but later I found myself thinking about it . . . I haven't been able to work at all these last days, because I've been obsessed by curiosity. How *could* they make anything of it? I kept hearing the things you said. I simply hadn't thought about it before. I refused to let myself go to the theatre, and yet I went. I can't explain.'

He was silent for a moment, and then his mind seemed to have jumped, because he said with abrupt despair, 'I shouted! I must have been mad. I couldn't stand it any longer – it was what those people said in the first interval – and then the talking and rustling – seeing it going on up there, with all those little sounds of incomprehension all round me in the dark . . .'

He stood up tormentedly and began to cross the room with stiff jerky steps which reminded me of Polly. The eiderdown clung round him for a moment, then fell off on to the floor. He reached the window and flattened his forehead and hands against it.

'It was so bad,' he said at last, in a queer, gentle voice. 'It was so badly written. They did their best up there, they brought something to it, love I suppose, and I hated them. It was like watching perfume being poured down a drain to cover up the smell. I kept thinking "What a waste! Why do you try, you poor, stupid, unperceiving sods, why don't you understand you're throwing yourselves away?" And it was unstoppable. That was the terrible thing. Once it started, there was nothing I could do to blot it all out, cancel it, make it never have happened. Every word they spoke I could remember dictating to you, I could remember how I'd laughed and the sly, dirty remarks I'd made to you about the Method boys and the poor silly sods in the audience who would be taken in, and how I told you I'd laugh my guts out at all of them . . . and there it was, happening, without anything in between to prepare me . . . oh my God, when I think of them rehearsing it, trying to find the thread, the mind, the sane graspable meaning behind it – trying to keep from drowning by clinging on to a soluble lifebelt that comes to bits in the hand . . . And those people aren't such fools. They knew. They all knew what I'd done. I heard them in the bar after the first act, I was drinking and drinking and trying to remember that it was all a joke, and two women were standing near me, so near I could smell their hair, and they weren't just ciphers, they were intelligent people, and one of them said to the other, "Would you believe that any literate young man could spend weeks and weeks turning out such a *polished* bit of charlatanism?" And the other one said, "The worst of it is, he can write".'

He began to beat with his hands on the glass, rhythmically, like a protesting prisoner.

'I had to force myself to go back after the interval. I'd avoided everyone I knew until then by standing at the back of the circle, but as the house-lights went down I found Polly standing beside me. She was wearing black, and with that gaunt face of hers she looked like a funeral mute. She just stared at me and then said "Why aren't you dressed?" I heard it as "Why aren't you dead?" It was like a nightmare, as if I had come to my own funeral. I was drunk by then because I'd had nothing to eat. None of it seemed real after that; I mean, it seemed real enough, but too awful to be part of real life, more like finding yourself in hell. Those words of mine kept flowing over me like hot metal, and sometimes Jo spoke them – my Jo – my wise, sensible girl, having to mouth that . . . and the agony was, she made some of it sound clever – she said it with such confidence, as if she were in on my obscene joke and were degrading herself by trying to help me . . .'

The beating stopped and his voice dissolved. My heart was wrenched. I longed to shout 'Be quiet! I can't bear to hear!' but I kept silent and listened.

'I didn't *decide* to stop it,' his voice went on, now blurred and jerking. 'I just heard my voice breaking into it, shouting – I saw all the faces below me turn in the darkness with a sighing sound, and I heard Jo's voice falter and then go on . . . and I knew nothing would stop it. Then I ran away.'

He turned very slowly to face me, and stood with his arms and head hanging, defenceless, surrendering to me, it seemed, as if to a judgement.

When I stood up to go to him, I nearly fell – my legs were shaking – I had to step over the eiderdown on the floor. As I walked carefully towards him he had time to say, 'I tore down the poster outside – the one with my name on it.' Then I had reached him.

I've tried to remember exactly how it happened, but the details are lost. When I was little, my parents took me swimming in the sea. I held a hand of each, and they led me out into the teeth of the waves, standing either side of me as tall and firm as trees, able to see the horizon; but for me, there was nothing ahead but a wall of water, and I can still remember the terror as a wave reared up before me. I couldn't cry to them to lift me up, and they were too far away to know how it felt to be shorter than the wave.

When Aaron and I came together it was like being engulfed by a weight of water – the sensation was as overwhelming as that of drowning. But that was afterwards. At first I held him in my arms and somehow we slipped to the floor and lay there clinging together; and I was in control. I cradled him and kissed him like a child, and with a child's disinterest and introspection he clung to me, almost unaware of me personally, as to something solid in an earthquake.

And then he changed. His shivering and the jerking of his shoulders stopped and his body no longer lay passive in my arms but began to turn towards me. He lifted his head and stared into my eyes, and his face was wild, a stranger's face, with a stark look of incredulity on it. That was when I saw the wave rear up. My lips moved in silent pleading not to let it happen, but I couldn't make a sound; and then his mouth and his body descended, and it was happening, it was all happening.

I remember the feeling of suffocation as his lips and his four limbs imprisoned me, my will impotently shouting in protest inside a body that seemed to have a will of its own – a body which put its arms round him in acquiescence at the very moment of the worst pain, and kept them there until long after it was over. It was without my agreement, and so were the other movements of submission. My mind was clear all the time, receiving messages of fear and pain, but my body acted and accepted without it, as if all the connexions had been broken.

At last he left me, rolling away to lie like somebody dead on the floor at my side. When his body wasn't touching mine any longer, the links between brain and function were restored, and I was able to stand up. Still strangely detached from reality I picked up the clothes from the floor and carried them into the bathroom. The discovery that I was bleeding didn't distress me. I attended to my damaged body as impersonally as if it were somebody else's. I washed myself, thoroughly and mechanically, and cleaned my teeth before putting my nightdress and dressing-gown on again. I felt nothing – no shame because I had had no choice, and no pleasure because there had been none. I felt calm, almost matter-of-fact. I didn't realize that this was the effect of shock.

It took no special effort to go back into my bedroom where he

131

was. He had recovered and was sitting on a straight-backed chair. He looked dazed; his face, turned away from me, was deathly white. A cigarette burned in his hand. I thought how good a cigarette would be, and crossed to take one from the bed-side box. The tray with my supper on it was still on the bed. I looked at it with a puzzled feeling; it made me uncomfortable and sad, as if the person who'd been eating it had just died.

When I'd lit the cigarette and inhaled that first, blessed draught, I carried the tray into the kitchen. I scraped the cold food into the garbage-pail and rinsed the plate, and then took a bottle of milk and two glasses back into the bedroom.

Aaron stood up this time as I came in. He shot a frightened glance at me.

'I'd better go,' he said beneath his breath.

'If you want to,' I agreed, wondering vaguely how I could make him feel better.

'Don't *you* want me to?'

The answer came, not from reason or emotion, but from some deep instinct. 'No, I think it would be better if you stayed here.'

After a pause, during which I poured the milk, he said timidly, 'Do you mean I can sleep with you?'

'Yes.'

I handed him his glass, and he took it, and we both drank. The cold milk pouring down my dry throat was even better than the cigarette, better than the warm, soothing water.

Aaron didn't speak again, but watched me while I drank, and then abruptly turned away and began to undress. I climbed prosaically into bed, and lay down to wait for him. I had never lain in bed waiting for a man to come in beside me. As I watched him folding his clothes, the numbness suddenly began to wear off, a process like the thawing of a frozen limb, at once a relief and an agony. As he turned silently round, almost naked and looking heartbreakingly thin and vulnerable, I put my hand out to him and smiled.

He made an odd little sound, as if of pain, took it swiftly and pressed it against his neck. His face, too, was full of pain, and I smoothed the lines off it with my other hand.

132

'Come in and get warm,' I whispered.

Then in the friendly darkness, the pleasure came – so unexpectedly. Why was it nobody told you about this part – the indescribable feeling of companionship and completion? The books describe, in cold medical language or the fever of purple passages, how the sexual pieces of the human jig-saw fit together, but they don't draw attention to the wonderful soft mechanism of the other parts, which knit and accommodate each other as if they were never intended to be apart . . . the way the chin of one dovetails into the smooth hollow of the other's neck, the curve at the waist which allows the arm to pass under and round, the ball-and-socket compact between armpit and shoulder, breast and hand; the upper arm providing the cheek's natural pillow, the comfortable intertwining of legs and feet, the crutch mounted with loving security upon the thigh. And every alternative modification brought about by the soft mutual caresses and movements of tenderness produce the same marvellous harmony of comfort and peace.

'Nothing else matters, does it?'

'There isn't anything else . . .'

'Not even words.'

'Only thank you. Thank you.'

He fell quietly asleep in my arms, and for a long time I lay half-drunk and afloat in happiness, aware of every inch of his skin which mine was touching, breathing in the scent of his hair, listening to the light, peaceful sound of his breathing and the muted beating of his heart.

It was the sound of the front door closing that brought me back to reality.

The shock was as violent as being sobered up with a bucket of ice-water. I'd forgotten everything that lay outside my room. Now with horror I thought of the hundred times Jill or Gwen had come into my room when they got home late, to mull over the evening before going to bed. The doors had no locks. I died a sharp little death every second as they came giggling and whispering along the passage. I wanted to wake Aaron, tell him to hide – throw my weight against the door – anything . . . but I was frozen by the frightfulness of the situation, and could only lie motionless, willing them to go past.

There was an agonizing moment when they stopped outside my door and conferred in whispers; but, thank God, they decided it was too late and that I must be asleep, and tiptoed away.

I relaxed with a sob, but the magic was shattered. The real world, held temporarily in suspension, broke round me, inevitable and cold and full of problems to face.

Now I began to see the realities clearly. People don't change their nature in an hour, however violent or full of emotion and unexpected beauty. I remembered all that had gone before – Anne-Marie, and Aaron's assertion that he never ventured on to dangerous ground – 'The kind pain grows in.' And later, Jo's horror-story had confirmed it, and founded it upon reason. Now he had broken his rule – abnormal pressures had pushed him into a love-affair with me. What would he feel tomorrow, when a new day brought the inevitable staleness and restored him to himself as he had always been?

He would look at me, and believe that he had – how did Jo put it? – that he had 'defiled' me. I was not the kind that 'lies down', or so he would believe, though now I wanted nothing but to lie down with him every night for the rest of my life. But it was useless to even think of it. With sickening certainty, I knew that either he would try to go on as if nothing had happened, shedding responsibility as a man will for some act he commits when too drunk to know what he's doing; or – and this was infinitely more to be dreaded – he would look on me as he did the others. He would make suggestive little remarks, and touch me casually, slipping into bed with me when circumstances permitted and he felt like it . . . because now I would be different. Our past friendship was meaningless now . . . no more than a build-up to a climax which had blown my life off-course but would leave his just as it was.

As tiredness brought me towards sleep at last, I determined that whatever attitude he took in the morning, whether sheepish or brazen, contemptuous or cold, familiar or merely casual, I would fall in with it. He would need something from me even if it was only an absence of complicity, a blotting-out of

134

memory. I would do my best. I would even be his floosie if that was what he needed. But as I lay there holding him, my arm numb from the weight of his head, I thought that, after all, I would be getting off easily. The impossible difficulties would follow if what he asked me for was love.

Part Two: Aaron

For Chaim

Chapter One

God, what a sleep! Like the sleep of the dead – or the unborn. No dreams; no starting violently awake in the empty darkness, expecting to find some unspeakable threat hanging over you. Just warm, padded depths, a lightness in the throat, and peace.

Waking up was good, too – like waking from the first healthy sleep after a long, feverish illness. It was slow enough to savour each stage: the awareness of nameless happiness first, then up through the layers of drowsiness to the knowledge of satisfaction and safety, and at last the detailed remembrance, the warm, soft, sleeping flesh in my arms.

I lay quite still, with my eyes closed, and let my hands and arms and body enjoy her closeness. Then I opened my eyes. I could only see her tousle of short, dark hair, and beyond it the dim curtained bedroom, the double hump that was us lying in bed together.

Even asleep, her hands were strong and firm on my back. I'd often watched them, always so swift and capable – attractive by themselves, so that I wanted to touch them, hold them, get strength from them, even before I knew I wanted all of her. When had I known it? Only in flashes, now and then. And I'd refused to recognize it. I never did recognize it consciously until I found her underneath me and knew how badly I wanted her and that it was too late to stop. My body took over from me. *Can it be one's own fault if one can't help it?* My life-long self-excusing inner cry. But this time there had been no punitive kick-back. I remembered steeling myself for her tears, her abuse, some crippling punishment of words, and instead there had been soothing, healing softness; no forgiveness, no reminder of guilt – almost a reward.

At the thought, my arms tightened round her and I felt her stirring and waking. I grew suddenly afraid that I'd get the punishment now, that last night had been some false reaction on her part and that this morning she'd hate me and weep, or, worse still, undo it all by being brave and forgiving and saying we'd forget it ever happened . . . Jesus, Jesus, I thought, don't let her do that!

I rolled over on top of her in an impulse to smother any such reaction at birth. She turned on her back, still not properly awake, and her face came round out of the pillow. As soon as I could reach her mouth I began kissing it frantically, keeping my mouth on hers and kissing as if to stifle her, to block the way of words. She made little sounds which vibrated up into my lips and tongue, and I could feel her hands, awake and aware before the rest of her, trying to explore me for the benefit of her sleepy brain, to tell her what was happening. I felt her get frightened, and I freed her mouth and whispered urgently into her ear, 'Don't say anything – don't feel anything – not yet. Just this. Just this.' And I took her very strongly, although she was half asleep and not ready and I had to hurt her and make the mountain of guilt and indebtedness higher, but I thought that while she was being hurt she wouldn't think, she'd only blame me for this, each thrust of pain, not for last night or the play or the past with Polly, and nor would she look ahead and be angry or afraid about what was going to happen now.

But at last I looked at her and saw her small face all twisted with trying not to cry out, and I stopped cold. I felt ill with disgust at myself, and came away from her suddenly, and lay with my back to her, wondering what to do, feeling the impossibility of even asking her to forgive me – yet at the same time, contemptibly, wanting to turn back and finish.

After a while I couldn't stand the silence any longer, and reached my hand backwards to feel for hers. It was there, and held mine tightly. I found the courage to turn round and look at her. Her eyes were waiting for me. It was too dark to be sure, but there didn't seem to be any reproach there, or tears, and after a moment she did a strange thing – she put my hand to her breast, and then, when I made a little involuntary movement towards her, drew my head down and kissed me.

The relief was so incredible that I felt as if I might bloody well cry myself. I thought there must be a catch in it. But her hands were gentling me, and my heartbeats grew calmer in spite of myself.

'Aren't you angry?' I muttered at last into her soft neck.

'No.'

'But I must have hurt you.'

'Yes . . .'

She was silent for a moment, stroking my hair thoughtfully, and then she said, without a trace of self-pity, 'How many times is it painful for, do you know?'

I lifted my head to look at her. Her face had changed for me overnight from that of a pleasant, warm, appealing girl into the face of a woman so infinitely important to me that I was amazed by the violence of my own reaction as I looked at her. I touched the concise, upturned lines with pain and astonishment. There was nothing extraordinary there, nothing remotely beautiful, and yet the poignant joy of possessing her was so acute I felt my bowels dissolve.

'It was my fault it hurt this morning,' I said. 'I promise it won't happen again.'

She frowned and turned her head away. 'I see.' After a moment she looked at me again and smiled – not very happily, but brightly, and said 'Well, it's up to you of course.' She pushed me aside quite gently and added 'I think I'd better get up. I'll have to start thinking about how to get you out of here.'

It was a cold morning, I suddenly noticed. She shivered a little as she got into her dressing-gown, the delicate movement making me want to drag her back into bed beside me. But something – the brisk way she was moving about, keeping her head turned away – stopped me. I lay there watching as she drew back the curtains, throwing a cold, grey light on the room and the bed. She lit the gas-fire, then went to the chest-of-drawers and collected some things out of it. Every movement she made seemed calculated to make me want her more, perhaps because she was quite unconscious of it. I realized suddenly that this was the first time since Oxford that I had actually slept all night with a girl and seen her going about things in the morning. I'd forgotten how good this part was, comforting and exciting both at once, especially when you could sleep with her again . . .

'Martha –'

'Yes?'

She said it as she said it at the office. I felt a ghastly misgiving.

'Come here!'

She hesitated, but came, and sat down with an incongruous primness on the very edge of the bed. I pulled myself out from under the covers and knelt on the pillow, so that my head was higher than hers, and gripped her shoulders.

'Listen, if there's going to be any come-back, ever, let's have it now.' She stared at me, her mouth slightly open. I shook her a little. 'I mean, don't get brisk! Don't tolerate me. If you're ever going to be furious, let's get it over, so we can get on.'

'Get on? With what?'

'Everything. Being together.'

Her face seemed to fall to pieces bit by bit. The strength just went out of it and tears flooded over her eyes. She suddenly flung her arms round my waist and held me tightly, fists clenched like a child, her face pressed against me. I could feel her tears running down my neck.

It seemed hours before she came back.

I heard the front door close; there was a longish pause, and at last I shouted out 'Hurry up!' She came in looking stern.

'You mustn't do that,' she said. 'It might not have been me.' But it was her, her cheeks and lips cold from the frost outside; even her hair was cold. But the skin of her back under her sweater was warm and silky, her breast even warmer.

She drew away from me and said uncertainly 'Are you really as pleased to see me as all that? I've only been gone a few minutes.'

'Christ, is that all?'

She searched my face for a moment, and then bent to pick up the papers she'd dropped on the floor when I grabbed her. 'I don't know how you're going to take these,' she said worriedly.

'What? – Oh, the notices. To hell with them, I couldn't care less.'

'I think you'll have to care,' she said. 'I think it's a success.'

More to please her than out of curiosity, I sat down in the armchair and began to glance through the papers. My outburst had made the front pages of the *Mail* and the *Express*. 'New

Author Harangues Audience' and 'Angry Young Playwright "Does a Behan".' I turned to the inner pages and read the reviews.

'This extraordinary play has all the earmarks of brilliance – but none of the tearmarks. Mr Franks succeeded in disturbing, intriguing, amusing, alarming and gripping me, with his vivid account of a Twentieth Century lost soul searching, Pirandello-like, for a body to accommodate it. But he did not move me, except to irritation at his own hysterical interruption of the performance. However, anything genuinely new, inventive and personally felt in the theatre is warmly to be welcomed.'

Another said: 'The author trying to shout down the actors might well have been part of the action. I quite thought it was. It would have been in keeping with a play which had already pushed me over the opposing brinks of exasperation and violent enthusiasm. The savage sensuality of the dialogue, flowing purposefully up first one blind alley and then another, by turns obscures and illuminates a stark plot concerning a slumming expedition through the flotsam of London. It was rather like watching Ionesco by flashes of coffee-bar neon.'

'Here's a wonderful one!' Martha said, sounding quite as excited as if it mattered. 'Listen: "Here at last is a play *about* something – a play whose author has set out to make entirely original comments on the modern human predicament. True, he has chosen to do so in symbols already done to death (I had thought) by such experts as Pinter and Beckett. A man goes in search of himself, and finds his own component parts – male and female, moral and immoral, juvenile and adult, cerebral and physical – in the form of chance encounters. All the characters in this play make up a complete personality, which I for one recognized all too clearly, with the same shock I might get if I could see my own subconscious staring me in the face from my shaving mirror".'

I let out a snort of incredulous laughter as she stopped. She looked at me, then shook her head and slowly reached for another paper. I intercepted her hand and pulled her on to my knees, burying my head and my laughter against her shoulder.

'Don't read any more!' I mumbled. 'Pinter – Ionesco –

Beckett – three separate and totally undreamed-of plots . . . it's too crazy, one can only laugh . . .'

She turned my face up. She still had that anxious expression as she frowned into my eyes.

'Why so solemn? Don't you think it's funny?'

'Have you forgotten so quickly how you felt last night?'

The bubble of laughter burst and my body went cold. I gathered her against me for warmth. She hugged my head gently in her arms and I could feel her chin resting on my hair. We sat like that for a long time. My mind was a deliberate blank, but my body was stirring again; my hands began to stroke down her back. She got off my knee quickly.

'Aaron, please let's talk. Let's think.'

I brought my mind back into focus with an unpleasant effort. 'What about?'

'Everything! Polly – the play – where we go from here!'

I tried to think about it, but it was all too big, too difficult. Besides, seeing her standing there, away from me, looking so childish in her skirt and sweater and flat shoes, I began to want her urgently. I stood up and followed her, putting my arms round her in a way she couldn't mistake.

She let me kiss her, but her mind was away from me, fretting. I felt a mild anger with her when she slipped out of my arms.

'Aaron, not *now*! It's not the right time.'

'Are you one of these girls who thinks it's indecent to make love in daylight?'

'I want you to make love to me whenever you like, only I think I'd do it better if I were easy in my mind – if we'd settled about the other things.'

She was trying so hard to be sensible that I couldn't possibly be angry. I sat down again and folded my hands in mocking obedience. 'Right, let's talk. You begin.'

She looked at me helplessly. 'You're not being very helpful, are you?'

'I don't want to talk about last night or about anything else that's happened to me until now. None of it seems very relevant this morning.'

'But Aaron . . .' She sat down opposite me, small and solemn and erect, and began to talk. I watched her mouth moving and

144

her hands fingering the pleats in her skirt or lighting a cigarette, and I listened to her voice as if it were music, a pleasant wave of sound without any directly intelligible meaning. She was so lovely and complete, so serious in her care for our future. She was mine. All that she was and did from now on would be for me; everything I was and did, she would accept and take care of.

My mind strayed to Polly. She had always taken care of things. For the first time I was prepared to admit how anchorless I had felt in the pub in Charing. I hadn't really done much work in that cold little room. I had sat at the window with my mind drifting aimlessly, unable to come to grips with the book or even with myself. I had found myself half-listening for those footsteps on the stairs, the astringent voice ordering me to get to work. Could it be that I'd missed Polly, or was it just that I'd missed the applied discipline, the circumscription of my life within her orbit?

Anyway, it didn't matter now. Now I had a new star, a bright one which would compel obedience through love. When the sound of her voice stopped I went to her and undressed her, kissing as I went, and she only protested a little at the beginning.

Chapter Two

The days drifted indistinguishably past. It was rather fun to think of life going on outside that room, without me. Strange how simple everything was, when you didn't move out into the stream of active life, but just sat still and let it rush past. I was totally happy. The room was a self-contained world, complete with a completeness I hadn't dared to hope existed.

Martha came and went. When she was not with me, the sense of completeness was missing, of course, but not alarmingly so, as I knew she'd come back and that as soon as she did, the half-pleasant aching hunger could be satisfied at once. When she was out I just sat, or lay in bed, and thought about her. It was like floating in a warm, endless sea.

Only sometimes Martha looked so worried and upset that I was forced to jerk myself back to her world, the world she went out into each day, and listen to what she wanted to tell me.

'I've had to tell the girls. How I hate other people knowing! They behaved as if it were something spicy out of the newspapers. Anyway, I've made them promise they'll keep quiet about you being here until I can find somewhere else for you to live . . .

'That was your sister on the phone again. I wish she wouldn't keep on and on – she knows you're here, I'm sure she knows it by instinct. Oh Aaron, the lies are so awful, I'm no good at them . . .

'Jo called round while you were asleep. We sat in the next room and talked. I do like her, I wouldn't have minded telling *her*, but I felt I shouldn't. She told me the story of the first night again from her point of view. They're all terribly worried about you . . .'

She brought me newspapers. I glanced through the stories without interest, as if they concerned some stranger. '"Stop-my-play"-wright Goes to Ground,' said one heading. The story ran:

What's become of the angry young author who stood up on the first night of his play and yelled to the cast to be quiet? Since this outburst, which failed to stop the play (most critics think fortunately) no sign has been seen of Mr Aaron Franks – he has gone to ground without trace. Reporters going to his home on Hampstead Hill have been turned away with a brisk 'No comment' from his sister Paula, who runs a gift shop in Regent Street. His secretary, Miss Martha Fletcher of Earls Court, likewise refuses to answer questions, except to say that she hasn't seen her ex-employer recently. Is Mr Franks too ashamed to show his face? Or is it that he's waiting to see whether the publicity he gave his first play is paying off, before owning up that it was just a first-night stunt? If so, I have news for him. You have a hit, Mr Franks, a very palpable hit. So come out and take your medicine, and with it, a bow.

I slung the paper aside. 'How can they write that crap!' I said cheerfully. It was so supremely nothing to do with me that I was surprised when Martha said with sudden sharpness, 'You wrote some crap too, you know, and people are paying to see it.'

I reached for her, but she dodged away. 'Aaron. This can't go on. You've been here three days, and you're like somebody in a stupor. Polly keeps phoning – she's frantic. The cool manner she puts on for the newspapermen is only a front. She thinks –'

'What does she think?' I asked tolerantly.

'Jo told me. She thinks you've killed yourself.'

That gave me a bit of a jolt, but only a bit. I looked at Martha's hands for a moment, and then was able to say lightly, 'I'm not the suicidal type and she knows it. Darling, don't let's bother about any of it. It's not important.'

'It *is* important, can't you see that it is?' I suddenly saw that she was close to tears – worse, that her hands were trembling. I started across to her and shut them between mine, gripping them too tightly to allow for trembling. The sight had scared me. 'All right, it's important,' I agreed quickly, to soothe her. 'So what? What can we do?'

She looked up at me. Her face wasn't strong, I saw; the

strength was all in her hands. 'Can't you show yourself – take whatever's coming in the way of publicity, and then . . .'

My stomach suddenly ached with anticipatory horror. 'God! And then what?'

'Get a place of your own.' I suppose she saw me go white, because she added hurriedly. 'I'd stay with you if you wanted me to.'

'It'd all be different outside,' I said. 'You know they wouldn't let us be happy, like here.'

'Who's they? Anyway, Aaron – I'm not happy.'

She might as well have spat in my face. I just stared at her.

'Darling, try to realize what it's like for me! I've got you here – living in my room – doing nothing for yourself – refusing to face up to things – it's such a responsibility, Aaron, I'm not ready for it! You just sit all day in a daze, and when I want to talk to you about things you don't listen, all you want to do is make love!'

'Don't you like making love?'

She twisted away from me, her face contorted. 'Aaron, for God's sake! You're not listening to me even now!' She stood against the window as if bracing herself, then took a deep breath. 'Listen, please listen. We've got to think what to do. Every time I go out to do a bit of shopping there's a reporter outside. You don't seem to realize what a stir you made by what you did.'

'Nine days' wonder. They'll soon lose interest.'

'You're not proposing to stay here until that happens? Don't you realize your sister's on the verge of reporting to the police that you're missing?'

'Poor old Poll,' I said indulgently. It was easy to feel indulgent towards her now she couldn't touch me any more. 'She always loved a bit of drama.'

She closed her eyes for a moment and then opened them again and said in a low, desperate voice. 'Aaron, please tell me just what you plan to do.'

I hated to hear that note in her voice, but I honestly couldn't see what there was to get so upset about. I knew I could soothe her and make her calm and happy if only she'd come to bed, but when I tried to caress her she pushed me away quite violently.

148

She'd never done that before, and I felt angry and hurt. I walked away and took a cigarette. I felt her watching me and I was uncomfortable. 'What do you want me to say?' I asked shortly.

'I want you to say that you're prepared to come out of your cocoon and start taking some of the responsibility. After all, the whole situation is your doing, not mine.'

Ah, so here it came, after all. I might have known it was all in cold storage, just waiting till she was a bit upset to come lashing out.

I wasn't in the mood to be apologetic. I bowed with mock humility and said, 'I'm terribly sorry I raped you. Please excuse me for taking your virginity, I realize it wasn't quite nice. I'll try not to do it again.'

She was looking at me with an air of helplessness. There was a long silence and then she said wearily, 'I wasn't talking about that.' Suddenly she brushed past me and went out of the flat.

I wandered about feeling miserable. Why couldn't things – just for once – be straightforward and simple, why did women always have to make everything so bloody complicated? I felt frustrated energy building up inside me and wanted her to come back so that we could have a damned good row followed by a damned good – Even at moments like this, I couldn't quite think of her in those sort of terms, but I knew clearly what we both needed. In the morning, everything would be clear and restful again. I lit cigarettes one after the other. How the hell could she say she wasn't happy with me? I knew bloody well I made her happy, otherwise she wouldn't move under me the way she did, or make those little sounds which healed the guilt because now they were from pleasure . . . How could she turn round after that and say she wasn't happy?

Well, there was nothing I could do except wait. She'd come back, sooner or later, and then I could explain properly how little it mattered about Polly or the reporters or anything else. Wandering restlessly about the room, I found a couple of library books on the shelf by the bed. I picked them up. I had them both at home. It gave me a pleasant sort of shock to see them here, books about Israel, which she could only have wanted to read for one reason. I was as pleased as if she'd brought home one of my handkerchiefs to keep. Idly I began to leaf through the pages of one of the books, a novel about the history and resurgence of the Jews. I re-read a few passages, despising the flat, characterless writing, yet getting caught up against my will.

What was it, I wondered for the millionth time, about us? Why did we raise this blood-blister on every country we settled in? Too easy to say, as Polly did, that we brought out the worst in other peoples because they needed a scapegoat, because they were jealous of our successes, afraid of our differences. Did they hate us because men must hate other men and we were a fixed target, a captive receptacle of hate, having nowhere to run to? Or had the very fact of having nowhere of our own made us provoke hate by stubborn refusal to blend, the bitterness of unbelonging making us defiant, clannish and arrogant?

But in that case, I thought suddenly, it was over. The cause was remedied, the effects nullified at source, the nightmare pattern of recurring hatred broken. As I read this uninspired account of the renaissance of Israel, I was moved in spite of myself by what it meant – not to the lifeless cardboard people in the book, but to the rest of us, for whom normality was possible now.

I heard the front door close, and without thinking dropped the book and ran to the bedroom door.

Outside was a girl, hanging up her coat. She spun round and stared at me, goggle-eyed. I recognized her then, vaguely; she was the one who had been left on guard the time I came to take Martha to the party.

She looked so startled at the sight of me that I wondered if I'd grown horns. But then she blinked rapidly and said, with a breathless laugh, 'Oh, it's you! The – the beard foxed me for a minute.' She was clearly embarrassed, but trying to show what a girl-of-the-world she was. There was a coy, almost giggly air about her, as if she'd met a famous roué at a party, knew she ought not to talk to him and yet couldn't resist.

'Those awful reporters!' she said. 'They just won't take no for an answer. I had one jolly near push right past me into the house as I came in just now.'

I felt vaguely uneasy. The world outside must not encroach. 'Perhaps they've got wind I'm here.'

'Perhaps . . .' She was looking at me curiously, almost sensuously, but more as if she were enjoying imagining what went on in that bedroom than wishing she were in there with me herself. She was a pretty little thing, all pert and blonde and cushiony, but it was like watching a very old film of a vamp, dead or aged long ago; it just didn't occur to me to want her. I supposed distantly that it would be like that with all women from now on, and I felt a faint pang for the loss of that ripple of indiscriminate, girls-in-their-summer-dresses lust. This girl's remote prettiness just titillated me for Martha. At the thought of her, I instinctively glanced at my watch.

'Do you suppose those bloody reporters have got her cornered somewhere?' I asked without thinking.

'Who, Martha? I don't know . . .' She hesitated. 'Are you hungry or anything? Maybe I could – you know – fix you something.'

I knew Martha would be angry if I started treating the whole flat as if I owned it. She'd told me firmly that I had to stay in her room. But I was annoyed with her, I remembered. And hungry.

'Thanks, could you?'

I followed her into the bootbox kitchen. As she opened a tin and put on the kettle she gave a little nervous giggle.

'What's funny?'

'Nothing, except – the reporters and everything, and you in here all the time like the Prisoner of Zenda or somebody.' I doubted if she'd ever read *The Prisoner of Zenda* or anything else written earlier than 1950, but I let it pass. I saw how intriguing it could seem to someone like her.

'How do you put them off – the newspapermen?'

She giggled again. 'Oh, I just say what Martha told us to say. That we don't know anything about it.'

'If you giggle like that, no wonder they don't believe you.'

'I can't help it – it makes you so nervous, the way they crowd round.'

'The fuss'll soon die down. I'm amazed it's lasted this long.'

'How long are you expecting to stay?' She asked it politely, like a hotel manageress.

'Oh, indefinitely.'

She gave me a startled look.

'We went to see your play,' she said after a moment.

'And?'

'It's terribly, terribly good.'

I grinned to myself. 'Did you understand it?'

'Of course! It was about a man going back into his past.'

That stumped me for a moment, but then I remembered. One of the wetter *Sundays*.

A little genuine enthusiasm came into her voice as she went on: 'It was madly exciting, listening to people in the audience talking and speculating about you, while we were the only ones who could have told them where you really were.'

'So long as you didn't.'

'As if I would!'

But she might. I felt the unease again as I sat down to some beans on toast. Odd to think of those beer-swilling vultures out there, and the girls having to think of ways to keep them off . . . Odder that I should get some genuine realization of how difficult, and how nasty, this must be, not from Martha who made light of it, but from this little dim-wit who thought of it all in terms of women's-magazine adventure.

Martha came in while I was eating. I heard her shut the front door, then go into the bedroom, then come out again like a whirlwind. I felt the shock of her anxiety in my own throat, and stopped eating. She burst into the kitchen. For a moment she looked from the girl to me; her face was white.

'What's the idea?' she shot at me, her voice breathy with anger.

I forced myself to go on eating, as if her anger didn't matter. 'Your nice friend found me in an advanced state of starvation, so . . .'

She gave her nice friend one look which acted like an ejector seat. When we were alone, which was two seconds later, Martha came and sat opposite me across the narrow table. She was giving me a look now, under which it was impossible to eat. To my fury I heard myself rattling off excuses. But she didn't let me get far.

'All right, Aaron, never mind that. Something awful's happened. Look at this.'

She thrust an evening paper at me, streaking the back of it with beans. A paragraph on the front page was surrounded by deep-cut pencilled circles.

Miss Martha ('I don't know where he is') Fletcher, midwife at the birth of that new-wave hit *Man in a Hole*, can't have looked very far for the runaway author. His present address, I learn on good authority, is 21 Kensington Crescent, Earls Court. This house contains four flats, in three of which he quite definitely is not. The tenant of the fourth flat? Miss Martha ('I don't know where he is') Fletcher.

I read it through three times simply to postpone meeting her eyes. I felt sick. I'd like to have gone outside and bashed open the head of the first reporter I saw.

'Aaron . . .?'

I looked up. Her chin was trembling but her hands were steady, clasped on the table in two controlled fists.

'Who the bloody hell do you suppose told them?'

She jerked her head towards the door and then looked down at the table.

'Silly stupid *bitch* . . .' I began, half-getting to my feet. But she reached over and stopped me.

'What's the use? She didn't mean to.'

I sank back. The anger and helplessness I felt was the first unpleasant emotion that had attacked me since the opening night – it was like falling into ice-water on a hot day.

'Those rotten sods . . . why can't they mind their own business?'

'They are – outside the house right this minute. I had to fight my way through. No wonder they're all back on the scent . . . a few more days and it would have died down completely.'

We sat in silence for long minutes. I held her hand, but it was cold and I felt she'd withdrawn from me. No wonder. They'd made it all mucky for her – and that was only the beginning. There'd be more, and worse, I felt her realizing it, felt her wishing that what they would imply about us wasn't true.

'Darling . . .'

She put both hands to her face in a swift, angry movement and gave a sob which she clamped down almost savagely. I could see her neck-muscles working.

'I know what you're thinking,' I said. 'That it's all spoilt and awful now other people know –'

With a thud her fists landed on the table.

'It *isn't* that!' she cried out. 'I don't care any more about other people! It's *us*. What are we going to do?' She was crying helplessly, turning her head backwards and forwards as if in some physical pain. 'She'll come for you! That's what I'm most afraid of! She'll come, and I won't be able to keep her out, and when you see her you won't be able to help yourself – you'll go back!'

The words were like an explosion in my head. I found myself standing over her, shouting.

'Are you bloody mad! You can say that after – you think she could make me go back *now*? Is *that* what you think I am?'

So that was how she'd felt and thought about me all those months! As Polly's lap-dog, to run and beg when she whistled. And the worst of it was, it was true . . . I felt something akin to hatred as I looked at that unspeakable reflected vision of myself in her face.

Suddenly there was a noise, a commotion out in the hall. Both of us turned instinctively as we heard a girl's voice.

'Can't you understand what *no* means? I've told you a dozen times, he's not here!'

It held a note of shrill desperation; the falsehood was palpable in it. Martha jumped up, clutching my arm.

'It's Gwen! Quick, shut the door –'

I didn't move fast enough. Along the passage I could see the struggle going on, and suddenly a man pushed his way past the girl. Just as I was on the point of closing the door of the kitchen, he saw me.

It was an odd moment – the moment of waking up. I felt a violent shock, followed by a fatalistic sense of peace. He was such a nasty-looking bit of work, fat and scruffy, with the little bright eyes of a pig at a trough. After all, did it *really* matter? Could anything that creature did affect us? I had a sudden rush of superiority to the head as I walked calmly towards him.

The stream of questions started when I was still only half-way there, but I just kept walking, and when I reached him I didn't stop but caught hold of his greasy trench-coat lapels with both hands and backed him forcibly through the front door.

He was even more unattractive close-to. His breath stank of stale scotch and tobacco. He had a little hairline moustache and the rest of his flabby jaw was covered with ginger stubble. The skin under it reddened as I half-carried him in front of me, like a cow caught on the front of a train, and his mouth started to splutter and issue threats. I got him along the passage outside the flat, to the top of the stairs. I was in complete control of myself and the situation, and handled him contemptuously with only as much effort as was necessary to get rid of him.

I hadn't planned anything so melodramatic as pushing him down the stairs – I wasn't angry enough for that. Only suddenly he seemed to draw himself together inside the shabby mackintosh and the oily pig's face spat out a short sentence:

'Hands off, you dirty yid!'

My arms did it, not me. I gave no orders, they simply acted. My mind stood aside as the man melted outwards and downwards, registering with faint surprise the solid noise he made as he hit the stairway – the clatter, the hard flesh-and-bone sounds. And yet he had melted before my instinctive shove like mashed potatoes.

I felt scared for a second. Not sorry, just scared for fear the fall would kill him. But when he reached the bottom he lay still for only a moment, then scrambled up and limped off without looking back.

I found Martha and the other two beside me. The others started to chatter hysterically, but Martha took my arm and led me quietly back into the flat. She didn't tremble. Without a word she took me into the bedroom and I heard the click of the bolt she had made me screw to the door.

Usually at this point in the rages, when I've done something violent, I shake all over – sometimes I find myself crying. It's always been the same – part of the release when it's over. But this time I didn't seem to be having any reaction. I felt quite calm. The blindness that had seized me at the top of the stairs was as dim a memory as a pain that's stopped.

But the words were still there. I took Martha in my arms and they were still there. I stroked her hair and kissed her and they

155

were still there. They were there like a brand on my ear-drums. For the first time when I tried to take her I couldn't. I could feel her, all soft and willing, waiting for me, and I longed for the forgetfulness of sex, but I couldn't do anything. The words stopped me. They were like a glass wall preventing me going on from one minute to the next. It was the first time anyone had ever said them to me, or anything like them. I had been lucky.

Father had not. He'd heard them plenty of times, on the way up. 'The quicker you climb, the oftener you hear them,' he'd said to me once. 'And shall I tell you something else? You never get used to them. Every time you hear them – every single time, even when they're not meant for you, even when you hear them on top of a bus from people talking about someone else – it feels as if somebody's sticking a knife in your guts. No amount of reasoning, no amount of success, stops that feeling. Every time.'

And he'd added, 'You can't get away from it, either. Not in this country, whatever people tell you, and certainly not in any other. Except one, of course.'

Except one . . .

Martha lay in my arms. I could sense her wondering what it meant, this limpness, but she didn't ask anything, only held me. Her quiet acceptance made me love her more than ever; but only in the distance. The words were too close to let me feel it properly.

I closed my eyes and thought about my trees.

In my imagination I watched them move, gently and coolly, stirring the hot blue sky; their roots kept the encroaching sand at bay. I counted them, painstakingly, as an insomniac counts sheep. There were thirteen. Father had paid for them to be planted on the day of my Bar Mitzvah. It had been a secret, because of Polly's furious disapproval of everything connected with that one exceptional country where you weren't a Jew as you were a Jew everywhere else, on sufferance . . . Father had bought me another present, and winked as he gave it to me, to let me know that it was only for show; my real presents were being planted in the rocky Judean Hills.

For ages I thought that they had my name on them, were somehow marked and identified as mine. And still I thought of them sometimes when I felt full of hate for myself and Polly and the way I lived; the idea of them was like a stiff drink – it lifted me out of the scrum of my own inadequacy and gave a different look to everything.

I thought of them now, and it worked as it always had, making me feel less desperate, more as if I had roots somewhere and were not drifting loose, helpless before every emotional current. *Their* roots, I realized with a deep sense of comfort, would be well-established by now, no longer in need of daily watering, but embedded firmly in the rocky ground.

'The wonderful thing is,' I said aloud, 'that after a while they make their own soil. The roots break up the rock and make the ground fertile enough for them to live on.'

Martha lay, puzzled and alert, but I was hardly aware of her. I was conscious of a dragging feeling, a magnetic pull. It was like being stretched at the end of a piece of elastic. The odd thing about it was the feeling that the tension had been there for years without my noticing it. I'd thought it was just a reflection of the ideas and longings of my Father. I suddenly realized it was my own, a personal and urgent need.

It was one thing not to be wanted in the place you were born in. That might not be enough to make you get out – it might only make you more stubbornly determined to dig in. But if there was a place that did want you – wanted you so badly it didn't even ask whether you had tuberculosis or a criminal record, let alone whether you were popular in the place you came from or whether you liked yourself or whether you had the guts to stand on your own two feet – then what sort of a bloody fool would you have to be not to go there? Surely there, if anywhere, you could start again with nothing chalked up against you, even in your own mind. There, perhaps, what went on in your mind wouldn't matter so much, anyway – you might have too many other things to concentrate on, to be peering inward the whole time. What an indescribable relief it would be, to find realities more important than that murky, squashy half-lit world inside your head! To emerge into the real world of hard work and clean air, of earned hunger and sleep instead of the sort which merely punctuates the days, of problems of *living* instead of feeling and thinking. I could see the belt of trees behind my eyes, and felt a sudden furious lust to stick my fingers deep into the dry earth, to lift rocks and to feel my own sweat running down my back.

But at the same time I seemed to be standing off from myself and sneering: Sweat down your back – Christ, that's marvellous! How long do you think that'd last, that fine flourish of Jewish land-hunger? About as long as all your other half-baked enthusiasms and self-improvement campaigns! Do you happen to recall that that splendid play is the only project of your life that you've ever actually *finished*? And you only managed that out of pure hate. You'd probably keel over in a dead faint at the first sign of a callous.

But the dream was still there. It was growing and taking hold, springing up fully-armed like a dragon's-tooth warrior. I could feel a sudden energy shooting through me; my lethargy was burnt up by it, like fog by a flame-thrower. I knew what I wanted. It was a knowledge which gave me unlimited power.

I turned to Martha and, holding her face against my shoulder so that she couldn't say anything, I told her what we were going to do. After a while I released her and her eyes stared into mine from about six inches away, huge and dark and quite unreadable. I thought she hadn't taken it in yet. But she said quietly, 'There'll be problems there, too.'

Again she was showing me what she thought of me, but this time I didn't feel angry. That was all part of the past.

'I'm not running *from* something,' I said. 'I'm running *to* something. It's a positive adventure, not a negative escape.'

She didn't say anything else, and after a few moments I started to talk to her about Israel. I told her things she knew already, and then things she didn't know – how it felt to be a Jew and to know Israel was there and to want to go. Or perhaps she knew about that, too; I'd described it very carefully in the novel about Father. Odd to remember that. I had no desire at all to go on with it. Presumably it had been a form of sublimation. Now I was going myself, there was no point in writing a long excuse for not going. This realization was like a yoke being lifted off my neck.

As I talked, I felt a bit uneasy that Martha wasn't arguing. She was just lying still and listening. I broke off.

'Haven't you anything to say?'

'What about?'

'Going.'

'No. If it's what you want, let's do it.'

Perhaps she would have welcomed any plan that got us out of London, away from the reporters, the slimy suggestions, the complexities. And away from Polly. I could face with complete detachment now the knowledge that that was still, for her, the deciding factor.

'You must go and see Theo and get some money from him.'

'How much do you think we'll need?' Obviously she was against going to Theo.

'Just enough for the fares.'

'But what will we live on?'

'You don't need money on a kibbutz.'

It seemed suddenly better to drop it into the conversation casually. Perhaps she didn't know what a kibbutz was, and in explaining it I could sell it to her, make it sound something less than a fundamental change in her whole way of life.

But one startled look from her told me that she knew a good deal. I started to explain anyway, but she rolled away from me and stood up sharply.

After a long moment she said, 'All right, Aaron. We might as well go the whole hog. It could do us both good.'

Thus, in the way of women, she swallowed the whole great pill at one gulp – which left me with a sinking feeling. Dreams are one thing; they're fine, very consoling and pleasant. But when it looks as though they might come to something, they can become very frightening indeed.

Chapter Three

Now the days were no longer passive periods of waiting punctuated by the sharp explosions of love-making. When Martha was out, arranging things, I paced the flat like a prisoner, my mind full of stabbing images and an all-but-unbearable mixture of fear and impatience. Each time she came in I would rush to meet her, but no longer simply to satisfy myself with the sight and touch of her. Now I wanted to hear what she'd been doing, what she'd accomplished; I listened to every word she had to tell me with an interest so acute I could hardly wait for her to get from one sentence to another.

The first problems came early. My passport was at home. This was quite a stumbling-block, until Martha thought of Bella. I chose a time when Polly was almost certain to be at the shop, and telephoned home.

'Boychik – boychik – boychik –'

I imagined the poor old face screwed up, the tears washing paths through the white powder on her cheeks. Everything suddenly seemed to cost too much in other people's pain.

'Don't go away – come home, darling – Bella loves you –'

I had to be stern with her, and sterner with myself. I told her almost curtly which of my things to pack, where my passport was, where to meet Martha with the suitcase. It wasn't until I had hung up that I realized that I would never see her again. I sat dumbly with my hand still on the phone, as if retaining a last contact, remembering things from years ago. I was alone at the time and I as near as dammit backslid all the way. But the thought of Martha's face when she found me gone was more compelling than the remembrance of Bella's pleas.

We had to travel cheaply. Money was the biggest problem. I learned by accident that it had been one for Martha since I accepted her loan. That's what it does to you, having all your bills paid by someone else – it simply hadn't occurred to me that Martha had given me all she had. It didn't make me feel any more enchanted with myself to learn that we'd been living on Jo's money. It all served to aggravate my fury when Martha came back and said Theo wouldn't hand over any royalties except to me personally.

'Blast his miserable soul, it's my money, isn't it?'

'And he's Polly's friend. He wants to get you out of cover.'

'I could almost be drawn, just for the pleasure of pushing his well-fed face in!'

We sat silently over supper in the bedroom. That room was growing oppressive. The same bits of shabby furniture, the same nondescript boring view from the window, the same patterns on the faded carpet – I was getting sick of all of it, and the impatience to get away was growing like the pressure of an abcess.

After supper, before clearing away, Martha went through her window-box routine. It was as inevitable as a religious ritual. She took the tea-pot and emptied the leaves and dregs on to the earth, spread them meticulously, then watered them in from a jug she kept on the window-sill. Then she snapped off dead heads, plucked out any unwanted shoots and went over the whole surface with a minute rake. I found this daily procedure both touching and irritating.

'How are your little perishers going to manage without their daily cup of cha when we leave?' I asked her now, half-mockingly.

'I don't know,' she said shortly. She wiped the earth off her hands and began clearing the table. After a short silence she said, 'What now? I'm just about stony.'

'We'll have to borrow. My credit should be good, anyway.'

'Who from?'

I hesitated. 'What about Dan?'

'Do you think he would?'

'Why not? He's one of the tribe, too, you know.'

She seemed uncertain.

'What's wrong? Don't you think he will?'

'I don't know,' she said, and added astonishingly, 'He admires Polly so much.'

'What makes you say that?'

'Something he said once . . . never mind. I can but ask.'

She came back from seeing him too subdued to match the wonderful news she brought. Dan had agreed to lend us all we needed.

I hugged her delightedly.

'God bless the old bugger! I knew he wouldn't let me down.'

She said nothing and started tidying the room.

'What's wrong? Don't you think it's terrific?'

'Yes . . . it means we can leave by the earlier boat. I'll go down and fix it tomorrow.'

I made her sit beside me. 'What's up? What did old Dan say that's worried you?'

She held my hand and said, 'Did you know he's in love with her?'

'Who?' I asked blankly.

'Your sister.'

After a stunned moment I said 'You're crazy!' But somehow it made a warped kind of sense. I knew she was right.

'He's in a terrible state. He broke down.'

'Broke down – old Dan? I can't imagine it!'

'Don't try. It was awful – like seeing a fat happy clown in tears.' Suddenly she began to cry herself. It did something strange to me. I felt a vicarious pain coming over me, so poignant I knew I should find it unbearable. I fought it off with brusqueness, giving her a shake and saying, 'Stop it, don't be ridiculous. Tell me what happened.'

She pulled herself together at once. 'Sorry. I'm a bit strung up, those bloody reporters and everything.' She seldom used bad language, and I felt another unaccustomed pang; that 'bloody' told me with sudden clarity what these days were doing to her – what I was doing to her. She went on: 'He said things have been really bad with Polly since the first night. She'd been pretty upset before, when you were in Kent, but nothing to what she's been like since all the publicity about us. She's letting the shop go to hell – hardly ever turns up, and when she does she's half demented, does strange unpredictable things, scarcely speaks to him . . . he wants so much to help her but hasn't known how. He told me he'd like to kill you. He said it as if he meant it. He said you were ungrateful and ruthless and selfish and that you didn't realize what a . . .'

She stopped herself, and I didn't press her to go on. Somehow I minded hearing what old Dan thought of me. I remembered him at Oxford, before he put on all that fat and started being Polly's pot-boy. I never had understood why he stuck her, and the job and everything, considering what a good brain he had. Incredible to think of anyone being *in love* with Polly. But then Dan always had been a bit of a masochist . . .

'But if he feels it's all my fault, why did he cough up?'

'He was quite simple about it. He wants you out of the way.'

'What good's that going to do?'

She hesitated, then said 'He seems to think Polly's feelings for you are unhealthy.'

I said nothing and she didn't look at me.

'He figures if you're right out of the picture, she might – you know –'

'Start looking for a well-padded shoulder to cry on?'

'That's roughly it.' She stood up and shook herself uneasily. 'I like Dan, but there was something rather – horrible about him this afternoon. Perhaps it was just the idea of anybody –'

'Yes, I know exactly what you mean.'

She suddenly put her arms round me and held me tightly. She'd never done it before in quite that way – turning to me as if the boot of need were on her foot instead of mine.

Chapter Four

Leaving the flat was strange – like getting out of jail. We left at night, in accordance with a carefully worked-out plan to elude reporters; not that they were particularly interested any more, but the poisonous piece written by the porker after I'd thrown him down the stairs had stirred them up a bit and one couldn't be too careful.

The last thing I did before we left was to write a letter to Polly. Martha knew what I was doing and as she packed her few things there was a suppressed tension about her which made me nervous. It wasn't as if she hadn't agreed that it was necessary to write. She understood my terror of being followed, sought out and dragged back before the new place had had a chance to work its changes in me. I wanted the journey to be as complete an escape as if I were changing planets.

'Martha and I are leaving London together. Please don't try to find us. You could, if you really put your mind to it, but it would do no good. I shall never come back.'

I stared at the words. Never was final. In secret moods that came and went, I wondered if I really knew what I was doing. Was this grand gesture anything more than bravado? Did I really have the strength to make it good or was I counting on Israel to work some miracle which would give me the strength? But it was too late now. And Martha had no doubts. Once decided, she went ahead like an arrow. Next to her, my doubts seemed so snivelling I couldn't ease them by confiding them. My qualms now about the finality of this letter seemed equally contemptible. I let the words stand. Doubts, I thought, were inevitable when one's whole life was being uprooted. Only by behaving as if I had none could I hope to get rid of them.

We took a taxi to a hotel near Victoria Station where Martha had booked two single rooms. I felt a desperate need to sleep with her and not alone, but she was remote and withdrawn from strain and tiredness; she kissed me briefly and went into her room.

As soon as her door closed, I had a terrifying feeling. All sense of purpose and stability seemed to ebb out of me. A kind of vacant will-lessness overcame me like a soporific drug, sapping my resolution. I stared round in horror at the drab, half-lit corridor with its vista of closed doors; I smelled its lonely smell of transience and dust. What was I doing here, what madness had brought me to this Styx-like point of no return between solid reality and the frightful uncertainty of a half-planned future? There seemed to be no ground under my feet. Nothing that had happened in the last fortnight really had anything to do with me as I had always known myself. If I had woken up suddenly in another man's body, I could not have felt more helpless and appalled.

I forced myself to go into my room, and lay down, fully dressed. The sulphurous lights made hypnotic, infernal patterns on the walls and ceiling. I stared at them blankly, scarcely thinking. Afraid of the blankness, I tried to concentrate on the thought of Martha, and became more afraid when I realized I couldn't visualize her. It was as if I had dreamt her, and woken to a great emptiness . . .

Panic scrabbled about in me like a crab in my belly. Something real, familiar, must be found, something to hang on to. Into my mind, like an answer, came a sudden vivid image of the white house on Hampstead Hill. I was giving it up for ever. It was unendurable not to say good-bye to it.

I left the narrow hotel bed with a jerk. My heart was beating thickly and my scalp prickled; I felt as if I were about to venture into the supernatural. It wasn't until I caught myself opening the door and creeping outside with furtive, cat-like caution that I realized the feeling came from guilt. I knew that Martha would be horrified and frightened if she knew I was going back into Polly's orbit. I paused in the corridor outside her room and tried to control the compulsion with common sense. It was three in the morning – the journey to Hampstead, the flesh-and-blood journey, would mean a taxi both ways. And when I got there – what? I felt a stab of panic. What if Polly saw me? She would stop me, she would make me reverse everything, the transmogrifying fortnight would be wiped out, familiarity would claim me with strong hands. I would go back.

For a moment I forgot the humiliation, the self-contempt, the babyish terrors. I remembered the comfort, the routine, the security and stability, the constant feeling of my ego. I remembered the roots of my life, still deep in that house, in Polly . . .

I must have been standing unmoving at the top of the hotel stairs for some minutes, frozen by indecision, when I felt a hand on my arm. It was trembling. I gave a great start – I think I even cried out in dismay that she'd seen me, fully dressed, standing there with my intention so ambiguous that she might well have thought I meant to run out on her altogether. Perhaps I had . . . I stared at her. She was wearing only her nightgown, a blue cotton one, very crumpled. Her face was puffy from sleep and her hair was pressed flat on one side from lying on it which made her look lopsided, rakish and funny. But I couldn't smile, or say a word. I was afraid of her, of what she was thinking and of what she would certainly say.

But she said nothing except 'Come to bed.' She turned away and I followed her dumbly back into her room. Without turning on the light she climbed back under the covers and, still with nothing to say, I took off my clothes and got in beside her. The bed was so small she had to press her back to the wall to make enough room for me. Our arms closed round each other and I began to kiss her as I had kissed her when I woke up on that first morning, ferociously, to blot out her thoughts.

The worst part of the journey was having to sleep apart from her. I had begun to depend on this new, three-dimensional sex like a drug, apart from her mere comforting presence beside me which was already a prerequisite to peaceful sleep. I had never experienced anything remotely so desirable or satisfying. Before, sex had been something I needed to do now and then, and did, like eating or relieving myself; it was a pleasure like the satisfaction of all physical needs, but nothing more – in fact something less, because there was always a faint uneasy feeling deep down that I was dirtying myself. I had never thought it could be more than that because whenever I looked at a woman I cared for as a person, and forced myself, experimentally, to think of her body as an objective, I felt disgusted and inclined to apologize to her. So I had gone on with my surface sex, using it, I now perceived, chiefly as a weapon of rebellion against my life-hating sister and perhaps even against myself. Incredible, when all the time there was this – this prismatic, participating love, this endless shared adventure in giving. It had nothing beyond the basic act in common with the defiant smutty tumbles I had had with shallow, gay, impervious little girls like Anne-Marie.

I sat close to Martha in the train, on the channel steamer, in the train again, holding her hand and occasionally leaning the few inches to kiss whatever bit of her head was turned towards me. Of the previous night's terrors, nothing was left but an uneasy wraith in my memory, blown away before the reality of this firmly-profiled figure beside me, radiating purpose.

When night came they made up the couchettes, and we and four other people slotted ourselves into them. They were like those cheap bookcases without enough space between the shelves, so that books have to lie on their sides. It was hot and claustrophobically cramped. By some mischance I was on a top shelf and Martha on a bottom, with someone in between; I couldn't even reach down and touch her in the night. Perverse as the longing for a cigarette when the last one has been smoked, came the desire for her; I felt I would go mad thinking of her lying so near and yet so unpossessable beneath me.

Next morning I asked if she had slept and she answered simply: 'No, hardly at all. I kept wanting you.' We went out without another word into the corridor, and, at the far end of the swaying carriage near the lavatories where we could pretend we were private, we fell into each other's arms and kissed until our mouths were sore.

The journey seemed endless. We got through all our station-bought reading matter before noon; it looked as if we were in for many hours of paralysing boredom before nightfall. Suddenly Martha reached up and bumped down her suit case.

'What are you after?'

'I've just remembered something – something you'll like.'

It was a teach-yourself book called *Hebrew for the People*.

'I got it in Foyle's yesterday – saw it in the second-hand section. Is it any good?'

I riffled through it. I had had a head start on Hebrew; every Jew brought up as I'd been knows quite a few words, and there'd been Father's efforts. I could read, slowly and with difficulty, the stilted sentences about Yaacov and David who worked in the fields, and the joyful children who planted young trees at the spring festival. They were not sentences one would ever use. The people they described were cardboard figures, all good, hardworking, community spirited, and full of an awful sort of phoney strength-through-joy which reminded me of the worst excesses of the Jewish Youth Movement meetings Polly had forced me to attend when I was at school.

'Listen to this. "Leah is a good Jewess. She gives money to the National Fund. She helps her neighbours and never expects thanks. She something – prays I think – before each meal. When times are hard she never complains." And may God preserve us all from Leah.'

'What! Where does it say that?'

'It doesn't. *I* say that.'

'Oh . . .' She laughed and hugged my arm happily. I looked down at her. We'd been on the train for hours, we were dirty and tired and thirsty and I personally was scared stiff, but she laughed like a bell ringing, as if she hadn't a care.

Brindisi was a flat, dreary little port which lay fossilized under a hard October sun. The boat – our boat – was not the old tub I had, for some reason, expected. It was glossy white and proud of itself, and it gleamed with cleanness from stem to stern. As we went aboard, a smart Italian officer bowed to us, and smiled appreciatively at Martha. The tourist-class cabins were small, with four people in each, but perfectly adequate. The other three men in my cabin were middle-aged, paunchy Austrian businessmen who could well have afforded better-class travel but were probably charging First and pocketing the difference. They talked German petulantly to each other and jostled politely for the best berth.

After I'd settled my few pieces of luggage in the minuscule space left by the Austrians, I came up on deck, feeling unaccountably furious and disappointed. I met Martha standing at the rail looking dreamily over the town. She tucked her arm in mine and rubbed her cheek on my shoulder.

'Isn't that a beautiful war memorial?'

I looked. I thought it quite hideous, and said so.

'We stop in Athens for hours and hours, and the next day in Rhodes – then the Greek islands – or is that before? Anyway, then Cyprus, and then Haifa. Oh darling!' She pressed the back of my hand impulsively against her breast so that I could feel the excited beating of her heart. She began to laugh, burying her face in my jacket.

'Wait till you see my cabin-mates! They are *unbelievable*. I somehow expected old women in black with goats and cheeses and babies being suckled like mad, or at least knapsacky students – after all, it *is* the equivalent of steerage – but no such thing. All chubby and blue-rinsed, my dear, and simply dripping with charm-bracelets. And the luggage! I felt like Dick Whittington by comparison. They keep talking about how they've never had such awful accommodation and if only their husbands had let them travel on the *Theodore Hertzl* like last time.'

'Bloody silly *bitches*,' I said violently.

'Oh, not really, they're rather fun. One of them's already busy running up a dress out of some material she bought in Venice, so she can get it into Israel duty-free, stuffing herself with liqueur chocolates the whilst . . . What's the matter, dearest?'

'I hate it being like this, all clean and touristy!'

'But why?'

I didn't answer. It was impossible to explain that I had wanted, and expected, the hardships and rigours to begin now, before we arrived. I would have welcomed crowded dormitories full of students and refugees with no possessions and stern, haggard faces, talking Polish and Rumanian. I wanted austerity, even dirt and smells; I wanted not quite enough of the simplest food. I did not want the rich five-course Italian meal served by immaculate stewards just after we sailed, nor the gathering in the saloon afterwards, the urbane businessmen and their bejewelled, jabbering women crowding round the bar in an atmosphere of thick-witted *bonhomie* as if this were just any ship on a Mediterranean cruise.

What I wanted, of course, was an immigrant ship. But I'd missed it by some fifteen years.

Chapter Five

Just as there was no dramatic or heroic element in the voyage, so there was none in what we found at the end of it.

I got up at dawn, eager for the first sight of Haifa Harbour, feeling that it would renew my sense of the importance of the moment. It happened to be a dull morning; even the B'hai Shrine refused to glint, and as for the rest of the town, it lay glumly in the haze, unlovely and unimpressive.

'Bloody dreary-looking place,' I said to Martha as we shuffled down the gang-plank on to the dockside, which was studded with Coca-Cola tops.

'For heaven's sake, give it a chance!' she exclaimed.

But my unreasoning disappointment grew. The first few hours ashore were scarcely in accordance with one's dreams of arrival in the Promised Land. We spent them hanging about in the crowded customs shed, queuing up and being shouted at or ignored by a variety of swarthy and bad-tempered officials. The booths selling sweets, tobacco, papers and souvenirs were sleazy and tatty. The fact that such places are awful everywhere did not seem relevant. Here, things should be different.

After a great deal of frustration, we learned that most of the headquarters of the kibbutz movements were in Tel Aviv, so following a two-hour wait on a dismal and grimy platform we got into a crowded train which chugged along the coastline for several more hours. The heat, which had been increasing ever since we left Brindisi, now became a nightmare. I tried opening a window, but a blast of sand and dust forced me to close it. After that I sat slumped on the wooden seat, hemmed in by fellow-travellers, sweating and dismayed. I didn't glance at Martha for fear of seeing her looking cool and comfortable.

In Tel Aviv the heat was even worse. We got into a sort of communal taxi, with five others, all smelling of sweat and ill-temper, and were taken to – of all places – the Y.M.C.A. It seemed to be the only cheap residence the driver knew of. Martha was allowed to stay there too; we were strictly segregated, of course, but I was too hot and exhausted to care about that.

By that time it was after four o'clock, and too late for any offices to be open. We had showers and, feeling a little better, went for a walk. The town was brand new, very brash and bright and busy, and rather dull. We sat outside one of the many garish cafés in Dizengoff Street; Martha ordered an ice-cream and I had a beer. All round us prosperous-looking men in white shirts and well-fleshed women with brown backs were drinking long drinks and eating ices, for all the world as if they were in St Tropez. The fact that we were doing the same thing irritated me deeply. It was all wrong, somehow. The fact that I was *enjoying* sitting in the shade drinking cold beer and watching the pretty women strolling past made it worse. I had known I'd have to fight the soft, self-indulgent side of myself, but I hadn't expected there to be any opportunities for it here.

Martha, who was gazing serenely at the people around us, suddenly said 'Funny – most of them don't look specially Jewish.'

I grunted. I'd been thinking the same thing. Not only that, they didn't look as if they realized where they were. There was no feeling of what had happened so recently to make their lives here possible. The place had no atmosphere – it was just a modern city. And the people appeared to be just people. That was wrong, too. They should have had a quality of intensity. I could hardly define my disappointment that it all seemed so normal and ordinary. My chief feeling was one of hollow anti-climax. Perhaps the kibbutznik we were to meet tomorrow would have some grandeur about him.

The office of the kibbutz movement we'd chosen at random was at the top of a lift-less five-storey stone block. It was small and untidy, lined with books and littered with papers. A hot, weary-looking Englishman of about forty sat bent over a large table, surrounded by trays of papers, writing feverishly, his glasses slipping down his nose, his thin hair stuck to his scalp. He looked up at us through the shadowed, red-rimmed eyes of a man whose sight is not good enough for paper-work but who none the less has to do it all day. He had no obvious grandeur whatever, just an air of extreme busyness through which kindness filtered as the barest tolerance for any interruption.

Any hope I had harboured that he might boost my self-esteem with an enthusiastic welcome was soon dashed. He evidently found our application to join one of his kibbutzim more surprising than exciting. Very few people, he told us, just arrived out of the blue wanting to join kibbutzim. Most settlers came over in groups, having prepared themselves for years under the auspices of one of the Zionist youth movements. Most of them already spoke Hebrew, had had some farming experience, and knew exactly which kibbutz they were headed for. The fact that neither of us looked very hearty, that Martha was not Jewish, that we'd made the decision very suddenly – these and other factors obviously led the secretary to suspect that we were half-baked dilettantes, likely to cause more trouble than we were worth.

He suggested that instead of going straight on to a settlement we should first spend some months at an adult language school, learning Hebrew. When I said we wanted to go straight away and pick up the language as we went along, he shrugged.

'I was thinking you might go to a desert settlement later,' he said. 'That's where we really need people. Of course it's a bit hotter down there, but that's where the real pioneering's still going on . . .' He looked at us hopefully.

I glanced at Martha. Before we left London, I'd have sworn I wanted the toughest sort of life available. Now I knew that I could not take the arid heat of the Negev without dropping dead at the end of the first day.

'What's wrong with sending us to one of your English-speaking places?'

He shrugged again. 'Oh nothing – if you want to take things easy. They're pretty well-established.' He yawned widely, showing strong white teeth. It looked to me like a gesture of contempt.

The following day we were told we were going to a kibbutz on the fringes of the Negev, but near the sea, called Beit Hashoresh.

'What does that mean?' Martha asked me.

'House of something,' I said.

Later, while I was waiting for her to come downstairs in the Y.M., I looked it up. *Hashoresh* meant 'the root'.

'House of the Root,' said Martha, as if savouring a new taste. 'I like that.'

From Tel Aviv we got a dirty, rattling old bus to Ashkelon. It was packed to the roof with taciturn Moroccans and Persians dressed in faded cottons and carrying bundles, swarms of grubby children, lots of soldiers, male and female, and a number of live hens tied together by the legs and stowed under the seats. Queuing was evidently unheard-of. I got Martha a seat by fighting for it, and when I gave mine up to a very pregnant, dark-skinned woman carrying a year-old baby she looked at me as if I'd lost my mind. I soon began to wonder if she was right. The roads were bad, my fellow strap-hangers not the most congenial or clean, and the driver, a ferocious character whose handling of the bus reminded me of Toad of Toad Hall, was apparently unable to concentrate without the stimulus of a radio playing at top volume throughout the journey. At last the pregnant lady got off, leaving the seat steaming slightly. A dying-fish squirm landed me in it before it had cooled.

At the Ashkelon depot, a desolate spot, the bus disgorged us into the full blast of the two o'clock sun. A few roofed benches provided the only shade, and these were all crowded with people waiting for buses. We dragged ourselves and our luggage to a small kiosk across the road which sold iced drinks.

'You realize you can die from doing this . . .' Martha gasped as we poured the healing stuff down our parched throats.

'Roll on, death!' I replied, holding out my plastic glass for a third refill.

There was an hour to wait for the twice-daily bus to the settlements. We set our suitcases in a patch of burning dust where I estimated one of the roofs would shortly cast a shadow, and sat on them, our wet hands loosely clasped. The heat-waves danced before my eyes, giving the barren depot with its

174

bright clusters of people a look of unreality, like a bad abstract painting. After a long silence Martha said: 'They change their names here. They take biblical names.'

'You've got one already.'

'Wrong Testament.'

'I'm sure there's a Martha in the Old Testament,' I muttered sleepily. I closed my eyes against the dancing white light and leaned back against her shoulder. After a while she woke me up.

'The girls have names like bells.'

'For instance?'

'Tamara, Aviva, Layla ...'

'Oh, very bell-like, I'm sure,' I straightened up. 'Look, what is all this? I like your name, you leave it alone.'

'Aaron, you see the thing is – I do very much want to be part of the life, and not be too different. I'm bound to be a bit of an outsider because of not being Jewish, but I don't want to be an embarrassment to you.'

'That's very thoughtful of you, but don't overdo it. I'm expecting to be a bit of an outsider myself, and I shall need you to keep me company.'

She kissed me. Her lips were cool.

'Aren't you roasting?' I asked her.

'No, not too bad. I like the heat.'

'Gawd!' The mild comment seemed as out of place as it would from the depths of a furnace. 'Listen, if you take to everything like the proverbial duck to water, I shan't have anyone to grouse with. Then I shall have to divorce you.'

She said in a tentative voice, 'That reminds me.'

I looked round at her sharply. She was picking at her hem, which had come down.

'Darling, as far as I'm concerned, we're married,' I said emphatically. 'I mean – we *are married*. Don't you feel that?'

'Yes,' she said. 'Sort of.'

'If you're worrying about sidelong looks from the kibbutzniks, you can stop. They threw those sort of formalities out of the window years ago.'

'They've brought them back in again recently. I read an article. They've gone dead conventional in the last few years –

175

all that free love stuff's a thing of the past. They're almost sub-urban now.'

I couldn't help laughing. 'Christ! Out of the frying-pan!' But after a snort of laughter her face went back to seriousness. I put my arm round her and kissed her ear. 'Some old rabbi will come along and do us,' I said. 'Will that be good enough?'

She kissed me back and said primly, 'Quite, thank you.' Then she added, 'Let's not be too suburban till he turns up.'

'In this heat?' I protested, half in earnest.

She smiled knowingly. 'The houses are cool,' she said. 'They run water down the windows, and have fans.'

'How do you know so much?'

'I've been doing my homework. You don't honestly think I'd come to a place that was too hot to make love in?'

Chapter Six

Kibbutz Beit Hashoresh stood on the slopes of low sand-hills amid cypresses and palms. Martha caught her breath as the bus drew up and we looked at the oasis of greenery through the dust-covered windows; she gripped my hand like a child seeing a fair for the first time.

'That can't be it!' she said. 'But it's beautiful!'

We navigated our scruffed suitcases through the hens and into the sand on the roadside. A very plain woman and a very good-looking young man got off with us; both wore long denims, faded shirts and hats like flattened dunces' caps. We followed them up a side-turning, through some gates in a barbed-wire fence, and up a long hill, past a basketball pitch and a string of sheds and outhouses.

At the top the road reverted to deep sand, on which, like a dropped handkerchief, a rough patch of grass marked the centre of the settlement. Round it was a random collection of low buildings, their utilitarian outlines softened by bushes and trees.

Our two fellow-passengers from the bus went into one of the buildings, and of the other purposeful figures we could see striding about none seemed inclined to pay any attention to us. Martha stood staring round, alert and interested, and had opened her mouth on some unmistakably favourable comment when we were startled by a sudden outburst of shouts and howls. Over the brow of the hill poured a crowd of adolescent boys, brandishing home-made weapons and charging down on us like a barbarian hoard.

'Look out!' I exclaimed to Martha, dragging her out of their path. But abruptly they halted their advance and walked decorously across the grass, trailing their weapons and exchanging self-conscious looks of innocence.

Looking round for the cause of this transformation I saw a

tall thin man with fair hair – unmistakably English – standing near us with grimly folded arms. I went over to him and told him who we were. He turned on me a steady blue gaze which reminded me, with its suggestion of entrenchment and superiority, of my first day at public school.

'You'd better see the *Maskir*,' he said. 'Moshe. He's probably in that building over there. Sorry, I'd take you, only I'm too busy to bother with visitors.' And he strode away.

'Who's he calling visitors?' I muttered. 'Bloody unfriendly twerp!'

Martha said reasonably, 'Well, he probably is too busy. Come on.'

'We'd better take our cases.'

'Don't be silly, who'd steal them?'

We found the secretary of the kibbutz tapping on an archaic typewriter in a wooden shed. He was small and dark, his teeth clenched on a pipe so ludicrously large that he seemed to be hiding behind it. He was expecting us, and was quite welcoming in an off-hand way.

'Shalom, shalom!' he said cheerily. It was about the hundredth time we'd heard that word in three days. 'Glad to see you. Got here okay, then. Hang on and I'll show you your binyan. Lucky for you we've just got one vacant one left, otherwise you'd have been dumped in a *tsrif* – a hut, you know. All right for the very young – me, I like a bit of comfort in my old age.'

He led the way out into the sun. 'Is that your clobber?' he asked. 'I wouldn't leave it about. We've got a bunch of junior fiends from Youth Aliyah with us just now – we call 'em the Vandals. We're meant to be civilizing 'em. They're okay, really, but some of them haven't exactly had a convent upbringing, poor little devils, they're mostly orphans or children of poor immigrants – there's no sense putting temptation in their way . . .'

Talking non-stop he led the way along a maze of narrow concrete paths between the white one-storey buildings. 'We only laid the paths last year. Before that it was sand to the ankles – or mud, according to the season. That's my place, down at the end there, so you'll know where to come when you visit us.'

'The gardens are gorgeous,' said Martha.

'Edna does ours. My wife. She's out picking just now, but she'll be back soon. You can have a shower and then come over for a Nes before supper and meet her and the kids.'

'For a what?' asked Martha, thinking no doubt that 'Nes' was some Hebrew word.

'Nes,' said Moshe, staring at us. 'Nescafé. Instant coffee.'

'Oh!'

'I hope you brought yourselves some?'

'No, actually –'

'Pity. It's gold-dust here – so damned expensive.'

We passed some crude but solid-looking air-raid shelters, their entrances choked with sand and rubbish.

'What about those?' I asked.

'Haven't been near 'em since Sinai.'

'How near the border are we here?'

'Oh, not far. About three kilometres.'

'Ever have any trouble?'

He shrugged. 'The odd infiltrator nips across now and then and tries to put our lights out so he can pinch a cow. Nothing to speak of.'

I felt a schoolboyish shiver of excitement at the proximity of danger, and at the casualness of local regard for it. But Moshe's next tack brought me down to earth.

'Dan, our chap in T-A, said you don't speak Ivrit.'

Martha said quickly 'It's only me who doesn't speak Hebrew. Aaron speaks quite a lot.'

'What kind of work can you do?' Moshe asked in Hebrew.

I caught the word for 'work' and guessed the rest. 'I'll do whatever you give me.'

'No, try in Ivrit.'

I brought out a word or two, stumbled, and dried up cold. Moshe gave a great bubbling suck to his giant pipe. It had an uncompromising sound.

'You'll have to pick it up as soon as you can,' he said. 'We're not all English here, by any means – we've got Hungarians, Brazilians – anyway, you have to speak Ivrit, I mean it's so much a part of the place.' After a moment's thought, he brightened. 'Here, I've got an idea! Maybe your wife could teach the kids English. Edna's doing it at the moment – she's dying to get

179

out of it. They don't listen to her anyway – know her far too well not to play her up. Can you be firm?' he asked Martha.

'I shouldn't think so.'

'Still, they might learn something from you before they find that out. Then, in exchange, Edna can teach you Ivrit. I'll talk to her. Here we are,' he added, turning up one of the branch-paths. 'Nobody's lived here for a while, so the garden's gone a bit native. But you can soon fix it up. Even the fence-posts sprout here, if you water 'em.'

Our dwelling – 'house' would have been too grandiose a term – was one of a row of four, joined into a small, low building. We waded up to it through knee-deep grasses and thistles. From the roof hung a heavy vine which half-choked the entrance and plunged the open porch into murky shadow. The adjoining porches were separated from ours only by a chest-high wall.

'This is your inheritance from the last occupant,' said Moshe, pointing to a big platter made of porcupine quills which was hanging beside the front door.

'What happened to him?'

'Left,' said Moshe shortly.

'Oh, why?'

'Wife made him. Couldn't take it.'

I glanced at Martha behind Moshe's back, and she made a comic face.

'These are the first permanent *binyanim* we built,' Moshe said, dropping the subject of the defector. 'We lived in huts before that, and before *that* – right in the Dark Ages, twelve years ago – in tents.' He pushed open the screen door on a squeaking hinge. I understood that he was preparing us to appreciate what we would find inside, by letting us know how much more primitive things used to be. Somehow I resented the reminder. 'Sorry there's no plumbing,' he went on. 'We've got it in the newer ones. We'll get around to you as soon as we can afford it.'

The one-roomed interior was small and nondescript. It contained a double bed, two contemporary chairs, a small table, a built-in cupboard and a lamp. On the tiled floor was a bright rug, its startling contemporary colours echoed in the cotton curtains and counterpane. On the wall, which was stippled in yellow and brown, was a picture made of different woods, showing a girl dancing under a palm tree. There was a bowl of fruit and a jug of flowers on the table.

Despite its smallness, it was not nearly so bare and austere as I had braced myself to expect. One could almost call it cosy – a cosy little box. I hated it at sight. I hated it as I had hated the boat. It was neither good enough nor bad enough. A barrack or a comfortable bungalow with just a few modern conveniences – either would have satisfied me. But this – the prospect of living in this little coloured egg-box – appalled me.

With only three of us shut into the room, it already seemed crowded. I felt I could scarcely breathe. Even the window had a screen over it. I went back to the door and pushed it open.

'The mosquitoes and moths get in anyway, I wouldn't make it easy for 'em,' said Moshe. I was obliged to let the door swing to. The squeak and clatter sounded like the closing of a cage. I suddenly knew how claustrophobiacs feel.

Moshe was wuffling on. 'There's a tap sticking out of the grass outside – you can drink from it – and the bogs are over there, beyond that hill. The showers are where we've just come from, in the centre of the kibbutz. Edna'll show you round later.'

'Who brought these?' asked Martha, indicating the fruit and flowers.

'Hadara, I expect – your next-door neighbour. She cleaned the place up for you yesterday, when Dan let us know you were coming. She's English, comes from Bradford originally, she'll give you any help you need. Nice girl. Widow. Sinai – we lost four fellows. Damn bad luck really, so few casualties. . . . Anyhow – if I see Hadara, I'll ask her to drop in after work and bring you round to us. You can meet my two monsters. Yoav's too young to react much to visitors, but Essie's dead keen on anyone new, so you'll get the full treatment.'

'Who lives on the other side?'

'Brazilian couple. Nice types, but no spikka English of course. Well, I must get back to my accounts. Nothing you need for the moment? See you later, then.' He took the pipe out of his mouth, waved it at us, and went out, letting the door bang behind him. As soon as he'd gone, Martha flung her arms round me.

'Aaron, isn't it wonderful! It's all *so* much better than I expected! Isn't it you?' Before I could answer this ungrammatical question she was dragging the cases in from the porch and starting to unpack. While she stowed away our clothes and re-arranged the furniture she kept up a flow of excited chatter.

'I *like* this room. It's so pretty – not cell-like a bit. And did you notice? Cool!' She threw me a happy, sensuous glance. 'I can't wait to get my hands on that garden. You know, the only thing I was sorry to leave in London was my window-box, but this'll be a million times better. Darling, help me hump the cases on to the porch, will you? There's another cupboard out there we can store them in.' I complied in silence. 'I love this porch idea, we can sit out here in the evenings after work – oh look, Aaron!' She turned from the cupboard, clasping to her breast an ancient, handleless electric kettle. On her face was a look of rapture. 'I didn't know you were allowed to brew tea for yourself, I thought everyone ate together! I'm so glad I can still make tea for you sometimes.'

'You're being very sweet about it all,' I said. I didn't understand clearly why I was finding her enthusiasm so irritating. Perhaps because it was untinged by the smallest uncertainty.

She looked at me curiously. 'I'm not being a bit sweet,' she said. 'I honestly think it's wonderful. I'm going to be happy here, Aaron. I can always tell.'

She was so damned sure of herself! 'Don't get too carried away, it won't all be cups of tea and summer evenings on the porch, you know.' The sting in my voice was startling, even to me. Martha stared at me for a moment with all the joy fading, then quietly put the kettle away.

I turned abruptly and went back into the room, cursing myself. What the hell was the matter with me, anyhow? Hadn't I wanted her to like it?

'Aaron, what's the matter?'

She was standing outside the screen door, looking in at me.

'Nothing, dearest. Sorry I said whatever it was.'

'I don't mind that. But what's wrong?'

Impossible to put into words the all-pervading uneasiness. I I put my hands in my pockets and said, 'Nothing. Really.'

'I'm sorry if I was too girlish and exuberant. I suppose it's relief at it all being so civilized.'

'*Civilized?* You call this civilized? No running water and a mile to walk to the loo?'

'Oh, *that*. That's nothing. I expected that.'

'Well, what do you mean, civilized?'

'A nice atmosphere. Flowers in a vase for us, time for kindness and gardening – you know. I thought it would be all terribly basic, no grace-notes, no private kettles.' She giggled. I heard the door squeak and bang to, and then felt her hands slip round my waist from behind. She leaned against my back. 'There's so much waiting to be learned,' she said softly. 'All of it good.'

'How on earth can you be sure?'

'Instinct!' she said lightly, and blew on the back of my neck. 'I must find the showers, or I shall begin to sprout like the fence-posts. I love you.'

I felt very much alone, and strangely disorientated, after she'd gone. I found myself wandering round the room in wary circles, like a dog in a new basket. More specifically, I felt like a Great Dane relegated to the basket of a Pekingese. The smallness, the constricting, box-like smallness! The walls that I felt I could push apart, one hand on each; the ceiling I could actually touch; the window muffled by bushes; the door looking out on to the gloomy, overhung porch . . . I felt a tightness round my chest, and lay down on the bed, closing my eyes.

Immediately came the insidious images. Spacious white rooms leading off one another through wide archways; great light-reflecting mirrors and high handsome windows and ceilings three times a man's height – and every object that met the eye, down to the smallest ashtray and fire iron, permeated with quality and craftsmanship . . .

I shook my head violently. That way madness lay. I must put all that behind me, the pleasant, hedonistic, cushioned years, they were over; the good as well as the evil in them must be forgotten, or at least not regretted. I must be like Martha (but Martha never had any of that, it was easy for her . . .). Martha was in every way better fitted for this violent change than I was. Her reaction to the kibbutz from the first moment showed that she meant to adapt herself, whatever effort it took, and fit in, for my sake. Or was it also for her sake? Was this place the round hole to her round peg? 'I can always tell,' she had said. Perhaps she was right. Perhaps she was going to fit in straight away, without friction or effort, while I would be left to file off my square-peg angles without even the consolation of sharing my period of painful adaptation with her . . .

To quench my uneasiness with purpose, I found my Hebrew book and began to study. In this, at least, I had a head-start over Martha which I meant to keep. But I couldn't concentrate; I got up and went outside. As I stepped out of the shadow of the porch, the sun, flagging as it was, seemed to hit me on the head. I looked round for the tap, and found it sprouting on a long pipe out of grass grown lush under its flow. I bent my head and let the cold water pour sideways into my mouth.

The roar of an engine made me look up. Through the gates at the base of the hill came a tractor, drawing a wagon without sides. It was loaded with young men and women, their brown skins glowing against faded cotton workclothes. I could hear their lively voices above the racket of the engine.

I glanced at my watch. It was 4.30 – the end of a working day. Quite a long day, too, as they probably started at dawn to catch the cool of the morning.

Perhaps tomorrow evening I would be on that flat wagon. My whole body, which now felt no more than mildly tired and hot, would be shot through with aches and pains, making me conscious of every muscle. I wished with desperate cowardice that tomorrow was behind me – tomorrow and many days after that. How marvellous it would be to look back after triumphing over all the obstacles! If there was one thing at which I must not fail, it was the physical work on which all respect in the kibbutz depended. My erratic temperament might not be counted against me provided I proved I could contribute my fair share of labour. But the very thought of hard, continuous work in this heat sapped my confidence.

As the wagon passed near me, I could see that none of its

184

occupants looked particularly tired. The girls wore the same clumsy, heavy boots as the men. Their shirts, too, were stained under the arms and round the waist. But their faces had the acute, vivid look of intelligence. I found in this another faintly disquieting factor. Many of these people were as well-educated, and had been raised in as much comfort as myself.

The contrasts and contradictions which had seemed so fascinating in prospect now, in proximity, seemed unnatural and a bit repulsive. Rough-handed intellectuals, smelling of sweat and talking about Turgenev . . . I pulled my thoughts up sharply, aware that they were instinctive and not rational. For the first time I wondered uneasily how much I had absorbed of Polly's natural snobbishness.

Martha came back, cool and smiling, her dress sticking to her.

'What an idiot! I forgot to take a towel.'

She stripped the dress off. Her wet white slip clung to her, making her almost unbearably attractive. I stood by the window watching her, wondering why I didn't take her in my arms.

'What are the showers like? Are they communal?'

'Yes, of course.'

'But with cubicles?' Somehow I hadn't prepared myself for the particular small humiliation of being naked before other men with stronger, better bodies than mine.

'No, just a big tiled room with showers at one end.'

She was naked, towelling herself unconcernedly. I drew the curtains sharply, and went out on to the porch. She laughed.

'You are silly, who'd look in? They'd have to crawl over all those *kotsim*, anyway, and I'm not the Sleeping Beauty exactly.'

'All those what?'

'*Kotsim*. Thistles. One of the female Vandals told me to watch out for them.'

Instead of being amused and touched by this comic beginning to her study of Hebrew, I felt a pang of uneasiness. I said, 'What are the female Vandals like?'

'Wild, but quite sweet. One of them lent me some soap . . . I'll swear she was an Indian. Are there Indian Jews?'

'Of course. Bloody Jews get everywhere.'

Unexpectedly, I heard her say, 'Shut up, Aaron.'

'Why?'

'That sort of joke's never struck me as very funny. Here it seems outrageous, somehow.'

Heat, fatigue and nervousness had made me edgy. I had an unjust impulse to shout at her, but just then a couple came up the path to the binyan next to ours. They looked at me curiously and said 'Shalom'. I hesitated, biting back what I had wanted to yell until they should go inside; but they got out their electric kettle, plugged it in, and settled down to make tea on their porch. I was only a few feet away from them and I suddenly realized that even indoors there was no real privacy. Our neighbours on either side would be able to hear everything we said above a whisper. A sense of genuine outrage wiped out the pinprick of irritation I had felt against Martha. I felt quite winded by advance frustration.

I stared openly at the couple sitting on their porch. The man was forty-ish, small and thick-set with very dark hair and eyes and a swarthy skin. His wife, also dark, with raggedly cropped hair, was smiling at me, her pale unmade-up mouth showing a gap between her front teeth. Both seemed to me quite unprepossessing, even ugly. These, then, were our Brazilian neighbours, two stocky unattractive little people with whom we would, perforce, share everything except our whispers from now on.

The man said something to me in halting Hebrew, grinning. He looked like one of those nodding dummies in a shop window.

'I don't speak Hebrew,' I said coldly in English. Then I walked away across the spongy grass. He shouted behind me, but I didn't turn round.

But a walk by myself and a shower – also by myself, to my relief – restored me to good humour. It was growing cooler, or at least less unendurably hot, and as I strolled back to our binyan I was filled with new resolve, pushing aside the anxieties and forebodings with determination.

Martha had dragged chairs on to the porch and was entertaining a tall, rangy girl with straight-cropped mousy hair and stern blue eyes who introduced herself as Hadara, our other

186

neighbour. The lack of make-up on the women's faces made most of them look featureless and puddingy, but this girl had such good bone-structure that it didn't matter. I noticed, with an inner start, that Martha had put on less make-up than usual; a touch of lipstick was all I could detect. It gave her a strange, indistinct look to my eyes, as if she were drawing away from me into the distance.

Hadara, having heard of our arrival, had gone specially to the communal kitchen to bring us some tea, sugar and milk – and even some 'Nes' from her own precious store. She was explaining to Martha how to draw supplies of everything from clothes to toothpaste, and Martha was avidly absorbing the information while at the same time mastering the technique of lifting a boiling kettle without a handle. When I rose automatically to help her, she flashed me the most dazzling smile and, with the aid of two cloths, held the rusty, ugly object up in triumph, as if she'd found the Holy Grail.

'I can manage!' she said in a voice of unalloyed happiness. I stifled a sudden feeling of fear, and turned to Hadara.

'When do we start work?'

Her very blue eyes seemed to pierce my calm façade and see all the uncertainties behind it. 'No hurry,' she said in her dry, Yorkshire voice. 'Best settle in first.'

'We're settled. I'd like to start tomorrow.'

She raised her eyebrows, but only said 'Okay, I'll take you along to Uri after supper tonight. He's works manager.'

She looked me over openly. 'What are you good for?'

The lust to stick my fingers in the soil had faded, but I couldn't think of anything else. 'Something in the fields?'

'Well, there's the guavas, they're coming ripe all the time. Or the bananas – but that's real work. Uri'll likely stick you on the *guyavot* to start with.' Then she turned to Martha. 'What about you? Fancy washing dishes for eight hours starting at six?'

Martha laughed and said, 'Not much! Is there any choice?'

'Don't tell me you want to fry in the sun too?'

'Well, of course, I may flake out after half an hour, but I can always have a bash.'

I stared at her enviously. How wonderful to be able to say that! Being a girl, of course, it didn't matter much if she couldn't take the work or the heat at first – no one would think any less of her.

I'd noticed Hadara kept glancing expectantly over her shoulder. Now she suddenly jumped up, and without excusing herself went dashing along the path. Two small boys were running towards her, and there was a rowdy collision as they both leapt, shouting, into her arms.

She brought them over to us. They were both tough, pudgy, snub-nosed and splashed with freckles, like baby pumas. They stared at us with a sort of blatant, bright-eyed curiosity as their mother introduced them.

'They speak English quite well,' she said, 'but they won't. Yossi, Eli, say hallo.'

'Shalom!' they responded in shouted unison, and then went off into peals of laughter. Hadara shrugged tolerantly.

'Well, I must leave you to your own devices for a bit,' she said, as the boys began tugging at her skirt imperiously. 'It's hard work, being Dad *and* Mum.' And she allowed herself to be dragged away across the lawn to take part in what looked like a very rough two-against-one sort of game.

'Disconcerting children,' I said.

'Just uninhibited. What about trying to find Moshe's house?'

We strolled along the maze of paths between the houses. The whole place, so peaceful and deserted an hour before, had come alive like a disturbed ant-heap. We passed a sand-pit swarming with children and grown-ups, all playing concentratedly together. Men and girls by the dozen passed us trundling home-made prams or being hauled along by one or more children. The large central green of the kibbutz had become a playground where the older children crowded on to painted swings, slides and see-saws, their lithe bodies moving with the grace of small animals through the golden light.

Martha and I stood under some trees, not touching each other, private in our own thoughts, watching the children. A man went past with a child on his shoulders and another at his heels. The younger one was hugging his head with blindfolding arms and crowing 'Aba-aba-aba!'

'What's "aba"?' Martha asked.

'Daddy.'

'So much for the theory that they don't know their own parents. Hadara says that's the first question American visitors ask – "Do your children recognize you?"'

'And what's the second question?'

She laughed a little shyly and said '"Do you have free love?"'

I turned to her. 'And do we?'

There was no one near us. She slipped into my arms and we kissed. It was ten days since we'd made love in the Victoria hotel.

'I wish we could lie down here, under the trees.'

'Me too!'

The shared longing, acknowledged so freely, was enough, for the moment. We strolled on, our arms round each other. It was the first taste of contentment I'd had for what seemed a very long time, and it intoxicated me into believing, for a moment, that everything was going to fall smoothly into place after all.

Chapter Seven

'*Shalom. Corim l'cha Aron?*'

A sturdy little figure, barefooted and self-possessed, blocked our path. I said yes, I was called Aaron.

'*Ani Esther, bat shel Moshe. Boh.*'

When we failed to respond at once to this instruction, she took my wrist firmly and pulled me after her.

'Esther-daughter-of-Moshe' came roughly up to my thigh. She was slight, wiry and had a grip of iron. Her straight fair hair hung to the base of her neck, and swung solidly like a bead curtain whenever she snapped her head round to see that we were following. She had the face of a highly intelligent angel, and the tough, grubby hands and feet of an urchin.

She led us through the bewildering maze of buildings and gardens to Moshe's binyan. He was sitting on the porch smoking his outsize pipe. while a Junoesque girl twice his size knelt on the floor playing with a baby.

'Shalom, shalom!' Moshe exclaimed, jumping to his feet. 'Thought you'd taken fright and gone home. Find the showers and bogs all right? *Tov.* Have some Nes.' He hurried to plug in the kettle.

'No, we mustn't take yours –' protested Martha, her eyes on the baby, who was golden-skinned and fair-haired and seemed utterly unrelated to either of its dark, semitic parents.

'Of course you will, don't be so daft,' said the girl, lumbering upright. 'Don't mind my rude husband. Since I lost my girlish figure giving birth to his son, he never introduces me to people. I'm Edna – shalom.'

'Shalom,' I said, shaking her brawny hand. Martha echoed me shyly. It was the first time I'd heard her use the word.

Edna gabbled something in Hebrew to her daughter, who was staring at us in frank appraisal. The child turned and opened the door into the house. '*Boh hena,*' she commanded.

'Go in and play with her while I make coffee,' said Edna.

Rather apprehensively, we obeyed. Essie was meticulously laying out her toys on display in a room similar to ours, but infinitely lived-in and with a flavour of culture – crowded to bursting-point with books, papers, pictures, clothes, a radio, a record-player, and a great many bits of old pottery. The result should have been chaotic, but every inch of space was husbanded and the general effect, though cluttered, was not untidy. The crowding of possessions was made worse by the fact that one whole corner was allotted to toys, largely hand-made, which included a rocking-horse.

Esther had evidently grasped the situation. She decided to teach us Hebrew.

'*Suss*,' she said kindly, pointing to the horse.

'*Suss*,' we echoed obediently. She rewarded us with a gap-toothed smile and went on to Lesson Two. By the time Edna came to rescue us we had mastered the words for doll, bear, brick, boot and truck, plus an extra word that could have meant Plasticine, or on the other hand it could have meant lump.

'Has she been a bother?'

'Not a bit,' said Martha warmly, and added: 'She's not much like an English child of four, is she?'

'God forbid,' said Edna fervently, 'poor repressed little brutes.' We started to go on to the porch, but Essie intervened quite sharply. Edna gave in at once. 'This is her time,' she explained. 'She likes company while she plays, and she wants us in here, so here we must stay. Better anyway, those mosquitoes love me. Moshe! Bring the monster in, will you?'

Moshe came through with a tray of plastic cups in one hand and the baby in the other. 'Have you been looking at my sherds?' he asked.

'Of course they haven't been looking at your blooming sherds!' his wife retorted. 'Him and his old sherds, don't let him get started, he'll bore you senseless.' She poured out the coffee. 'I won't offer you cake before supper, but later I must give you my recipe. You have to save eggs from breakfast, and bake it in a special portable oven –'

'Talk about boring,' said Moshe. He sprawled on the bed on his back with his son athwart his stomach. 'Actually you can't help getting interested in archaeology here. Every time you trip over something it's a bit of history. I've found some things that'd even make the big boys sit up. Now take this for instance –'

'Give a man a hobby,' said Edna, 'and kill conversation. Please don't encourage him, I go meshuggah from him as it is. That and his theories on child-raising. He's dead worried at the moment because Yoav's bowels don't move when the book says they should –'

'Wonderful conversationalist, my wife,' said Moshe. 'Got it down to a fine art. Archaeology, no. *Bowels*, on the other hand, yes. Look at this.' He rolled over on his side, the baby in the crook of his legs, and showed me a small piece of stone. 'Two thousand B.C.,' he said diffidently. 'That's approximate. Could easily be older.'

'What is it?'

'Well may you ask!' said Edna contemptuously. 'It's a piece of stone four thousand years old. Most pieces of stone are. And we'll put this on for the roof.' She was on the floor, building a complex house of bricks and books for Esther.

'For God's sake, woman!' exclaimed Moshe, suddenly noticing what she was doing. 'Don't do it for her. You'll inhibit all her creative impulses!' Essie suddenly fell on the house from above with a cry of glee, razing it to the ground. 'There, you see? That's her protest against your interference!'

Edna roared with laughter. 'What can you do with a man who turns everything to his own account?' Yoav began howling. 'Now whose fault is it? So busy worrying about Essie's creative impulses, you let your little lad cry himself into fits.' She lifted the baby into the air and shook him above her head. His cries became gurgles of delight. 'Was his old bowels non-conformist, then?' she crooned. 'He's his mother's boy. Here, have one of Aba's nice sherds to eat.' She presented him with a piece of handle, worn smooth by aeons, on which Yoav immediately began gnawing. Moshe let out a roar like a wounded buffalo.

'Christ! He'll break it! He'll choke himself!'

Edna held the baby, plus sherd, out of reach, laughing deep in her throat. 'You notice which he mentions first!'

They wrestled for Yoav like two dogs for a bone. Essie leapt about, stiff-limbed with excitement, shrieking with laughter. A pile of magazines went flying. The whole small room seemed to be full of rioting figures. Martha and I had to take refuge on the bed, but it was a refuge which didn't last long, because after a moment Moshe, Edna, Yoav and Essie landed on top of us in a wrestling heap. I received a sharp jab in the stomach from Edna's elbow and felt for a moment as if I were trapped in a mad-house.

But it was quickly over. Edna could have given Moshe twenty pounds, and so emerged victorious, if wildly tousled. Neither the baby nor the sherd (which was Moshe's share of the spoils) appeared to be any the worse.

'You'll think we're barmy,' panted Edna happily. 'We're not all as mad as this, here, you know. Very sober lot for the most part. It's just this poor old husband of mine, he has to work off his adolescent feelings of aggression.'

Moshe was hunting for his pipe. 'Come on, we must get them back now. All this messing about.' He took Esther by the hand, opened the screen door to let Edna go out, and aimed a skelp at her as she passed. She dodged it, laughing and cuddling the baby against her face. Moshe gave us a sheepish grin. When we followed them outside, their heads were bumping together as they tucked Yoav into his orange-box pram.

As we formed up to process to the babies' house, Essie fell in beside me. She kept grinning up at me with a sort of flirtatious smugness quite disconcerting in such a little girl. She appeared to have all the instinctive wiles of femininity already. I disap-proved strongly of her precocity, and yet against my will I was drawn to her. When she abruptly tucked her bony little hand into mine, I found myself feeling flattered, as by a confi-dence from an equal.

Edna carried Yoav into the babies' house to feed and bed him down, and Martha went with her to watch. Moshe and I went on with Essie to her small communal residence, which she shared with six other children of her age. I was not asked in. Through the window I watched as Moshe, with what looked very like deference, accompanied his daughter on to her own territory. She greeted her friends, allowed Moshe to help her wash, and then settled down at a small table laid for supper. All the furniture was keyed to the size of the children; there were no adult-sized chairs, and Moshe and the other parents stood about looking rather *de trop*. The slight but capable girl in charge didn't encourage them to linger, and neither did the children, who kissed them good night with a distinctly dismissive air. I felt again the ludicrous sense of gratification when Essie, noticing me at the window, condescended to wave to me.

'What do you think of her?' asked Moshe at once when he came out.

'I'm not much good with children,' I said evasively. Nothing would have made me admit how much that bossy, cocksure child appealed to me.

'Wait till you've some of your own,' said Moshe, a casual remark which somehow startled me.

He led the way towards a large building which dominated the central green.

'Ready for a nosh?'

'Yes.'

'Nothing to what you'll be this time tomorrow.' The uneasiness, dimmed by the robust friendliness of the last hour, returned like a backwash of nausea.

Streams of kibbutzniks were trooping towards the dining-hall from both sides. Most of them had changed out of their working clothes into others, no less faded and shabby, but clean and pressed. I wondered how long it would take me to get used to the sight of women looking so – somehow – colourless. Even their brown skins could not save them from looking peasant-drab. I suddenly saw Martha coming towards me among a crowd of other girls. Even the trace of lipstick she wore made a startling contrast to all those naked female faces. Her dress, a vivid print, stood out among the washed-out cottons, giving her an air of unbridled flamboyance.

I felt a wave of pride. She looked twenty times more feminine, more attractive and pleasing to the eye than any of the others. She looked as if she cared for her appearance, and had the leisure and means to make the most of it. She looked as a woman should look. The men noticed it too, and kept glancing at her, their eyes irresistibly drawn.

'Your wife looks like something from another world,' said Moshe. He spoke non-committally, not giving away whether he

194

approved or disapproved. But I approved. I wanted, suddenly and sharply, to be certain that she would go on looking different, that she would never blend in with the others, become dowdy and faceless like them. I hurried over to her, my eyes praising her.

She met my look critically. 'Darling, you must have that beard off,' she murmured as I came up to her. 'It looks terribly off-beat here.'

I don't think anything she'd ever said to me had dismayed me quite so much. Certainly I'd never had this cold, shocking realization that, however much we were in love, basically we were separate people, different and alone in our distinctive attitudes to life. For a moment I stared at her aghast, feeling totally estranged from her. Then Edna came barging up.

'Come on, you lot! I'm perished with hunger.'

Martha said 'Me too,' as she had said 'Me too' an hour ago under the trees. I saw how useless it was to worry about trivialities in the face of a fundamental need. I would shave off my beard, I would shave myself down to the bone if she liked. What did it matter? What mattered was that tonight we'd be in bed together.

Martha and Edna went ahead of us, and Moshe suddenly said 'Lucky you got married before you left England.'

'What? Why?'

'Well, your wife's not Jewish, is she? And there's no civil marriage here, the rabbis see to that, may they rot.' I looked at him, startled and, deep down, a little shocked. He went on: 'Of course you know this whole country's *rov*-ridden. Who do they represent, in fact? A small group of parasitical lunatics in Jerusalem, and a lot of emotional vested interests abroad. And yet there they squat, firmly astride the Coalition see-saw, upholding all the old shiboleths . . . you wouldn't find one who'd marry a Jew to a non-Jew –'

Edna loomed beside us. 'And that's the third thing that meshugganates me about him – rabbi-phobia. Here, here's a table – let's cut the politics till after supper.'

The dining-hall was bigger, and noisier, than a factory canteen. There were about forty tables, all crowded, but Edna had secured places for us. One of the four people already at the table was the fair, supercilious type who'd been 'too busy' to cope with us when we first arrived. He turned out to be Uri, the works manager. He seemed more agreeable now, and pushed big bowls of salad, bread and fish towards us.

'Don't get used to this service,' he advised. 'After your novelty value wears off, you'll just have to grab.'

Martha ate very little. She toyed with the fish, peppers and yoghurt, abandoning each after tasting it with little dismayed grimaces. When the eggs came along, we were given the choice between 'cold' and 'hot'. 'The choice,' said Edna, 'is actually between eggs cooked for ten minutes, or for thirty seconds. I prefer a cold bullet, myself, to an egg-shellful of hot water.' Martha's disgust at her raw egg was palpable. She whispered to me: 'How could anyone eat them like this? And that horrible vinegary fish – I'll starve!' I replied, 'I love it. Give yours to me.' I was aware of a strange relief at finding something that I liked and that she didn't.

After the meal Uri lost his off-duty amiability and became brisk and businesslike.

'Edna says you're ready to start work tomorrow. You'd better come along to my office and I'll see how I can make use of you.'

His office was a cupboard-sized hut with room for no more than a table, a chair, and the works schedules. Uri stood consulting these for some minutes, tapping his teeth with a pencil and cogitating. Eventually he said we could both have a bash at the guavas to start with.

'Do you want to do just the half-day tomorrow, to see how you get on?'

He regarded me with cold cobalt eyes; his mouth turned up faintly at the corners with an irritating hint of quizzical contempt. With a full stomach and in the cool of the evening I felt once again ready for anything.

'Hell, no. We'll do a whole day.'

'Speak for yourself,' muttered Martha, but she didn't protest as Uri marked us down at the bottom of one of the columns. When he'd gone, we lingered.

'Which is me?'

I showed her her name and she stood for a long time, staring at the unfamiliar caligraphy. When I put my arm round her, she gave a little shiver, and threw me a quick, nervous smile.

'Anything wrong?' I asked.

'Not really.' After a moment she said, 'I'm a bit scared I won't be able to take a whole day, working in the heat.'

I felt suddenly very confident and very much in love with her. I hugged her shoulder and said, 'Don't worry, you'll be fine. They won't expect too much of you at first.'

'We'd better get an early night.'

'Yes.'

We began to stroll back through the dusk. The porch lights were on now, but few people sat outside, and we soon realized why. Mosquitoes settled on us in a devouring hoard. We both lit cigarettes, but the smoke did little to deflect our persecutors.

'It must be because we're new.'

'Full of rich English blood,' said Martha, slapping. 'God, they bite clean through two layers of cloth! Never mind, our blood'll soon thin out on the diet here, if tonight's meal was anything to go by.'

'Mopping and mowing already?'

'*Yes.* I love good food, and – get out of it, you little fiends!' She bent and swiped at her bare ankles.

'What do you think of Essie?'

'Attractive but spoilt. Is she a typical kibbutz child, do you think? If so I think I'd rather wash dishes than try to teach them anything.'

We walked on for a few minutes. I had no idea even what direction we were walking in, but Martha led the way to our binyan like a homing pigeon. I reached for her hand, thinking ahead to being alone with her. The horror of that little closed-in room had faded before the need to shut a door behind us – any door – and renew acquaintance with our private world.

Suddenly she said: 'I wonder if, when we've been married for ten years, we'll be anything like Moshe and Edna.'

I laughed and was about to say 'Let's hope not!' when she said soberly, 'It's something to aim for – a love like that after ten years.' I wished she wouldn't make these odd remarks. I never quite knew whether she was joking, or whether she and I really saw things so differently.

Chapter Eight

We went to bed early so as to be up early. At least, that was the original idea.

When our Brazilian neighbour knocked at our door at 5 a.m., I had had an aggregate of about ninety minutes' sleep. I came to the surface with the reluctance of a determined suicide being dragged out of the river.

'Time stop sleep!' he called in cheery, wide-awake tones. I'd have throttled him, if that could have been achieved without the smallest physical effort.

Martha lay curled against me, warm as a new-born puppy and with her eyes just as tightly closed. I knew I must wake her, and felt a surge of guilt. It was entirely my fault that we hadn't gone to sleep at a reasonable hour. She'd tried her best to remind me how we'd feel in the morning, but it was impossible for me to think beyond the needs of the moment – the one, to remember the magic of mutual ownership, and the other – equally urgent – to forget everything else, including the day ahead when the true trials would begin.

Now the fought-off morning had arrived, finding me limp and hollow-throated with exhaustion. I rolled off the bed, pulled on the coarse working trousers I'd been given the night before, and pushed open the screen door. The morning was cool and still. The sun was just over the horizon, and long bright-edged shadows extended from the buildings and trees. Condensation lay sparkling everywhere. I stumbled off the porch and put my head under the tap. The cold water rattled past my ears, sending shock-waves down my cringing spine. Around me, doors were squeaking open and banging shut; straightening, I could see men moving about down by the cattle-sheds. Beyond, the sandhills were smooth and clean, the colour of cider; their curves, the random arrangement of palm-trees against them, and the distant sparkling blue line of the sea, struck me with a sudden impact of delight. I stood staring in a sort of trance, the cold water warming as it ran from my hair down my chest and back.

Suddenly I heard the nearby roar of a tractor, and saw the flat truck with its load of pickers go bouncing and tilting down the hill. I stood appalled. They were going without me! I would be left behind, disgraced, on my first day.

Rushing back into the binyan I almost dragged Martha from the bed, flinging on my shirt and trampling into the stiff boots while she stood, naked and dazed, in the middle of the floor.

'Hurry up!' I said frantically.

Without a word she began to grope her way into her clothes.

Lacing my boots, I said, 'What are we to do? We *can't* go and tell Uri or Moshe we've missed the bloody bus. We'll never hear the end of it.'

'Maybe we could find our way on foot.'

She stood in the doorway, tousle-headed in the dunce's hat, her legs straight and childish under shorts like a schoolgirl's bloomers. The strange faded uniform might have been made for her; it transformed her instantly into a *sabra*, a native-born Israeli – a very young one, almost a Vandal. I felt a fleeting astonishment at the passion concealed in that small, barely-adolescent-looking body. For a split second I actually resented it for having exhausted me – and her for managing to look so right, so much as if she belonged to the new life, while I found myself unable to rise above the discomfort of the boots, the coarseness of the shirt next to my skin, and the petty but unpleasant knowledge that my trousers had been worn by others before me.

'Come on, then.' She had shaken off fatigue completely and was now bright and eager to be off.

'How are we to find the way?'

'Ask someone. *Efo guyavot?* I know that much.'

Luck was with us. We were hardly out of the gate before we heard the rattle of wheels, and a cart pulled by a dusty pony drew up. Driving it was a taciturn middle-aged man with heavy Mongolian features. When we asked directions to the guavas, he turned his impassive Ghengis Khan face towards us and jerked his thumb at the cart. With a groan of relief we clambered on the tail, our feet barely skimming the dusty road as we jolted forward.

'Have you any idea how guavas grow?'

'You could pull them up like carrots, for all I know,' said Martha cheerfully. She sat on a filthy sack, from which she rose vertically every time we hit a pothole. I did the same, without benefit of sack. But Martha was unaware of discomfort. She held firmly to the rusty iron rim of the cart and gazed round, pointing excitedly at things we passed – baby orange trees protected from the sun by screens of sacking; lush-looking banana groves; whirling sprays above the fields of maize. Once we passed a small, ragged Bedou child riding a heavily-burdened donkey. Martha opened her mouth on another cry of 'Look, look!' and said instead, incredulously, 'We're here!'

I suffered the sun in my eyes, the dust in my throat and the cutting edge of the cart under my thighs, and said nothing.

The two hours before breakfast weren't bad at all. It was still cool among the leaves, and the work wasn't hard in itself, though it involved a lot of bending, reaching, lugging of loaded satchels and fighting through sharp, resistant branches. By the time Ghengis Khan motioned us on to the cart for the drive back I was feeling quite cheerful and self-confident again; any old urban aesthete, I said to Martha, could cope with this.

In the crowded dining-room nobody took any particular notice of us. We ate avidly; Martha swallowed everything in sight without turning her nose up once. Edna was on trolley-duty, bringing round more of the ubiquitous eggs. She did a double-take at the sight of Martha.

'You look dead genuine! Never take you for a new-comer.'

Martha thanked her as if for an accolade.

Edna asked if we'd like to borrow a pair of sunglasses each. Before Martha could answer I'd let out a derisive hoot.

'What do you take us for, American tourists?'

Edna shrugged her broad shoulders and laughed. 'You'll be sorry!'

We were.

During the aeons of vacant dawdling time that stretched between eight-thirty and half past one, my well-being slowly but steadily deteriorated. The sun rose; the yellow fruit seemed to be embedded in its fiery depths. I closed my eyes to slits, but the rays entered like spears, piercing the eyeballs until they seemed to blister in their sockets. The weight of the shoulder-bag, insignificant at first, grew until I felt that I was filling it not with guavas but with lumps of granite. The trips to the ends of the rows to empty the pickings into crates took on a treadmill quality of repetitive drudgery. The branches clawed at me, scratching my arms and neck, snatching off my hat. The trees grew so close together that I could never find my place again and Ghengis would come scowling through the leaves to drag me back and point out ripe fruit I'd missed. He became impatient, scolding me incomprehensibly. There was nobody else to talk to; Martha had been stationed on the far side of the grove, and the majority of pickers were across the road – I could hear their faint laughter, like mocking echoes. My face began to smart with sunburn. My clumsy feet skidded on fallen fruit. Thirst became a problem which the juiceless, foul-smelling guavas couldn't solve.

But nothing was worse than the atrocious boredom I felt as the monotonous hours crawled on. I would glance at my watch, find only three minutes had passed since I last looked, and determine not to look again until I'd filled and emptied my bag twice more. This should take half an hour. But it didn't; it took less than fifteen minutes, which counted like a passing day in a life-sentence.

But at last it was over. The racketing ride back on the pony-cart was like a beating; my aching body now felt the jouncing shocks as blows. Martha lay on her back, regardless of the dirt; her head bumped on the boards and her hair filled with dust. She had put her hat under her bare knees to prevent the iron rim, now burning hot, from touching her. I watched her for a while and then said:

'Are you all right?'

'Yes, fine thanks,' she said in a bright conversational tone, her eyes closed.

My healthy appetite of breakfast-time had vanished. Even after having slaked my thirst and run cold water over my scorched arms and face, I could stare with repulsion at the hot meat pie and rice that the others' were ravenously eating. The whole business of kibbutz feeding seemed suddenly nauseating.

Funny that I hadn't noticed before that central bowl into which all left-overs, solid and liquid, were thrown. Soon bits of meat-pie were swimming amid globules of fat in the slops of soup. By the time the mushy centres of guavas and swollen cigarette-ends had been added, I could scarcely go on chewing at a piece of dry bread. I sat crumbling it in my hand and wondering why in God's name I hadn't said yes to the charitable idea of starting with half-days.

I looked at Martha. She was eating soup very slowly, as if each spoonful were a burden to lift. Her eyes kept closing. There was a dark patch on her blouse down the centre of her back.

'How do you feel?'

'Bloody, thank you,' she said without looking at me.

'Are you going back this afternoon?'

'Can one not?'

'I expect Uri would let you off, if you asked him.'

She sat in silence for a while, slumped over her arms on the table. 'Are *you* going to ask him?'

I didn't answer. I felt as if I were moulded in one with the bench, as if my boots were soldered to the floor. I felt incapable of the smallest movement.

Ghengis Khan scraped his plate into the garbage-bowl with a crust, ate the crust, and rose ponderously. He fixed his expressionless eyes on us and stood there, waiting.

'It'll get easier,' said Martha. 'It's got to.'

We put our hands on the table and levered ourselves to our feet.

Chapter Nine

It was all very well for Martha to say it would get easier. For her, it did. Two days later she was taken off field work and made a trainee English teacher under Edna. She told me it was difficult and alarming, that she dreaded the time when Edna would leave her alone with the children, that it was the hardest thing she'd ever done. I didn't contradict her, but I felt she had been let off lightly. How could she know what work felt like, real work, day after day after day of it? Soon I was too exhausted to listen to her talk about her teaching, anyway. I was absorbed in the task of keeping going.

After a week of the guavas had stiffened every muscle in my body, I was shifted into the banana plantation to replace a man who was in hospital with snake-bite. Here, the sickening boredom of ordinary fruit-picking was somewhat eased – partly because the work of humping the green bananas was infinitely harder, and partly because I found I couldn't be bored while suffering continual secret terror of treading on a poisonous snake.

The days started at dawn, when the long leaves, sharp as scythes, were dulled with a bloom of condensation. The growing heat soon evaporated this, filling the dense air with moisture. It was like working in a greenhouse, or a jungle. The ground underfoot was as full of obstructions as an obstacle course – huge chunks of the severed banana plants, left to rot, constituted hundreds of stumbling blocks. Mosquitoes throve in the rank atmosphere. Their merciless attentions, and the razor-edged leaves, made it necessary to wear heavy trousers and shirts with the sleeves rolled down. Sweat poured off me as ever I had romantically foreseen, but it gave no trace of satisfaction, only a feeling of inner dehydration – a kind of withering or drying-out of my reserves, even of my personality.

The tiredness soon became a permanent condition which sleep hardly affected; it reached into my very brain, making it impossible to talk or even think much. I dragged myself through the endless hours of the endless succession of working days with a blank mind; some dogged and remorseless inner automatic-pilot kept me on my feet, and grunted 'Fine' when anyone asked me how I was getting on. Between bouts of work I would devour food like an animal, often under a shelter in the fields; I soon lost my fastidious horror of the clouds of flies which crawled and hovered over the sausages, margarine, cheese, fruit and *halva*. After work I stood crushed among other sweating men in a cattle-truck dragged by a tractor, which threw back blasts of oily heat into our faces. My legs ached and trembled and threatened to collapse under me as I jumped off the truck in the centre of the kibbutz; I couldn't make myself walk back to my binyan for soap and towel, because the only tolerable experience of the day was waiting – the shower.

Back at the binyan I would fall on the bed and sleep like a corpse until supper-time. After supper all I craved was more sleep, but not daring to admit my weakness I would go with Martha to visit Moshe and Edna, Hadara, Uri and his dumpy wife Ruthie, or one of the other *ménages*. Sometimes, incomprehensibly, our hosts would elect to sit outside on deck-chairs, when mosquitoes, their sullen whine filling the air, would close in on my already intolerably bitten body. At other times we would go indoors – six, eight, even ten of us crowded into the small bright boxes. After a few minutes I would be seized by a craving to get out, even the persecution of the mosquitoes seeming preferable to the sense of confinement indoors. But Martha's enjoyment of these evening sessions was so patent that I felt I had to endure them. And indeed, if I had not been so deeply and engrossingly weary, I would have enjoyed them too – the endless tea and coffee and yellow cake and the flowing, many-coloured patterns of conversation.

They talked with excitement and perception about politics, about plays in London which they would never see, about books, about archaeology, about articles in The *New Statesman* or The *Observer*, about art, about everything. I heard it all across a gulf, through cotton-wool layers of tiredness, trying to admire their intellect and their articulateness, while longing only for utter, total and unbreakable silence in which I could sleep for a week.

These sessions often broke up at midnight or later. Sometimes I would mumble an excuse and leave early. When Martha came in later, I could scarcely move my leaden body to make room for her.

She seldom slept in the afternoons. Dimly I would be aware of her coming in from her shower, changing, brushing her hair, softly closing the screen-door after herself as she went out – incredibly, unnecessarily – into the hot, work-free late afternoon.

I found this infuriating. Her lack of fatigue was an implied reproach. One day I lifted my heavy head and called her back.

'Where are you off to?'

'To my lesson.'

I felt a stab of guilt. 'Is Edna teaching you Hebrew?'

'Of course. I told you.'

Had she told me? I couldn't remember holding a coherent conversation with her for weeks. Through the layers of descending sleep I forced myself to ask how she was getting on.

'Not too bad. It's awfully hard, though.'

'Why bother? You'll pick it up automatically in time.'

'"In time" won't help me against the little devils in my English class. They take the mickey out of me unmercifully, and I'm completely helpless until I know what they're saying.'

'Are you on your own with them now?'

She stared at me. 'Aaron, of course! I *told* you.'

When she'd gone I lay feeling guilty about my lack of interest in her recent doings. The truth was I had no energy to spare for mental activity of any sort. Even the guilt was soon submerged in sleep.

But two days later I had to listen. I came in from my shower and found her huddled on the bed crying despairingly.

'Darling, what's wrong, what is it?'

She flung herself against me. I could hardly understand what she was saying for her sobs.

'I can't do it!' she kept gasping. 'He hates me – I don't

know why – the others'd be all right if it weren't for him. He sits there with that funny, shut look on his face – he's so ugly, he's got a face like a goat – and I know something's going to happen – I get so frightened I can't think straight – and then he says something and they all – laugh – and he keeps sitting there . . . I can't go back any more, I can't, it's so awful, I don't know how to deal with it . . .'

I calmed her down, feeling helpless before the passionate storm of her crying. I kept saying, 'Sh, it's all right, someone'll hear you –'

'I don't care! I won't go back any more, he's a horrible evil little beast and I'm afraid of him!'

'Who, who is he?'

She pulled away from me and blew her nose, her breath still coming in gasps. 'His name's Shmuel. He's one of the Vandals. He's not just – naughty. I can't explain.'

There was a tap on the door. Hadara was outside on the porch.

'None of my business, of course, but – anything I can do?'

I let her in.

'If it's domestic row, I'll keep out.'

'It's not.'

'That's what I thought.' She sat next to Martha on the bed. 'What's wrong, love? Kids playing you up?'

She nodded, ashamed of her outburst, unwilling to say anything. But I felt a fierce protectiveness for her.

'Who's this boy Shmuel?' I asked Hadara.

'Oh, it's him, is it? Yes, he is a bit of a handful, Edna should have warned you.'

'She did, but it doesn't help.' She turned to Hadara, her face hard and unfamiliar. 'He's a horrible child!' she said passionately.

'He's a bit of a trouble-maker, I know, but he's had a hard life. His parents are poor immigrants from Tunisia –'

'I know all that. Lots of them are poor immigrants. None of the rest are like him. He's not just difficult, he's rotten. There's something fundamentally rotten about him.'

Hadara's face seemed to close, and she stood up and moved away.

'That's rubbish,' she said firmly. 'There's no such thing as a bad child. There are just children who need more love and understanding than others.'

I said 'There are children who need a good clout more than others.'

'I don't think force is any kind of an answer,' she said, 'not where children are concerned.'

'Shmuel's not exactly a helpless infant,' said Martha. 'He's sixteen, and big and strong for his age, as the littler ones have found out to their cost.'

'What do you mean?'

'He's a bully, that's what I mean. He's got them all where he wants them. And that goes for me too. I'm terrified of him.'

'That's quite ridiculous! If he goes too far, you call Moshe or one of the other men.'

'Who'll do exactly what?' I inquired sarcastically.

'Reason with him.'

Martha gave a short laugh. There was a silence.

'You're making good progress with the English, anyway,' said Hadara in a gentler voice. 'Edna says so.'

'I can't do it any more. Not after today.'

'Why, what happened today particularly?'

'At first, nothing more than usual. He puts his hand up when I ask a question. If I call on another child, he stands up anyway and the other child sits down. Then he says something in Hebrew, with those goat's eyes fixed on mine, and the others – the older ones – all begin to laugh. Some of them are embarrassed. I can tell from their reaction that he's saying something disgusting. Then today I saw a paper being passed round. I tried to confiscate it, but they screwed it up and kept throwing it over my head from one to another. Eventually there was complete chaos, the children running all over the room throwing the ball of paper to each other. In the end Shmuel had it. He suddenly threw it straight at me. It was a drawing of me. Not just – an ordinary drawing.'

Hadara frowned. 'Have you got it?'

'No, I destroyed it.'

'How?'

'I took it up to the front of the class and set fire to it with a match. They all grew quiet, watching it burn. I felt as if I might be sick with sheer frustration and disgust. I managed to finish the lesson . . .'

'Good. That was all psychologically good.'

'But never again. I'm beginning to hate him. And I'm not cut out for it, anyway. I feel at such a disadvantage, not knowing what they're saying, and whatever Edna says I don't think they're really learning anything.'

'You've got to make them *enjoy* learning,' said Hadara.

I laughed, outright and rudely, at this. Hadara looked at me inquiringly. 'Sorry,' I said, 'but really those sort of theories are terribly old hat. However, it's none of my business, all that interests me is that Martha shouldn't walk into that lion's den any more. She'll be a nervous wreck.'

With the abrupt perversity of women, Martha sighed deeply and said, 'Oh well. It's not all that bad, I suppose.'

'I thought you said it was?' I asked in bewilderment, the wind leaving my sails.

She said nothing for a moment, staring out of the window. Hadara glanced at me, a congratulatory glance, as if I'd deliberately engineered this *volte-face*.

'Perhaps it's just a matter of getting the hang of it,' Martha said at last. 'They were awful to Edna, too, at first. Besides, one hates to give up.'

'That's the ticket,' said Hadara.

'The hell it's the ticket!' I said hotly. 'You can't just foist the job off on someone totally untrained and expect her to cope somehow! It's asking too much, and I'm not going to let –'

Martha turned and met my eye. She had a pleading expression. 'Darling . . .'

'What?'

'Let me have another go.'

I literally threw up my hands. 'Good God, I'm not trying to stop you! I thought you said –'

Hadara began to laugh, and Martha grinned too, sheepishly. I gave up.

That night it grew hot in a new and frightful way. The air in the binyan lay heavy and stifling as stagnant water, unruffled by so much as a breath of breeze. When I woke at five I was already bathed in sweat; the sheet under which I'd been sleeping naked was almost soggy. I lifted my head and felt as if it had split down the back like a roasting chestnut. My mouth was a sandy burrow. I wondered if I had some sort of fever, but then Martha rolled over heavily and groaned. 'What's happened to the weather? I feel as if I were buried under a ton of sheepskins!'

Outside the air was not desert-clear and sparkling as usual in the early mornings; an ominous glinting pall lay over everything. The sun hung dulled behind something that was neither cloud nor mist, but looked more like grey dust; the effect was of a huge dirty brass disc. There was a threatening feeling in the air. Oppressive was hardly the word for it.

I soon found everyone was affected. People dragged themselves into the dining-hall for their early tea on leaden feet.

'What is it?' I asked the man who flopped next to me at table.

'*Hamsin*,' he said briefly. 'You're lucky you haven't had one before. We usually get them all through October.'

'What's a *hamsin*?'

'Hot wind from the desert. Worse than any ordinary heat-wave. Has funny effects on people, almost like drink. You never want to take any notice if people are fractious while a *hamsin*'s on. If an Arab kills his wife on the seventh day of one, they let him off. They say the *hamsin*'s the murderer.'

Nobody talked much on the trip out to the bananas. The hot stale air seemed to get into your throat, choking off speech. The usually friendly, alert faces round me were sullen and shut in. I kept taking deep breaths, but it was like breathing through flannel.

Under the dense banana foliage the heat was almost unbearable. We all seemed to move in slow motion; every movement was an effort. After half an hour I began to feel sick. My head throbbed; the sweat dried on me almost before it had left my pores. I grew clumsy. Once when my foot slipped and I bumped my load of bananas against somebody's shoulder, he turned on me and snarled, 'Why don't you bloody well look out!' I felt ready to drop the bananas and bash his head in, but it was too hot to bother. We both turned away.

By breakfast-time I felt as I normally felt after working all day. I could scarcely hold my head up, and yet through my exhaustion I was aware of an ominous seething irritability which made me almost want an excuse to lash out at some-body.

Yehudah, a red-faced Cockney giant who was in charge of the banana workers, came up to me as I bathed my face and arms in the dining-room basin. He avoided giving me his usual greeting – a hearty slap on the back – and said gruffly, 'Ruddy 'orrible, isn't it, mate? Worse when you're not used to it. Tell you what. You call it a day. Take your Shabbat, and you can make it up when this perisher blows itself out.'

I wandered back to the binyan, savouring freedom and relief. I'd taken a leisurely shower – having the place to myself at that hour – and was feeling calmer and more at peace with the world; I planned to spend the day reading and sleeping and generally not moving very much.

Outside the binyan I paused, noticing for the first time that things had been done to it since we moved in. The vine had been cut back, giving the front a much tidier, less overhung appear-ance; the thistles and long grass had been scythed, and evidently Martha hadn't wasted any time putting our minute garden in hand. Three sturdy rose-bushes had been freed of weeds and a dark, sunken circle round the base of each indicated daily waterings. There was a pleasing conglomeration of other flow-ers, too, round the edges. Idly I snapped off a rose; I'd put it in a cup beside Martha's side of the bed, to show her I'd noticed her good work.

I stepped on to the porch, and just at that moment the screen door opened and a man came out.

Half-blinded by the harsh sunlight I couldn't make out more than his outline in the dark doorway. For a second I thought I'd come to the wrong binyan; but something in his stance told me that he had no right to be there. Then my eyes grew used to the shadows and I saw that he wasn't a man, but a boy, though tall and heavily built. He had something in his hand which he instantly thrust behind his back; his eyes, which were a strange slanted shape, darted first one way, then the other, and he started to back away into the room.

'What are you doing?' I asked sharply in Hebrew.

Suddenly he made a dive to get past me. Instinctively I shot my foot out and he landed sprawling on the path. The thing he had had in his hand fell out of his reach, settling softly and whitely in the damp patch round one of the rose-bushes.

For a moment I stood staring at it numbly. The boy lay as if paralysed, looking up at me sideways from out of his odd, opaque eyes. Then with a sudden scrambling motion he gained his feet and began to run.

He got two yards before I grabbed him. I turned him to face me, gripping the collar of his shirt. He twisted his head, avoiding my eyes, and made a wild attempt to pull free. The shirt tore, but I got him by the arm. He began to pant heavily.

I dragged him to the rose-bush, and with my free hand reached down for the thing he had dropped. As I touched it, a black rage seized me.

'What did you want these for?' I asked between my teeth.

He wouldn't answer, just stood panting and sweating in my grasp. His eyes flickered sideways; they were set in the side of his head, like a sheep's, or like a –

'Are you called Shmuel?' I said suddenly, and when he was silent I shouted 'Answer me!'

He mumbled 'Yes.'

I thrust my arm over his shoulder and held the thing he'd stolen dangling before his face.

'What did you want them for? If you don't answer I shall break your arm.'

'It was only to play a joke on her,' he muttered, hanging his head. His dirty neck with a bright boil on it was a few inches from my face. I could smell his terror.

'A joke? What kind of a joke?'

I had to jerk his arm again before he answered.

'Just a joke. I was going to . . . one of the others dared me to take them.'

'Liar. What were you going to do?'

He was beginning to tremble. His wrist was slippery.

'Just – give them back to her – pretend that I'd – found them – somewhere.'

I understood. Slowly I let his arm go.

'Don't try to run,' I said. 'Turn round.'

He obeyed. He didn't look at me. His black hair hung over his goat's face as he stared down at his wrist to which the colour was just returning.

I put the pants into my pocket. I was shaking with anger, but it was not like the rages. I felt grimly calm.

'I'm going to knock hell out of you,' I said.

Suddenly he looked up at me. His face was livid.

'You can't, you can't beat me!' he screamed. 'You're not allowed to! They won't le –'

I was lying on the bed when Martha came back. I kept my cut cheek turned away from her. He hadn't given a very good account of himself, but he was heavy, and the one blow that landed had hurt.

I could tell she was happy by the light way she ran across the porch. She didn't even remember that it wasn't my proper day off.

'Aaron, I was right! Everything went marvellously this morning, and all because Shmuel-the-fiend wasn't there.'

'Didn't turn up at all?'

'No.'

'Fancy that. Perhaps he fell down the well.'

'You're just saying that to cheer me up.' She curled up on the foot of the bed, her sunburned face glowing. 'You know, it was quite different without him. I could actually make them concentrate for as much as ten minutes at a time. I can suddenly see what a satisfying business teaching could be . . .'

I felt the beginnings of the familiar resentment, the left-out feeling. I got it several times a day, whenever she was pleased or happy about something on the kibbutz, or whenever she made even a minor adjustment. I got it about quite trivial, ridiculous things, like her telling me at breakfast that she was beginning to like watery eggs . . . Yesterday when she had cried so hopelessly, when she had clung to me like a poor swimmer out of her depth, I had been – I recognized – happier by far than I was now. It was fear, this unworthy feeling; fear, which had been growing from the beginning, that I was losing her, that she was growing away from me into the life of the kibbutz where I could never fully follow her.

'Hey,' she said suddenly. 'What happened to your cheek?'

'Nothing.'

'Come off it.'

'Bumped it on a banana.'

She looked at me with deep, serious eyes, reached over and touched the bruise, wincing herself.

'Aaron . . .'

'Hm?'

'What's wrong?'

'Good heavens, it's nothing! A little bruise –'

'No, not that.'

I knew what she meant, and with her hand touching my face so gently it was suddenly possible to say, 'I think I've hated you for not being tired.'

She moved her hand on to the side of my neck and said 'I see.'

We looked at each other. There was no reproach in her face, but great tenderness. I remembered that she was easy to talk to.

'Martha, you're very happy here, aren't you – in spite of Shmuel and his ilk?'

'He hasn't an ilk. As far as I'm concerned, he's the only fly in the ointment.'

I gazed at her, lonely to my very bones, longing hopelessly to understand, if not to share, this incredible opinion.

'But what exactly is it about the place which – which *satisfies* you enough to make all the drawbacks unimportant?'

'What drawbacks?' she asked, smiling.

I turned away. 'Just tell me what you like.'

'Everything! Well, let's see. The people. Any place is its people, when you come right down to it. The people here are simply the most sincere, the most honest, the –' She stopped. 'I'm gushing. Let me put it this way. They're the *only* people I've every known who *really live* what they believe in.'

'But do *you* believe in it?'

'What?'

'The dream – the political ideal.'

'Oh . . .' she sounded vague. 'No, I don't think so. I mean, I think Communism's a horrible evil if it's forced on masses of people who don't want it, or who aren't the right sort to make it work. But it does work here, because it's a small community, everyone knows everyone, they all do their share – and they chose it. Each one, as an individual. Idealism keeps it going, and mutual respect – and responsibility – that's what's in the air you breathe here, that's what I love, the feeling of people living their chosen way, and finding it just as good as they'd hoped. Every action, every single day, is a dream fulfilled, to them.'

'But you – don't you feel – a bit of an outsider? I mean, not being Jewish –'

She blinked. 'Funny you should say that. I have to remind myself every now and then that everyone here is Jewish except me. They don't seem like the sort of Jews one meets in London. I never noticed it before coming here, but Jews at home are – well, different, a race apart. There's a sort of *straining* feeling about them, as if they were always trying to prove something to someone. I think I *would* feel strange in a closed community of English Jews, in England. But here they're just like other people. I mean they're normal. I never think about it.'

'But what you call the ideal – it can't mean anything to you. Zionism and socialism and all that?'

'I suppose not, though I love the intelligent, articulate way they can all explain what they feel about it. Perhaps I'll absorb it in time. In the meantime it's not political to me, it's personal. It's *them*, Moshe and Hadara and the rest – they're . . . oh damn it, Aaron, you know what I mean! It's not that they're self-right-eous or holier-than-thou; they're real people, they make mistakes, they're pig-headed, they have rows, they do all the things other people do, but at the bottom of it all is a foundation, a – a quality you don't find anywhere else – at least, I never have. It's happiness, and it's something else. Sureness, self-respect . . . or maybe it's just a basic – goodness. Imagine how they'd howl if they heard me say that! But it's true. And apart from that, there's something stimulating about getting right out of the world where commerce and materialism are the fundamentals, into a world where you never use money. It shakes up all your values, makes you think everything out freshly. That's what I've done, and I've decided – well, you can see what I'd decided. I want to stay here all my life,' she said simply, 'and I'll never be able to thank you enough for finding my place for me.'

She was not so grateful to me an hour later, when she came flying in with her eyes bulging and her breath coming short from running all the way from Edna's.

'Short lesson today,' I remarked, my heart hammering.

'Aaron! What have you done? Are you crazy? Why didn't you tell me?'

I put my book aside and lay back on the bed.

'How did you find out?'

'How could I help finding out? The kibbutz is seething with it! Edna couldn't think of anything else!'

'Did you tell them it was me?'

'Of course I didn't, what do you take me for? But Shmuel will. Moshe and David are in with him now, and they'll soon get it out of him.'

'I'll bet! He's probably only too eager to drop me in the soup. Who's David?'

'You know, that aesthetic-looking young fellow with glasses, who looks after the Vandals. He's their guardian angel, and the most passionate defender of the love-and-kindness method in the entire kibbutz. Edna said he'll have whoever did it expelled! Oh, Aaron –'

'Now don't flap.'

'*Flap!* You don't seem to realize! There'll be the most appalling row – you've no idea how strongly they feel about this! What on earth made you do it? No, don't tell me. Oh God, it's all my fault – why did I have to come blubbering to you, why couldn't I have kept hold of myself –'

'Darling, now stop. This is my responsibility, you've got to let me cope with it.'

She came slowly to me and took my hand. 'I do love you,' she said suddenly.

'Even if they chuck us out?'

Her face clouded. 'They won't, will they?'

'I doubt it. But supposing.'

'Yes,' she said, 'even then.' But she paused before she said it.

Chapter Ten

The storm was not long in breaking.

As we walked hand-in-hand into the dining-hall for supper, I felt an electric atmosphere. Several people stopped eating to watch us as we went past. Shmuel was there with some other Youth Aliyah boys. His eye was black and his jaw swollen. He was bent over his plate, shovelling food into his mouth, but as I approached his neighbour nudged him and he looked up at me. His yellow eyes followed me and there was a faint, malicious smile on his face.

We had hardly sat down when Moshe came over to us. He champed on his pipe and said shortly, 'Word with you after supper in my office, all right?'

'All right.'

It was difficult not to be apprehensive. Nobody at our table looked at or spoke to us except one man, a Yorkshireman called Wilfred, who pushed the 'garbage bowl' in my direction and said laconically, 'You might as well just jump in there now and have done with it, old lad.'

'You're bloody encouraging,' I said. He grunted.

'Tell you one thing – there's not one of us that's had any dealings with the little booger that's not itched to have a go at him one time or another. And that goes for David and all. Still, that won't stop 'em filling *you* in, I fear.'

Outside Moshe's office we paused. 'Do you want me to come in with you?' Martha asked. It was the first thing she'd said for half an hour.

'No. You're not getting mixed up in it.'

She tightened her grip on my hand. 'It was my fault in a way. I'm coming in.'

Nothing would dissuade her.

I recognized David when I saw him. He was a nondescript young man with very mild, myopic blue eyes and bad teeth.

He had a compelling voice, however, which brought his whole personality into focus while he was speaking. It was doubtless with this that he kept some sort of order among the Vandals.

'Look here,' he began at once, 'Shmuel Ben Yaacov says you beat him this morning. What about it?'

'*What* about it?'

'Did you?'

'You don't suggest he could conceivably tell a lie?'

Moshe and David exchanged glances.

'I wonder if you appreciate just what you've done,' said David.

'I wonder if you appreciate just what a little bastard your Shmuel is.'

David flushed angrily and Moshe said, 'Let me do this.' He cleared his throat and knocked out his pipe with a number of irritating bangs while we waited. 'We all know Shmuel's character leaves a considerable amount to be desired,' he began. His stilted pompous phraseology reminded me irresistibly of shop stewards on television, talking as no human being ever talks in real life. 'Unfortunately we can't pick and choose, we have to take what Youth Aliyah sends us, and do our best to undo, in many cases, a lifetime of harm that's been done to the children.'

David, unable to keep quiet, chipped in. 'Take Shmuel, for instance. Now his background –'

'I've heard all about it,' I said.

'Have you heard that his father's in jail now for ill-treating him?' He paused. 'No, I thought not. That boy's no stranger to beatings, believe me, he's had them all his life. That's what's wrong with him. So Youth Aliyah takes charge of him and sends him to us, and for months we try to make him understand that he's no different from any other child, *we* like him, *we* trust him to behave well. Of course he doesn't believe it at first, he's set in bad ways, he's defiant, he keeps provoking us to see how far he can go, trying to find out if we really mean it when we say we won't beat him like his father did. And just as he's beginning to believe us, just as he's reaching the peak of badness after which he may very well climb down and begin to respond, what happens? What the hell happens? You come along. You with your damned Victorian ideas –'

Moshe interrupted. 'Let me do this,' he said again.

'Is nobody going to ask why I did it?' I asked.

'It doesn't matter why,' said Moshe slowly. 'Plenty of people here have had provocation from the boy, myself included. The point is, it's all wrong to give way to that kind of impulse. Doesn't do anyone any good.'

'It did me a lot.'

The reaction to this was another meaning look between the two men. Then David, still scarlet with suppressed anger, took off his glasses and began polishing them.

'What do you think that makes you? There *is* a word for it, you know,' he said in his vibrant voice.

There was a heavy, antagonistic silence. Then Martha said, 'He did it because of the way Shmuel tormented me in class. You'd feel the same if it was your wives.'

'It *was* my wife for a long time,' said Moshe quietly.

'You've undone eight months' work in ten minutes,' said David. He was still looking down at his glasses. I realized it would be useless to describe the incident which had touched off my action. If I'd caught the little horror trying to rape Martha, I'd still be told I ought to have controlled myself.

'Well, now what?' I asked after another long painful silence.

'Are you willing to undertake not to do anything like that again?'

'Good God, no. How can I? You're not willing to undertake to control the activities of that depraved little savage, are you?'

David half-rose to his feet, his fair skin brick-coloured.

'Looks as if you've got a few Victorian impulses yourself,' I remarked.

Moshe said in Hebrew, 'Sit down, take it easy.' Then to me: 'The Committee could easily kick you out for this, you know.'

'It can go ahead,' I said without thinking.

I heard, or rather felt, Martha's reaction at my side. It was little more than an involuntary intake of breath, a tiny contraction of the muscles of her hands. It was enough to draw Moshe's eyes.

'What do you say?' he asked her.

After a long pause she said flatly, 'It's for Aaron to decide.'

'Don't you like it here?' Moshe asked me. The question had a plaintive, almost naïve ring, as if he could scarcely credit that anyone could *not* like it.

'There's plenty of aspects of it I don't like.'

'What, for instance?'

'Well it may be fearfully reactionary of me, but I like privacy. I'd like to be able to shut myself into my room and know that nobody would come knocking on the door to borrow something or ask a question or just settle down to chat. I'd like to be able to raise my voice once in a while, or make love to my wife, without the whole bloody place knowing all about it. I'd like to have a meal at home sometimes that isn't the same thing two hundred other people are eating. And I'd like to be able to take a punch at someone who asks for it without being hauled over the coals and ostracized as if I'd committed sabotage.'

'That's just what you have done!' said David.

Moshe looked at me sadly. 'Looks like you've come to the wrong place altogether,' he said.

Martha suddenly went out of the room. Moshe jerked his head after her.

'*She* wants to stay,' he said. 'You know that, I suppose.'

'*She's* worth having,' said David furiously.

I stood stiffly, staring at them with no expression. I felt armoured and encased in pride. Not even the knowledge of how much it meant to Martha could drag out of me so much as an implied apology.

After a while Moshe, clearly embarrassed and tired of the whole thing, began banging out his pipe again, and said 'We'll just have to put it up to the Committee, then, that's all.'

'Leave to go, sir?' I asked sneeringly.

Moshe sighed heavily and said, 'Try to grow up a bit, mate, why don't you? We're all too busy for that sort of crap.' I felt myself break into a sweat, and turned to leave. As I went through the door Moshe said, 'If you change your mind about the undertaking, the Committee doesn't sit till next week.'

Martha was already in bed, and apparently asleep, when I got back, after a long walk round the less frequented parts of the settlement to calm myself down. But when I woke up in the morning and looked at her, I could see she'd spent a large part of the night crying. I lay on one elbow looking down at her swollen eyelids with a sense of hopelessness, thinking: *It's all too hard. I can't do it. It's too hard.*

My pride held out for three days against Martha's quiet misery. Then I went to Moshe and promised not to lay a finger on Shmuel again providing he kept away from my binyan. Moshe said he thought that was fair enough.

'We don't like to lose people,' he said. 'Maybe we've been working you a bit too hard. It's not easy at first, we all know that.'

A few days later, Shmuel ran amok and attacked a little girl. Fortunately he was caught before he could do too much damage. Within a few hours two Youth Aliyah representatives arrived by car to remove him. That night David came to my binyan. His eyes were bloodshot behind his thick glasses.

'I want to show you something,' he said.

He took me to the infirmary where the little girl was. She was asleep. Her face was white and withdrawn, like the face of a corpse; she had the stillness which comes from heavy sedation. Only one blue eyelid twitched periodically. David lifted the thin sheet and undid the plain nightgown so that I could see the bruises.

'You did that,' he said.

The Committee forgave me. But David didn't, and nor did the rest of the kibbutz, not for a long time.

I was no longer welcome at the evening talk-sessions. I was glad not to go, but the reason shamed me so deeply that I became bitterly resentful. I spent my spare time in the binyan, often alone; Martha's effort to be loyal to me at all costs made my guilt so much worse that I forced her to go out and about as before and behave as if nothing had happened. I read a great deal, and studied Hebrew from the book Martha had bought. The fact that it was so deadly dull, so full of pompous worthiness, seemed perversely satisfying. For my reading I got Martha to borrow some of the paperback classics in which the kibbutz abounded, the sort of books one keeps meaning to get around to and almost never does. Now I sweated them out, first out of a grim desire to inflict a harsh discipline on my mind, and later because they took hold of me and gave me a mental satisfaction I hadn't known since the rigours of tutorial reading at Oxford.

Martha, meanwhile, became more and more immersed in the life of the kibbutz, and drifted farther and farther away from me. I learned the hard lesson that you can live with someone in the closest contact, talk to them, sleep with them, and yet have not even an illusion of true intimacy. Sometimes she made an effort; she would try to communicate her pleasure in some small triumph or personal victory, such as when her class brought her presents on her birthday, or the first time she was able to hold a 'serious' conversation in Hebrew with Essie. But for the most part it was clear that my outburst to Moshe had in some way made it impossible for her to go on confiding her excitement and enthusiasm to me. And it was also true, on my side, that her uncritical delight in everything she did and found on the kibbutz irritated me deeply. She was beating me hands down at what should have been my own game. From the outset she had been part of it, while I, whose need had brought us here, whose Jewishness should have made it easier for me than for her, remained stubbornly and hopelessly aloof; the kibbutzniks' tentative efforts, gradually resumed, to absorb me only served to turn me into a more complete alien. Martha knew this, and as, despite a conflict in loyalties, she became more and more closely identified with the others, I felt an outsider even from her.

Even our lovemaking lost some of its magic. In the past we had delighted in talking about ordinary things before and afterwards, as a contrast to throw the extraordinary sensations of union into relief. Now we talked very little, and the sex-bridge was no longer an effective link across the widening gulf that divided us. More and more often, it seemed, she would resort to the little time-honoured tricks of the unwilling woman – a headache, sleepiness . . . she was very gentle and humorous as she put me off, but this didn't soften the agonizing hurt her rebuffs caused me.

My body was used to the work now, and my eyes to the sun. My muscles no longer ached, nor my system crave more sleep all day. Nor did I feel the same painful self-consciousness about my thin pallid body when I took a shower. I knew that the physical toughness I had sought was growing all the time. But I got no special satisfaction from it. It was just one less thing on the debit side of my life, that was all.

In any case, something had replaced the gnawing muscular aches – something worse; a constant emptiness which I slowly realized was the worst loneliness of my life, a loneliness I hid from myself but which expressed itself irresistibly and insidiously in dreams of the white house on Hampstead Hill, and of Polly, grown plump and kindly like the pictures of my mother, holding me in her arms . . . In these shameful dreams, which made me cringe when I remembered them by day, I was always a little boy, rather sickly and helpless, often lying in the big feather bed in my old room muffled in the huge warm continental quilt, calling for small services – and having my wants instantly attended to by this maternal, satisfying person whom I called Polly . . .

Sometimes in the morning Martha would look at me oddly. I wondered, with an uneasiness bordering on horror, if I ever talked in my sleep.

Chapter Eleven

As November ended the weather became cool, and work, correspondingly, almost a pleasure. The screen windows were covered with glass, and each household was issued with a temperamental but, once bested, quite efficient oil-heater called a *Ptilya*. Summer clothes went back into the communal store, and we drew out instead warm heavy shirts and trousers, sweaters and underwear.

In recent years, kibbutzniks had begun to have their own marked clothes instead of communal ones. As I had brought few more than I stood up in, it was suggested that I might try to get some warm things sent from England. It wasn't until the crate arrived from Bella and I began to unpack the silks and cashmeres, cavalry twills and Donegal tweeds, that I realized I might have saved her the trouble for all the use they'd be to me here.

The sight of my old clothes gave me a strange pang; it was like unpacking the belongings of some dead relative, permeated with unpleasant associations. But Bella had interlarded the layers of clothes with little love-gifts of sweets and cigarettes, tins of coffee and the condensed milk I had loved to eat with a spoon when I was a small boy. She had sent a lot of my books, too. Right in the middle of all the padding, my exploring hands encountered a large, heavy object, which proved to be my portable typewriter.

It gave me a thoroughly nasty jolt – the kick of conscience.

Martha, who was sitting in a corner sorting the books, saw the typewriter as I lifted it out. She flashed me a look so full of meaning that I couldn't meet it; then, without a word, got up and went out on to the porch. I heard the household cupboard open and shut. She came in again carrying a long, thick envelope. At the sight of it I felt a heaviness descending on my spirit, the hopeless weight one feels in the face of an unanswerable challenge.

She drew the foolscap pages out and laid them beside the typewriter. Then she turned and looked at me levelly.

I shook my head. 'Not a hope, darling. Please don't hope. I'll never finish that, it's quite out of the question.'

I expected argument, pleas, but none came. She left the manuscript where it was and went on arranging the books on the floor. After a while she said in a bright, let's-change the-subject-for-the-moment voice, 'Have you heard? We're all getting bookcases soon. It's the next thing. They voted for them at the last meeting.'

I sat on the bed and watched her, remembering how every move she made had once delighted me. Now she seemed somehow less controlled, less graceful. She was squatting on the floor, her slacks drawn tight across her buttocks, her stomach blown out by her recent meal, her knees wide apart. For a moment I saw her as if she were just any woman, having no special meaning for me at all. It was a frightening moment of detachment, born of the weeks of mental separateness. Fear that she might be losing the enchantment, in the literal sense, that she'd always had for me, made me suddenly say more sharply than I'd intended: 'Are you putting on weight? You've got a belly on you like Mother Earth.'

Her hands stopped moving and she looked up at me with a strange kind of curious pain. She began to say something, stopped, and went back to the books.

I felt ashamed, as always after a piece of my periodic blind insensitiveness. The unbidden words that had hurt her couldn't be recalled. But perhaps I could make her forget them . . . Looking round for something to distract her, I saw the pile of clothes lying on the bed.

On impulse I shucked off the battered denims and pranced into a pair of narrow Italian trousers, which clung to my legs and would scarcely fasten over my newly-developed stomach-muscles. Over my sweaty shirt I drew a long, soft pullover which hung on my hips, and filled in the neck with a silk cravat.

'Look, darling!'

She looked. I minced up and down the room, thinking, *She'll laugh. I haven't made her laugh for weeks.*

But she didn't laugh. She stared at me gravely, with an

abstracted frown, as if trying to place me, her hand toying with the corner of the mat.

'Do you miss it all very much?' she asked.

I suddenly felt a fool in the incongruous clothes, and flushed like a man whose best joke has fallen flat. The implied reproach was always there – the harking back to the physical indulgence that I had fought away from. I bitterly resented being reminded of it, the more so since, despite myself, my skin was welcoming the half-forgotten softness, the luxurious smell of quality that rose from the expensive clothes. I looked at the coarse working trousers lying on the tiled floor and felt an instinctive revulsion, not so much from their cheapness as from the fact that they were the same as everyone else's.

But before I could answer, there was a tap on the door and Uri walked in. His eyes lighted on me, and he stopped in his tracks.

'Ying-tong-yiddle-i-po!' he said softly, like a whistle of mockery. 'Get a load of His Lordship!'

Uri had been one of the first to resume friendly relations after the Shmuel episode, and I knew with my reason that he was only sending me up and was not getting at me. But I felt a wave of humiliation go over me, as if the clothes betrayed to him the whole of my past life. As I started to explain, I was aghast to hear myself beginning to stammer, something that hadn't happened to me since adolescence.

'My dear chap, don't apologize! I envy you wholeheartedly. Only wish they were mine. Nothing warmer than a good tweed. Wow, look at this!' He held a suède jacket against himself. 'I say, you chaps, let's mosey down to Pelham Cres. and gate-crash the Hon. Caro's coming-out binge, eh what?' He laughed delightedly at himself. Then he noticed the books, and immediately lost all interest in the jacket, which he dropped on the floor. 'Ullo-ullo! What have we here?' And he levered his long body on to the mat and began to disarrange all the piles again, avid with interest to see what new reading-matter the kibbutz had acquired.

Martha straightened herself slowly, rubbing her back. 'Coffee, Uri? We're having some.'

'You've got some smashers here! What's that? No, no coffee,

dear, I came on business actually.' He became momentarily immersed in *Lord of the Flies* and then wrenched himself back with an obvious effort. 'Two things. First, we're in a hole you can get us out of. We need someone to do a week's guard-duty starting tonight.' He looked up at me.

'It's been years since I handled a sten.'

'Oh hell, that's nothing, you mustn't use it anyway unless they're coming at you in Centurion tanks. It's mainly for show. In any case I'll show you the drill. What do you say?'

'Sure, I'll do it.'

'Thanks, I thought you would.' He hesitated and then went on, 'The other's really David's pigeon, only, er – well, he asked me to ask you. Rumour's got round that you're a scribe.'

I shot a look at Martha, but she was getting out the cups and refused to meet my eye.

'You know Hannukah's coming up. We don't keep these feasts on any religious basis, but the kids expect some kind of festivities, and we thought we'd have a bit of a play. You know, just some nonsense. The Committee wants you to dream something up.'

'You want me to write a play in *Hebrew*?'

'Not if you can't – David'll translate it. We want some parts for the kids themselves in it – and a nice meaty plot – only not too meaty – hell, you know the sort of thing. You can have a free hand.'

'And some free time?'

He looked at me for a moment, and then offered me a cigarette. 'We normally arrange these things in our spare time.'

'If any!'

'You get a hell of a sight more than most,' he said mildly. 'The rest of us are pretty well all on a committee, or we hold some office, or we're responsible for organizing something or other . . . spare time's a fairly rare commodity on a kibbutz.'

'Its very rarity gives it a considerable value.' It wasn't that I wouldn't write their play. I just resented the calm way Uri assumed I'd agree – almost told me I'd be doing it, like an order.

'Value to whom?'

'To me. Does that make me a Fascist?'

'No. It just makes me wonder.' He stood up, absently slipping

Lord of the Flies into his pocket. 'It's making us all wonder. I mean, you've been here nearly three months now. You work hard, yes, but that's only the first essential. What we have to ask ourselves, before we accept you as a candidate for full membership, is – is he good material, on a long-term basis? Will he take his share of responsibility?'

You pompous bloody ass, I thought. I suddenly recognized Uri, I felt I'd known him well for years. Good home, good schools, cricket eleven, debating team. . . . I nearly laughed. He lost all power to disconcert me when I realized that we were equals. His background was precisely like mine.

'Of course,' Uri said, 'nobody *wants* to take on extra work. Only somebody has to do it, so normally we just vote the best man into the job, ignoring his modest protests that he isn't up to it, and wait for him to get on with it.'

'"I want volunteers – you, you and you?"'

He rubbed his nose and grinned. 'That's about it. Well, will you do it or not?'

'I'll go on watch, of course. But not the play.'

'Why not?'

'I'm not up to it,' I said smoothly.

He stopped grinning. 'And supposing we think you are?'

'Think on, comrade. It won't get the play written.'

He looked at me, his well-bred lip beginning to curl in disdain. Utterly unaffected, I smiled back into his cold eyes. I felt my own, my old personality and power flowing back into me again. This was like the battles of wits with Bill, or with anyone from the old life. I was me again, an individual, back on the home-ground of defending my individual rights, and knowing I couldn't lose, not if the whole bloody kibbutz tried to high-pressure me into writing their play for them.

'You know, you're a funny type,' said Uri. He spoke casually, but I could tell he was baffled and annoyed. 'I can't make you out. *You* chose to come here, we didn't invite you. You must have known you'd be expected to do more than put in a few hours' work every day – that's not communal living.'

'If I'm not earning my keep –'

'Oh, you're earning your *keep*.'

'Right, then –'

'Only you're not earning a place here, not a permanent place. Martha, on the other hand –'

He left the sentence unfinished, breaking off abruptly at the look of pain on Martha's face. 'I'll see you at my office in half an hour. Dress warmly.' He started to go out, but I stopped him.

'I think you have my book in your pocket.'

God knows what possessed me. It was simply to prevent his having the last word. I knew perfectly well that everyone shared their books freely – Uri himself had lent me at least a dozen.

He looked at me now for a second in such blank amazement and unbelief that I knew at once I'd put myself totally in the wrong. He reached slowly into his pocket and took the book out, still staring at me as if he couldn't credit his hearing. For a moment he held it, giving me the chance to retract my words. Then he held it out to me.

'I'm *so* sorry,' he said, putting such a wealth of mockery and contempt into his voice that I felt myself break into a sweat under the arms. Not since Polly had I heard such sarcasm, or been so floored by it. He held out the book at arm's length until I was forced to take it from him.

'You needn't bother about tonight,' he said politely. 'I can see you've got a lot of reading to get through. I'll get one of the girls to stand guard. Shalom.'

He turned on his heel and walked out, leaving the screen door to swing to with an eloquent crash. Martha stood rigid, a cup in her hand. In my mouth was the familiar backwash of anger, the sour taste of defeat.

But this time we didn't go silently to bed, and Martha didn't wait to cry until I'd fallen asleep. She flung herself down in such an anguish of tears that I thought she was being ill – her sobs seemed to be retched up from the very depths of her body.

I went and sat on the bed beside her. When I touched her, she twisted herself over on to her back and stared up at me with rage and bewilderment distorting her face.

'Aaron!' she gasped. 'I can't stand much more of this! When are you going to stop? When are you going to grow up?'

'I'm sorry, I lost my temper –'

'I'm *sick* of you and your bloody lost tempers!' she said shrilly, clenching her fists and striking the bed with them. She heaved herself ungracefully up until she was crouched on the bed, her eyes level with mine. 'Why did we come here in the first place?'

'You know why –'

'Yes, I thought I did. I want to hear it from you.'

I said nothing.

'All right, I'll tell you then! We came because you couldn't stand yourself the way you were in England. Yes? You were nothing but a weak-kneed, spineless, gutless appendage to Polly. Her lap-dog, her little puppet. You were Peter Pan incarnate, only with tantrums you couldn't control instead of sweetness and light. You knew it, and you hated yourself, and you realized that only by getting right away from her could you save yourself from being a drivelling weakling for ever.' She stopped and took a breath. Her eyes were red, and every now and then she seemed to choke on her torrent of words. 'So. You decided to come to a place where you'd *have* to look outside yourself, you'd *have* to be disciplined – where hard realities would be more important than what went on in your own mind. You chose Israel so you could forget about being Jewish; you chose a kibbutz so you could soak yourself in hard, satisfying work and learn how to live with other people on equal terms and grow into a real person yourself.' She suddenly thrust her face into mine and shouted harshly 'God damn you, you haven't even *tried*!'

I felt stunned by her violence. After the long weeks of feeling so separated from her, this sudden attack had the impact of a battering-ram.

She got off the bed and began to stride about. The size of the room made it impossible to take more than a few steps before having to turn, and the effect was of a caged animal, at once pathetic and magnificent. The tears were streaming down her face and her breath came in gasps; she beat her fist into her palm to try to ease her anger. I could see it would give her great satisfaction to beat me instead. I almost wished she would.

'Ever since we got here I've waited for you to start contributing something. Not just to the kibbutz. To yourself – to your own transformation, the thing you came here for. At first it seemed enough that you kept yourself on your feet. I could see what the heat and the work and the sense of being shut in were

230

doing to you. Did you think I didn't see? But I knew if once I started sympathizing you'd get sorry for yourself and give up. Then came the Shmuel business, and after all you had the humility to back down and apologize when you saw you were in the wrong, and for my sake, and I thought – I hoped it was a good sign. But instead of taking it as a victory, you chose to think of it as another defeat. You retired into your shell. Even when you'd proved to yourself that you were well up to the physical side of the life, you didn't go on to the next stage – the real battle to turn yourself into a –'

She suddenly stopped. All the angry energy seemed to drain out of her.

'Into a what?' I asked under my breath.

'Into a man.'

She stood still with her arms limp, looking at nothing, and then said with sudden terrible tiredness, 'I don't want to go on talking about it. Oh dear,' she said on a rising note, with new tears coming, of a different sort, 'I wish there was just somewhere I could go to now and shut the door . . .'

'I'll get out,' I muttered. It was an effort because, in a sudden sickening ferment of self-hatred, I wanted to hear it all, every lacerating word of it. 'It isn't that I don't want to change . . .' I began, but she just stood there with her head drooping as if she were too exhausted to move. I went out without touching her.

Hadara was standing out on her porch, still as a statue in the dusk. She beckoned me over. The flashing realization that she'd heard everything – probably the part with Uri as well – should have seemed more important than it did. I could only think of Martha. Hadara took me into her room and made me sit down.

'Will you listen to some straight advice?'

I nodded, putting my face in my hands.

'No–leave Martha alone. Go and find Uri –' I raised my head sharply, but she gestured me to shut up. 'Go and find Uri, and *crawl*. Beg him to let you stand guard. Apologize to him – tell him you'll write his play for him. Tell him you know what an ill-tempered bastard you are. I'll bet you ten to one he promptly tells you he's a worse one.' She put her hand on my shoulder and smiled at me kindly. 'As it happens you'll both be liars. But you've got to make a start in the right direction soon or you'll

231

leave here a failure, and something tells me you won't survive that. Here, have a drink before you go.' She poured me a stiff brandy which I drank. 'And when you get back from watch at 4 a.m.,' she added, as I got slowly to my feet to go, 'wake Martha up and ask her if she's got anything to tell you.'

Chapter Twelve

That first week of guard-duty was a turning-point. To begin with, I liked the job. The long, peaceful watch in the cool darkness, the sense of doing something at once useful and (in theory, at least) dangerous, the fact of being alone without any anti-social stigma – all these aspects made the long nights a pleasure. They gave me a chance to be quiet, to think and to sort myself out.

My days were free. I used the first three to write the play, and when Moshe read it he was delighted.

'In Ivrit, too! Bloody good for you, mate. We'll do you proud, don't you worry. Be worthy of a West End run by the time we've done with it.'

'Never thought you had it in you,' said Edna. 'Must be the prospect of fatherhood. It did wonders for Moshe.'

It was obvious the kibbutzniks had decided to give me another chance. They were a very good-hearted bunch, straightforward in their reactions and, at bottom, ready to give one the benefit of every doubt, even if they weren't always specially tactful. It occurred to me that the coming baby might well have helped them see me in a more favourable light. Children were undoubtedly the kibbutz's most important product; the rest of the world may love a lover, but the kibbutz loves nothing so much as a pregnant woman.

My own feelings on the subject were confused. My first reaction was chagrin at being the last to find out about it – the baby, due in six months, must have been conceived on the night we arrived. I felt Martha's unwillingness to tell me was all part of the shutting-out process which had come to a head with Uri's visit.

However, that was now over. The relief was acute. For the first time I realized that it was my love for Martha, more than hers for me, that really mattered to my self-respect. I needed to

233

know that I was capable of loving like that, so fully and whole-heartedly. And I did love her again. The feeling of detachment, almost of dislike, had been only passing; the resumption of her confidence brought an almost unbearable return of love.

I wanted the baby; I was genuinely happy about it, when I could make myself believe in it. Our acts of love had always seemed so complete in themselves, it was hard to realize that they were only a beginning.

After the week on *shmira* I went back to day work. Either by accident or because he'd realized I liked working alone, Uri put me to shepherding. There was a lot more to it than I'd imagined, but I worked hard, and after a period under supervision they let me go out alone on Rifka, a laconic old grey mare who knew so much about herding sheep that I couldn't have had a better teacher.

Now that my Hebrew was better I began to make friends of my own. I liked the circle Martha had formed round herself, largely of our earliest acquaintances on the kibbutz, but I soon found others with whom I had more in common. There was Yigal, a Hungarian painter, who had a studio in one of the deserted *tsrifim* and got one day off work a week to paint. He, too, liked to be alone – so much so that he was that freak of freaks by kibbutz standards, a bachelor. I liked his work and recognized a strong Chagall influence in it, which pleased him and made him willing to discuss art with me. I could sense that he was starving for the cultural life which only a big city provides, and he made me describe, in halting Hebrew, my impressions of the last galleries and exhibitions I'd visited before leaving London.

Then there was Wilfred. Wilfred he was born and Wilfred he remained, throughout all the idealistic name-changing; it was unnecessary, he declared, to change one's good Yorkshire name for something with a hawk and a spit in it in order to prove oneself a Zionist. His political philosophy seemed to me to be based on a paradox. He was an ardent Socialist, and so automatically obeyed the will of the majority, but he reserved the right to believe that the majority were fools who could invariably be counted on to arrive at the wrong decision. He was for ever pressing for reforms, like allowing children to sleep at their parents' homes, yet when outraged left-wingers called him a reactionary heretic, he was furious. Moshe used to conclude ferocious arguments with Wilfred on this and kindred subjects by repeatedly slapping his bare knees in agitation and shouting, '*Tov*, good, fine, vote for it then, let's call a committee meeting and you can vote for it – but *by God* if we ever have it here, all I can say is it's the end of the kibbutz movement and I shall leave and become a bloody *rov*!'

However, nobody really held his eccentric ideas against Wilf, and although Edna especially moved heaven and earth to get Yigal married, his unorthodoxies, too, were tolerated. We all lived too close together not to make allowances for each other, and I, once I began to show willing, came under the same benign régime.

All in all I began, first to resign myself, then to accept, and finally to enjoy the life – up to a point. But I was still a foreigner, even if I was the only one who knew it.

When the rabbi made his bi-annual appearance to 'regularize' any liaisons which had cropped up since his last visit, he flatly refused to marry Martha and me.

'*Y-efshah!*' he exclaimed, tugging his beard in horror. 'Impossible. Marry a Jewish boy to a *shiksa*? You can ask such a thing of me? Out of the question.' And he turned his rusty black back on us with finality.

I expected Martha to be very upset, especially with the baby coming; her conventionality had been deeply ingrained. But although Moshe's triumphant fury knew no bounds, Martha was philosophical. Perhaps it was the rabbi himself, a scruffy little man wearing a dusty trilby and a torn sweater under his ancient coat; I must say I felt his services wouldn't have meant much.

We watched three other couples being 'done' *en masse*. There was a great deal of scuffling and suppressed giggles. One of the boys, obviously quite unversed in the form, didn't know what was happening when his bride was led round him seven times, and started to turn round after her, which nearly broke up the ceremony. When the moment arrived to smash the glasses, I wondered where these had come from, as I hadn't seen a real, non-plastic glass since coming to the kibbutz. The paper bags containing them, however, when dropped, made a most satisfactory crash, and it wasn't till afterwards that Martha told me they contained spent light-bulbs.

'So it wouldn't have been a proper wedding anyway,' she said, with what seemed to me the height of feminine obscurity.

The kibbutz gave us a 'wedding' after their own fashion, and that, Martha said, made her feel as married as she ever would.

Hannukkah came, and with it tremendous festivities. My play was staged on top of a huge old Arab well, all that remained of the village which had once stood on the kibbutz site. I went in a spirit of indulgence, expecting rank amateurism; but before it was over I was forced to realize that the play, dashed off as it had been, was barely good enough for the staging and performance it was given. It was a great success, and I felt rather dazed by the wholehearted applause.

At the party afterwards, toasts were drunk in sweet Carmel hock, and *horas* by the dozen danced to the music of an old-fashioned accordion, a tambourine and several drums. I entered the *hora* circles reluctantly, at the others' insistence, feeling self-conscious and clumsy in my ignorance of the steps; but the rhythm and the vivid, melancholy tunes were infectious. As I danced round and round, in a sort of trance induced by dizziness and the throbbing drums, my lingering pleasure at the success of the little play seemed to dissolve backwards into a sudden acute memory of that other evening, when the applause, to my ears, had been tinged with contempt or bewilderment, the laughter ambiguous, and my own emotions numbed by guilt. Tonight I'd seen in microcosm what that other night might have been if only I'd written a real play instead of a three-act insult. For the first time in months, I remembered that I had a skill, and that I was letting it rust.

We left the party early because Martha was tired. After she'd fallen asleep, I got up and read my unfinished novel through. I felt completely detached from it. It gave me the same uncanny feeling one might get from looking at an old photograph which no longer bears any resemblance to one's face in the mirror. I had wanted to alter myself, but this proof of how much I had changed was disturbing. I felt I could never finish it. It would be broken-backed, as if two different people had written it.

When I'd finished reading, I felt bewildered and depressed, and decided to get out of the stuffy little box and walk the devil out of myself. The party was still going on on the central green, though most of the older *chaverim* had gone to bed hours ago. I could hear the singing and laughter, and I stood for a moment on our porch, listening, sensing the deep content of the people around me both awake and asleep. I envied it, and wished with my whole mind that I could share it totally. Could it be done, without sacrificing some essential part of oneself, one's individuality and freedom? Or would I, for one, be better without that part – that ego – which I had always clung to in the belief that it was the *sine qua non* of responsible living? Not that I was exactly an expert on that subject.

I strolled down the hill towards the sheep-fold. There was an old ewe on the verge of lambing and I thought I'd have a look at her. I had no great affection for my charges, with their maddening, motiveless behaviour and almost total lack of personality, but I'd begun to know them, and felt secretly happy when a few, less stupid than the rest, stopped fleeing from me in indiscriminate terror and sometimes even pressed their curved bony faces against me.

When I reached the shed, though, I decided not to go in. In another hour, at 4 o'clock it would be time to start milking them, and there was no sense in disturbing them until then. I decided instead to go across to the stables and pass the time with Rifka.

But as I turned away from the sheep-fold, I heard something.

It was little more than a subtle change in the sounds made by the drowsy sheep, an intensification of the rustlings and patterings, as if the herd was beginning to stir and get up. Perhaps they'd actually recognized my step! Feeling mildly gratified, I took out my key to open the door. But to my surprise it wasn't locked.

Inside, the first thing I noticed was that the whole herd was on its feet, many of them beginning to trot round in uneasy circles uttering low bleats. I wondered what had made them restless, and as I walked in from the open door I felt a sudden instinctive twinge of fear. Then I heard something move behind me.

I swung round, just in time to see a robed figure flitting out like a ghost, outlined for a second against the pale whitewashed wall of the stable opposite.

My first thought was a curse that I wasn't on guard, and armed. I had done this round a score of times with my sten under my arm, and found nothing. But as I rushed outside, and saw the figure, bent double, darting from one building to another in an effort to keep cover, I felt relieved that I had no gun. I might so easily have shot without thinking, simply because the target presented itself.

I shouted '*Atzor!* Halt!' The Arab instinctively stopped for a moment, his body frozen into a grotesque statue of flight, then just as instinctively ran on.

I chased him beyond the barns to the perimeter of the kibbutz, expecting to nab him at the fence; but as he got to it, only twenty yards ahead of me, he seemed to melt through the place where it should have been, like a ghost passing through a solid wall, and almost at once disappeared into the dark shadow at the foot of a sand-hill.

When I reached the fence I saw that the wire had been cut and the ends dragged apart, leaving a wide gap between the fence-posts – wide enough, I realized, to drive sheep through. The second fence had had the same treatment. He must have done this in advance, as a preparation for stealing the herd while the party kept us busy. Moshe had told me that marauders usually chose feast-nights when the guard was at a minimum. By the time I reached the foot of the hill, I'd already seen his hunched, flapping figure hump itself over the crest against the stars, and when I got to the top, he'd gone.

I walked back with my heart beating heavily. I was excited, relieved and disappointed at once. I regretted that I hadn't collared the intruder, and was not now dragging him back in triumph to Moshe. On the other hand . . .

I'd never given much thought to the people who'd once lived here. I only knew they'd fled without firing a shot. Perhaps the would-be sheep-stealer from Gaza was one of them? I knew he was much more likely to have been a *fedayeen*, one of Nasser's paid thugs . . . but in that case, would he not have had a weapon?

Of course I never admitted to the others that I was not altogether sorry I hadn't caught him. But I told Martha, and she understood.

After that I was one of them, as far as they were concerned, and if I still didn't feel completely absorbed it was not their fault. Martha's tranquil gaiety no longer made me feel irritated and shut out. On the contrary it pleased me because it showed that at any rate I'd done the right thing in bringing *her* to Beit Hashoresh. Her contentment often seemed the only really important and creditable thing in my life, which otherwise continued to have an odd flavour of unreality, of impermanence.

But I was far from unhappy. I had proved to myself at least some of the things I had needed to prove. And I was safe. No one had come to dig me out or drag me back, and now I belonged here, at least nominally. Eventually – perhaps after the child was born – I hoped to feel my roots going down, instead of just clinging to the surface for day-to-day sustenance as they were now.

Chapter Thirteen

The short, mild winter ended, and the land was suddenly smothered in growth. Even the mean-spirited sand showed its advantages – the rain drained quickly and gave way to flowers. The weather was perfectly balanced between the damp chill of winter and the unremitting blast of summer, which we had yet to prove we could take.

In the meantime Martha and I asked if we could have a week's leave at Passover to see a bit of the country before summer and parenthood curtailed our movements. The Committee gave it to us, the more readily because I had recently 'come into money' from which the kibbutz could pay for the trip and still show a profit.

The money came from Jo, to whom, after consulting Martha, I had written. I knew from the *Observer*'s Quick Theatre Guide that *Man in a Hole* was still running, and I saw no reason why the royalties should sit rotting. So I sent Jo Power of Attorney, and in a remarkably short time she had managed to get sent to me through my bank a sum which really rocked me. It rocked the Committee, too, when, after a certain inner struggle, I handed it over to them.

'Christ!' said Moshe, with a reverence quite unconnected with the Deity. 'We've got a bloody capitalist in our midst.'

Of course in a community where nobody even thinks of minding their own business, some explanation had to be given for this sudden wealth. I let it be thought I'd inherited it from a defunct aunt. The small deception gave me a secret thrill; I felt like an escaped prisoner who at long last begins to feel safe and free, securely hidden in his double life.

Our week's leave was undoubtedly the happiest time of my whole life. We spent it chiefly in acute discomfort, jolted by wild driving over bad roads, scrambling up stony tracks towards countless views, listening to a dozen guides discoursing on every aspect of the country's history, from Christ's miracles to Preminger's, and sleeping in a variety of unaccommodating beds. But we did it all with a mutuality of reaction which was the antidote to all irritation. We seemed to be in such complete accord that this in itself became a source of laughter. We looked at the natural beauties and the new developments with all the pride of ownership, and grew furious together at such blots on 'our' landscape as the omnipresent litter, the American tourists in all their horrid glory come to inspect and criticize the application of their dollars, and the shoddy souvenir shops which had mushroomed to make the most of them. We found places where we wanted to buy a house and live for ever, and places we couldn't wait to get out of. They were always the same places for both of us.

'O let's ask how much it would cost to have a studio here!' Martha begged in the artists' quarter in Safed, after we had explored the narrow cobbled passageways and picture-hung courtyards. We asked; we chose the very one we would buy, its court on three levels linked by low archways and short flights of steps, with geraniums cascading from cracks in its whitewashed walls. Standing on the top level you could look over the wall across the whole glorious panoramic valley.

'Shall we have it?' she asked, her eyes sparkling.

'Of course,' I said seriously. 'It's settled. I'll send the deposit tomorrow.'

We went back to the bus and on to the next place.

'You wouldn't really want to, would you?' she asked me that night in bed. It was eight hours since the studio in Safed had been mentioned, but I knew at once what she meant, and said, 'No, not really.'

She made a little contented sound and curled up against me.

We finished up with a day and a half in Jerusalem, staying at a fearfully Kosher *pension* filled with quiet, pious couples and their hoards of unspeakable children.

'Why doesn't somebody stop them?' moaned Martha at eight o'clock on Shabbos morning, when the racket which had awakened us had risen to a deafening crescendo. 'What are they *doing*, anyway? Wrecking the building?'

What they were doing was racing up and down the stairs,

241

screaming in unison and slamming every door they passed. The row had long since drowned out the gentle, mosquito-like humming their devout fathers were making in the little *schule* next door. Their mothers, plainly, had neither the desire nor the ability to exercise the smallest control. Suddenly our bedroom door burst open and three little boys fell in, skullcaps askew, sidecurls flying. I rose in my wrath. The two slowest left howling and clutching their behinds.

Martha, who had watched with deep satisfaction, now mimicked David's shocked tones. 'Don't you realize that force proves nothing except that you have no other argument? That it's an anachronism left over from an age of brutality? That it sets up an unconscious hatred of authority?'

I said a short, rude word and climbed back into bed.

'Quite,' said Martha primly.

We lay in an aura of pleasant accord in the last of the short silence won by my bestial act. I picked up a week-old *Observer* from the floor and began browsing.

'Our child,' said Martha, 'will be born an Israeli. It will nevertheless be blessed with an English upbringing.'

'What, on a kibbutz?' I asked abstractedly, deep in the book reviews. 'Just try clipping its bottom once in a while. You'll have every woman in the place down on your neck.'

'I'll revolutionize the system,' she said.

But I'd stopped listening.

There are few things more startling, and in my circumstances more appalling, then carelessly turning a page in a newspaper and coming face to face with a photograph of oneself.

For half a second I stared stupidly at it, wondering why it looked so familiar. It was an old one taken at Oxford, showing me in rowing shorts, grinning like a greyhound and looking pleased with myself – the result of somebody's talentless enthusiasm for candid camera shots. A cold shock ran over me as my subconscious recognized it before I did.

I read the column it was attached to with my mind so numbed by apprehension that I could scarcely take the words in. It was a piece about freak runs in the London theatre. The writer had set out to prove that inertia was a strong factor in the success of certain plays. He cited various thrillers and farces which became standard fixtures, running on and on, not through merit, but from the weight of the years behind them. Another category, he went on, included plays which were somehow given an initial push – some publicity stunt, or a striking review which made it a conversational necessity to have seen them – and kept gathering speed from their own momentum.

Man in a Hole was one of these. 'It opened six months ago at an outer London theatre. A fracas on the first night, and the subsequent brou-ha-ha over the disappearance of its author, gave it a spurious attraction which set its success in train.' For anyone the least bit interested, the writer added, the author was still more or less missing – he was believed to be living abroad, 'on the profits'.

I let the paper fall off the bed and stared out of the window. All round the *pension* grew tall pines, closing the place in like a ring of watchmen standing shoulder to shoulder. Martha had said what a pity, because they cut off what would otherwise have been a beautiful view across the valley to the new Hebrew University; I agreed, but secretly I loved the protected feeling, just as I had begun, lately, to be glad of the double row of barbed wire that enclosed Beit Hashoresh. Now, as the panic of imminent discovery crept over my skin in a cold white tide, I remembered, ludicrously, the words of the old song:

Close the door! They're coming through the window!
Close the window! They're coming through the floor . . .

Everything seemed suddenly full of cracks, through which tell-tale information could infiltrate like poisonous gas, and security leak out. At least three copies of the *Observer*, airmailed by relatives, reached the kibbutz each week, and were read and re-read from cover to cover until they were falling to bits. Somebody had already remarked that my name was the same as the author of *Man in a Hole*, the original notice of which they had all read. It was one chance in a million that nobody would recognize me from the photograph.

Martha was still lying with her arms behind her head, soliloquizing happily about our child's future. For a moment I had the wild urge to tell her we wouldn't be going back to the kibbutz, ever, that we were going instead to Safed, or Haifa, or

Tel Aviv, to start again our search for anonymity. I thought of the jostling same-faced crowds in Dizengoff Street, and the thousands of little lighted balconies, each a world of its own, a private, cell-like, inviolable world where people lived unknown to their neighbours in the way of city-dwellers. There we could get lost, uninvolved in anyone else's life, responsible only for ourselves – under a new name perhaps, faceless except to each other, self-contained, anonymous, safe . . .

Safe from what? From Polly? I no longer feared her. When I thought of her now it was tolerantly, almost with affection – after all, she'd only done what she thought was best for me. No. What I was afraid of was that if the wall of secrecy, of violent change, between my life in London and my life here, were to be broken, if the two lives began to mingle, I would lose all I'd gained, would become somehow a disintegrated mixture of the two people I had been. Only it wasn't as simple as that. At the back of my mind lurked a deeper fear, one I would hardly acknowledge to myself, a fear that if some echo from the past interfered with my resolute forward-looking, I might be dragged backwards like a pin to a magnet – to what, I wasn't sure. When I thought of it, it was like thinking of suffocating in some hot, dark hole. Hateful, sickening – and yet somehow, obscenely, desirable. I seemed to have experienced something similar in dreams which were too obscure to remember clearly.

I knew I should tell Martha about the article, warn her. But when I looked at her, so serene and hopeful and loving me again with a new pride and trust, I couldn't do it. I couldn't bring myself to remind her. There was always that million-to-one chance that no one would spot it.

All the way back on the bus Martha chatted happily. She was longing to get home, and her conversation was as full of excitement and speculation as if we'd been away for months.

'Nothing will have changed,' I said, as if by saying it I could make it true.

Beit Hashoresh looked very attractive on its hill as the bus brought us into sight of it. The cypresses stood tall, rolling a little like sailors in the soft evening breeze. The low buildings, glowing in the late sun, had a look of permanence and security.

As we passed through the kibbutz lands, so neatly tilled and husbanded, I felt a sudden surge of confidence, even pride, that fruit-bearing trees had been coaxed out of that unyielding yellow sand.

'I thought you said nothing would have changed!' Martha said triumphantly. 'Will you look how those orange-trees have come on!'

'It's wonderful,' I answered. I used the hackneyed word, for once, in its true sense. I felt, for a rarefied moment, filled with wonder at the sight of those masses of shiny dark leaves burgeoning up from roots which gained a living where nothing had grown before. The miracle had become commonplace through too-close acquaintance, but after the separation it suddenly reassumed its deep importance. The feelings of awe, consolation and stability I had had in London about my Bar Mitzvah trees returned now, only with greater validity, having their roots in real life and personal effort.

'Glad to be back?' Martha asked me. She'd been watching my face.

I pressed her hand hard against my thigh.

We slipped through a hedge and direct to our binyan, bypassing the centre of the kibbutz. Someone – Hadara, probably – had swept our porch and put some early roses into a big stone vase. Apart from that, everything was as we'd left it. All our familiar bits and pieces – the painting Yigal had given us for a wedding present, the porcupine-quill platter we'd inherited, a clay ashtray Essie had made for us in her *gan* – seemed to welcome us. I leaned against the door and took it all in, watching with a sense of almost unbearable well-being as Martha bustled about, unpacking and setting things to rights.

'You're all right, darling, are you? Not too tired?' I asked, overwhelmed with a tenderness I could scarcely contain.

'I'm feeling marvellous. Go and fill the kettle and let's have a cuppa.'

I wandered along to the tap, passing our Brazilian neighbours, who welcomed me back and asked about our trip. I looked at their dark heads and sturdy smiling faces and wondered how I had ever thought them ugly. As I stood savouring the good solid sound of the kettle being filled, Hadara's sons came tearing round the corner, stopped dead at the sight of me, then hurled themselves on to me with shouts of glee. Beyond them, I could hear the faint evening sounds of conversation and laughter that pervaded the place, and quite suddenly I felt an onrush of such strong emotion that my chest tightened with a desire to weep. I stood holding the kettle, letting the water overflow into the lush grass, and the thought came to me quite distinctly that this was, after all, my place, and that if I had to die for it, I would.

The sense of being powerfully possessed was alarming and uncomfortable, and I pushed it quickly aside, hurrying rather shamefacedly back to Martha's brisk and practical presence. She had just unpacked a paintbox and a packet of coloured Plasticine.

'I've just remembered, it's Essie's birthday today. Never mind tea, let's go and see her and give her our offerings.'

We met Edna half-way. She did a lumbering sort of dervish dance when she saw us.

'Thank God you're back! Essie's just beginning to get offended.'

Essie seemed far too occupied with being the centre of attention to worry about us. She accepted our gifts as royalty accepts its due. Moshe stood back on his heels, his pipe stuck straight forward as if for balance, and beamed on her as if he'd built her with his own hands. It all had a comfortable, home-like feel.

'Can't I stay for the party?' Essie suddenly asked.

'You've got your own party to go to,' said Edna, quite sharply for her.

'What party's this?'

'They always have a do for the whole *kitta* when there's a birthday.'

'Aaron meant, the other party,' said Essie slyly.

Edna said in English, 'Little devil's given the game away. It's nothing really, just a few people dropping in after supper to welcome you back. *Meant* as a surprise,' she added in Hebrew, pinching Essie.

Essie instantly broke into a game she and Edna often played, in which she pretended to be terrified of her mother, and fled from her, shrieking. They circled the lawn and rushed in and out of the house with Edna shouting dire threats and waving her fist. Suddenly Essie, for whom the game, as always, was beginning to be real enough to frighten her deliciously, rushed at me screaming 'Save me! Save me!' and leapt up on me like a monkey, clinging with her legs and arms and burying her face in my neck. I could feel the excited, half-fearful trembling of her warm sharp-cornered little body. I looked over the blonde head at Martha, who looked back at me over her pregnancy. We experienced a mutual flash of understanding, each sharing the sudden, vivid anticipation of the other. I hugged Essie till she squeaked. Happiness surged through me, ousting all self-doubt.

I think that was the last really happy moment I remember.

We returned to Moshe's binyan after supper, bringing coffee and sweets and various other luxuries imported from 'outside'. The walls were now draped with left-over *Pesach* decorations Yigal had painted – a huge bright poster depicting Moses leading the Children of Israel out of Egypt, and another illustrating the Twelve Tribes. I stopped in the doorway to admire them, even while the unnatural atmosphere in the room was raising every hackle on my neck in nameless anticipation.

'How pretty!' Martha exclaimed, and then noticed how her voice rang out in the silence although the room was full of people. They were all looking at us with a strange, almost shy self-consciousness, which could not be accounted for by the normal welcome-home atmosphere.

'Here comes the dark horse of Beit Hashoresh!' said Moshe jovially.

Stupid of me to have relaxed. Insane to have let myself believe for a moment they hadn't found out. I felt myself drowning slowly under the tide of their cheerful wisecracks and congratulations. They gathered round, pounding me on the back, grinning, making good-natured jokes. Moshe kept talking about 'the modest celebrity in our midst'. Martha was half-laughing, bewildered, asking how they had found out . . . she was taken off-balance, too. I wished I'd warned her, so that it wouldn't have been such a shock. But then slowly I saw that it was not a shock to her, only a surprise, that she was accepting the congratulations on behalf of a man she'd forgotten, this Aaron Franks they were all chatting and asking about. I felt the loneliness sweep over me again, like the loathsome prelude to a recurrent disease.

Edna pushed through the crush, handing out cake and wine. There seemed to be a score of people jammed together in the small space, and the noise and laughter were attracting still more. Every few minutes the door would be forced open, there would be cries of 'Shalom, shalom! Come in! Have a drink!' and more back-poundings and jokes and questions . . .

'Renouncing fame and riches for the simple life, eh? You're a right old William Morris after all, then!'

'Or else he's a right old lunatic. So that's where all your lolly came from, eh? Rich auntie flaking out, indeed! Talk about ill-gotten gains –'

'Why'd you chuck it up, lad? Surely not just for (sob) our sakes?'

'Course he didn't. Must have been the critics. *Statesman* didn't reckon much to it, as I recall –'

'That's it, he's no hero at all really, just another lacerated ego fleeing the Tynan scourge –'

'We didn't know we had such a modest celebrity in our midst –'

I kept forcing on myself the words 'They mean well. They mean well,' like a charm to keep the destroyer at bay. But they were pressing too close, pushing and staring, their faces were becoming masklike and inane like the faces round a fatal accident, or an animal in its cage. I began to feel I couldn't get my breath, that I was literally going to suffocate. Sweat was running down my face, and Martha was nowhere, she'd been swallowed by the crowd, waving lightly to me over their heads . . . Suddenly I could think of no one but Polly. Her image, dimmed by distance and long months of rigorous mental rejection, danced before my mind's eye. I found myself thinking about her almost with longing, as a man might about the prison cell from which he's escaped after many years, only to find himself incapable of coping with freedom.

All this time I was standing quite still, a fixed smile like a grimace on my mouth, holding the plastic glass in one hand, the sticky yellow cake in the other, fighting a losing battle against the black rage that was claiming me again, irresistibly. It was welling up like blood from a badly-healed internal wound. I fought, knowing that, if I lost, I would lose everything, that I would be back where I had started. But what they were doing was monstrous. They were cheerfully stripping me of my obscurity and bringing me face to face with the thing I had run from, against which I had built up, slowly and painfully, a whole new life and personality.

The Twelve Tribes were dancing now, jigging up and down above the heads of the crowd, through a stinging mist. It was so long since I'd been drunk that I didn't recognize the symptoms. I only felt aware of a dangerous distortion of vision and feeling. I tried to get out and couldn't – I was hemmed in. Panic seized me. Panic and blind fury.

'What about a speech from the modest celebrity in our midst?'

I swung round suddenly, my elbows out to scythe a little space for breathing in. Moshe grunted and doubled up, his pipe dropping on to the floor.

'Here, watch out! You nearly did me an injury!' And he aimed a friendly punch at my shoulder before ducking to retrieve his pipe. But someone jostled him, and the punch, innocently meant, struck my nose.

It hurt, it hurt incredibly. It outraged me. In my drunken vulnerable state I hated him. The hate built up in me like an approaching orgasm, ending in a flushing sense of climax and release as I lashed out.

Moshe caught my blow on the side of his head as he straightened up, and staggered back with a look of blank amazement on his face. Instantly I was sober. The sting in my knuckles, the sudden horrified silence, brought me back to normality. Moshe sprawled on the floor between people's feet; his pipe had snapped. Somebody helped him up and he stood looking at me, absently jiggling the two pieces of the pipe in his hand. There wasn't another sound in the room.

I knew everything was over. Instead of minding, I felt nothing but a defiant joy. I was able to pretend to myself that I had *decided* to hit Moshe, as an act of nonconformity, of protest. I must still have been a little drunk, because I remember thinking, without any sense of self-delusion, that I'd done it for Martha. It seemed quite logical and honest. They had taken her; I had fought to get her back. It was, in that moment, a simple, satisfactory justification. Only the slow, hollow, ugly sound of her being violently sick across the room gave me an inkling of the indefensible reality.

Chapter Fourteen

'Well – what do you think of it?'

Martha looked round the room. As cheap flats in Tel Aviv go, it wasn't bad, as I knew after a fortnight's flat-footing round; but her eyes were dull with indifference.

'It's fine.'

She spoke with a shrug in her voice. It was the same shrug that had been in her whole body and manner for two weeks.

'Come through into the bedroom.'

She followed me obediently. The bedroom really was quite nice, with rugs on the tiled floor by the bed and plenty of cupboard space. A small room for the baby led off it. There was a balcony, too, from which, by leaning dangerously over the edge to one side, you could just see the sea.

I showed her this, going through contortions in an effort to get a smile out of her. But she only stared out across the acres of white blocks and hardly seemed to notice me.

'My new employer swore you could see the sea – can't sue him, I suppose. Though I don't know how he'd know – he's so fat he'd roll off like a ball if he tried to lean over.'

She nodded absently, as if I'd made a perfectly serious comment, and went back into the bedroom, where she sat down on the bed. Recently she always seemed to sit down whenever she could. She was now seven months pregnant and it was only natural that she should often be tired, but just the same her air of perpetual exhaustion worried me like a reproach.

'It's better than that bloody little hotel, anyway,' I went on, as if she were arguing. 'At least it's ours.' I kept hearing a note of desperation in my voice when I talked to her. Our conversations were nearly all one-sided. She wasn't 'not speaking' to me or anything of that sort; it was more as if she was too listless to talk.

'It's fine,' she said again.

She sat there with her hands curled in her lap and her head bent. The gnawing anxiety and guilt I had felt since our disastrous last night at Beit Hashoresh renewed itself sharply whenever I saw her doing nothing. In all the time I'd known her, I'd never seen her anything but active and vital, her hands always busy, her face vivid with some lively emotion. Now she was like a peasant wife, speaking when I asked her a direct question, doing what I told her, unable to take the initiative in anything. Her passivity nearly drove me crazy sometimes; but there was nothing I dared say or do for fear of provoking the punishment of recriminations which I deserved so richly but as yet hadn't had. Sometimes I wished she would say it all, shout, rave, get it over with – anything seemed preferable to this terrible washed-out emptiness. But I still felt so bruised from my own failure that I couldn't bear to risk her anger.

'Why don't you lie down for a while, and I'll make some tea?' I suggested. She looked at me blankly for a moment as if the words took time to register, and then shook herself slightly and stood up.

'No, I'll make it.'

'Better let me, and you unpack. You know where you want to put things.'

I didn't press her to rest. It reassured me when she was busy, though I knew it was a false reassurance. We worked with a wall between us. Even the sounds of her movements were subtly different; they were muted, lacking in briskness. Sometimes she seemed to run down altogether, and I could imagine her in that slumped position on the bed, head bent, hands curled and idle.

We had tea in the unlived-in living-room. Irresistibly I remembered that within ten minutes of our arrival at the kibbutz Martha had begun to make the binyan her home. Now she had apparently unpacked only the utilitarian essentials. A perverse desire to confirm this made me ask: 'Where are you going to hang Yigal's picture? I thought over the desk.'

She said after a moment, 'Did you bring it?'

'Didn't you?'

'No.'

'What about the quill platter and our other things?'

'I suppose they're still – on the porch.'

I thought of the long evening ahead before we could decently end this misery of non-communication in sleep. We had spent fourteen such evenings in Tel Aviv. I had thought there would be so much to do after moving into our own flat that this evening, at least, would be less silent and terrible than the others; but somehow everything was already done, the few clothes put away, the suitcases stowed under the bed . . . we might merely have changed hotels.

'We're likely to be here for some time, you know,' I said, following up this thought. But neither of us could make it seem real that we were starting again in this strange white block of cells. Martha gave a little shiver and did not answer.

'Would you like to go out for a bit this evening? Have dinner somewhere?'

'If you like.'

'Actually, we'll have to go out. We've got no food in.'

'It doesn't matter. I'm not hungry.'

It was the simple truth – she wasn't trying to punish me. She wasn't hungry. She had lost all her appetites, all zest for living.

I had meant to avoid Dizengoff Street, but somehow we gravitated towards it as towards a magnetic centre. We found ourselves helplessly drawn to the same garish café, even the same table, where we had sat six months ago while waiting, with such hope and trepidation, for our 'posting' to a kibbutz.

'It's stupid to come here, they don't even serve meals,' I heard myself objecting.

'I'm not hungry.'

'Well, I am.'

But we didn't move. We sat in silence and drank coffee; I had two brandies. We kept turning our heads as people passed in front of us, backwards and forwards drearily as if we were hypnotized. I wondered if she was as unhappy as I was, or if she was really as numb as she seemed.

The futile desire to re-establish contact forced me, against my will, to keep making conversation.

'You haven't asked me about the job.'

Reluctantly she stopped watching the passers-by and turned to me with an attempt to show interest.

'It's definite, then?'

'Yes. Not bad, either. Four hundred and eighty pounds a month – that's about sixty English pounds.'

She was still looking at me. 'Do you still do that?' she asked curiously.

'Do what?'

'Change Israeli money back into English.'

I felt an unreasonable confusion. It was as if she were accusing me of treachery. 'We haven't handled money for so long –'

'We handled it on our holiday.'

The holiday, with its happiness and intimacy so recently lost, was too painful to think about. I wondered that she could mention it. I always marvel how people can maintain that happy memories are a comfort in times of misery.

'Anyway,' I said lamely, 'I start on Monday.'

She didn't ask any more questions.

Moshe had offered to give me back my money intact. Of course I'd refused, so we'd arrived in Tel Aviv with barely enough to keep us for a few days. Fortunately a small royalty cheque had been waiting for me in the bank. But obviously the play wouldn't run for ever, and it had been necessary to get work – not only for financial reasons, but to try and shore up my self-respect.

The job had come from an estate agent I went to in search of a flat. He was sleek and plump as a young seal, with the same sort of amiable, pug face, and a trace of American accent. I arrived just as he was going out to lunch, and for some reason he took me with him.

When I told him I'd been on a kibbutz, he laughed sympathetically and said, 'Stuck it six months, did you? That's six months more than I could take, fella, I can tell you that!' He went on to give me his views. Paradoxically, he seemed to resent the easy life lived by kibbutzniks – 'milk and honey' and 'fat of the land' were two of his favourite phrases. 'Everyone's supposed to fall down dead with gratitude because they were in the front line during the war, but I'll tell you something, fella. The war's over, and now what? They think they got problems? Eight hours' work and that's it? Listen, they should try living my life. Take some *real* responsibility for their wives and kids, instead of letting us tax-payers subsidize them. Try worrying about school bills and the wife's clothes and paying the rent and every other god-damned thing. They don't know what problems are.'

I said nothing, and he took that for agreement. By the end of the lunch I knew a lot about him, none of which I particularly liked, but when he suddenly said, 'You're a nice agreeable sort of guy. I could do with someone like you around the place. Like a job?' I said yes. I wasn't really in a position to be fussy, especially when he offered to 'work' a flat for us.

'You wouldn't get anything like as good as this for the money without a bit of protexia,' he mentioned as he handed me the key, 'but I believe in looking after my own.'

His name was Friedrich Zimmermann; I was instructed to call him Freddy. He told me he was a Yecce, a German-born Israeli.

'They hate us here, you know,' he said cheerfully. 'Oh yes! Did you cherish the illusion that you were leaving anti-semitism behind you? They got it here too, fella, they got it here too. With just the one little difference . . . here when some guy hates you for being a bit smarter than he is, he's a Yiddisher fella himself. Keeps it in the family – like incest,' he added gaily.

The job turned out to be money for old rope. All I had to do at first was sit in a small office from eight till four sorting out files, which Freddy, who'd run a one-man business till he took me on, had allowed to lapse into confusion since his father's death a year before.

'Great guy, my father,' Freddy would say jocularly. 'Built the business up from nothing when we came over from the States in '48. "System, Freddy," he used to tell me. "System, and getting in on the ground floor right after a war. That's the secret of success in the property business. A good war and you need never look back."'

I disliked him heartily. But I didn't see much of him, and a job was a job. Another reason I stuck it was because it got me out of the flat; for eight hours a day I didn't have to be with Martha. I missed her every minute like you'd miss an arm, and invariably ran up the stairs of our block, all five flights, at the end of each day; but by the next morning I was glad enough to run down them again.

We lived on the surface of the flat. Every evening when I came back I was struck anew by the unnatural naked tidiness of our three rooms. They continued to be like unused hotel rooms, spotlessly clean but depersonalized. The only thing Martha had done to stamp her own personality on the place was to buy a trough, fill it with earth, and make a miniature garden of it out on the balcony. Her attachment to this was slavish; it reminded me uneasily of the window-box she had tended in her flat in Earls Court. She certainly gave far more time to it than to preparations for the baby, which seemed to be nil. Any time I asked her when she was going to start buying things for it, she brushed the question aside. She seemed unwilling to be reminded of it at all.

One evening as supper ended I watched her gather up the dishes, drawing them together and piling them before making the effort to rise from the table. It was an effort which always made me want to look away. I was sure it wasn't normal to be so tired, even in the eighth month; on the kibbutz, women – but I didn't let myself think about the kibbutz.

'You look awfully tired, darling. Have you been working hard today?'

'Not particularly.' She carried the dishes into the kitchen, her body tilted slightly backwards for balance. It gave her a proud, almost insolent carriage. I remembered the evening months ago when I had noticed the beginnings of her pregnancy and found her clumsy and unattractive. Now that she was really misshapen, really heavy and awkward, it seemed to me I'd never loved her so much, or needed her more. My desire for her, too, had never been stronger, regardless of her grotesque size and the fact that she made no effort beyond cleanliness to make herself attractive. But I never tried to touch her, except to kiss her cheek. I knew that was all she would tolerate, and that it was not just natural fastidiousness or care for the child which made her hold me off. Without a word or a gesture she made it quite clear that she didn't want me. Sometimes it seemed to me that she wanted nothing except to be left in peace.

I went to help her wash up. It was useless to offer to do it myself; she would just answer in that flat, drained voice, 'No, leave it, I'll do it.' After we'd worked in silence for a few minutes I suddenly asked:

'What do you think of Freddy?'

'He's a worm,' she said.

I was surprised. She'd only met him once, and then just for a minute.

'What makes you say that?'

'Isn't it obvious?'

I felt vaguely irritated by this snap judgement. After all, he had helped us. 'Just because he's anti-kibbutz –' I began.

She turned on me, her face going an ugly red. 'He would be! Common little city-slicker! He *would* be anti anything he couldn't understand – like people actually working for something that wasn't money!'

This was the longest and most emotional speech she'd made for weeks, and although I knew we were on very dangerous ground for me, I felt I must draw her out; there were actually tears in her eyes and the sight filled me with sudden hope of dragging her out of whatever limbo she'd sunk into.

'You must realize that, from a city worker's point of view, the kibbutzim are rather pampered, what with subsidies and tax relief –'

She stared at me with her mouth open, and then turned her head sharply away, the tears spilling over into the washing-up water. 'Shut your face,' she said harshly.

I was scared of her, but I couldn't let this moment pass. I grabbed her shoulders and forced her to turn and face me. Her eyes were blind with tears and wretchedness. I was shocked at the misery in them.

'Darling, talk to me!' I begged. Her head twisted away. 'Talk to me – say all of it, and let's be together again, *please*.'

For a moment she trembled on the brink of an outburst that would have done the trick, however scalding it was while it lasted. I felt her tense herself. But suddenly she seemed to go dead between my hands, slipping away, and the moment went by.

'Leave me alone,' she said dully. 'I'll be all right.'

I went out. I had nowhere to go, so I just walked. I walked away from the bright centre of town through narrow, ill-lit streets, and eventually I came to Jaffa. It was squalid and anonymous down by the docks, and I sat in a bar and drank brandy until I felt my thoughts beginning to grow numb. A girl came and sat with me; not a pro, just a warm, cheerful little tart, a sort of dark-skinned Anne-Marie of the streets. But fortunately by that time I was too drunk to do anything about her. Perhaps I wouldn't have anyway; I don't know. I didn't feel justified in giving myself credit for anything.

Chapter Fifteen

After a few weeks, Freddy's friendliness seemed to grow warmer. He began, somewhat ostentatiously, to 'trust' and 'rely' on me in a way which made me feel not so much flattered as obscurely uneasy.

He acquainted me with the rudimentary details of his current deals, and told me to cope if anything came up while he was out of the office – which was frequently. One day one of his associates arrived in a great hurry with a deed for the sale of a piece of property which he wanted me to register at once with the Land Registry Office. I felt I couldn't do this without Freddy's okay, but when he came back and I told him about it, he was quite angry. I argued that I had no authority to sign documents on his behalf, whereupon he calmed down at once, said of course that was true, and with great amiability suggested that it was time to make me his junior partner so that I could deal with these little matters in his absence.

I was far from sure that I wanted to be Freddy's partner, but in the end he offered me a lot more money and I agreed. There was a lot we'd be needing for the baby. Besides, I couldn't see why he should raise my salary if I wasn't worth it, and allowed myself to accept his explanation – that although I was a beginner I was so promising that he wanted to 'snap me up' – on its face value.

Now, abruptly, I found myself promoted to paper work – so much of it that sometimes I hadn't time to wade through everything, translating the small print, before signing it. Freddy said it was just standard, routine stuff.

Every time a piece of property changed hands it had to be registered, and nearly always it was I who signed at the Land Registry Offices as witness to the transactions. I noticed that there were sometimes remarkable discrepancies between the sum Freddy was paid for a property, and the amount he handed over to the original owner. But when I ventured to ask about this, he merely smiled indulgently and put his arm across my shoulders.

'Listen, fella,' he said paternally. 'Listen what I'm telling you. There is nothing dishonest about making a profit. You buy, you sell, you take your profit, and the better you are, the bigger it is. Would I involve a nice kid like you in anything not straight? Would I?'

He looked me straight in the eyes as he said this, and for a second I knew the truth. But I shut the knowledge out. I think, looking back, that I expected – almost wanted – what was coming to me. It was a kind of death-wish.

One evening I got back to find Martha lying on our bed, reading a letter. She thrust it away when I came in. It hurt and angered me, the way she always did this – I knew perfectly well the letters came from the kibbutz. Usually I ignored this instinctive gesture of exclusion, but tonight I heard myself saying jocularly: 'Well, what's Edna got to say for herself?'

'Nothing much.'

'May I see?'

'If you want to.' She got up laboriously, leaving the letter where it was, and smoothed the counterpane. Its wrinkles had been the only signs of human habitation in that hideously tidy room. Abruptly I flung myself down on the bed and rumpled up the counterpane again.

Martha stared at me, a little puzzled frown appearing on her face. On a wild impulse I grabbed her wrist.

'Darling, sit down here for a minute.'

'I have to get supper.'

'Bugger supper.' I pulled her down. She sat stiffly on the edge of the bed, not looking at me. 'Martha.'

'Yes?' she said politely.

'What's that thing you've got on?' But I could see what it was, it was one of my shirts. Now I stopped to think about it, I realized she'd been wearing it, repeatedly washed and ironed, for weeks. 'Why in God's name have you never got yourself a proper smock?'

She shrugged. 'I don't know.'

'Well, get one tomorrow.'

'It's not worth it for a fortnight.'

'A fortnight . . .' As soon as that! I sat up. 'Darling . . .'

'Yes?'

I wanted to shake her. That polite little 'Yes?' tied me hand and foot. I couldn't say any of the things I wanted to.

'Have you got any lipstick?'

'I suppose somewhere.'

'Then do put a bit on. You look like a bladder of lard.'

She gave me a long, blank stare, and then tried to stand up. I still had hold of her wrist and wouldn't let go.

'Martha!' This time she said nothing, and I felt able to say one of the things I'd wanted to say for weeks. 'Don't you want the baby?'

She was shocked. For a moment I really got through to her. Her eyes focused on me, and she answered, calmly but with real feeling, 'Yes, I do. More than you can imagine.'

'Then why aren't you getting ready for it?'

She needed to think carefully for a long moment, and then she said, 'I suppose because I can't believe I'm going to have it here.'

'Where do you want to have it?' She didn't answer; I didn't give her time to answer. 'What's wrong with here, anyway? Is it too small? I'll talk to Freddy about a bigger flat. Now I'm a partner . . .'

'I'd rather we didn't owe him any more favours,' she said.

Little things assume outrageous proportions when you're at rock bottom. That 'we', even in that context, made my heart leap with hope.

'Darling, you know, I've got a nasty suspicion our Freddy's not quite on the level.'

'I told you ages ago that he wasn't.'

'You didn't.'

'Well, you knew it anyway, didn't you?'

I was silent. After a while I said, 'But what can I do? He's got me in his clutches.'

'Clear out. He can't stop you.'

'I'm not so sure. He's got my signature on a lot of papers.

Besides, how else can I earn a living for us? I'm utterly untrained for any money-making pursuit.'

'Except one.'

'What's that? Banana picking?'

'Writing.'

I put my cheek against the counterpane and lay for a long time staring at the weave of her cotton skirt. I'd let go her wrist but she sat on patiently, as if waiting to be told she could get up.

'I can't write any more,' I said at last. 'You know that.'

She gave a sharp sigh and stood up.

'In that case, you'd better stay where you are. Get up, Aaron, will you please? I want to straighten the bed.'

Chapter Sixteen

The time for the baby to be born came and passed with no sign of it. Suddenly, Martha changed. Her introverted lethargy gave place to a growing restlessness, a nervous fidgety anxiety that never let her be still. Every day she seemed to grow more agitated. She was like an animal searching for a warm, private place in which to give birth, and finding nothing but glaring lights and hard, cold concrete.

For the first time she grew careless about the flat. I would come home to find it dusty and untidy (but no more homelike for that) and Martha either roaming up and down like something in a cage, or out. She tired herself with long aimless walks, and yet at night she couldn't sleep. She would get up and prowl about the flat, moving tensely from room to room in a way that nearly drove me frantic.

'Darling, what is it, what's the matter? Can I get you something?'

'No, it's all right. Go to sleep.'

Pause. Fumblings in the darkness.

'What are you looking for?'

Reluctantly – 'A cigarette.'

'There are some in my jacket.'

She'd stopped smoking without apparent effort early in her pregnancy; now she'd begun again, far more heavily than ever. I saw her hand tremble as she struck the match; there were frowning lines between her eyes and her whole body seemed taut and over-charged with bottled-up nervous energy.

'Why don't you go into the baby's room and sit there for a while? It's cooler.'

The nights were very hot and often oppressive, and the days all but unbearable. Perhaps it was the heat which was making her like this. I was jumpy myself.

She wandered through into the other room and I heard a

263

creak as she sat down in the wicker nursing chair. We had finally got the room ready. I'd done most of it. It had given me unexpected pleasure to choose things and bring them home, hiding from myself each time the obscure hope that they would kindle some spark of enthusiasm in Martha. But she would just glance at whatever I'd brought and say 'Oh – sorry – I meant to get that tomorrow.'

I lay awake for a long time waiting for her to come back to bed, but she didn't. Finally I went in to her.

'Martha, if it's the heat – I mean, I could sleep on the sofa –'

She shook her head sharply, almost irritably. 'I'm all right. Why don't you go back to sleep?'

'It's too hot.' But it wasn't that. I couldn't any longer sleep without her.

I went out on to the balcony. The scent of Martha's flowerbox filled the hot night. There was scarcely a trace of movement in the cloying air, which seemed to lean against my face and chest with a tangible, clinging weight. The star-heavy sky looked convex and oddly solid, as if it might fall. I kept drawing deep breaths down into my lungs, but it was no more satisfying than drinking salt water.

The big, thriving, impervious city of Tel Aviv stood round me. I reflected how well it had fulfilled the purpose for which I had come to it. I had wanted to vanish without trace, to be buried in its complex of stone boxes, and for that I could have chosen nowhere better. One could live here for years, I imagined, without ever making a friend, without finding a single corner of the city that one would mourn if it were destroyed. It was a city of business men, built to make money in, existing and growing for the same cold motive. One could be more completely alone here than in the middle of the Arctic.

It had given me anonymity. I was a cipher here – a flat number, a bank account number, a number on a city register. My employer didn't regard me as a person, but as an adjunct, a certain improvement to his business which equalled a sum deducted from his income. Even to my wife . . .

I turned and looked into the darkened room where Martha was sitting. I could only see her dimly, the little glow of her cigarette-end coming and going like a distant beacon, remote and aloof. Once I would have known what she was thinking, or if not I could have asked her; or else we would have been content with silence and a privacy mutually respected. Now the privacy had become total isolation, and, for me, a loneliness so profound that suddenly I felt I would risk any hurt rather than let it go on for another moment.

'Are things ever going to come right between us again?'

I heard my own voice with a pang of alarm. As long as I had kept from asking it, there was always a little hope; I could even pretend that the need to ask it didn't exist. But now it was out, and the answer could be dooming.

It came after a long moment. 'Once I would have said it was up to you. Now I don't know any more.' She sounded very tired.

'What do you mean, you don't know?'

She sighed as if she had to gather herself together. 'Just that it can't come right while you're running away.'

'But I've stopped running.'

'Have you?'

She didn't say it sarcastically, just wearily, as if she no longer cared one way or the other. It was that terrible note of defeat in her voice that made me realize for the first time how completely I had failed her.

The despair was slow to come, like pain following a blow; but after a few moments' numbness it spread softly, almost luxuriously, like a burn creeping over the skin. There was no escape from it. There was no cure, no alternative to the dead-end I'd fled into. Having explored my own possibilities in every situation, and found myself wanting in all of them, there was now no way left to run. No forward way, at least . . .

I stood for a long time, staring at the city, not seeing it any more but seeing the white house on Hampstead Hill. After a while I smelt burning. Martha's cigarette had fallen on to the wicker arm of her chair and was smouldering gently while she slept, her head sunk uncomfortably on her shoulder. With difficulty I carried her to bed; she grunted a little, and for a moment it seemed that she turned towards me in her sleep, nestling her face into my neck. I kissed her hot cheek as I put her down on top of the bedclothes and straightened her damp nightgown over the huge bulk of the child.

Then I went into the living-room, closing the dividing door. I sat for a while in the darkness. I wanted urgently to drink, but I realized the futility of it. Eventually the need for some kind of action became too strong. I turned on the light and wrote a letter. I only wrote it as an outlet – I never meant to send it; but I carried my fantasy too far. I addressed an envelope, put the letter inside, and sealed it down. Then, instead of tearing it up, I put it in my brief-case.

It was lunch-time the next day before I remembered it. But by that time the office boy had found it on my desk and sent it off.

I lived through the next days in a haze of shock. I was appalled and stupefied by my folly. But after sending off a telegram aimed at nullifying the letter, there seemed to be nothing else to do; I could only wait, and the process was hellish. I tried to bring my mind to bear properly on what I'd done and what the result was likely to be, but it was too awful to contemplate. At the same time I couldn't think of anything else.

As a result, my work at the office received scant attention. I followed Freddy's orders mechanically, and hardly noticed that he himself was decidedly distrait.

For some weeks, he'd been preoccupied with a very important deal concerning a valuable piece of land right on the sea-front which had unexpectedly come on the market. Freddy, jubilant, had shown me a Power of Attorney he said he'd received from the owner, a man called Gault who lived in Argentina.

'A great site, a great site!' he kept chortling. 'A dozen offers already, they're bidding their heads off. I think I'll settle for the hundred thousand offer from those hotel schlemeils. Such a hotel they're going to build, the Sheraton will look like a Kansas City cat-house.'

But only two days after the deal had been signed, sealed and registered by me at the Land Registry Offices, something happened which wiped the grin right off Freddy's face. It was a telephone call from a man called Gault, and it didn't come from Argentina. Five minutes after I'd put it through on his private line, Freddy emerged from his office glassy-eyed and palely sweating. His hands shook and he leaned on my desk like an old man.

'That bastard,' he kept saying. 'How could I know he'd turn up? In a million years was there ever such a piece of luck? That *bastard*.' He poured a drink, spilling half of it on my desk. 'And those nebbishers haven't even paid me yet, only the deposit. What time is it? Listen what I'm telling you, get down to the bank and see if they cleared the deposit cheque yet.'

'But what's happened?' I thought I knew. Gault, thought to be safely remote, had come to collect his money and check up on the exact selling-price. Freddy would thus be done out of his 'cut'.

He flew suddenly into a rage. 'Never mind what happened, you don't have to know so much! You go down to the bank and if they cleared the cheque ring me here – at once, you hear what I'm telling you? Now get out and don't bother me with questions!'

I shrugged and went out to the bank, telephoning Freddy to tell him the deposit money was in his account. He gave a sigh of relief.

'Listen, I got to go see that bastard now. You come back and see to things here. Don't leave the office. If Gault calls, stall him, tell him I'm on my way.'

I sat out the morning in the office. Gault called twice. So did a man called Ben-Ze'ev, from the Land Registry. I was too pre-occupied with my own dilemma to worry about Freddy's, which wasn't one anyway, so far as I knew. He'd been prevented from swindling Gault, if that had been his intention.

Just as I was going out to lunch, the office boy announced the arrival of three *adonim*. Two of them were Gault and Ben-Ze'ev. The third was a detective.

Ben-Ze'ev was a pleasant-looking man with enormous, slightly crooked white teeth and glasses. He rubbed his hands and grinned at me genially.

'Ah, Mr Franks, isn't it? I've seen you at our offices.'

We shook hands and I offered chairs and cigarettes all round. I had no qualms. I didn't even develop any when the situation was made clear to me. It seemed this Mr Gault was not the original owner of the property, but his nephew, who had only recently discovered that he'd inherited it. He had not authorized Freddy to sell it; in fact he'd never heard of Freddy until this morning when he'd gone into the Land Registry Offices and discovered that the site no longer belonged to him.

Mr Ben-Ze'ev asked to see the Power of Attorney, and I looked for it in the files. I'd seen it only that morning, but now it was gone. The detective found the remains of it – some very fine ash in Freddy's big glass ashtray.

Mr Ben-Ze'ev grinned toothily. 'Never mind, we still have Mr Franks's signature.'

'Mine?'

'You witnessed the Power of Attorney at our offices, when the sale was registered. Surely you remember that.'

He didn't look in the least accusing. He sat back on his chair, his hands folded on his stomach, his expression positively benevolent. It was that almost avuncular air of good nature that made me realize for the first time that he had me, and that he knew it.

Needless to say my increasingly frantic efforts to contact Freddy were a waste of time. I didn't really expect they would be any use. While I telephoned Freddy's home and everywhere else I could think of where he might possibly be, Mr Ben-Ze'ev sat placidly watching me. Plainly he thought I was putting on a not very effective act of desperate innocence. I kept apologizing, idiotically, for keeping him waiting.

'Quite all right,' he would answer cheerfully. 'Take your time. I'm in no hurry.'

At last when I could think of nowhere else to try, Mr Ben-Ze'ev smiled sunnily and said, 'All finished? Then I should telephone your lawyer, if I were you. That'll be much more useful.'

I stared at him, the full horror of the situation dawning on me. 'But I haven't got a lawyer,' I said. I realized how absurd it sounded.

The Government official stopped smiling. 'You *haven't got* a lawyer?' he repeated slowly. 'But the firm has one, presumably?'

I could hardly think straight. 'I suppose so.'

'Well, telephone him,' he said, sounding impatient for the first time.

'I don't know who he is,' I said helplessly.

Ben-Ze'ev suddenly snatched off his glasses and peered at me through screwed-up eyes. His composure seemed shaken. He leaned back again in his chair and rubbed the bridge of his nose.

'*How* long did you say you'd worked for Mr Zimmermann?'

'Nearly two months.'

'What were you doing before that?'

I told him. He stared at me, all benevolence gone, a puzzled frown deepening into something like anger.

'You say you signed these on Mr Zimmermann's behalf,' he said, gesturing towards the contracts. 'Did you read them first?'

'Usually.'

'Well?' he almost barked.

'They seemed all right to me – Mr Zimmermann told me they were standard contracts, just a formality.'

'And you believed him?'

I nodded.

'You *trusted* him?'

'Not – well, at least –'

'At least what?'

'It's hard to explain. I knew he was a bit sharp –'

'Oh, you knew that much! Excellent!'

'But I swear I didn't know he was breaking the law.'

'You just thought he was bending it a little.'

I couldn't think of any answer.

'And you needed the job, I suppose?' he asked with heavy sarcasm.

'Yes.'

'Wife and kids – no experience – all the rest of it?'

I said nothing.

'You poor *messhugenah*,' he said.

They took me in and charged me, and then let me go home.

'Aren't you afraid I'll run away?' I asked.

'You'll be in worse trouble if you do.'

I almost smiled. No more unconsciously pertinent words had ever been said to me.

But when I got outside into the commonplace sunlight, all philosophy and sense of proportion deserted me. I stood on the edge of the kerb, buffeted by the lunch-time crowds, and asked myself how, having failed at so many smaller fences, I could hope to find the strength to surmount this one. Clearly I had managed, quite accidentally, to convince Ben-Ze'ev that I was only guilty of gross stupidity and carelessness; but the fact remained that technically I was in the soup up to my neck. Even if they caught up with Freddy, who was slippery enough to make this unlikely, my signature was still irremediably on those papers . . .

The word 'irremediably', as I thought it, struck some chord in my memory.

'"Irremediably"? Did I say "irremediably"? I meant "unreversably" . . .'

Suddenly and clearly I could picture Martha's prim dark head bent over the desk in that room above the shop. I could feel again my impatience for her eyes to turn on me, like well-lit mirrors, to show me myself by her reactions to me. She was untouchable then, unknowable, despite her warmth and enthusiasm – self-complete, remote, and yet vulnerable, as only virgins are.

I had a lot to answer for, having taken that girl and changed her, making those eyes dull and devitalizing those hands. I had not meant to do it, but that didn't lessen my culpability. I had ruined her in a sense far beyond the usual one. Grimly I reflected how gravely I had underestimated my own powers of destruction when I had kept myself from physical involvements with certain women for fear of despoiling them with sex. Just about the only facet of our relationship which had *not* despoiled Martha had been our love-making.

And now I had a new degradation in store for her.

I tried to imagine myself telling her that I was in line for a jail sentence. It was not even as if I could claim to be entirely blameless – she knew that I had known what sort of man Freddy was. The prospect of inflicting this new humiliation on her, and especially now, was so unendurable that the old, automatic reflex made my mind instantly begin to dash about, seeking a way of escape. But the panicky clockwork mouse ran down almost at once. I seemed to have reached the ultimate dead end, where the urge to run dies of its own futility.

I walked back to the flat, not pausing until I reached the cool dimness of the stone stairway in our block. I stood for a moment half-way up, relieved of the remorseless noon sunlight, trying to analyse some deeper relief that I was aware of. There was a surprising inner dignity, even strength, to be found in not even wanting to run away any more. Suddenly I wasn't afraid to tell Martha. I realized that I made her suffer most simply by being too weak to stand my ground in any situation. The trouble I was in now couldn't reduce her opinion of me any further; in fact I might even make a start at restoring her belief in me by facing up to this with a bit of courage.

That she would stick by me I had no doubt at all. This outside attack, as it were, might even draw us closer together. Once when we were in bed together she had said to me: 'What I like best about being in love with you is the feeling that we're partners against the world.' Surely that sort of love couldn't be killed, even by me, in a few short months. If it were not still alive in her somewhere, she would have left me.

Unreasonable, instinctive hope filled me at the memory of our past happiness together. We would start again – not in a new place, not with flight as the first pre-requisite, but here and now, in the very storm-centre of the mess my idiocy had got us into. This was all she had ever asked of me, I suddenly realized – that I should stay in one place and put down roots that nothing could tear up.

I ran up the last stairs, the key ready in my hand. I had all the words ready too, the words that would make the new beginning. I threw the door open, and burst into the living-room.

Polly was sitting by the window smoking a cigarette.

Chapter Seventeen

The sight of her gave me the worst shock of my life, though I should have been expecting it.

'Christ Almighty, what are you doing here?'

She turned her head and looked at me calmly.

'You sent for me, Aaron,' she said.

I'd forgotten the letter. For two whole hours I'd actually forgotten it. Instinctively I motioned her to be quiet, and glanced at the closed bedroom door.

'Yes, she's in there,' Polly said without lowering her voice.

I rushed at the door. It was locked. I could hear Martha moving about beyond it . . . not her muffled, weary movements, nor her more recent jerky pointless ones. These were brisk and decisive. I heard the rustle of tissue paper, the firm closing of a cupboard door.

'Martha, let me in! What are you doing?'

'She's packing,' said Polly.

I turned on her. 'Get out!'

'No, Aaron,' she said gently. 'Not after your letter.'

'I sent a telegram telling you the letter was a mistake!'

'Did you? I didn't get it.'

'You're lying.'

Her mouth turned up at one side. How well I remembered everything, now I saw her again! The softened image of her that months of homesickness and irrational self-delusion had produced suddenly dissolved into this hard-edged reality with the bony head and square shoulders and thin, nervy hands. The triumphant possessiveness in her face turned me sick at the stomach.

I pulled myself together sharply and stood in front of her.

'Listen, Polly,' I said, my voice sounding harsh and uneven. 'That letter was written one night when I was so unhappy I didn't know what I was doing. I didn't mean to send it, even. Everything's changed since then.'

'In four days?'

'Things can change in an hour. I'm sorry you've had the journey for nothing, but you'll just have to go back. I don't want you.'

Her lopsided disbelieving smile didn't waver. Without taking her eyes off me she took my letter out of her bag. I stared at the envelope with a feeling of outrage. That thrice-damned thing had travelled half-way round the world and betrayed me without my volition. It was as unfair as if she'd read my mind. Not even my normal mind, but some subconscious unacknowledged thoughts, dredged up and filched against my will.

She put on her glasses and began to read in the quiet, toneless voice of perfect confidence, like a barrister with incontestable proof in his hands.

My dear Polly, nothing ever turns out as one expects. In all my advance suppositions about this venture, the one thing I didn't allow for was that I should miss my home so much. I even miss you.

She glanced up at me, lifting one plucked eyebrow ironically. I wanted to scream at her to stop, but something kept me silent.

We've always been so different that it's quite impossible for me to imagine how your mind has been working since I left. Perhaps by now you've convinced yourself you never had a brother. I know I failed you dismally as I seem to fail everyone, but what you asked of me wasn't reasonable; that's why I'm not apologizing for making such a mess of it. If you knew how much worse a mess I've made since I got here, you'd regard my behaviour in September as too trivial to bother about. At times like now, I'm so unbearable to myself that I wonder why I bother to go on living. Only the thought of you and home brings any measure of peace. *If only you were here*, I might be able to take my bearings from you, like a lodestar.

My God, had I really written that? It was as revolting as having one's stale vomit thrown into one's face. I literally thought I might be sick as she reached that snivelling bit at the end. But at the same time, the shame only went down to a certain point; beyond that, it couldn't touch me. That letter didn't really belong to me any more, except as proof that I had touched bottom and that there was nowhere to go except up. The knowledge that she was reading it simply to humiliate me into submission filled me with strengthening contempt.

I looked at her when she'd finished. Her smile was still there, calm, confident, almost caressing. She folded the letter up and put it away; it was the gesture of a blackmailer, or of a killer sheathing his knife.

'You know, you're really a very unpleasant woman,' I said. I hadn't planned to say that, it was just the result of the genuine dislike that I felt for her, for the first time unmixed with dependence and uncomplicated by whatever warped love had bound me to her all my life. 'Now you really must go, because I want to talk to my wife.'

A quiver of uncertainty passed across her face.

'You're married?'

'Yes.'

'Legally?'

I hesitated for one beat – too long. 'We're married.'

The smile reasserted itself, a kind, indulgent, reasonable smile.

'Then why is she packing?'

'No doubt because you read her that letter.' I shut my teeth on the words *You bitch* which had almost added themselves automatically.

'And that simple, human cry for help is enough to make her leave you? She must love you *very* much.'

Simple, human shit. But again I didn't say the words aloud. I couldn't afford to lose even that much control of myself.

'How much she loves me isn't your concern.'

'Nor yours, any longer,' she said immediately.

'What do you mean?'

'Just that you'll be doing the leaving. I've come to take you home.'

I caught my breath and stared at her. My thoughts threshed about for a moment in confusion. Then, to my infinite relief, I heard myself answer with a confidence that matched her own:

'This is home.'

We looked at each other. It was invigorating to watch the sure knowledge of defeat come into her eyes. But she didn't face it at once, of course. The conversation went on for a long time. I stopped enjoying it long before it was over, because by the end she was fighting desperately and without dignity; she had abandoned her characteristic techniques and was degrading herself with abuse. Most of it was directed towards Martha.

'Why do you imagine she attached herself to you? Allowed the whole thing to start? I suppose you think it was spontaneous combustion. Or perhaps you even flatter her to the extent of calling it love. That pathetic, commonplace little girl, what does she know about love? She knows one thing, the only thing her upbringing would teach her – how to look after herself. She saw in you a man who could take her places. She saw the brilliance I've always seen, only I saw it disinterestedly. She saw what it would mean, one day, to be married to you. Thank God you had the sense not to go that far. Thank God you're free. And don't imagine I had anything to do with her wanting to leave you. She's the sort that would walk out, as soon as she saw she wasn't going to get what she was after – it would have happened before long anyway. Love! She doesn't know the meaning of the word, common little leech that she is!'

I didn't bother to defend Martha against all this; none of it touched her. I sat still, looking into Polly's face twisting with malice as she spewed out her poison; I was hardly hearing her any more, just wondering, as she got more and more out of control, how she could expose herself like that. Almost, I could be sorry for her; but at the same time I felt a grim amazement that I could have belonged, in any way, at any time, to this unhappy, pitiable, loathsome woman.

At last she stood up, gathering her things together with hands that shook. Her whole body seemed drained and exhausted by our struggle of wills. She kept her eyes lowered. To break her grim and defeated silence, I suddenly said:

'By the way, how's Dan?'

'I sacked him,' she said. 'Dirty little lecher.'

And so she would deal with, and had dealt with, any and every man who might have warmed her with his love.

She raised her eyes and looked at me.

I had never seen her cry in my whole life, and the sight of the tears which only final failure could evoke gave me a pang of pity. But pity is not, to me, a kind of admirable emotion. It's a detestable feeling, quite unlike sympathy, associated with futility and despair, the emotion roused by those who are beyond help, the irretrievably lost and damned. It had been pity for my own condition which had been crippling me for so long. I recognized that suddenly, when I experienced the same sick hopeless feeling now for my sister.

She left saying that she would be back, that I would change my mind. But I knew she would not be back, just as she knew I was now fixed and firm and indifferent to her, independent and beyond her reach for ever.

I stood for a moment after the door closed, aware of myself as if I'd entered a new body. Despite everything I felt exultant. My heart pounded as if from a triumphant exertion. I thought of the police, and felt a surge of exhilaration, almost joy. I felt so secure in my new self-confidence that I rejoiced at the prospect of a real battle that would confirm me to myself. And to Martha.

The triumph dispersed a little. None of it would be fully concrete and permanent until I had taken it to Martha and she had ratified the change in me. And Martha was packing to leave me.

I realized it without in the least believing it. I knew I could stop her. It was Polly's arrival that had been the final straw, and small wonder – but when she discovered that I had rejected Polly, and when, furthermore, I told her of the trouble I was facing, then she wouldn't consider leaving. I seethed with confidence and certainty; this threat of the ultimate disaster only put me on my mettle.

I knocked on the door again. 'She's gone, darling. Let me in, I've got to talk to you.' My voice sounded different, there was no querulousness in it. It was only to be expected that she would open the door immediately, and so she did.

I was so full of what I had to say to her that at first I didn't really notice how she looked. I saw that she was different, but I thought it was a reflection of the difference in me. She had a large suitcase and a hold-all in her hands.

'You won't need those. Put them down. I've got a lot to tell you.'

I tried to take the heavy suitcase away from her, but her fingers seemed to be welded round the handle. Then I saw that her face had the same quality of rigidity, a sealed-in look, impenetrable as a locked safe. Without intending to I found myself touching her face, verifying with my finger-tips the stiff, closed muscles. She had shut her face against me before, but never with quite such an impression of finality.

I felt a little afraid, but only for a moment. I touched her arms and said very quietly, 'Please, darling.'

She put the cases down with a little shrug, and walked away from me to the settee. Her walk still had that proud, back-tilted look, but it was no longer slow and indecisive; she moved now with clarity and certainty. When she turned and sat down, it was a poised, almost balletic movement that made her skirt flare. She sat with her hands on her knees. They didn't lie there limply, but were placed one on each knee with purpose; they conveyed a definite impatience to be gone.

I kept staring at her hands. They made it hard to begin.

'I won't disown the letter. I only want to tell you when I wrote it.'

'I know when you wrote it.'

'Then I don't have to explain that I wasn't my normal self when I did it.'

'On the contrary, Aaron, you were never more yourself.'

I was flabbergasted by the change in her. She had recovered all her old positiveness, but without the warmth. She met my eyes as politely and coldly as a stranger.

'Of course she didn't tell you that I sent a telegram after it to cancel it . . .' But I realized at once this was a futile line of defence. I had written the letter. Even if it had never been sent, that was weakness enough to condemn me.

'Well, anyway, what you must believe is that I didn't really want her here. I didn't mean what I said in the letter. The sight of her made me feel sick.' None of this sounded right, and there was no response at all on Martha's face. It was attentive, polite, as if she were listening out of good manners to a story which bored her. I began to realize that it would be difficult to convince her that the change she had waited for for so long had come suddenly about. I had a fear that, if I started at the beginning, she would get up and leave through lack of interest before I reached the important point. It seemed better to start at the end, with the final proof.

'The main thing is, darling, she's gone. I've sent her packing for good.'

'She'll be back,' Martha said at once.

'She won't, and even if she is, it won't do her any good. She's beaten and she knows it. Nothing on earth would make me go back with her now.'

'Oh, but why not? I think it would be the best thing in the world.'

Fear, real fear, began slowly in the pit of my stomach. 'The best thing for whom?'

'Well, you, of course. You'll be better off in London with Polly than alone here.'

The terror, distinct and persuasive in my throat, had to be shouted over. 'You're not going anywhere!' Her cool stare forced me to control my voice. 'Listen, please. You've got to believe me. I did write that letter in a moment of weakness, but it was my last – I mean my last of the sort that's bedevilled us from the beginning. Don't you see, something's happened to me? I'm able to withstand her now – and if I can withstand her, I can do pretty well anything.' Her imperviousness was destroying my conviction. I went over and gripped those two impatient hands, feeling the life in them again, a life that was anxious to take her away from me. I shook them, and saw her body move slightly, like a tree when you shake its branches; but I knew suddenly, as Polly had known with me, that I could not root her up from her purpose.

But I had to try. I talked. I told her everything, everything that I thought would sway her – all except one thing. I didn't tell her about what had happened in the morning. It was there all the time, pressing forward to be told, the trump card jumping into my hand as I struggled for this all-important trick; but I didn't play it. She had to stay because she wanted to, because she believed in me, not because I was in trouble. The horrible debasing emotion of pity was still sour in my memory. If I roused it now in Martha, and she stayed because of that, it would prove nothing, I would be lost before I started.

She listened to everything, and let her hands stay in mine. But in the middle of a sentence I felt a slight movement of her wrist, and saw her glance at her watch.

'I'm afraid I have to go now. If I miss the 2.15 bus I won't get the connexion at Ashkelon.'

I hadn't asked her where she was going, because I hadn't expected her to go. Now I realized with a sudden shock what I had known and yet not let myself know, for months – that all this time she had been hungering with all her heart to go back to Beit Hashoresh.

She was looking at me now a little more softly, a little less impersonally. 'There's still time,' she said, with a strange trace of shyness. From it, I knew that she didn't mean time to catch the bus, she meant there was time for her to get home before the child was born. This realization robbed me of the will to argue any more. It would be like asking her to wrench up her roots for me. She had done it once, when we left England; but the roots she had put down in the kibbutz were deeper and stronger. They were her very life. I saw fully, only now, what I had made her suffer by tearing her away from them.

'Oh my darling! I'm sorry!' I cried out, feeling her accumulated pain strike me as I came to understand it. 'I should have known. I should have taken you back. Christ, I should never have made you leave!'

I craved the comfort of her arms and her forgiveness. I felt a yearning for her love that was a present agony and a terrifying foretaste of future loneliness, both so strong I felt my head reel. I groped for her blindly, but the stiffness of her shoulders brought me to my senses. I mustn't force her. I mustn't cling to her, or make any more demands on her in the name of need. I drew back into myself, leaving her alone.

'I'll find a taxi and take you to your bus,' I said.

We stood at the bus-stop as part of a bulky, disorderly queue. The sun was at its hottest, a heavy, stifling burden the carrying of which left little energy for speaking or moving. All round us was noise, confusion, sweltering bodies, the flashing of reflected sunlight on passing cars, an affliction to all the senses at once. It was like a modern image of hell, all heat and glare and racket, with an inner pain which stabbed and stabbed with the knowledge that this was nothing, this was only the start.

She stood beside me, small and contained, with her huge

279

overdue burden under my tightly-stretched shirt and the blue *kova tembel* on her head like a label proclaiming her destination. Under it, her small, tidy face was in profile, staring ahead, expressionless and very pale. I stood looking openly at her, aware of everything, that she was really going and that in a few minutes I would have to go back to an empty flat full of things for our child which would never use them. There was no possibility even of a dignified or private farewell.

'Are you sure you'll be all right on the journey?'

'Of course.'

'But your luggage –'

'Someone will give me a hand.'

Her voice was strained, and when she saw how I was looking at her she turned her head sharply away.

'I hate letting you go alone.'

Her hand groped for mine, closing on my thumb, and just for a moment we were together, as if nothing had happened.

'I know,' she said.

Our hands were still locked like drowners when the bus rattled up. The queue immediately broke and there was the usual scramble for seats. I left Martha and fought my way into the stifling interior, grabbing a place next to the window by means of an eel-like slither under the arm of a fat man who was heaving his bundles on to the rack.

'Here, that's my place!' he said roughly.

'Then you should be sitting in it,' I said shortly. Through the window I motioned to Martha, who hurried to relieve me. The man, who was preparing to get nasty, altered his manner as soon as he saw that the seat was for her.

'Sorry, *Adoni*. I didn't realize –'

He moved his own things and put her suitcase on the rack for Martha before I had a chance to. He smiled and bowed to her.

'There's a place free here –' she said, indicating the seat beside her.

'No thanks, *Geveret*, I'm too big, I'd make the journey uncomfortable for you.' He struggled off along the congested aisle.

'Kind,' said Martha.

'Very,' I answered.

She smiled at me, rather tentatively, as if we'd only just met.

Then she began settling herself, pulling her skirt straight under her and winding down the window to get a breath of air. I stood in the aisle leaning over the empty seat between us, being jostled and pushed and sworn at, but unable to leave her a moment before I had to.

'Is there anything I can get you – something to read?'

It was an idiotic question. Who could read on an Israeli bus? She shook her head, still smiling, but now her eyes were bright with tears, and she turned away again quickly, pressing her face against the window. I felt an agonizing pain in my chest and sat in the empty seat beside her, holding her thin trembling shoulders.

'Don't cry, my dearest,' I whispered. 'When you get home, you'll be all right.'

'I *have* to leave you, I *must* do it,' she muttered indistinctly.

'Yes. It's all right. It's the right thing.'

Suddenly she turned round to face me. 'Aaron, come –'

'Are you travelling, *Adoni?*'

A thin, sour-faced woman was standing over me.

'What?'

'That man down there said this seat was vacant, that you weren't travelling.'

I stood up slowly, feeling Martha slip out of my hands. 'That's right.'

The woman sank fussily on to the wooden seat, distributing her belongings round her. I stood helplessly, the seconds passing. Martha blew her nose.

I leaned behind the woman. 'What were you going to say?'

Martha said 'Nothing.' She sat motionless with her hands gripping the seat on either side of her.

'Would you like anything to eat or drink?'

She saw that these last moments had to be filled if they were to be endurable. She pointed through the window at a swarthy little man selling oranges.

'Would it be terribly anti-social of me?'

'Of course not.'

I hurried out and bought her half a dozen oranges, a stupid thing to do as they'd only be another thing for her to carry. The seller had no bags. I had to cradle the oranges in my arms, and at once began dropping them like a comedy juggler. As I bent to pick one up, another would roll away. Two disappeared under the bus, and several people began to laugh.

I reached the bus just as the driver closed the automatic doors.

'Quick, through here!'

Martha's hand appeared through the narrow crack at the top of the window. I thrust an orange into it; but her hand with the orange in it was too big for the crack. She tried to wind the window down further, but it was stuck. I began a struggle to push the oranges through, one at a time, but they were too big. They were all too big.

By this time the bus was beginning to move. I ran alongside, still trying to force the fruit through. Everyone inside was watching this farcical performance with shouts of laughter. The orange-seller was at my elbow, yelling advice, picking up the oranges as I dropped them. And all the time I could see nothing but Martha's hand, reaching out through the top of the window; I could think of nothing but the desperate urgency of my need to give her what she'd asked for. It seemed so little – one orange – she must have it; but I couldn't get the fat Jaffas through to her, and her hand stayed empty.

At the last moment before the bus pulled away, her hand withdrew. My heart turned sick with despair. But then, quite suddenly, I saw her kiss her palm and press it whitely against the dusty glass. Her lips formed one word:

'Write.'

I was left standing in the exhaust fumes with one squashed orange in my hand.

The orange-seller, his toothless face creased horizontally with laughter, bent and picked up another one from the gutter. It was streaked with oil. He wiped it on his sleeve before handing it to me.

'Too bad,' he cackled. 'But you keep it for her. Keep it for when you join her.'

'Thank you,' I said.

'May the rind not be dry,' said the old man.

I walked back to the empty flat, holding an orange in each hand. When I got there I sat for a long time at the desk where I had written the letter to Polly, turning the oranges this way and that until my hands were covered with the sharp, invigorating smell of the oil. Then I put the fruit carefully on the window-ledge in the sun. They would dry there, and not go bad, and in due course, when whatever was coming to me had come and gone, I would take them to Martha.

What had she meant by that one word, *write*? Letters, to keep a link between us? Or had she meant that I must scrape the rust off my one skill and use it to help in my restoration? Perhaps both. I thought of Yigal, intent and absorbed in his cobwebby studio. It would make quite a difference to kibbutz life to have one's own work to keep one from sinking in too far. I somehow didn't want anonymity any more.

Abruptly I began to search the flat. First I hunted through the various drawers in the living-room, putting off the moment of going into the bedroom, but in the end it wasn't too bad because we'd never made love there. Still, the empty spaces where her things had been inflicted a muffled ache, through which I kept doggedly searching. Nothing.

I went through into the little room with the baby's things in it. That was harder. I stood staring round, fighting the sharp lonely pains. There was nowhere there she could have put what I was looking for.

Just as I turned to go back into the living-room I noticed something odd on the balcony, and went out to look. It was her flower-box. All the plants had been uprooted and left to shrivel up in the sun.

I looked down at them for a long time. Some of them already looked dead. Squatting down, I picked them up and began inexpertly re-planting them in the jagged holes they'd left in the orange earth. They drooped; some lay down, hanging over the edge, their blooms half-closed and fading. I straightened up, feeling helpless and exasperated. Silly, useless things – let them die, what did it matter? But for some unknown reason it did matter. I found myself hurrying into the kitchen for a jug of water.

At once I saw what I'd been looking for – the foolscap envelope, its scuffed top sticking upright out of the garbage pail. I lifted it out. The bottom edge was black with wet tea-leaves.

It was like a slap in the face, and yet I almost laughed. She hadn't even enough malice for a really subtle insult. *Right, my girl*, I thought. *Scorched-earth policy, eh? Right. We'll see.*

Carrying the jug of water in one hand and the manuscript in the other, I went back on to the balcony. I scraped off the tea-leaves round the roots of the wilting plants, and watered them in.

'Live, you little bastards,' I said grimly.

Then I went back indoors and started shifting the desk into a better light.

Other books by women writers in Penguins

HOLY PICTURES
Clare Boylan

In the Dublin of 1925, the Holy Scriptures are about to be superseded by moving pictures. To fourteen-year-old Nan the cinema appears as a miraculous rescue from the confines of her Catholic upbringing. But growing up into a world of immoral, unreliable adults is not easy. Neglected by her mother, bullied by her increasingly eccentric father, buffeted by aristocratic nuns, unwelcome house guests and an uneasy knowledge of the facts of life, the last year of Nan's childhood moves from the burlesque to the tragic ...

'Sharp as a serpent's tooth ... it is a very long time since a first novel of such promise, of such fun and wit and style, has come so confidently out of Ireland' – William Trevor

VICTIM OF LOVE
Dyan Sheldon

Paul Sutcliffe has one wife, two children and two lovers. He is a sensitive, kind and intelligent man who has always been committed to equal rights for women. Women do not threaten him; he is one of their biggest fans. Also, he believes in love.

Linda Sutcliffe is in her thirties (though on most days she feels closer to sixty). She has a career and a family, mostly because Paul thinks she should have them. Everything Linda does, she does for love.

Why is it that, suddenly, everything is conspiring to let Paul down and Linda is filled with dreams of being the person she has never had the chance to be ...?

Lynne Reid Banks's poignant trilogy

THE L-SHAPED ROOM

Unmarried and pregnant, Jane Graham is cast out of her suburban home. Lighting dejectedly on a bug-ridden room in a squalid house in Fulham, she gradually comes to find a new and positive faith in life.

THE BACKWARD SHADOW

After the birth of her son, Jane exchanges the L-shaped room for a remote country cottage. She is joined by Dottie, and together they embark upon an enterprise that is to change both their lives.

TWO IS LONELY

Now the mother of an eight-year-old, Jane finds she has to grapple with the increasing problems of single parenthood.

and

CHILDREN AT THE GATE

Gerda is a Jewish-Canadian divorcee alone in a miserable room in the Arab quarter of Acre. She is thirty-nine but looks far older: emotionally her life is a shambles. Her sole comforts are drink and an Arab friend, Kofi, about whom there is considerable mystery.